The RULE of KNOWLEDGE

Important note to readers:
Whenever you see this symbol,
you can access additional chapters
at www.ruleofknowledge.com

The RULE of KNOWLEDGE

SCOTT BAKER

First published in Australia and New Zealand in 2013
by Hachette Australia
(an imprint of Hachette Australia Pty Limited)
Level 17, 207 Kent Street, Sydney NSW 2000
www.hachette.com.au

This edition published in 2015

10 9 8 7 6 5 4 3 2 1

National Library of Australia
Cataloguing-in-Publication data:

Baker, Scott.
The rule of knowledge / Scott Baker.

978 0 7336 3447 5 (pbk.)

Teachers – fiction.
Secrets – fiction.
Suspense fiction.

A823.4

Cover design by Luke Causby, Blue Cork
Cover photograph courtesy of Arcangel Images
Typeset in Sabon by Kirby Jones

PROLOGUE

Pain.

Searing, unbearable pain.

Nothing.

Light. Brilliant and white.

Nothing.

What's that sound? Is that my heartbeat? Stop, it hurts.

Nothing.

God, I'm so thirsty.

Pain.

There's something I have to do …

Nothing.

Something I …

Panic.

Who … Who … am I?

PART I

ANOTHER DAY IN HISTORY

'And when they come, they'll find me here.
I will not run, they will not see my fear.
And I will fight, to the very end.
Before that wind, I will never bend.'

'Eastern Wind', Christopher Davison

Rome, 33 AD

The wind whipped the arena sands into a frenzy, stinging his skin and catching in his throat, but the condemned man paid it no heed.

Bronze-tanned and rippling in the sun, Saul the gladiator strode forward. He squinted as perspiration trickled into his eyes, borne not of exertion but rather of fear – the fear that came with knowledge of certain death. Death itself was not the problem, but instead, what it brought with it. In death lay defeat, and in defeat lay failure.

Failure was not an option, and yet there seemed no way he could survive this battle. His gaze curved in a slow arc around the arena. There were a hundred gladiators here, but it felt like a thousand. A lucky blow, a knife in the back, a slip on some slick pool of blood ... it could be over in an instant.

Jets of perfumed water blasted into the air, propelled by a miracle of Roman engineering. Drums and trumpets electrified the air until finally, looking down on the whole scene from his place in the crowd, Caesar himself stood. In moments the Royåle would begin, and a hundred gladiators would fight until the red elixir of life was emptied from their limp bodies by last beats of their failing hearts. The sands would be stained, and they would all be dead.

Death. Defeat. Failure.

There was more at stake than anyone here could know. Striding forward once more, Saul thought of his mother ...

CHAPTER 1

North Carolina, United States, 2014

Shaun Strickland was breaking the speed limit, and not just by a little – nearly double – as he navigated his way out of the city. His mind was elsewhere, racing through the growing possibilities. He squinted as perspiration trickled into his eyes, borne not of exertion but rather of anticipation of what was to come. This was it. Finally.

His mind drifted back to an hour ago, to the moment before his phone rang as he made his way to the staff lunch room at Masonville High. The physics class he had been teaching stampeded out of the room like cattle at the sound of their beloved bell. The bell was about the only thing that was always on time in this monotonous, backwater town.

'Perhaps they should scrap GMT and use the Masonville High school bell to coordinate the rest of the world,' he had thought as he began to pack up his belongings from the desk.

Perhaps indeed, his brain agreed. It often spoke to him, either to aid in his work or to chastise him for some shortcoming or folly. What it had to say wasn't always what Shaun wanted to hear, but usually what he needed to.

At just thirty-three, Shaun Strickland was the very manifestation of a human sigh. He had gathered an armful of papers and let his hand drift down to his pocket, his fingers fiddling with his keys and the novelty keyring he had received for his last birthday: a lighter in the shape of a pistol. He didn't smoke, but he found it useful for lighting Bunsen burners in chemistry class. He had considered taking the pistol to the carelessly completed class quizzes he was now carrying; it would save him a whole lot of time marking them tonight, but he decided against it. Barely.

Despite having the ability to push the boundaries of science, Shaun had made his choice to stay in his hometown long ago. Though he often felt under-appreciated, he tried not to focus on where he would be if he had left town as his brother had. In fact, the high-school science teacher was content to bide his time, because when he left work at the end of the day he went home to the most beautiful and amazing woman he could have ever hoped to meet. No, it really wasn't so bad. He thought about her at each frustrating tick of the clock as the hours stretched away, and inevitably a smile came to his lips. Lauren.

He was walking up the stairs thinking about her as his cell phone rang. Speak of the—

'Hey!' he said, instantly smiling. 'What's up? Making sure I get the apples? I'm all over it—'

'Shaun, listen to me,' she cut him off. 'You know how you said that if anything arrived in the mail that looked important, I should open it?'

'Uh, yeah ...'

'Even if it's addressed to you?' She sounded unusually excited about the mail.

'Lauren, what's going on?' He pictured her gold-streaked hair framing a mischievous grin. Something was up.

'Well, a letter came today. It's from England. From Cambridge University.'

He paused on the steps. 'What did it say?'

'Even if it's addressed to you.'

'Stop holding out!'

'They want you to go to England!'

'What?' Shaun shouted, oblivious to the sudden stares of students moving past him.

'Really! They say something about you sending a paper there and they want you to deliver a speech – at some sort of conference.'

The blood drained from Shaun's face. He was still holding the phone, but he could no longer feel it in his hand. He knew exactly what Lauren was talking about.

Early on, he had found out that trying to describe the beauty and elegance of complex physics theories was challenging; always fraught with misinterpretation. He knew that he needed to show the theory for it to be grasped. Like a painting, words could not do what a cursory glance could; show the painting and instantly the intangible is understood. He longed to have the ability to test his theories, to show the world rather than have to try to explain complex mathematics in a language as inadequate as English.

He took comfort in the fact that most of the great ideas in physics arose long before the means to test them existed. Einstein called it the 'thought experiment', and was a huge fan of running a train of thought through to its logical conclusion to prove his ideas. The catch was, of course, that until you tested something for real you never really knew. So it was Shaun's late-night study sessions that became thought experiments: page upon page of complex theory explained in painstaking detail.

If his days were spent battling teenage lethargy, his nightly work was a complete euphoric escape. When Lauren fell asleep, which she did around nine-thirty most nights, he would retire to his study, click on a Beatles or Pink Floyd CD and start to write. He would write and research and test and calculate and work his brain like an athlete works their muscles. It was a space where his mind could run without restriction, where he could speak a language few others understood.

During the long evenings, revelations flooded his dust-coloured room with light. But they were his alone. His conceptual ability would have been astounding if anyone around him had understood enough to be astounded. No one did. There were two downfalls to this: it made him frustrated, and it made him bitter.

He was bitter that there was no one to share his ideas with, no one who could join him. He was bitter when he heard students talk about the whimsical stories they heard in church on Sunday. The ridiculous superstitions made him want to scream. If they understood anything about the science of the real world, they wouldn't waste their time.

The other teachers always thought he looked a little sad, prompting concerned questions such as, 'Everything all right, Shaun?' or 'You look a little tired, Shaun, you sleepin' okay?' He always smiled and nodded pleasantly.

Lauren would look in on him occasionally, late at night, squinting at the scrawled pages stacked on his desk. She knew that he wouldn't abandon a half-explained theory, so she would tell him the time and ruffle his hair and trundle back to bed with a concerned frown on her sleep-crinkled face.

Most of his ideas, he knew, were too fanciful to be taken seriously, and far too impractical to ever be tested, at least in his lifetime. He sent the papers out anyway. He had sent them to anywhere he thought there might be minds that could understand them – to universities, research institutions and private companies – but he had never heard back. Not once. Not until now.

'There's just one thing,' Lauren said, still on the phone. 'They want you there tomorrow.'

'What?' Shaun snapped back to reality.

'It says here. Hang on, let me read it to you:

'Dear Mr Strickland,

I am writing to formally invite you to present a lecture at our annual Worldwide Developers' Conference, to be held on 14 June here in Cambridge. The conference is a convergence of the latest advancements and theories in science, and after having received your paper entitled "Holes in Space", we think you would be an excellent candidate to deliver our keynote presentation.

Should you accept our offer, please contact our office during business hours.

Your expenses will be covered by the university and your flights have been pre-booked pending your confirmation.

We look forward to receiving your acceptance and seeing you in person on 14 June.

Sincerely,

Professor MS Landus, Phd

'... then there's some phone numbers and an address,' Lauren finished.

Silence.

'Shaun? Shaun, you still there?'

His mind reeled, and although he commanded his mouth to move, it wouldn't respond.

'Shaun? This is good, right? This is one of the places you sent your work to?'

'Ah, yeah, this is good,' Shaun finally replied. 'I'll be home in twenty minutes. I've got to ...'

But he wasn't thinking about the phone anymore; he had already hung up. He turned slowly, looking back down the stairs towards the front office. The professor who had sent the letter was someone whose work Shaun admired, listening to hours of his podcasts over the years, but the research paper the letter mentioned had been sent to the university in Cambridge more than seven years ago. Right now he wasn't able to register how strange that was.

He had to ... had to what? Had to, yes, get his classes covered, and something about getting apples ... would Lauren still want to bake the pie? Would she be mad at him if he didn't bring home the apples? The shock of her call caused him to lose all perspective.

Walking through the front office to the car park, he called back to the receptionist.

'Gladys, I think you might want to find a sub for me for a couple of days.'

A small lady with trifocal glasses looked up from the screen she was staring at.

'You sleepin' all right, Shaun? You do look tired. Not feelin' well?'

'Uh, yeah, not too well at all.'

CHAPTER 2

Shaun's Chevron screeched to a halt in the driveway of his home. The drive had given him some time to process the information and let it sink in.

'Lauren!' he bellowed as he burst through the door to find Lauren in the lounge room bending over two open suitcases and folding a pair of jeans. He kicked off his shoes and slid dramatically across the wooden floorboards. With arms outstretched he came to a stop, 'I forgot the apples!'

She looked up and laughed before rushing over to him, throwing her arms around his neck. 'Oh, baby, I'm so proud of you! We're gonna have the best time. I've never even been out of the state, and now we're going to *England*.'

He hugged her tiny frame and kissed her passionately. Then, and only then, he heard what she had just said.

'We?' He looked down at her, holding her shoulders and searching her face. She was beaming.

'Of course we! You didn't think I was going to miss out on a chance to go to England, did you? Shopping in Soho and Knightsbridge, riding on the red buses and seeing Big Ben, maybe we can visit Buckingham Palace?'

Shaun looked past her and saw the two suitcases open on the couch next to their passports. Sure enough, one was filled with a neat stack of his standard attire: plain T-shirts, jeans and a couple of button-down shirts for what she called 'fancy' occasions. The second case was nearly empty, but almost all of Lauren's wardrobe was piled up next to it.

'Uh ...' He unhooked Lauren's arms from around his neck. He found it hard to look into her eyes to deliver the news. 'You know I'd love you to come with me more than anything, but we just can't afford a plane ticket to England right now. I'm not even sure if I'm going yet. I've still got to call and confirm and see if I can get on a flight.'

'All done! And they've booked me a seat next to you. We don't have to pay for a thing.'

Shaun turned his head a little and looked at her sceptically. 'You've already called the university?'

'I called them right after I called you. Well, maybe a bit before, but the point is that it's all done. Though they seemed a bit puzzled because the woman thought we'd already confirmed last week. Anyway, we've got tickets on a flight out of Charlotte tonight.'

It was all happening so quickly. His analytical mind ticked through the strangeness of the circumstances, but he didn't dwell.

'Tonight? But we only just found out. And Charlotte? I can't get a flight to Charlotte now; there won't be any domestic flights out till morning.'

'That's why I packed us a bunch of turkey-and-cranberry sandwiches. I've been starving lately and we won't have time to stop for dinner if we're going to get there by eleven. See, you're finally going to get the attention you deserve, and the world will see how smart you are.'

'Eleven tonight?' Shaun did the math in his head. It was a six-hour drive to the airport in Charlotte, and they were supposed to check-in well ahead of time. He looked at his watch. 'We'd have to leave now. *Right now.*'

'We?' Lauren looked at him with the girlish glint in her eye he had come to love and mistrust all at the same time.

A broad smile spread across his face. 'How quickly can you pack?'

The road to Charlotte seemed endless: a mass of greenery and bends that made Shaun motion sick as he thumbed through his manuscript.

'What did you tell your dad?' he asked when he finally paused to look up again at the horizon to try to stop the world from swaying.

'I didn't.'

Shaun looked across at his wife. She kept her eyes steady, but the muscles in her jaw twitched as her mouth became a grin.

'He just would have hassled me about work. I'll call him in the morning and tell him I can't be there on Monday.'

'In the morning we'll be on a plane, Lauren. You know how hard I've worked to get him to accept me, so if he thinks I've dragged you away from work for nothing, that'll be it.'

'It's not for nothing, it's for your big break. And I've already married you, remember? You don't need his permission anymore. We're not teenagers, Shaun; he can't keep me locked up in that little town forever, and he definitely can't keep me from shopping in Soho.'

Like Shaun, Lauren dreamed of travel, of getting out of Masonville. She fantasised about moving to LA to do make-up and special FX for the stars. She loved cinema, costumes and the theatre. At college her tutors had told her she was bursting with potential, but her father had seen an end to all that, insisting she work in the family business. But she still dreamed, and Shaun loved watching the way she sparkled when she spoke of ignoring her parents' expectations and doing something really interesting – something more than raising kids and baking pies. She would make people beautiful.

Shaun knew that she hated working for her father's business, and didn't see tobacco farming as a noble pursuit in life. But he also knew that she was determined to honour her family, at least until she and Shaun had the money to move. And, as she always said as she slumped on the couch after a day of meetings, 'Life is full of sacrifices.'

She turned back to the road as Shaun sighed and rubbed his eyes. It was already seven, and getting dark outside. He looked back down to his papers and sighed again. He had moved on from the field of space–time years ago after becoming frustrated with an impasse he could not breach. Doing a crash course in his own theory again after so long was tougher than he had expected.

'They're going to have questions about this stuff,' he said. 'They're going to have a whole bunch of questions I can't answer.'

'There's nothing you can't answer, baby,' Lauren beamed with her trademark optimism.

'I wish that were true.' Shaun forced a laugh. Every day he faced questions he could not answer, but not because the questions were hard.

To Shaun, the science of how the very fabric of space, time and the universe was formed was as intuitive as breathing. He could not imagine anything *more* interesting. But then, he did have a problem. Apart from not realising that he was intellectually swamping his students, Shaun Strickland's problem was – he did not realise that he was brilliant.

Shaun was reminded of a lesson just this morning as he struggled to get through to his class.

'... it's called the "Doppler effect", and so the sound of the siren gets higher as it approaches you, because it's catching up to the soundwaves it's making. It's moving towards them and therefore they're shorter, and a shorter wavelength means a higher pitch. Then the ambulance passes you, and ... vaaarooommm, it's moving away from you, so it's soundwaves are stretched out, making them longer and therefore the pitch is ...?'

He took a moment to stare at the board. A neat scrawl of his handiwork and a logical, coherent train of thought, all there in white chalk. He knew that when he turned around, not one of the blank faces from North Carolina's Masonville grade ten would have a clue what he'd been talking about. He therefore savoured the moment for just a second longer before he turned.

And there it was.

'So, it gets deeper like?' It was Tom Charbell, a boy who resembled a tree, who spoke. It was actually more than Shaun had expected. He sighed, smiled and took a breath to answer.

The bell. The stampede.

Shaun continued as if his class were still sitting before him, instead of halfway down the hall.

'That's right, Tommy. The same thing happens with light,' he sighed. 'An object moving towards us is catching up to its light waves, making the wavelength shorter and tinting the object blue. An object moving away is the opposite. The light arrives with its waves stretched out, and has a shift towards red. It's how we know the universe is expanding ...'

'Why do we have to learn this stuff anyway?' He heard someone grumble as the kids shuffled past. That was the question he couldn't answer. If they didn't know why, he couldn't tell them.

No, it wasn't that the questions were hard. What was hard was motivation.

They had been on the road just shy of four hours when the last rays failed. They had agreed that Lauren would drive until it got too dark for Shaun to read. Unlike many people, public speaking wasn't something that fazed Shaun. Probably, he thought, because having an audience that was keen to hear him, that had a vested interest in what he was talking about, was a luxury compared to ninth-grade boys who seemed to have mastered little more than the projectile physics of throwing 'spit-balls' at the board.

Now, though, Shaun was tired. Lauren was going strong, and insisted that he should get some rest and that she could sleep on the plane.

Shaun's wife knew he was brilliant, although she often didn't understand what he was talking about. Not that it mattered. There was no one she would rather be with. Some girls were impressed by muscles, but it seemed that Lauren got off on neurons, on having someone who always knew what to do, someone she could trust completely.

Shaun's head bounced against the window in an irregular rhythm ... *thunk thunk*, *ka*, *thunk thunk* ... he didn't really notice. He was tired and knew that he should drive soon. Waking from a minor doze, he adjusted the papers on his lap so he could put them into his bag. Through weary eyes he looked up at the road ahead, just in time to see something burst from the forest and out into their headlights.

Lauren never had a chance. She screamed, shattering the blanket of lethargy in which Shaun had wrapped himself. The tyres screeched as the back end of the Chevron fishtailed, but it was all too late. The impact came with a sickening thud, and it happened while the car, weighing more than a tonne, was still travelling fast. The full momentum of the vehicle slammed into the object, sending it sailing down the road. Papers flew from Shaun's lap, slamming against the dashboard and exploding in a frenzy of white chaos. His arms sprang out against the roof and side of the cabin to secure himself as Lauren fought the wheel, struggling with the weight of the car and trying to keep them straight to avoid rolling. The coffee she had been sipping splattered on the inside of the windscreen, burning her face as it splashed back over the cabin.

Then it was over.

All at once the car came to a stop.

Silence.

Lauren's hands gripped the wheel, her knuckles white, her breath coming in short, sharp gasps. Even though the car had stopped, Shaun found his arms wedged in place. His heart pounded in his ears. He felt sick, the aftermath of receiving a sudden jolt of adrenaline into his tired body. Breathing deeply, he looked over at Lauren. She stared straight ahead.

'Are you okay?' No response. 'Lauren.'

She flinched back with a short yelp and looked over at him, her eyes focusing.

'Are you okay?' he repeated, slowing his own breathing.

She paused as if doing a self-assessment. 'I'm okay, I'm okay ...'

'All right, just breathe ... I think we hit a deer.'

Lauren stared straight ahead.

'That was no deer.'

CHAPTER 3

Mist rose up from the ground, causing the thick yellow headlights to appear opaque in the surrounding darkness. The car shot its beam diagonally across the road, firing into the trees. The road that could be seen was empty, and the buzz and click of forest insects punctuated the silence. Thirty feet from the car an object lay still, large, unmoving.

The sound of Shaun's door opening creaked loudly as it resonated in the night and pierced the air. His feet crunched on the gravel as he stepped forward cautiously, leaving the door ajar in case he needed to retreat. The engine rumbled to life as the car started up again. He looked back at Lauren's silhouette moving her head around trying to get a clear view.

'Just back up a bit, straighten her out.' Shaun could see his breath carried off by a gentle breeze as he spoke. He shivered involuntarily, and zipped up his jacket, all the while stepping slowly towards the object lying still on the tarmac. The large black four-wheel drive reversed and swung around so its headlights pointed out onto the road ahead. He squinted off into the darkness beyond the lights. Whatever they hit was still out there, at the edge of the cone created by the low beam. He edged forward.

'Switch it to high,' he called back to Lauren. She had never been good with shocks, and moving the car was keeping her mind occupied; he didn't want to give the panic a chance to take hold.

Coming around the front, Shaun saw the windscreen and grille. They were covered with blood. The coffee spilled on the inside of the windscreen had initially obscured their view, but now he saw it clearly.

'Je-sus!' Shaun exclaimed at the sight. Then, as Lauren flicked on the high beam he followed the light to the object on the road. It had flown so far – a full thirty feet from where the car had stopped – and now lay motionless. Large, brownish and steaming from warmth in the cold night air, it looked like an animal. Whatever it was, it was alive, or had been until they hit it. He moved forward. What was that? Was it wrapped in something? He started to move faster as a chill shot through his body. No, no, no.

Shaun broke into a run for the last twenty feet. He could not believe it. He looked back over his shoulder and waved to Lauren to bring the car up. It was his turn to panic. As the tyres crackled and popped on the asphalt he looked down at the shape at his feet. It was the shape of a man.

At first he didn't believe what he was seeing – nothing could have prepared him for this – but with a quick shake of his head, Shaun threw off the remnants of shock and knelt down, reaching out with one hand to check for a pulse. He hesitated as he got a better look at the figure under the increasing light of the approaching headlights. My God, he thought, who *is* this guy?

The figure lay in a fetal position facing away from the car. He was clothed in what appeared to be layers upon layers of rags. He was impossibly dirty, filth, grime and now blood covering the tattered clothing. A leather cap was pulled tightly over a mass of tangled hair, and the figure's closed eyes were barely visible between his bushy eyebrows and overgrown beard.

Shaun snaked his hand down into the rags around the man's neck, worming his fingers in search of the warmth of skin. There was so much blood. The rags the man wore were slick with it, his hair matted, and his beard was covered in fresh streams. Then Shaun's fingertips found flesh, and he waited.

Lauren stepped out of the car, but kept the door open as if it were a shield. 'Shaun, that's not a deer, is it?'

Shaun looked up. 'He's alive, but only just. Call 911, my cell's on the back seat.' A tingling sensation made Shaun look down at his fingertips. They were now dotted with small bumps. He tried to wipe them off but could not. What were they? Blisters? Did this guy have a disease?

He didn't want to risk moving the man in case there was some kind of spinal injury, but he brought his head down to see if he could detect any breathing. He immediately wished he hadn't.

The gentle breeze stopped. The smell hit him like a runaway bus. He gagged and fell backwards.

Popping her head up from the Chevron, Lauren saw Shaun sitting back covering his nose and mouth. 'You okay? Shaun, what happened?' she asked urgently.

'This guy smells like piss!' The comment broke the tension a little, but Lauren didn't laugh. He could barely see her face, but her voice was too high. He knew she was feeling nervous.

'I can't get a signal,' she said. 'It's not even showing one bar, and I've turned it on and off a couple of times.'

That was Lauren's answer to anything technical: turn it off and on again. Funnily enough, it usually worked. Usually, but there was nothing usual here.

'Ah, shit,' Shaun said as he sat up to have another go. 'Move around a bit, stand on the car, see if you can get anything. It's got a hot-switch for emergencies.'

'No, nothing,' Lauren called after climbing on to the roof.

'How long has it been since we passed another car?' Shaun called back as he sat up, satisfied that the man was breathing.

'I haven't seen a car the entire time we've been up in the mountains. At least a couple of hours.'

Damn. *Damn, damn, damn.* Shaun knew what this meant even before he dared to think it. *You can't leave this guy here*, Shaun's brain cut in. *You'll have to take him to the nearest hospital.* Who knew where that was?

'Lauren ...' he started.

'Oh no.' She knew.

'It's a man. It's a guy and he's hurt really bad.'

'Shaun, we have to get to the airport.'

'Baby ...' Shaun left it hanging. He knew that it was only token resistance. She was clinging to the belief that their plans had not been totally disrupted. But, *damn.* What was a raggedy old man doing out here in the mountains in the middle of the night? And what the hell was he thinking running onto the road like that?

'Can you bring the car round? I don't want to carry him in case he's ...' *What?* Shaun's brain interjected. *In case he's totally fucked up? Too late for that.*

Shaun stared at the body as the lights of the car came around. The engine buzzed loudly and he wondered if the man would be roused. Part of him wanted the shape to move, and part of him was glad it didn't.

He examined the rising and falling chest, and then with a start noticed that the man wasn't just curled up, he was curled around something, clutching it tightly.

'How the hell did you hang on to that?' Shaun wondered. He looked closer and saw that the man was holding a large bundle. Keeping his eyes on the man's face as if it might suddenly spring to life, he reached down. He moved first one arm, then the other. Unconscious, the rag-man offered no resistance. A limp forearm fell away and Shaun removed what the man had been holding. It was about the size of a large shoebox.

There was something wrapped in rags and leather, and it smelled almost as bad as the man who had been holding it.

'What's that?' Lauren asked as Shaun carried it over to the car, holding it away from his body as if it too might spring to life at any moment.

'Don't know. The old guy was hanging on to it for dear life.'

Lauren screwed up her nose as Shaun placed the parcel on the passenger seat. 'Eeww, that smells dead! Is that animal skin?' She winced as she opened the back door. 'Are you sure we should touch that?'

She jumped down and moved around to the man's legs. The mingled grime, blood and dirt nearly overwhelmed her as she helped Shaun carefully lift the man's dead weight into the back seat.

'How are we going to drive with that smell?' she asked.

'We'll just drive until we get a signal, then we can call the paramedics. I mean, there's got to be a town round here somewhere – how the hell else did he get out here?'

Lauren raised an eyebrow. 'Are you seeing this guy? He's probably lived out here for years. Smells like he hasn't showered in a decade. You couldn't tell who he was even if you did know him, under all that hair and grime.'

She was right. Still, Shaun agreed that it was weird. He checked his watch: 8.53 pm, so they had about two hours to get to the airport, and this was going to change things. Damn.

Crazy old fool, what the hell was he thinking?

Shaun opened the driver's-side door as Lauren made to climb into the passenger seat, but stopped dead at the sight of the bundle sitting there. A sense of foreboding filled her. 'I am *not* touching that thing,' she protested.

'Just put it at your feet,' Shaun offered, keeping one eye on the inert form now lying across the back seat. The man was hurt badly, bleeding from everywhere and nowhere; it was impossible to tell under the mud and blood caking his clothing. The cap he wore looked like a hunter's cap that peaked at the front but came down to cover his ears and neck. Clearly he had been in bad shape long before they hit him. He looked like he had been through a war.

They sped on through the winding mountain roads, both feeling stunned after the accident, but relieved the man was alive.

Lauren shuffled her feet uneasily, trying not to touch the wrapped bundle that was slick with the man's blood.

'Who do you think he could be?' she asked to break the silence.

'The more I think about it, the stranger it seems. I mean, there's nothing around here for miles, and it's not like he was trying to wave us down or anything, he just ran out. He ran straight out!'

'Perhaps he was running away from something?'

'Maybe. But it's not like he didn't see us. I mean, one road, loud noise, bright lights, we kind of stand out.'

Lauren was silent. Her eyes were fixed downward. They were both thinking the same thing.

'I don't want to touch it,' she finally said after a long pause.

The bundle slid on the floor towards her, bashing into her shins. She recoiled.

'He was hanging on to that pretty tight,' said Shaun. 'I went through his clothes for a wallet or something, but there's nothing. I'm betting that whatever that thing is, it'll tell us something about this guy. It's got to be important. You don't get slammed by a speeding SUV and think of nothing but holding onto a package if it's not important.'

Lauren made to protest again, but then sighed. The initial shock had subsided somewhat, and now she was curious – and, despite the horror of the whole episode, a little excited. She fumbled through the glove box for something to cover her legs with, finally settling on a patchwork of paper napkins, receipts and Kleenex. She reached down and hoisted the bundle onto her lap. It was heavy, as if it bore the weight of a terrible secret.

'There's definitely something inside this lining,' she said as she handled the animal skin. 'Several things, by the feel of it.'

After one more glance at Shaun, she began to peel away the layers.

In the chill night, the big Chevron sped through the hills, taking the turns with determined speed. Somewhere far behind, another vehicle pulled to a stop. It was a dull matte black, and if not for the headlights it would have been invisible in the darkness. The passenger door opened, and a pair of shiny black shoes stepped out onto the asphalt. They paused a moment, then spun, walking to the front of the car to stop at a large stain of blood. Their owner crouched to look closely, before standing and returning to the open door. With a satisfied spin of the tyres, the car leaped forward, followed closely by three identical dull black vehicles. They seemed to suck light into them and appeared as three holes in the night. In the darkness it was impossible to tell what they looked like, but it did not matter. For the cars' drivers, all that mattered was that they were closing in.

As Lauren peeled back the outer layers of the bundle on her lap, she wrinkled her nose. A release of stale air exhaled from the package and filled the car. It even overpowered the smell of urine and grit coming off the man who was breathing steadily in the back seat. Layer upon layer. There seemed to be an outer coating of fresh animal skin surrounding an inner layer of old leather.

Eventually, Lauren peeled it all away to be confronted with a semi-transparent sack. Inside she could see a large pile of what looked like papers, books and parchments.

'What the?' Shaun started as he shot a glance over at the sack, then at the man in the back. He seemed to be breathing a little more easily now, and his head was gently rocking as the car bumped over the road. The blood that had been wet and flowing was slowly drying on his beard and face, creating yet another caked-up layer.

'What *is* this thing?' Lauren asked, holding up the translucent sack.

Shaun looked it over. 'It looks like the stomach of some kind of animal.'

Lauren looked down and let out a short sound of disgust. 'A stomach? Why would anyone put books inside an animal *stomach*?'

'I don't know, but I'm really not sure we should go any further.'

'Oh no, I'm not getting my hands all grossed up for nothing. I'm opening this thing and finding out what's in it.' Then, digging her nails into the stomach sack, she punctured it.

The odours they had encountered before were mild in comparison to what now seeped out from the pile on Lauren's lap. Air that had been trapped for longer than either of them could have dreamed raced out to fill the cabin.

Shaun gagged and pulled the car to a stop, quickly opening his door to get out. Lauren, however, had anticipated the smell and pulled her sweater up over her nose and mouth.

'Oh, man!' Shaun took a good lungful of the fresh night air before dropping back onto his seat. 'And I thought they smelled bad, on the outside!' Shaun mimicked in his best Han Solo voice. 'That's rank,' he blurted.

'No, rank is you after a high-fibre breakfast. *This* is interesting.'

Shaun stared at his wife, not wanting to believe that she was actually enjoying this.

'Well, look who's changed their tune. While we're stopped, can you check the cell again?' Shaun asked as he slipped the car into first and got them moving again. Lauren pulled out the phone and checked for the signal bars. Still nothing. She turned her attention back to the open bundle on her lap.

Sitting in a neat pile, protected for who knew how long from the elements by an airtight seal of animal and leather insulation, was a stack of documents. Books, papers, texts, all appearing impossibly old and delicate. Lauren carefully opened to the first page of the manuscript sitting on the top of the stack. It was a collection of symbols that she did not recognise, and she was certain she had never seen anything like it except maybe in one of the museums Shaun had taken her to. The writing looked a little like Arabic.

'Oh my God,' Lauren said as her head came up suddenly. 'What if he stole these? What if this stuff is from a museum or something and he was running away from the police?'

Shaun did not argue. It seemed as plausible as anything. Lauren continued through the stack. There were single loose leafs of old parchment, three crude leather-bound books held together with thin leather strips and a multitude of tightly rolled scrolls. Some contained what looked like diagrams, while most were filled with different kinds of writing.

'It looks like some sort of collection,' Lauren began, 'and there doesn't really seem to be any order to it. The writing looks different from one page to the next on these loose sheets ... and then there are these ones with pictures—'

Bleep! Lauren's train of thought was lost. *Bleep!*

It was the sound of a message arriving on the cell phone, which meant they had a signal again. Lauren fished around for the phone in the centre console of the car, looked at the screen and then handed it on to Shaun.

'Voice messages,' Lauren said matter-of-factly. 'Your brother and my dad.'

Shaun winced. Her father only ever called Shaun's cell phone when he couldn't get a hold of Lauren at home. As for Shaun's brother Tim, why was he calling now? They hadn't spoken in years.

'Well, we'll listen to those later,' he said as he thumbed the disconnect key. He dialled 911 and waited. 'Where are we?' he whispered to Lauren, nodding towards the map in the open glove compartment.

She wrestled with the map for a second then handed it over. For all her wonderful traits, he thought as he flicked on the interior light, reading a map wasn't one of them. He steered with his knees while holding the phone in one hand and spun the map in the other.

'Ah,' he told the operator when prompted, 'we're about twenty miles west of the Greensville junction on the old Southern Road ...'

Bleep, bleep, bleep.

'Shit!'

'What?' Lauren looked over as she saw him take the phone away from his ear. In disgust he flipped it closed and tossed it in her lap.

'Signal dropped out. Keep an eye on it, would you, and if it comes back, hit redial. We're ... here ... ish,' he said pointing to a spot on the map as he handed it across to her.

Lauren turned her attention back to the bundle and continued to sift through as Shaun refocused on the road ahead. He soon noticed a sign, the first they had seen in miles. It was for a place called Motel 6, fifteen miles ahead. He smiled. At least they would have a landline and perhaps a shower. They might be able to leave the hobo there and still make the airport if they really pushed it.

'Hey, do you still have that coupon book you were talking about before? That had something for accommodation, didn't it? Maybe we can ...'

Lauren wasn't listening.

'Lauren?'

She stared at her lap, her large green eyes wide.

'You okay? What is it?' Shaun asked, his heart starting to race.

Slowly and seriously, she looked up at Shaun. She then lifted what she had been looking at up to the dashboard in front of him so he could read it. It was a book like the others, although maybe not quite so crude, but just as old. It was bound with some kind of animal skin that still had the remnants of hair on it, and it was thick.

A peculiar symbol was imprinted on the book's cover: a vertical line with a cross-bar, and two loops, a larger one, and a smaller one, hanging from it like teardrops. It was not the appearance of the book, however, that caused Shaun to slam on the brakes; it was the words written on the page:

'This diary will be found on the 13th of June 2014AD, more than two thousand years from now. My name is Graeme Fontéyne, and I remember everything.'

CHAPTER 4

The motel wasn't big; it only had twelve rooms, and Clive could not remember the last time they had all been full. Five-star it certainly was not. It wasn't even a member of the Hotel 6 chain, the owners had simply used the name to sound more reputable, and they relied on no one bothering to sue.

Clive rocked back on the legs of his wooden chair and stared at the small television on the counter. Twenty-six, overweight and balding, Clive thought he had it pretty good at the reception desk of Motel 6. There were only a couple of chores to do on the night shift, about an hour's worth of work. Then for the rest of the night, he watched porn. Loads and loads of porn. He found it helped the time pass, and no one ever came in after midnight anyway. There was no rain tonight, and the stars were out. Yes, he liked tonight. He probably wouldn't have changed a thing, which was fortunate, because this would be the last night of his life.

He had got the chores out of the way early and started to watch *Indiana Bones in Her Temple of Poon* when he heard tyres on the gravel outside. It was with mild surprise and irritation that he pushed his chair back and strained his neck to peep through the venetians at the bulky SUV outside.

With a groan, Clive returned all four legs of the chair to the ground and heaved his considerable bulk forward to flick the DVD off. He'd once left one of his discs in the 'in-house movie' player, just to see if anyone complained. No one did.

As the screen door swung open, Clive got to his feet. The man who entered appeared to be about Clive's age, perhaps a little older. He seemed agitated and rushed. Clive caught a whiff of foul human stench as the man leaned towards him, his eyes wide and desperate.

'I've got to use your phone, there's been an accident,' the man said.

'Cost of a local call is thirty-five cents,' Clive stated in a drawn-out Southern accent. 'Unless 'course you wanna get a room, then I just puts it on your bill.' The man fished around in his pockets, pulling out a handful of change and dumping it on the counter. Clive slid the green rotary-dial phone across the counter, eyeing the man suspiciously as he hurriedly dialled.

'Operator, yes, there's been an accident. We're at Motel 6 ...' Clive listened to the man relay his story to the emergency call centre, and noticed the blood covering his hands and clothes. The agitated man hung up. Only now looking into the face of the unsympathetic receptionist, he asked, 'You got somewhere we can get cleaned up?'

'Only thing I got is this board right here with a whole lotta keys on it. If you wants one of them keys, you gotta pay eighty-two dollars for the night.' The rooms only cost forty-five, but Clive knew a sucker when he saw one.

The man frowned, clearly irritated. 'I don't need a room, I just need to get cleaned up. There's an ambulance on its way and we've got to get to the airport.'

'Not tonight, you don't. You didn't hear on the radio? There was that big blackout at the airport. Closed the whole thing down till morning.'

'What?' The man said exasperated. 'Are you sure?'

'It's been on the TV every five minutes. You're welcome to stay and watch it for a while if you want.' Clive spun the television around on the counter. Almost on cue the programming went to a commercial break and a news bulletin flashed up:

'... half the city. There's no explanation as yet as to what caused the massive blackout, but authorities haven't ruled out a terrorist attack. According to Charlotte's chief of police, major public services will resume in the early hours of the morning and she urges everybody to stay calm. Just repeating once again: a massive blackout has hit the city of Charlotte, causing power loss to over thirty thousand homes and major transport services. The central railway station and the airport have both been closed until further notice.'

'Oh no, no, no! You've got to be kidding me!' Shaun cried as he stared at the screen.

The night was spiralling out of control. Suddenly his biggest concern had gone from getting his page numbering right, to having a half-dead, bloodied hobo in the back of his car. Now it looked like his flight had been cancelled, or at least postponed, until the morning. Of course there was a terrorist attack on the airport tonight, he thought – in case their plans hadn't been derailed enough. Shaun rubbed his neck anxiously, then thought of Lauren sitting in the cold car with the half-dead man. He knew she needed a rest, and it looked like this was it.

'Okay, fine, I'll take a room, but tell the ambulance where we are when it arrives, okay?'

Clive reached up to the top corner of his key rack and grabbed a key. 'There you go, room twelve, all the way down the end. That ambulance is gonna be a while, ain't no hospital for at least an hour. Oh, and payment's in advance.'

'You're kidding,' Shaun said.

'You don't get this key till I get paid. It's motel policy.' Clive pulled the key back.

'Yeah, when it suits you, no doubt,' Shaun said, only half under his breath. He pulled out his wallet, found two fifties and threw them across at the counter.

'Oh, we ain't got no change. Correct change only. Or you can see Heather in the morning to see if she's got some change for ya.'

'Forget it,' Shaun growled. 'We're gonna be making a whole bunch of phone calls from the room – keep the change to cover those.' Shaun snatched the key from Clive's raised hand and rushed back out the door. Clive smiled and slid the cash into his pocket.

'Did you get through?' Lauren asked as Shaun jumped back into the driver's seat and gunned the gas, obviously irritated.

'Jackass!'

'*Shaun*?'

'We're going to have to stay here for a while,' he started. 'The ambulance is on its way but could be about an hour, and there was a goddamned blackout at the airport.'

'What? A blackout?'

'Took out half the city, apparently. It was on the news. No planes are flying till the morning.' Shaun set his jaw and shrugged, grinding the gear stick into reverse and spinning quickly on the gravel.

Lauren grabbed the sides of her seat, alarmed. Trying to soothe Shaun, she offered: 'At least we'll get a chance to freshen up.'

Shaun looked over to her and relaxed just a little. Always a positive. They drove slowly past rooms eight, nine and ten, which were fronted by hillbilly trucks and beaten-up station wagons. As they approached numbers eleven and twelve they saw a large metal dumpster out the front, so Shaun eased the car into the free space outside number seven.

He gave Lauren the key and climbed out, debating whether to move the unconscious man or leave him peacefully breathing in the back. He decided that he did not want the guy waking up in his car, so he hoisted him over his shoulder, the man's arms dangling down Shaun's back, then closed the back door with his foot and headed for the room.

It was modest, to say the least. A double bed, one small counter with an old rusted metal chair pushed up under it, and a phone. There was a television, but a large hand-written sign gave notice as to its state of disrepair. One thing it did have, though, was a shower.

Shaun carried the ragged man on his shoulders over to the bed and laid him down as gently as he could. They agreed that Lauren take the first shower, but not before she ducked back out to the car and returned with the bundle that had been sitting on the front seat.

'I really don't know if we should,' Shaun said, but he knew it was futile. They had both seen what piqued Lauren's interest: one of the books, as old as the rest, was written in perfect English. They knew that it was impossible, that either the whole bundle was a fake or ... or what? Shaun racked his mind for a logical explanation.

Lauren carefully placed the bundle on the floor and took out the animal-skin-covered book. It was remarkably well preserved – or not as old as it appeared to be. But then Shaun looked at the figure still unconscious on the bed. He was definitely not fake.

Lauren perched on the rusty chair and opened the book to the first page. It was the thickest of the books, and it could have been centuries since it had seen the light of day, but then there was that first line: 'This diary will be found on the 13th of June 2014AD, more than two thousand years from now.' That was today. Shaun glanced over at the bed again, then moved behind Lauren, leaning over her shoulder to read.

CHAPTER 5

My name is Graeme Fontéyne, and I remember everything. I am writing this book as much for my own sanity as to complete what I have started.

The first thing I will say and the most important is this: the human mind is not designed to live in two places in time. I tell you this so they might know what happened to the others, if they are not found.

The first thing I remembered was pain. Unbelievable pain, as if the weight of the entire universe were trying to crush me from all sides, and there was no reprieve. I woke up naked, freezing and thirsty. I was so very thirsty. It's hard now to even think about it. It felt like every nerve ending in my body was screaming. In all human existence, there is no pain like it.

Then it was gone.

Then came the thirst. I'm not sure how long I was lying out there before I could move, but it must have been several hours.

No part of me was broken. I had no cuts, no injuries – just thirst. I finally stood up and looked around. It was dark, cold, and I was naked – funny how the facts stated themselves so clearly. The moon was large and full, and lit the grass-covered hills surrounding me. The place was dry, and the grass was arranged sparsely in tufts and tangles against the dust. A breeze tunnelled through the dirt and whipped particles lightly against my bare feet.

I walked. There was nothing else I could do. I walked aimlessly all night, with nothing in my mind but the thirst. After hours of trudging through unwavering terrain, I saw a light. As I moved closer, I heard voices, I heard laughter and I saw three men seated around a fire. I approached them slowly, and their laughter stopped, as one after the other they turned and looked at me. After a pause, they burst into laughter again, and this time, it was at my expense. One of the men said something.

I remained silent.

All at once they roared with a fresh peal of laughter. It was the strangest thing: I knew that the man was not speaking my language, and yet I understood exactly what he said. I will write it here for you in English, but know that that was not the language we were speaking.

The first man spoke again, with a broad grin. 'I said, "Cold night?"'

'Very cold,' I replied, shocked at my own voice. The three, uproarious now, clutched their bellies, laughing until tears streamed down their weather-worn faces. It was then that I realised that they were referring to my nakedness, and more specifically the effects of the cold upon it. I smiled. For some reason, I smiled, relieved.

'Water?' I asked then. The rasp in my throat betrayed the fact that there was next to no moisture in my body. The laughter stopped and the one who had spoken looked more closely, appraising me.

'What happened to you?' he asked, his eyes wavering between suspicion and concern.

'I ...' I did not know what to say. I had nothing to say. Indeed, I had not asked myself this question since I woke up. With my head the way it was, all I could do was speak the truth.

'I don't know,' I said simply. The man who had spoken watched me from beneath bushy black brows, and pursed his lips under a thick black beard. Then, having made a decision, he said something very quickly to his companions and stood up, looking me in the eye.

'Friend, come and sit with us by the fire and warm yourself. Yosef will fetch you some clothes,' the man put a hand on my elbow and guided me into the circle. The warmth was incredible. A moment later one of the others, a taller man with lighter hair and a dimpled face, brought a grey robe to me. I put it on silently and sat. A moment after that, the other man, shorter and balding, handed me a wineskin. I drank deeply and quickly. I drank and drank and soon toppled over sideways.

When I woke I was warmer. I was inside a tent. The sun was shining through the fabric prickling my eyes and my head pounded. There were no voices outside but I could hear the pops and crackle of a dying fire. I rose and opened the tent flap, blinking in the strong light.

Alone in front of the cooling embers sat the taller brown-haired man. He was perched on a large stone and played with the ashes of the fire with a long stick. He stood when he saw me.

'How are you feeling?' he asked.

'My head hurts,' I replied.

'You drank a lot of wine,' he replied, laughing, and I realised that he was not much more than a boy, although his skin was weathered.

'Where are your friends?' I asked.

'My father and uncle are with the flock. They said I should stay and help you if you woke up. They will be back soon.' The boy's speech was plain. Even in this strange language I somehow understood, I could tell he was a simple man.

'They said I should give you some food if you want it.' He turned and reached into a basket at his feet, pulling up what looked like a loaf of bread. I took it gladly. Despite the pain in my head, I was beginning to think more clearly.

'Can I ask your name?' I looked at the boy, who was still staring at me.

'My name is Yosef. My father is Jonah and my uncle is James.'

'Yosef? Yosef what?' I pressed.

'Yosef what? What do you mean?' The boy looked confused and tilted his head to the side a little.

'What's your last name?'

'The last name my father gave me was Yosef. I don't think I had one after that.'

I let it go.

'What is your name?' he countered. I was now lucid enough to realise that I had no idea where I was, why I was here or – and this thought struck home with Yosef's question – who I was. What I said next came out as if by its own free will.

'Saul. My name is Saul.'

At that moment, the bleating of sheep made me look out to my left. I saw the other two men, Jonah and James, coming over a nearby rise followed by a group of docile animals, their white curls dust-coloured, their heads stooped low with exertion.

I smiled and waved as the men approached, offering them my thanks for their kindness.

'You seemed fairly confused last night, but a few wineskins and good rest appear to have done you good.'

'I feel much better, thank you,' I said. 'I think I was robbed, but I don't remember anything. I woke up with nothing.'

'Yes, we saw that. These parts are a little dangerous to be travelling alone. We come from a village two days' walk to the west. We've had to move the flock every couple of days. Haven't had any rain for more than a month now.' Jonah removed the scarf he had wrapped around his head and placed it on a stick, which was standing upright in the ground.

'I am going to guess and say that you are not a shepherd. And also by your look, that you are not a Jew.'

It was the first time that I had thought about what I looked like. Despite my confusion I had a strong sense of my physical appearance. I felt confident that I could make decisions even without remembering anything before the previous day. I knew basic things such as my moral code and my likes and dislikes.

I knew with certainty that I did not look like these men. I was taller, and although my features were dark my skin was fair. I looked down at my body. It was that of a physically well-trained man. I knew also that it worked. It worked well. I knew that I could run, that I could fight and that if I had to, I could walk across a wire one hundred feet above the ground without falling. I felt sure of myself and my abilities, but I did not know my name.

'I am from the east,' I lied. 'I think I was hit on the head very hard last night. I am looking for family in the west.' I hoped that this explanation would give me some semblance of credibility.

'Which town are you looking for, brother?'

I paused, and looked blankly back at them.

'Well, if you're heading west, you'll come to our village of Chorazin, then a half-day beyond that is Capernaum. You might like to start there. It's a big town near the water and you can find my brother Simon there. He works as a fisherman and will help you. Of course you are welcome to stay with us for as long as you need, but we are moving this flock today and heading further east.' He untied a pouch he was carrying around his waist and offered it to me. 'Here is some bread. Please take it.'

I reached out to take the pouch and as I did Jonah grabbed my wrist and held it firmly.

'There is something about you, friend,' he said as his eyes held my gaze like his hand held my wrist. 'There is something very strange about you. These are unusual times and you have some part to play.'

He released me, both from his grip and from his impromptu evaluation. 'Go with God.'

I was a little taken aback, but sensed no malice from this shepherd, and so I smiled.

'Thank you for your kindness, and for the food. I will remember you.'

With this I turned and walked west.

A groan.

Shaun and Lauren turned together towards the bed. There had definitely been a groan. Shaun moved to lean over the figure. 'It's okay, buddy. Take it easy, you're safe now. The ambulance is coming.'

It was of no consequence. The groan had come, but the man had not regained consciousness. His eyes remained closed.

'He's still out. Keep going.'

They were both hooked. Despite the strangeness of the evening and of this book, their eyes returned to the page.

CHAPTER 6

For hours I walked west in the beaming sunshine and saw no one. The ground turned crimson under my feet as the sun sank over the horizon.

I heard the village before I saw it. A distant scream split the silence – not the scream of a child, nor that of a woman, but the deep, guttural, animalistic scream of a man. Terrified. Then abruptly, the sound ceased.

I heard hooves. I heard terror. I heard the screams of more men. I started to run, and as I moved, the shouts became louder. I smelled smoke. I ran faster.

I rounded a bend in the road and skidded to a stop. The decapitated body of a man lay unceremoniously on the road, strewn like an animal carcass. Ten feet away his head rested, a hairy, bloody mass staring into the sky, mouth agape. I gagged, looking quickly away. The man was dressed in robes not dissimilar to my own, but his body was perforated with wounds. The stretch of road around him was littered with hoof prints and clumps of wet, bloody dirt.

As the sounds grew louder I ran on, mindful now of the danger that was all too apparent. I felt unknowing purpose and it drove me forward. When I reached the village it was burning, the buildings flecked with flames.

I moved on, coming to the houses and the confusion on the streets. Terrified people ran everywhere. I walked through the centre of town, unnoticed amid the carnage. Then I saw a woman slumped on the ground in front of a crudely constructed house. She was wailing over the body of a man, cradling his limp torso in her arms and stroking his face. Compassion took me. I knelt down in front of her and she quieted, looking up into my face apprehensively through wet-lashed eyes. The man was alive, but bleeding badly from a wound in the leg. I pulled off my shirt and tore it into strips. I wrapped the strips around his leg and fastened them tightly, using the remaining fabric to bind a wound in his side. The pain would have been intense, but I knew these wounds were not fatal.

The woman watched me, her eyes searching my face, and darting again to the man as he groaned. He opened his eyes to look at me.

'You are not one of them.'

'No,' I replied, figuring if I did not know of whom he spoke, it was a safe assumption.

'This hurts, but you will not die from these wounds,' I said.

The man shook his head. 'They have Mishca, they have my son!' He coughed with the exertion of speaking. His face was that of a man who had fought with all he had, and lost.

'Who has your son?'

'They took him, they took him away,' the man repeated, overwhelmed by grief. 'He's only twelve years old.'

I turned to the woman. 'Where did they take him?'

She stared at me wide-eyed, and raised her arm, pointing. I ran bare-chested, following her gesture.

The scene around me was a montage of fights, fires and agony. I saw men from the town join together, holding short swords of iron, battling against two or three of the enemy, but it was this enemy that caught my attention.

Dressed in red cloth and gold-sculpted armour strapped with leather, they moved like warriors. They were merciless, and looked to be winning whatever battle had taken place here. I ran down the street looking for the boy, avoiding the armoured men taking wild swings as I passed. I only slowed when I saw a small boy struggling in the grip of a large guard, who I now know to be a Roman soldier.

A group of Romans languished in the final throws of their pitched battles, and then fell into line behind the man who was now dragging the boy through the dust with a firm grip around his torso. The boy kicked his captor's legs but was no match for the centurion, a thickset man with broad shoulders and a tall plume on his helmet. He paused long enough to backhand the thin boy not once, not twice, but three times across the face to knock him into submission. The boy went immediately limp – and my blood boiled.

'Let him go!' I shouted, furious. Even above the clangs of metal and the screams of the butchery, the man heard me. He stopped, turned and looked at me as I stood alone, unarmed with a torn robe. Then a strange thing happened. The man spoke to me. He spoke to me but not in the language I had heard from the shepherds. He spoke to me in a deep baritone voice in an offhand way as he turned his back on me. And yet, once more, I understood.

'Run along, dog,' he said. 'I do not want to waste any more time on this wretched outpost.'

What happened next was even stranger. In this new tongue, I spoke back: 'Then leave quickly, and leave the boy where you stand.' The words came out like I had been speaking the language all my life. The soldiers all turned. The man holding the boy scowled, unsure of what to make of me.

'If you are a Roman, you are a long way from your post,' he said.

'Leave the boy,' I replied firmly. I did not know if I was a Roman or not, but I knew that this boy had to be free. The heavyset centurion studied me for another moment, then turned and waved a motion to the guards behind him. He walked on towards a cage of iron a few hundred feet down the street.

On his command, two of the guards approached me with their swords drawn. The centurion felt the boy start to struggle again and raised his hand to solve the problem when I called out to him once more.

'I said, leave the boy. You do not touch him again.'

The big man turned, shocked to see me standing unharmed above his two guards unconscious at my feet. He waved his hand again and the remaining four guards approached me. This time the centurion did not turn away. He watched long enough to see the first guard thrust his short sword straight out towards me. He watched long enough to see me twist my body in time with the blow and lock the man's arm under mine, bringing my other palm around on his elbow. His arm broke cleanly and offered no resistance as I twisted it back the other way to bury the blade up to its hilt in his stomach.

The second and third attackers came at almost the same time, one stepping in with his sword raised high above his head, the other with his blade tip lower directly behind the first man. The centurion watched as I continued the turning motion I had started with the first attacker and shot a back kick straight out at the armour-covered mid section of the second attacker. My heel made solid contact with his breastplate and sent the guard flying, directly on to the tip of his colleague's sword. The blade severed his spinal cord and his body sank to the ground, the third soldier's sword still buried in it.

Still watching with disbelief clouding his face, the centurion saw that I was already moving, running up the body of the falling man and with the weight of the third guard's sword dragging his hands lower, I snapped the ball of my foot into the man's exposed face, immediately knocking him out. The fourth guard hesitated as he approached, then stopped.

The sound of thundering hooves filled the street and the battle cries of at least twenty men shattered the strange spell that had befallen our corner of the village. The centurion turned and ducked out of the way of a slashing sword levelled just above his shoulders by one of the riders who now thundered past. As he ducked, the big man pushed the boy into the path of the riders. I saw the first rider evade the boy, but I knew that the others would not be able to see him. I raced into the path of the charging animals and their slashing riders and crashed into the falling boy, tackling him through the closed window of a house lining the street.

CHAPTER 7

Shards from the window exploded as the body sailed through it and landed hard on the tarmac outside the reception area. The sound of shattering glass snapped Shaun and Lauren back into the present.

'What was that?' Lauren gasped. She followed Shaun to the window of their hotel room and took in the scene: the hotel receptionist lay prone on the ground; three black cars were parked out the front of the hotel; and next to the cars stood four men clothed head-to-toe in black.

The men stood still and silent. With their feet shoulder-width apart, and their gloved hands clasped in front, they stood watching the same thing Shaun and Lauren watched. They watched the beaten motel clerk groan, roll over and slowly raise himself on all fours. They watched as another man in black strode from the front of the reception door to where the clerk knelt, rocking back on his haunches at the man's approach. Shaun could not hear him, but the body language was clear: the clerk was begging – shaking his head, his hands raised, palms outwards. The man in black stood directly in front of him and raised one arm out towards his head, and it was then that Shaun saw it. It looked like the man was pointing a long-gloved finger at the clerk, but it was no finger. The muzzle flashed twice and the clerk dropped. Dead.

'Holy shit!' Shaun exclaimed. Lauren stayed silent.

The other men strode into action. Two of them moved up to the body and checked it over, removing small items from the clothing. Another two marched to the first motel-room door and kicked it in. Shaun and Lauren could not see the muzzle flash this time, but they heard the screams of a woman and the yells of a man. Both were silenced by the *BLAM! BLAM!* of pistols.

Lauren made to scream but Shaun put a hand to her mouth and looked around the room for another exit. There was none. As the next door was kicked in, the scream of sirens came around the corner and the red lights of an ambulance flooded the area. The large white van screeched to a halt in the centre of the car park out the front of the line of rooms at the motel. Shaun and Lauren watched as one of the paramedics climbed out of the passenger side of the van and approached the man standing over the dead motel clerk. The paramedic looked as if he was speaking.

He was silenced as the man in black raised his arm and shot the paramedic through the chest, twice. Without missing a beat he fired at the ambulance driver before he had a chance to react. A second later the driver slouched on the wheel and the whole ambulance leaped forwards, heading straight for them.

Shaun pulled his wife away from the window. His hand still covering Lauren's mouth, he looked into her eyes and hissed, 'We've gotta get out of here!'

She whimpered and then nodded, trying to control her breathing.

Shaun let her go and searched the room for something, anything. They could hear the gunmen outside, systematically kicking in the doors, executing the people inside.

'They're just ... they're just shooting everyone! Oh, Jesus!' Lauren panted, beginning to panic. 'Oh, Jesus!'

At that moment they heard a massive crash outside their window. Shaun dared a look and saw that the ambulance had smashed into the dumpster right outside their room.

'They're coming,' he said matter-of-factly, watching the men disappear into another room, then reappear moments later, then move on to the next.

SMASH! They kicked in the door. Screams, scuffle, *BLAM!*

Room four.

'Okay, we have to try and get to the car,' Shaun said finally.

Room five.

'Go *towards* them?' Lauren breathed.

Room six.

'We'll wait till they go into a room and then ...' He looked out, playing it out in his mind. Their SUV was fifty feet away. They would never make it. They did not have time.

'Shit! Shit! Shit!' he cursed. Then he saw it. Right there, blazing with its flashing red lights. They would never make their own car – the men in black had just gone into room seven – but the ambulance was only fifteen feet away.

'Okay, we have to time this right,' he said as he reached up for the door handle. Just then they heard another groan from the bed.

Shaun spun around. He had completely forgotten about the hobo. He paused, uncertain.

'Shaun, we can't. You can't carry him.'

He knew she was right, but ... 'They're gonna kill him if we leave him.' Shit, shit, shit.

You run now you might just make it to the van, but you leave a man to certain death. You try and take him and you might all die.

Shit.

What kind of man are you?

Stupid brain.

Shaun half-crawled, half-scrambled across the floor over to the man on the bed. He had rolled over slightly, but had not woken up.

'Lauren, when I say so, open that door fast.' He heaved the man up onto his shoulders. 'I'm going to race for the dumpster. The second I'm through the door, you follow right behind me, you got that? *Right behind me*. If they see me, I don't want you stranded in here.'

Lauren nodded. She was already exhausted after the accident and did not have any more energy for fear.

'Now!' Shaun rasped.

Lauren opened the door and followed Shaun as he raced for the dumpster. The area of exposed ground between the room and the cover offered by the large metal trash unit was about ten feet, but it felt like a marathon. Shaun's thighs burned as his shuffling steps rang loud in his ears. After the longest second of his life, he slid to a crouched halt behind the dumpster. Lauren landed beside him, breathing quickly.

They waited.

She peeked around the edge of the dumpster and saw the black-clad men enter room nine. No one there. They emerged. Room ten.

They hadn't seen them. God, they hadn't seen them! Shuffling on his knees Shaun rounded the far side of the bin, coming over to the passenger side of the ambulance, the hobo weighing heavily against him. His wife was not behind him.

'Lauren!' he called sharply in a whisper. But she was not there. He panicked, a feeling of dread filling his stomach. He had not felt it since the day he heard that his parents had been killed. He went dizzy with fear, and his vision began to blur as Lauren appeared at the edge of the bin. She held something tightly against her chest.

'God, what are you doing?' Shaun spat in a mix of relief and fury.

'The diary,' she said simply. He had forgotten all about it, and right now he could not believe that she had run back into the room to get it. Was she insane? She had married him even when her father threatened to cut her out of the family fortune, but this was a whole new level of crazy, dashing across open territory in front of people who would shoot her if they saw her.

Unfortunately, this time they had.

The first shot hit the edge of the dumpster on the far side. It had come from someone over near the black cars outside the motel reception, a good hundred and fifty feet away. With that shot, all of the gunmen were alerted to their presence. There wasn't time to sneak about now, no time to think, just time to rush up to the passenger-side door and shove the hobo inside. He fell across the bench seats awkwardly as Shaun climbed over him. The dead paramedic was still slumped at the wheel, and Shaun heard three slugs bury themselves in the body. Lauren threw the diary in and leaped for the open passenger door.

Reaching down to the column changer, using the paramedic's body as cover, Shaun slammed the still-running van into reverse. He opened the driver's door and hurled the dead man out, spinning the wheel away from the motel. The body went flying as the front end of the van spun around. He kept the van circling so it faced the car-park exit, and as it whooshed past the line of black cars bullets rained on the front and side of the vehicle.

As the back of the ambulance came level with the dumpster, Shaun slammed the transmission straight into second and gunned the gas flat to the floor. It took about half a second for the torque to kick in, and then the powerful engine pulled the van forward. The tyres smoked and screeched as they spun, and the hail of bullets was relentless. *BLAM! BLAM! SMASH!* The rear windows blew out. He sunk even lower into the seat. With each second, the ambulance put distance between itself and the gunmen in black.

Shaun slammed into third, then fourth and then, with a sound like the slowing of popcorn popping, the impacts became fewer and further between. Finally, they stopped.

They were clear.

'What the hell's going on?' Lauren asked as Shaun looked around for the paramedics' radio. It sat on the underside of a large box hanging from the roof in the centre of the cab. He cursed. Both the radio and GPS unit had taken on the multitude of bullets that entered the cabin during their escape and were barely recognisable.

Shaun glanced in the rear-view mirror. The cone of a car's headlights turned out onto the road from the motel and pointed at them like the glowing eyes of a demon.

'Shit!' Shaun cried. 'They're coming. Stay low. Do you still have my cell?'

Lauren patted her pockets and pulled out the phone. 'Flat,' she said, defeated.

'Okay, okay. Hang on, we can't be too far from a town now.' Even as he said it he knew it wasn't true. It had taken the ambulance more than forty minutes to get to them, and he wasn't even sure which direction it had come from.

They pushed on into the night, without any idea where they were going or how long it would take to get there. They had a good start on the car chasing them, maybe a minute, but when the road straightened out, they could see the headlights gradually getting closer.

'Why were they killing everyone?' Lauren asked.

Shaun thought about the way the men had systematically burst into each motel room. One door at a time. Killing anyone who happened to be in there. They weren't taking any chances on missing their target.

'They were looking for something,' Shaun answered. 'They were looking for something or someone. They didn't look like street hoods, they're organised and calculating.'

They were both thinking it. The hobo lay slumped between them, his body curled awkwardly in the centre of the bench seat. He was breathing heavily again, and making the occasional groan, but he had not woken up.

'How can he sleep through all this?' Lauren asked, her pitch betraying her rising panic.

'Do you still have that book?' he asked.

'Yes,' she replied, pulling it up off the floor in front of her.

'I think ... I think that whatever's in that book is the real thing, or at least someone thinks it, and they think it's important.' He looked at Lauren. 'Important enough to kill for,' he said, looking down at the crudely bound volume again, doubting himself, even as he spoke.

'Keep reading it,' he said. 'There might be something in there that can help us.'

'If this is what they want, let's just give it to them,' Lauren said, her voice sharp.

The thought had occurred to Shaun, but he dismissed it.

'You saw what they did. Probably shot the clerk for being a smart-ass to them, then they killed everyone at the motel. Hell, they even shot the paramedics. I don't think just handing this stuff over would make them stop, or save our lives.'

She knew he was right. Shaun paused, feeling more confident in his course of action. Although it seemed absurd to be reading while being chased, Lauren too knew that their pursuers would not stop. This diary might be their only chance to find a way out. At least for now they were out of range of gunfire.

'Read it aloud, will you? And hang on.' The battered ambulance sped down the mountain road at incredible speed. Now forty-five or so seconds behind, another car sped after it. Closing in.

Lauren fumbled for the switch on the interior light and opened the pages with tears blurring her eyes. She wiped them, and focused on the words.

CHAPTER 8

'Are you okay?' I asked the boy. He was crying and his face was purple with bruises, but he nodded his head. 'Mishca? Are you Mishca?' He nodded again as I took him by the arm and helped him to his feet, and the wooden shards from the window scattered to the floor around us. The hut we were in looked like a storage shed. The thunderous roar of battle filled the street. Whoever the men on horseback were, they were fighting the Romans – swinging and slashing and kicking, less skilled than their adversaries but outnumbering and overpowering them.

I pulled the boy out into the street and led him back the way I had come. He followed, limping, at a good speed, fuelled by anxiety and the thrill of an unexpected escape.

We soon came across the boy's parents lying in the street. The fighting had moved on from this area of the town and all along the streets people tended to the wounded and cried over the dead. On our approach, the woman wailed and threw her arms open. The boy forgot his limp and ran to catch his mother's embrace. From the ground, the boy's father reached up and pulled the boy down to him. I stood there, watching, glad for a moment to be a witness.

Looking around the dead and wounded people, I felt compelled to help. Leaving the boy and his father in a bloodied and heartfelt embrace, I did what I could for the people closest to me. One victim was no more than sixteen, cut down with purposeful strokes. Another, a man around thirty, lay near the boy, still gripping a crude digging tool, a trowel of some sort, in his limp hand. It was the tool of a farmer, not of a warrior. I dressed the wounds of the injured as best I could and then moved on.

As I fixed a splint to a man's leg, I felt a hand on my shoulder. I turned and saw Mishca's father leaning heavily on his son. He beckoned me.

'Stranger, you have saved my son. I cannot ever repay you, but now you must come inside. The soldiers will return at any moment.'

Sure enough, as the words left his lips, a melee exploded around the corner. A Roman guard was fending off two attackers who slashed and struck with relentless ferocity.

I followed Mishca and his parents into a doorway across the street as the fighting travelled closer. I raced back across the street to help some of the wounded into the house, while those who could walk unaided hobbled to their feet and followed. Inside, we slammed the wooden door closed and locked it.

'The zealots have come,' said Mishca's father. 'They battle the Romans, but they only bring greater wrath upon us.'

At that moment, I heard the thundering of hooves blast by the door, and the group in the house sank back. Once the sound passed, the man spoke once more.

'You have saved my son, you have tended to my friends, and yet we do not know you. What is your name?'

I paused, then opting for consistency, said, 'Saul. My name is Saul.'

Over the next few days, after the zealots had driven off the Roman attack, I learned more about where I was. It was a small village in the land of Palestine. This felt right to me but I did not know why, and I guessed that perhaps Palestine was my home. The people were a mix of Jews and Arabs, but the whole area was under Roman occupation.

I was told that normally in this area there were only a couple of sentries, and the people were left to themselves, but recently bands of religious zealots had attacked Roman posts in small towns like this one. Several days before the attack, zealots had stormed a town to the north, and in response the Governor of the region sent a legion of Roman soldiers to a neighbouring town to assert their continued authority over the land.

That is what had happened here. The village's name was Chorazin, and it had borne the brunt of Rome's retribution for an attack on a Roman outpost at Thella. They started by taking the children, killing anyone who tried to resist. Of course the families fought to keep their children, and as a result many people died. In the case of Chorazin, the zealots had followed Rome's pattern and anticipated the attack; they had mobilised and struck at just the right moment, winning the battle but escalating the war.

I stayed with Mishca and his family for several weeks. I had no need to leave. My search was one of self-knowledge. I needed to know who

I was and what I was doing, and Chorazin seemed as good a place as any to start that search.

Mishca's father, Mycha, suffered from his wounds during those weeks. I had patched his leg, but he had a broken rib that was slow to heal, so I helped him in the fields where he worked. It was a good arrangement: I got to work and in return was given food and a place to stay. All the while, I hoped my memory would return. After nearly a month, it hadn't.

One morning, as the sun bore down on me in the field, and sweat poured off my bronzing back, Mishca ran up to me. We had grown close in the time that I had been there. He was intrigued by this mysterious traveller who had saved him from the Roman cages.

'I do not understand,' he said as he panted up to me with water. 'You told my father that you travel west, but you tell me you do not know where you travel!' He was always full of questions. Especially ones I could not answer.

'Yes, you have it right.'

'Then, why do you travel at all?' he looked quizzically up at me.

I smiled and winked at the boy. 'I do not know where I am going. But you must not tell your father that or he will have me working the fields for him all year!'

The boy smiled, showing his bright white teeth. 'You do not look very much like a Jew,' he said. 'Did you come from far away?'

I stopped and studied the boy for a moment. There was a keen intelligence in his eyes. I made a decision to confide in him then, both because I was growing frustrated with making up new lies and, for reasons I could not articulate, I trusted him.

'Mishca,' I said solemnly, 'can you keep a secret?' The boy's face lit up.

'What I am about to tell you is a secret between you and me. Do you understand?' The boy nodded eagerly.

'I have your word as a man?' He nodded again, without hesitation. I looked him squarely in the eyes.

'Mishca, I woke up last month with no clothes, no food and no idea who or where I was.' I paused. His eyes narrowed. 'I do not even know my own name.'

'But you said your name was Saul.'

'I made it up.'

'But you saved me from the Romans.'

'I saved you because you were in trouble, not because you were a kinsman.'

'But ... then ...' his mind grappled with the idea. 'Then, how do you know what you're doing? Who are your parents? Where do you live?'

I looked at the boy and smiled. Then shrugged. Mishca shook his head and turned it over in his mind. Then he surprised me.

'Surely you can work a lot of it out?' he started. 'There are things you know about yourself that must help. You speak our language, so you must come from near here. You called out to the Romans in their tongue, so maybe you were one of the ones they captured as a child to join the army. My father says they do that. They take young boys from families and bring them up as Romans, or train them to fight in the great games.'

'Games?'

'It's where they make men fight against each other to the death, or sometimes they even fight great ferocious beasts from strange lands. I mean, you know how to fight, so maybe you were in the army, although you didn't fight like any Roman I've ever seen.'

For all the rambling, the boy was right: I needed to work to solve the riddle myself. Despite all the unknowns, there was one thing of which I was certain: there was something I was here to do. I had a purpose, a sense of it. There was a reason.

For the past few weeks that I had been in Chorazin, a feeling had been steadily building in me that something was going to happen. It had grown from a twinge, but now it was an uncomfortable frustration. I knew I was here to do more than dig fields. I looked into the boy's face.

'You are right, Mishca. You are absolutely right. And you know why it is that I have to go now.' I had dreaded telling the boy. His attachment to me was very strong, and I too was fond of him. His eyes dropped. He understood, but he wasn't happy about it. Then he brightened suddenly.

'That's okay. When you find out who you are, you can come back and visit. Maybe you're very rich!'

I laughed. 'Maybe I am.'

At that moment there came a yell from one of the other workers in the fields. A man ran towards us, shouting frantically and pointing back behind him. As he approached, I heard him clearly.

'Romans! The Romans have come back! They are coming here, a whole legion! The Romans are coming!'

My reaction was immediate. I scooped up Mishca in one arm and ran to where his horse was tied to a tree.

'Ride straight home,' I urged him, unfastening the animal. 'Take your family to the grain store, hide in there. You understand?'

Mishca's eyes were wide with terror.

'Mishca!' I barked at the boy. He refocused on my face. 'Do you understand?' I asked again. He nodded.

'Straight home.' I smacked the animal on the rump and it lurched forwards, kicking up dust as it sped off, the boy's skinny body clinging tightly.

This road was the only way into the town from the Romans' base at Capernaum, so I knew that Mishca had about a five-minute start. Workers ran from the fields and clambered into the surrounding trees to hide. I did the same, but with a different intention. The attack was unusual. The Romans usually took retribution on the neighbouring town only when they had first been attacked by zealots – following this pattern, the zealots now waited for the soldiers at Bethsaida to the south, leaving the people of Chorazin defenceless.

I picked up a sharpened metal hoe and ran to the trees near the edge of the road. I swung the hoe into the trunk of a tall, bushy tree not a foot from the edge of the road. I drove the hoe down again into the mark I had made, cursing the ineffective implement. A small chip flew out. Then I heard it.

It was the sound of horses, like thunder over the rise of the field. I swung the hoe again, and again, and again. I could hear the shouts of the vicious men now. They were only seconds away. Again, again, again. There wasn't time. More chips flew, and I could see the dust cloud rising over the nearest hill. I had fifteen seconds, maybe ten.

I drew the hoe up high above my head, concerned more now with power in the blows than accuracy. I swung it down hard – the hoe's head flew free and I smacked into the tree with the blunt end of what was suddenly a useless stick. Five seconds.

In frustration I drew back from the tree, then ran hard and planted the stick in the ground, using it to launch myself up into the air like a pole-vaulter. Curled in a tight ball, I kicked out sideways and struck the trunk. Finally the tree fell across the road.

I dove back into the thicket on the side of the road just as the first figure appeared around the bend, followed by a second, then a third. I looked at the tall, thick-bushed tree lying across the road and then at the riders as they slowed, reining in their horses. A shout went back through the ranks, and the train of soldiers stopped. The column parted, and a single rider came up through the ranks.

It was the centurion I had watched beat Mishca. He had obviously survived the zealots' attack, and his appearance suggested that he could survive most anyone. His jaw was square and his nose looked like it had been broken more than once. He gave a short, sharp command and two of the riders dismounted. They walked to the tree and drew their swords, taking turns to hack at where the tree's trunk still clung by splintered shards.

My eyes traced along the line, counting thirty men, and I was sure that the road around the bend held many more. Only a moment passed before the two guards sawed the tree in two and dragged the pieces off the road. My plan to slow them had gained Mishca only a couple of minutes. It wasn't enough.

The centurion rode up to the tree and dismounted. He looked at it carefully, a mere fifteen feet from where I lay in the grass, my heart pounding. He examined the trunk as one of the guards held out the head of the hoe I had used to fell the tree. The centurion took it and rose to his full height, at least six-and-a-half feet. He looked at the end of the sharpened digging tool as I gripped its shaft in my hand.

'This was done on purpose, and done only just before we arrived. Whichever one of these—' he held up the iron tool head again, 'farmers—' *he spat the word, 'did this, they are still here. I suspect very close.' His voice was deep and menacing, and commanded the full attention of his troops. I did not need to hear anything more. I knew that if they looked they would find me in a matter of moments. I had no choice. I felt around my body, and my hand closed around a fist-sized stone.*

I threw it back along the tree line, clenching in my other hand what was now a thick staff, and rose up to one knee. The stone crashed in the bushes, drawing the soldiers' attention as I hurled the staff like a spear at the man mounted on the nearest horse. The moment it left my grip, I set off in a sprint, chasing it. With his head turned back towards the sound of the stone, the man bore the full brunt of my carefully aimed throw. The thick staff connected with his cheek and threw him from his mount, sending his legs skywards.

I was on the horse in seconds, and immediately dropped forward and hugged its neck to avoid the swing of a short sword levelled just above my shoulders. At the same time I dug my heels into the animal's flanks and was jolted forward as the muscled beast sprang to life, galloping through the column and bursting out the front like a stone from its sling.

I heard the calls and knew that the legion was following me. The horse sped along the road, keeping just ahead of its pursuers.

CHAPTER 9

The ambulance sped along the road, keeping just ahead of its pursuers. They were losing ground fast. Headlight reflections in the mirror had brought Lauren out of the story.

'Shaun, they're coming,' she called.

'How far?' Shaun asked, speeding and struggling to maintain control of the broad van.

'Maybe two hundred feet. I don't know, but those lights are getting really bright.'

'I see them,' he said, looking in her side mirror. They were only about five seconds behind now, and the road was starting to straighten out, taking away whatever advantage Shaun had by using the corners of the road to shield them from gunfire.

Lauren put the diary down and disappeared into the back of the ambulance.

'What are you doing?' Shaun called. She did not answer.

The chase car was gaining now, and the first spatter of bullets started to hit them intermittently. Shaun was frantic now. He could not outrun them – the van just wasn't fast enough.

'Lauren, what are you doing?' Silence. 'Lauren!' he shouted this time.

'I'm looking,' she replied.

'Looking for what?' he asked, trying to focus on the road ahead rather than the headlights getting closer in the rear-vision mirror. A bullet smashed into his driver's-side mirror, shattering it and making Shaun swerve dangerously. The car was gaining on them, but at least the ambulance had a low rear bumper that prevented their pursuers getting a clear shot at the tyres.

He heard Lauren moving things around in the back. 'Lauren, get out of there! One of those bullets is going to come right through that door at this range!'

'We can't outrun them, Shaun,' Lauren finally replied, surprisingly calmly. 'They're too fast. We have to let them get really close, and then smash them.'

'Then *smash* them?' Shaun parroted.

'Let them get close, then slam on the brakes,' Lauren said, as if it were the most obvious thing in the world. Shaun was about to protest, when he stopped himself. She was right. They might just screw up the chase car enough to stop their pursuit.

He hazarded a glance over his shoulder and saw Lauren strapping a long metal cylinder to the gurney.

'What the hell? What's in that cylinder?' Shaun asked.

'Oxy-acetylene. They use it for cutting metal to get people out of wrecks.'

'Really?' He tilted his head and jutted out his bottom lip, impressed by the random things she knew.

'Ready?'

Shaun steadied himself, checking again in the rear-view mirror. Two headlights stared back at him.

'Okay, now!' she yelled, grabbing tightly onto the surrounding shelving. Shaun lined up the pursing car as they rounded a bend in the road, and as they both sped up again, he slammed on the brakes. The van screeched and groaned in protest, but lost speed instantly, its tyres smoking up clouds of burned blue rubber as Shaun fought to keep the vehicle straight.

Taken by surprise, the car slammed hard into the back of the ambulance, its nose crumpling with the force of the impact, its back end leaving the ground entirely. The car's chassis twisted and buckled as it took the momentum. When the velocity was finally sucked out of it, the rear end came down and met the road with force.

Inside the ambulance Shaun and Lauren had time to brace for the impact, but unsecured, the hobo in the centre of the seats slammed up against the front dashboard, knocking two of his teeth clean out.

Lauren, who had wedged herself in between the shelving and the back of the passenger seat, was hit by several medical vials, but leaped into action again the instant the van settled. She reached up and found a heavy metal case, which she used to bash the top of the cylinder until the nozzle blew off. A rush of highly condensed gas hissed in a white plume. She unbolted the back doors and yelled to Shaun as she pushed them open: 'Give me your keys.' He looked at her quizzically. 'Your keys!' she insisted.

Shaun had no idea what she was thinking, but reached into his pocket and fished out his bunch of jangling metal keys. He tossed them back to her. Coming alongside the gurney, she kicked its brakes to unlock it, and then quickly sorted through his keys and found his novelty, pistol-shaped lighter.

Without hesitation, she pulled the trigger on the mini pistol and thrust the flame in to the white jet of gas that was rushing out of the cylinder's nozzle. The result was instantaneous: where there had been a whooshing mist of gas, now shot a roaring torch of flame. The orange jet pushed furiously outward, reaching a full six feet from the nozzle and forcing Lauren to lean back against the pressure. The heat was intense and the noise was an angry growl, like an animal had been woken roaring a tongue of flame.

Shaun realised what she was doing and leaped through the seats to help Lauren push the bed backwards. With a surge of combined effort, they sent the whole contraption – bed, cylinder, flame and all – crashing through the back doors and onto the windscreen of the black car now crumpled against the van. Screams filled the burning interior of the car. The light from the flame illuminated the inside of what they could now see was a sleek, black BMW – or had been. The sound of death and popping, burning flesh mixed with the cloud of blue–grey smoke that billowed from the car's shattered windows.

Mesmerised by the heat and the light of what lay just beyond the open ambulance doors, Shaun had to force himself to climb back into the driver's seat, Lauren following quickly behind. He gunned the engine and the ambulance lurched forward, leaving the medical contents to spill out of the open doors and onto the road.

Before they rounded the next bend, he looked across Lauren into the passenger-side mirror – the only mirror still intact – and saw a flaming body emerge from the driver's-side door and take a step, before falling to the ground.

Still, burning, dead.

CHAPTER 10

Through the silent night a white streak hugged the road. Punctured, shattered and riddled with bullet holes, the ambulance was in need of an ambulance. A parody of itself – it was hard to believe it still ran. Right now it ran. It ran from the carnage it had left behind, and it ran with the fate of three lives in its cabin. Then, it ran out of gas.

Shaun stared ahead at the road, not knowing where he was driving, but wanting to get there fast. His mind raced, images flashing in his head like gunshots. *FLASH!* Slamming into a man in the middle of nowhere. *FLASH!* Lauren's face as she read the diary. *FLASH!* The man in black executing the motel clerk, and then the paramedic. My God, Shaun thought, realising that even he had used the dead driver's body as a shield. What was happening? The rules were changing.

The first splutter came accompanied by a sudden lurch as the ambulance lost power ... then it recovered.

'What was that?' Lauren asked as she wrestled with the unconscious hobo for more room on the seat. Shaun did not need to look down. He had noticed that the gas was low, and now as they were being chased by nameless, faceless murderers in the middle of nowhere, they were about to run out.

At least you all survived, even the hobo, Shaun's brain commentated.

'He *is* still alive, isn't he?' Shaun asked.

Lauren was staring at the fuel gauge, preferring not to say anything, as if talking about it made it true.

'Yeah, he's still alive. I hate to think what he'll smell like when he's dead.' She checked herself. 'I mean, if he dies.'

She had just barbecued a car full of men. Shaun knew that that had not sunk in yet. He was losing perspective too. The van sputtered again.

'We're not going to make it,' Lauren finally voiced.

'We'll make it,' he said, not sure where 'it' was. 'No ambulance would leave a hospital without enough fuel to make a—'

BEEP! The red fuel light switched to orange, and right next to it a word lit up: 'Reserve'.

'Reserve?' he asked the console. 'Reserve?' he repeated. Then he looked at Lauren, his mouth spreading into a broad grin. 'Of course. Reserve,' he beamed.

The release of tension was welcome.

'What are you doing?' he asked his wife.

'Well, like you said, I think that we're being chased because someone is looking for something. I think it's this book, or this guy,' she said, gesturing at the hobo, 'or both, and I think that we should try and find out why that is. I think it's ...'

But Shaun had stopped listening. Lauren had seen it too. Headlights. Behind them in the distance. She took a breath, and as if to counter the inevitability of the situation, she opened the book. The ambulance rounded a bend ...

... at breakneck speed, with only open road before me. The horse whirled the other way, taking the next bend even faster ...

The headlights closed in on them.

... but I did not relent. A spear sailed past my ear and lodged itself in a tree to my left. Riding out in the open, I knew it was only a matter of time before one of the spears found my back, so I did the only thing I could think of: I spun the horse off the road and charged full speed into the thicket lining the path.

'We have to get off the main road. We can't outrun them like this.'

I ducked the branches that slapped at my face, hoping that at least some of the riders would follow. I had to lead them away from the town.

It was then that I heard calls behind me.

'That's him. He's the one we want!'

It did not make sense. I burst clear of the trees and into a clearing, and too late I realised, into a trap.

The ambulance spun hard to the left, taking the first fork off the main road they had seen yet. Shaun switched off the headlights and turned sharply again as another signposted road came into view: 'Charlotte

13 miles'. Civilisation. So close, and yet behind them, he saw the headlights take the first turn. 'How did they get here so fast?'

I asked myself the question, but I knew the answer. They had been waiting. As I looked at the long line of horses stretched across the clearing, it became obvious. I reined in my steed; I had nowhere to go. Behind me, my pursuers burst clear of the trees and slowed, seeing that I was now all but surrounded. I realised that they had not wanted to attack the town at all. They had come for me. It was at that moment I heard a feverish yell from somewhere down the line. My eyes told me what it was, but my heart did not want to believe it.

Kicking and screaming, Mishca was being held by two large guards. As I watched, one struck him across the face. I turned my horse slowly to face them. The complete line of mounted soldiers, maybe twenty of them, kept their animals in check, watching from a distance. I moved closer.

The ambulance came over a rise and the road dropped away steeply. It seemed that whatever new direction they took, it was a shortcut to the outskirts of the city.

'Look for a map,' he said. When Lauren did not respond he spoke again, loudly. 'Close the book and look for a map to the hospital! All ambulances have them. Something that shows them all the alternative routes if the main roads are blocked.'

Lauren searched the glove compartment. A street directory sat on top of a hand-held radio and some official-looking papers. 'There's a map here!' she said, as she held up the radio and pulled the directory out.

'See if you can get someone on the radio, and then you're going to have to navigate me to the hospital.'

They were well and truly in suburbia now. Houses, streetlights and other cars blurred past. It brought Shaun some comfort, thinking that their pursuers were less likely to open fire with other people around. He was wrong.

The first shot went high, taking out one of the red lights atop the ambulance.

'They don't care,' Lauren said, reading his mind. 'Okay, there's a main road coming up. Go left.' She fiddled with the radio in her hand, raising nothing but static. Shaun pulled hard on the wheel, shooting across a line of traffic that hadn't seen him coming. A bottle of something flew out from the back of the open van section and smashed on the road, and cars swerved to avoid it.

'Right up ahead,' she said, turning the map over, 'or maybe left.'

'Lauren!' he snapped. He glanced in the passenger-side mirror and saw that the BMW had made the turn.

'Right. Definitely right,' she said with less conviction than her husband liked. He spun the wheel hard, just as two more slugs slammed into the side-rear of the van. Shaun flinched and ducked instinctively as the bullets rang out in the cabin, then he looked up, straight into a wall of oncoming traffic.

'Arrrghh!' he screamed as the first of the three lanes of cars began to swerve out of his way, blaring their horns.

Lauren spun the map round and said quietly, 'Oh, it *was* left.'

Without missing a beat Shaun reached over and flicked a switch. Immediately sirens and the lights that still worked blared to life, alerting the oncoming traffic to its presence. Like the parting of the Red Sea, the road opened up before them.

The black BMW used a very different approach to clear its path into the oncoming traffic: automatic gunfire. Even with the sirens blaring, Shaun and Lauren could hear the rapid-fire explosion as the machine guns sang their tune of destruction. The BMW literally punched a hole through the centre of the traffic by shooting directly into the centre lane.

Vehicles with bursting tyres, radiators and drivers' heads swung out of the centre lane and into those cars on either side. Some made flips like a Hollywood stunt show. Cars clipped other cars, people did not quite get completely out of the way, and the cars in front acted like ramps to the speeding cars behind, sending them skyward, flipping and rolling in the air, propulsion intensified by gas tanks exploding mid-air from collisions and bullet impacts. The colossal mass of destruction, which would be later called the 'Charlotte Derby' on the evening news, was the cumulative effect of hundreds of drivers panicking, dying and losing control of their speeding vehicles.

The pursuing black BMW sped through the carnage, cutting through the mass of traffic like a knife. For about ten seconds.

An oncoming Lotus, known throughout the world for its sleek pointed hood and design, seemed to emerge from nowhere and burrowed under the front of the BMW at full speed. The BMW's resulting somersault was cut short as it was hit flat on the roof by another car flipping in the opposite direction. The two roofs came together, just off-centre. The BMW's forward rotation stopped dead, and it started to spin around its vertical axis at incredible speed. Like a drill falling from the sky, it bore down into the carnage below, burrowing awkwardly into an open-top convertible that contained an elderly lady with blue hair. Then the BMW exploded.

Shaun saw the whole thing in the mirror.

'Holy-fuck-me-shit,' he muttered, wide-eyed and disbelieving.

Lauren, horrified and thrilled at the same time, was too glued to the horrific scene behind them to chastise him. Through the open back doors she watched the smoke, fire and carnage disappear into the distance before losing sight of it altogether as they rounded the next bend.

It was only then that she looked down at her blood-soaked blouse.

Then she felt it; across her right arm, just below the shoulder. A bullet had caught her and she hadn't even noticed, but she noticed now. It throbbed. She stared as the blood spread over the white of her shirt. Shaun noticed too, and with a wave of fear he spoke, trying to keep his voice steady.

'Lauren. Focus,' he said as he brought her back to the moment. 'I need you to guide me to the hospital. We need to get to the hospital.'

'Something tells me they're going to be busy tonight,' she said slowly as she turned around, holding her arm. There was no humour in her voice, only horror and incomprehension. They were supposed to be going to England tonight. Shaun was supposed to be brushing up on his speech right now, not dealing with this ... whatever this was.

Ten minutes of speeding later, he spun the wheel into the hospital's emergency unit. He entered just as another six ambulances left, sirens screaming.

They were met immediately by medical staff rushing out. The staff looked shocked at the state of the paramedic truck but did not question it. The news had obviously reached here about the shoot-up on the freeway.

Good, fewer questions, Shaun's brain voiced.

Gurneys and wheelchairs were waiting for them as they fell out of the ambulance in shock. He refused the chair, instead dragging the hobo out of the ambulance cabin and hoisting him onto one of the wheeled beds. Lauren, however, merely fell in a heap into the wheelchair that was offered to her. She sank down into the vinyl cushioning, and though her body stopped at the seat, her heart, mind and soul sank all the way to the floor. Within moments of the immediate danger passing, without the desperate need for survival, she burst into tears, overwhelmed.

Shaun stood on shaky legs as his wife, along with the man they had hit, were wheeled away by medical staff. He made to follow but his legs failed him. His first step held his weight; his second did not. Shaun fell to one knee alone in the middle of the emergency driveway. Both hands went to the ground. With chaos all around him, Shaun Strickland was alone, overcome with grief and unable to move.

Weeping uncontrollably, he sank to the ground.

CHAPTER II

BRUSSELS, 2008AD

The shovel penetrated the damp earth, slicing it as it went down. The archaeology student pushed hard, levering up another chunk of dirt. He had been digging all day, and had earned nothing but sweat for his trouble. He had come on this trip to Brussels thinking that there would be a lot of French, German and Belgian girls who would want to spend time with an Italian guy like him. His French was pretty good too, and he wanted the chance to practise it.

But there were no sexy French women here. There was little else but dirt and history. The site was close to the city, and right near the site of the famous Battle of Waterloo, but he did not care. He did not expect to find anything of interest. The site had already been dug so many times.

Silvio looked across at the nerdy guy he was partnered with. Alec was earnestly digging away, sweat beading on his freckled shoulders and dripping down his weedy arms. If only he would shut up about the history of the place. He was like a living textbook. The story might have been interesting too, if only it wasn't coming from someone quite so annoying.

'In 1814, twenty-five brutal years of war came to an end with the surrender of the French General Napoleon Bonaparte.' Alec was in full swing. 'Captured and banished, he was imprisoned on the Mediterranean Island of Elba. The remaining allied European powers then set about restoring the mainland continent to the earlier peace it had enjoyed.'

If the runt would do more digging and less talking, they might actually get through their required quota of holes before the afternoon break, which meant that Silvio could get home to prepare for tonight. He had heard about a bar not far from the hostel and he was keen to try his luck.

'Things were all pretty good for a while, but then on the first day of March in 1815, Napoleon escaped from his island prison on Elba. Some say he bribed the guards, some say he was rescued by loyal subjects, but no one really knows who braved the waters to get him. He sailed to France, and people treated him like he was some sort of god. Nineteen days later he was Emperor again. His army rallied to him. The soldiers who had been captured during the years of fighting had been released, enabling Napoleon to reform his Grande Armée. The European allies prepared to resume war and to overthrow the Emperor for a final time—'

'Seriously, do you ever shut up?' Silvio grunted.

Alec ignored the interruption. 'Napoleon resolved to attack the British, Prussian, Belgian and Dutch armies before the other powers could come to their assistance.' He was getting excited now, his eyebrows leaping about on his face and his voice reaching a fever pitch. Silvio continued to dig broodily.

'The Duke of Wellington took up a position on the Brussels road where it emerges from the woods of Soignies south of Waterloo. On the road at the southern side of the valley, below the second crest, stood La Belle Alliance Farm. That farm is where you and I are standing today.'

Alec finished as if waiting for applause. He did not receive any. Silvio was on his hands and knees using a soft brush to dust away at something. Alec peered down. He had never seen Silvio so interested – perhaps all his lecturing was finally having an impact. He did not really expect to find anything on this dig, he just loved the thought of being where it had all happened. He craned to make out the shape as it emerged from the dirt. There was no mistaking it. It was a human skeleton.

'Does everyone die in this position?' Silvio asked rhetorically some time later as he carefully removed dirt from around the hip area. The skeleton was almost complete and lay in the classic 'white chalk outline' pattern that looks like it's running.

Alec was silent. They had been meticulously uncovering the form for about twenty minutes now, and had agreed not to let anyone know they had found something until they finished. They dared to hope and believe that it was a soldier. They would be heroes.

As they prepared to victoriously reveal their find to their supervisor, Silvio came across something else. Brushing away tentatively at the porous head of the right femur, he caught a glint of silver. His soft-bristled brush flicked away the dirt specks and more metal was revealed. A bullet! They had found a ... wait. Silvio did not say anything at first, but within moments he alerted Alec to the shiny metal cylinder embedded in the bone. Silvio brushed frantically, intrigued.

Barely an hour passed before the two students sat back on their haunches, surveying their find. Complete with a decayed musket still clutched in its hands, lay the bones of a soldier from the Battle of Waterloo. Along the length of his right femur, a thin cylindrical object ran about a tenth the length of his thigh. It was the circumference of a dime and had several small markings, holes and, strangest of all, lights. One thing was certain: it did not exist in 1815.

San Francisco, 2011 AD

David Black was about to hit 'play'. This was his moment of truth. Five years of development had gone into cracking the encryption.

As one of the world's best codec development software engineers, this moment was akin to winning Olympic gold. It hardly mattered to him that no one really understood what he did; he most often described himself as a 'digital magician'.

'Codec', short for 'compress–decompress', referred to an algorithm that encoded video data to get a better picture quality for less storage space. Five years ago he had received this tiny circular disc, and he had been pretty sure it contained video data. The pattern of the blocks on the disc was sequential, meaning that something continuous was recorded, rather than chunks of data randomly placed fragmented all over the disc.

And now, finally, he thought he had it. Figuring out this compression sequence had been one of the most incredibly demanding tasks imaginable. It was so far beyond anything he had seen – like finding a rocket ship well before the Wright brothers ever soared down Kitty Hawk Beach.

Each new codec that came on the market had brought him closer to understanding the marvellous little disc, but the data had been woven into the molecular structure of the disc itself. With a little over two years of calculating, tweaking and recalculating, he had finally worked it out. It had become much more important to him to solve the equation than to actually see what was on the disc. He was into the math, which was lucky because his instructions stipulated that he was not permitted to see whatever images the disc held. He was well paid and working at the frontier of his field, so he did as he was asked.

The small room in which he now sat was dimly lit, with a couch at one end and several other comfortable chairs. At the other end was a large plasma screen. Sitting back, with his supervisor, he asked the two

Europeans who had commissioned the project if they were ready. They nodded, leaning forward, their eyes glued to the screen. David hit play.

Nothing. Black. *Shit.*

David did not know what to say. He had promised them that he had cracked the codec, and he knew he had. There *was* data on the disc ... but then white text appeared on the screen:

IDENT: 0012
SUBJECT: Napoleon Bonaparte
OFFICER: X10

It appeared for five seconds and then the screen returned to black. They all sat there stunned. The fact that there was only five seconds of image did not matter in the slightest to him; with technology like this, you either got it or you did not. David had retrieved the data from the disc, and he felt extremely pleased with himself. He only started to feel nervous when the visitors continued to sit in silence. He shuffled uncomfortably in his seat. What did they expect?

Finally, one of the men said something to the other in Italian. The other grunted. Then the first man spoke again, his thick accent making it difficult to understand what he meant.

'Of this, you have made another video?' he asked David directly. It was his supervisor, Randy Bilis, who answered.

'Ah, no – this is the only player in the world that can play this disc. As you requested, we only made one unit.'

The Italian spoke again, explaining to his counterpart. The second man, silver haired and larger than the first but without his associate's thick, black beard, nodded slowly. Then he spoke. The first man interpreted.

'My friend here, something different was expecting to see. Something with more picture. There is nothing else you have found?'

Randy, a forty-two-year-old Texan who prided himself on getting things done, slid off the table where he had been sitting, and stood above his clients.

'This, gentlemen, as per your instructions, was the first time anything has been played from this disc. I have to tell you it's hard to work on a codec when you can't actually look at the picture you're trying to see. We copied the data and monitored the signal with vector scopes, histograms, parades, you name it, until we were sure there was an image of some sort. Of course without being able to—'

'The images are not of concern to you.' It was the second man who now spoke. Randy and David looked at him in surprise. He had never spoken in English before. What's more, his English was perfect, his accent French, not Italian. 'There is nothing else on the disc. You are certain of this?'

'The rest is just black. It's funny, actually. I've never seen compression like this. That disc is capable of holding about twenty hours on each of its fifty platters – all up, that's a lot of data,' said David.

'I see. And all this space is unused?' the question was directed at David.

'Ah, yeah. There's no data there.'

'Then,' the large Italian man said, standing, 'I think our work here is done. Thank you for all your expertise. We will take this unit, and as agreed, you will be receiving your final payment today.'

'So, that's it?' David asked, as much to Randy as to their clients. 'There's no more? I mean, there's some incredible stuff we could do with this codec. We could make a camera that records in it and sell the patent to, like, Sony or Panasonic or someone.'

'That won't be necessary,' the Italian man said. 'I'm sure the non-disclosure agreements you signed will be honoured, as we would hate to encounter any legal difficulties.'

'Of course,' Randy said, jumping on the grenade.

David looked at his boss, suddenly realising how in the dark he had been kept. Randy had joked about this whole thing with David, about striking it rich. David was being well paid, at least by his standards, but he suddenly wondered whether he was getting stiffed on the payments too.

Hands were shaken and the unit – David's pride and joy – was handed over to the Europeans like a farewell present. When the doors were closed and the mysterious clients were out of earshot, David exploded.

'What the hell is going on? Not tell anyone about it? Randy, that compression is unlike anything I've ever seen. It's genius! Whoever invented it needs to be given a Nobel Prize, and now they're going to beat us to the patent and we're going to miss out. You said this was our ticket!'

Randy looked at him directly. He had known that this day was coming for a long time, but he had needed David to complete the project, and the only way he would do that was with the promise that he would get royalties from the inevitable sale and marketing of the new compression system. David was one of the only men on the planet who could reverse engineer the codec simply from the small amount of data found on the disc.

'David,' Randy said, looking as if he were about to give the explanation David deserved. 'You're fired.'

With that he turned and walked out the door, to be replaced by two burly-looking security guards who grabbed David firmly by the arms and escorted him from the building. As David's protesting screams echoed through the empty hallways, Randy stepped out of the building and blinked in the sunlight, a satisfied grin spreading across his lips. He was set for life. Several million dollars had already been deposited in his bank account, and now, with the success of the codec, another fifteen million would hit it today. Randy knew that David was so brilliant in some ways, but so naive in others, and he felt nothing but overwhelming relief that five years of on-spec research had paid off. Five years since the Frenchman and Italian had approached him. It was a big risk, but he had done it, and no one knew. His clients had stressed the need for secrecy. He did not know or care why – the numerals on the first bank cheque overcame any initial misgivings. After that, he just didn't seem to have any more.

David sat at the bar and signalled for another Southern-and-dry. The barman obliged even though he knew he shouldn't. The straggly-haired, heavyset man who had been here all afternoon had confided that he had just lost his job, so the barman cut him a little slack.

Through the alcohol fog David saw something familiar on the television behind the bar. The picture blurred in and out of focus.

'I haven't been drunk for shhevral yearsh,' David continued in his four-hour confidence. 'I've lived the last two years going shhtraight home after I finish, but not today, no sireee, not today. Not home today. Shhayy ...' he said, with one eye open staring at the television. 'That's my home just there,' he said, motioning his floppy arm towards the television.

'That's your home?' the barman said as he towel-dried a glass. 'Man, that house got shot up tonight.' He reached and turned the television up, taking a closer look at his unsteady patron.

'... no one home. Police are urging anyone with information to contact them about the whereabouts of the house's sole occupant, a Mr David Black.' An image appeared on the screen: David last summer.

‘Hey,’ he said, pointing, ‘datsh mee!’ With this he promptly slid off the stool and crashed into an unconscious heap on the floor. David Black fell into a deep sleep, oblivious as the television went on without him:

‘... also killed this evening. One of the four other victims who worked with Mr Black at Newcom Technologies was his supervisor. Forty-two-year-old Randy Bilis is survived by his wife and two children.’

CHAPTER 12

When Shaun woke, the first thing he felt was the pain. Even before the light. His eyes were heavy. Impossibly heavy. He was lying flat. His head fell to the side. He saw a man standing next to a bed. He saw the man reach out and brush the hair off someone's face who was lying on the bed. His eyes were so heavy.

He fought to focus. To see the face. To see Lauren. To see her alive, lying on a bed next to him. The man walked to an open elevator door at the end of the hall. The door started to close. The man turned. Shaun couldn't see his face, but thought he looked familiar. 'God, how long have I been asleep?' Shaun refocused as another man walked over to Lauren's bed, this one was wearing all black. He raised his hand and pointed; pointed with the long silenced muzzle of a—

Shaun woke from his dream. More pain. How long had he been asleep? He was slouched in a chair, his jacket around his shoulders. He had been dreaming, but he couldn't remember what. He refocused. Looking over, he saw that Lauren lay on a bed not far away.

'My God, how have we survived any of this?' Shaun asked himself.

Strength of will, his brain answered.

Indeed. Through strength of will he forced himself to stand. He had sat for almost twenty minutes while they stitched up Lauren's arm. They had asked him to stay away while they worked. He had protested, but when he saw the chaos going on around him, he decided not to push the issue and to let the doctors do their work. It had given him a moment to regroup. To get a drink, to charge his phone and to stop. He took a seat across the hall and must have fallen asleep. He was drained after their ordeal; it seemed unreal.

Except for the fact that he was still holding the diary. He looked down at it now, clasped firmly in his hands. He knew that it was important. Important enough to kill for, but not to die for, not to him. His finger traced the symbol on the front cover. It flowed up from the bottom before being guided around the first small loop, then around the larger loop, before returning to the centre line and drifting upwards into the unknown.

He tucked the book into his inner jacket pocket and brought his fingertip up to his face. There was the bump. It looked like it belonged there, like it was part of his finger, but he knew it hadn't been there a few hours ago. He had tried to get someone to look at it, but the triage nurses had other priorities.

He walked over to the strange man who lay on the bed next to Lauren. The curtains were still drawn around her cubicle, and he guessed she was sleeping.

No one buzzed around the rag-man lying on the bed. *The smell*, Shaun's brain reasoned. The doctors couldn't explain why the hobo was still unconscious. He had hit his head, sure, but the trauma to his body was far more than it should have been. Many of the wounds were older. The doctors explained it away as extreme exhaustion.

Shaun absently ran his thumb over his fingertips. He had only checked the man's pulse and now … Seeing that no one was around, he reached down to the man's collar, and started to pull down far enough to—

'What are you doing?' The nurse startled Shaun, approaching from behind.

'Ah, my friend … he was …' he started.

'He's your friend? You brought this man in? Good, then I have some paperwork for you to fill out. Beds in this hospital are not free, young man, and we'll be needing some of your details too.'

She produced a document and clipboard as if by magic. She was a woman in her early-to-mid forties, he guessed, and had long ago had all the sympathy sucked out of her. She thrust a pencil towards him and marched away.

The frazzled teacher sank back down in his seat. He had to wait it out until Lauren recovered, so he may as well do the paperwork. Sighing, Shaun looked down at the forms, and then at the diary.

He had to know if it really was the book these people were after. Shaun shook his head, remembering that he was a logical man, a scientist. Maybe this had all been random, but that seemed implausible given how many strange events had occurred over the past few hours. It was all too coincidental, and the thought that all this was an accident was nearly as hard for him to stomach as the thought that it *wasn't* all an accident – which was a thought that was very hard to stomach indeed. He figured his stomach was in for a rough time.

Putting the paperwork aside, he opened the diary.

CHAPTER 13

I was faced with ninety feet of open ground lined by Roman soldiers. At the far end was an innocent boy being used, I knew, to spur me into a fight. I smiled and thought that a blow to the head might jog my memory.

My heels hit the horse's flanks hard. I did not bother to speak, did not bother to call for them to let him go. I knew now that this was all a ruse. They had probably not even planned an attack on the village, but why go to such trouble for me?

The first challengers came from the right. Two soldiers spurred their mounts into action and lifted their short swords. I charged straight at them. Their confusion showed, but they did not slow. They both raised their swords. I aimed my approach directly between them, and as they reached me they were forced to split apart, one passing on either side. They each swung at my neck, their blades parallel to the ground. As the steel whistled towards my collarbone, I laid back on my animal and watched both blades sail harmlessly overhead.

My horse was still galloping full speed to where the soldiers held Mishca. Two riders sprang from their line to intercept, then two more after that. Mishca screamed my name, the only name I had ever known, but was silenced by a blow to the mouth. I could see that I was going to crash headlong into the wall of four riders now in front of me. They held their reins tight and would not let my charge pass between them. I had no choice. Already lying flat on the back of a charging stallion, I lifted my legs and tucked up hard, the momentum forcing me into a backwards roll that took me off the back end of the horse. While upside down I had time to see the first two riders whirl their horses around. My legs came all the way over and I hit the ground running, now sprinting along directly behind the tan-coloured stallion. The horse pulled up as it came to the charging wall of Romans. The fifteen-hand stallion turned side on, forcing the four riders to go around it. They reached the horse moments before I did, and set to swing their swords down at me. The gap my horse had created was all that I needed. From my sprint I dove into a forward roll, right between my horse's legs and came up on the other side. I ran harder.

Now with six mounted guards behind me, plus the ones who had chased me from the road, I found myself running with a mass of red and leather close behind. Ahead, a line of men had formed, dismounting from their steeds to face me on foot.

They started to converge from the edges to form a wall. There was no going through the body-length shields they held side by side, nor past the long spears that jutted out intermittently along the advancing line.

I slowed, my sprint becoming a run, then a jog, then finally a walk. My chest heaved with effort and I sucked in lungfuls of air. Behind me, the chasing soldiers also dismounted, and before I knew it there was a ring of legionnaires around me, slowly closing. I was surrounded, still not knowing why these men pursued me.

Then it started. One man came into the circle. No sword, no spear. I didn't understand, but as he ran at me I didn't have time to think about it.

I stepped back with my right leg, and as he charged, I pushed forward, tucking my knee and driving my foot out hard, directly into the man's face. The effect was dramatic. His head went backwards while his body kept on coming. He did a complete backflip in the air, landing flat on the grass next to me. He didn't move again.

Another man entered the ring, slowly, sizing me up. He also was unarmed. Coming within a few feet of me, he dropped into a wide-stanced crouch. He leaped to tackle me and caught me on the chest with his shoulder. I fell back, but as I did I brought my knee up into his sternum and gripped the straps on his shoulders. The big man flipped over me through virtue of his own attack. He landed flat on his back, winded. I straddled his chest, reaching out with my hands to his chin and the back of his head. The twist was sudden and definite as the man's neck cracked. I got to my feet, ready for more. Then I heard a call.

'Enough!' It was the deep baritone of the centurion I had seen on the road, who had tried to take Mishca in Chorazin. 'Bring him.'

From behind the ring of tightly packed soldiers a net came sailing over to land on top of me. It was made of thick rope and weighted by stones at its rim. The weight surprised me, dragging me to my knees. Within that moment a guard rushed forward, and I looked into the fine wood grain of the butt of his spear.

CHAPTER 14

The curtains hissed as they were drawn back. Shaun's head snapped up, shaken by the metallic sound of the railings. There was no butt of a spear to greet him, only several nurses walking out of the cubicle. Lauren was awake and lying flat on a bed. Her wound had needed sutures, so they had stitched her up and let her sleep for a couple of hours. Now, though, with more patients coming through after the carnage, the bed was needed for more serious cases. He closed the diary, leaving a hospital flyer to mark his page. With a broad grin he stood up and crossed the small hallway to where she lay, looking better after her rest.

'Hey, baby,' Shaun smiled. 'Nice sleep?'

'Mmm, I was swimming at the Olympics. The pool was all warm and made of chocolate and the other competitors were complaining,' she answered dazily.

'Not you, though, huh? I've never heard you complain about chocolate in your life.' He looked down at her. 'Hey, look at your arm all stitched up. You'll be able to swim again in no time.' She wriggled in the bed a little.

'I just wanna go back to sleep,' she looked over at her shoulder. 'I didn't even feel it, Shaun. I don't know when it happened.'

He could not believe that his wife had been shot. The thought terrified him, but he forced a laugh. He recalled the single most frightening moment of his life prior to tonight – when he had asked Lauren to marry him. They were up in the spectacular Blue Ridge Mountains of North Carolina, and they had snuck out from under her father's nose for a drive.

Lauren always said that there seemed to be more stars the further into the mountains they drove, and she loved to imagine what the world beyond was like. Shaun knew that her father wasn't a bad man; he just wanted the very best for his daughter, and to his mind, Shaun wasn't it. And so they had dated in secret for almost two years before

Lauren plucked up the courage to tell her father she was in love with the town nerd.

They were on a chairlift overlooking some of the most glorious scenery in the United States when he had turned to her and said, 'I brought you here mostly so you couldn't get away, but also ...' And then he did it. Or tried to.

Before he had got the next word out, she had said, 'Yes. Yes of course I'll marry you – so you can stop sweating now.' Then she laughed and pointed at an eagle swooping in a gorge below.

He was so happy and relieved that he had forgotten about the ring in his back pocket until later that day when he sat on it in the car. He would never forget the unceremonious way he slipped it on her finger in the car park at the base of the huge Grandfather Mountain, and remembered thinking that this girl, who had said yes, was sparkling much brighter than any ring. This girl who was now lying on a hospital bed with stitches in her shoulder.

'I know, baby. Things were a little crazy.' Shaun stroked Lauren's cheek. 'They still are; and this place is filling up quickly. The crash has been all over the news.' He paused for a moment and then said, 'I think they're going to ask us for the bed soon, so I should try to find a hotel. Then you can go back to swimming pools of chocolate, huh?'

'Mmm, I think I was winning too. Or coming a really close second.'

'There's a hotel board in the lobby. I won't be long.' He made to leave, but Lauren reached up and grabbed his hand.

'Don't leave me, baby. Just a few more minutes.' Shaun brushed the golden hair that had fallen across her face out of her eyes.

'I'll be two minutes. You want the Hyatt?'

Her eyes lit up. 'Only if they've got a pool!' she said, letting his hand go with a smile.

He smiled back, then turned and headed for the elevator. He knew he couldn't really afford the Hyatt, but after tonight they needed a splurge.

It's not every day your wife gets shot, he thought as he held the close-door and lobby buttons simultaneously. He had heard an urban myth that this trick gave an express ride to the desired floor, so he thought he would try. Shaun turned as the door shut, staring back at his sleeping wife.

In that moment, the world stopped. This moment would be etched in time forever. The only thing that still moved was the elevator door. Closing. Closing on his view of Lauren and the man in black who now stood next to her. A cold surge pulsed from the small of Shaun's back, up his neck and rippled goosebumps into the rear of his scalp. It was the most sickening, nauseous feeling Shaun had ever known. The colour drained from him as he opened his mouth to scream.

Slow motion.

The door continued to close. The man in black stood over Shaun's sleeping, oblivious wife. He raised an arm and pointed towards her chest. The elevator door was about to close.

From the back of the elevator Shaun leaped forward to stop the door, screaming as he shot out a hand.

It was too far gone.

The gap was barely an inch. There was no chance.

It was too late. He was too slow.

The muzzle spoke.

Shaun crashed into the metal door just as he heard two shots ring out.

'No! Nooooo! Arrrrghhhh!' Shaun slammed his fists against the door as the elevator descended. 'Arrrghhh!' His scream was pure agony. Unbelievable pain, terror, sickness. He slammed his fists on the door again, slammed them as he sank to the floor. *SLAM! SLAM! SLAM! SLAM! SLAM!*

The lift continued downwards, uncaring. Tears and saliva streamed from his face as the horrific moment replayed again and again. Shaun Strickland had just seen his wife die.

Shot.

Murdered.

Real.

CHAPTER 15

The elevator was unbearably slow. Screaming hysterically and kicking, bashing at the door, a small-town school teacher was reduced to a primal, roaring beast. Chemicals and hormones flooded his system and all functionality broke down. This was shock. This was terror. This was hysteria. This was real.

He lay on the floor kicking the door, trying to pry the inner lining open with his fingers and gurgling in desperate sobs. The elevator moved on steadily, uncaring. It travelled from the ninth floor to the ground floor where the lobby and emergency entrances were located.

Ding, ding, ding ... it was taking an eternity. He reached up and hit the buttons for all the floors until the bottom, but his trick had worked, and the lift sailed all the way down without stopping. He watched desperately as the floors ticked away.

Bzzzzzzz, ding, bzzzzz, ding. He stood up and paced in the small room, staring at the lights, willing them to move down the levels faster.

'Come *on*!' he screamed at them. Level Three ... *Bzzzzzzz, ding* ... Level Two ... *Bzzzzzzz, ding* ... Level One.

It had taken less than a minute, but it was the longest journey of Shaun's life. Slowly the elevator decelerated and gave a jolt as it stopped. The door finally opened to a lobby full of administrative staff, patients and visitors, all milling around, oblivious to the single most devastating event in Shaun Strickland's life. The door stayed open. It had been agony coming down, but now he had to go back up.

Finally the segmented metal sections began to slide from within one another to seal the small room.

'Young man!' Shaun heard a middle-aged woman call as she marched over to the elevator door. 'Young man, you hold that lift for me right now!' Her tone was insistent. He didn't react. 'I said, hold that lift!' The woman, dressed in a suit and clopping her high heels on the hard tiled floor reached her hand in to stop the doors closing.

Sensing a blockage in its path, the door began to open again. This caught Shaun's attention.

'Now, step back, I have a very important—' *WHACK!* She was silenced by his palms slamming into her chest, knocking her backwards out of the elevator and onto her backside. He pressed the close-door and ninth-floor buttons and stared back up at the level indicator, willing it upwards.

Bzzzzzzz, ding! Level One. The lift stopped, the doors began to open—

'What?!' he screamed. Then he looked at the buttons on the inside panel. He had pressed nearly every floor on his way down in an effort to get the elevator to stop. It hadn't responded on its way down, but it was responding now. The elevator was going to stop at every floor, then take about twenty seconds to go through the ritual of aligning, doors opening, staying open, closing, then starting to move again. He didn't have time for that.

In frustration, as soon as the doors opened on Level One, Shaun burst out into the hallway. He crashed into an orderly who was wheeling a bed coming the opposite way, barrelling the man to the floor.

'Jesus, man, watch out!' the small, black Londoner said, looking up from the floor where he had landed.

'Stairs!' Shaun commanded in a tone that took the man off guard. One look at Shaun's white, tear-streaked face and the orderly pointed.

Shaun ran, slipping and crashing, as fast as he could to the stairwell. He took them four at a time, reaching out and pulling hard on the handrail. Sweating, heaving and panting, Shaun flew upwards. Step by step, flight by flight, he headed up. People moved out of his way, hearing him coming like a crazy man on the loose. He didn't care. He was focused only on reaching the next platform at the top of the flight of stairs. Up, up, up. His thighs burned, but he pushed harder.

His right hand reaching at the handrail, his left hand swinging hard, Shaun Strickland was possessed of strength of will that few men experience in their lifetime. He could not lose her. It was all that mattered.

Fifth floor ... sixth floor ... The horrific moment replayed again, as it would thousands of times to come. His angel, his love, his safely sleeping wife ... *BLAM! BLAM!* Seventh floor ... The details, all the details. So sickening. She didn't even have time to see it. She was dreaming. How could no one notice? Why didn't they notice? How could a man walk straight up to a patient and shoot her?

Eighth floor ... *God, come on, legs!* They were failing him, all their stores of energy gone. Adrenaline surged again ... so close.

Ninth floor. He fell at the top of the stairwell and burst into the hall. The diary spilled out onto the floor. He absently grabbed it and dragged his burning legs towards her bed, moving frustratingly slowly as his limbs refused to work. He staggered around the corner to the elevators.

BING! The light blinked on, and the metal door slid open. It had arrived at the same time he did. The irony was wasted on Shaun as he passed through the ward. He barely noticed as he tucked the diary into the back of his pants, moving again towards Lauren.

Black uniforms surrounded her bed. Shaun slowed, not daring to face the moment he had so desperately rushed to meet.

'Lauren?' he called. The heads of several cops turned as one. There were four of them.

'Lauren?' he said again, stumbling as he walked now, like a drunk man trying to make it home. His eyes were fixed on the bed he could not see, the wall of uniforms stopping him.

'Lauren? It's okay, baby, I'm here now.' His face was streaked with tears. One of the police officers, a woman in her twenties, walked over to meet him, putting her arms out to slow his progress and get his attention. Shaun was about to push past her when he caught sight of the bed. It was empty. He stopped.

'Lauren? Where is she?'

'Mr Streetlunds?' the female officer asked. Shaun didn't respond.

'Are you Mr Streetlunds, sir?' she repeated. He looked at the woman for the first time.

'Where is she?' he asked. 'What have you done with her?'

'Mr Streetlunds, calm down. Come over here with me.' The officer put her hand on Shaun's shoulder, pressing uncomfortably hard, and made to turn him away from the scene. He fought past her.

'Where's my wife?' he demanded, staring at the patches of blood dotting the bed. The cops around the bed all looked a little strange; they weren't saying anything or taking notes.

'Mr Streetlunds,' the woman continued from behind him.

Don't trust her, his brain warned.

'Max, my name's Max,' Shaun lied.

'Max, your wife's body and that of your friend have been taken to the morgue. I'm very sorry.'

Shaun turned back to her, confused. The morgue? How had they moved Lauren so quickly? How had they got here so quickly? And what about the hobo? What had happened to him?

'We can take you down to identify the body in a moment.' The female officer spoke in sympathetic tones. 'I'm very sorry, but first we have to ask you a few questions.'

She spoke with an Italian accent. Shaun's suspicion gave him focus. The policewoman turned to him and gestured to a couple of chairs at the corner of the ward. She led him there and pulled one out for him and one for herself. She sat and offered for him to do the same.

He sat cautiously, hoping his face wouldn't betray his growing suspicion.

'Mr Streetlunds,' the officer began, pulling out a small notebook.

'It's Streetland,' he corrected her as a test.

'Streetland, sorry.'

She doesn't know who you are, his brain interrupted.

Her pen seemed to act independently of the rest of her body. With her mouth she was asking questions, but with her notebook and pen she was working feverishly, writing, annotating, describing.

'We believe that the people who shot your wife were looking for something. We believe they followed you from a motel out past Whitesville and were looking for ...?' she searched his face. The sympathy she had shown was gone and her expression was cold.

'What sort of something?' he asked.

'Something very, very important,' she said in measured tones.

'I really don't know what you mean,' Shaun lied again, growing more suspicious. The woman smiled. She was pretty. Dark hair fell out from under her hat and curled across her forehead. Her eyes were an emerald green and lined with dark lashes.

'I know it's been a hard night for you,' she continued. 'Your wife has been killed, and your friend was shot also. These people killed your wife, and we know they will not hesitate to kill you in order to get what they want.'

Is this the way cops usually speak to victims? Shaun wondered. *Something's up*, his brain warned. He clung to his suspicion; it gave him something besides the shock and grief.

'Why don't you tell me about your friend? The man with the beard. How long have you known him?' Her pen was still working overtime, and she had filled three pages by now. He caught a glimpse of what looked like meaningless scrawl. What was she writing? The harsh fluorescent lights in the ward flickered. Shaun found it hard to focus.

'I don't know him,' Shaun began. 'We were driving and we hit him with our car. He ran out in front of us.' The pen continued to move, but for the first time he noticed the light on the end of it. A small red light ... or wait, was it green? It seemed to change hue depending on the angle. His eyes followed it.

'Yes, you hit him with your car, didn't you? You hit him with your car and thought you'd killed him. But he wasn't dead, was he?'

'No, he wasn't dead,' Shaun repeated her words. She wasn't so bad.

'Then you took him in your car, didn't you? You took the man in your car and drove him to a motel.' The pen kept moving. It was very interesting. He wondered where he could get one of those pens. Maybe they gave them out at the police academy.

'And you took him to a motel, didn't you?' she said again. 'You took him to a motel and he was carrying something. He was carrying something very important, wasn't he?'

'Yeah, he had a whole bunch of books and papers and stuff. They looked really old.' He had stopped crying now. He felt better. Maybe it was better to talk about it, to tell the cops everything, to get it all off his chest.

'So, you took the man and the books to the motel, didn't you?'

'We took the man and the books to the motel,' Shaun heard himself say.

'Then what did you do?'

'Then we called the ambulance. We took the man to a room.'

'You took the man to a room and then the bad men turned up, didn't they? The bad men turned up and shot everyone. They were very dangerous men, weren't they?'

'They were very dangerous,' Shaun agreed. She really was a very sensible police officer.

'The bad men killed everyone and then you escaped, didn't you?'

'We escaped.'

'You took the man with you but left the books, didn't you?'

'We took the man and left the books.'

'Did you leave *all* the books?'

Shaun struggled a little. Did they leave them all? No, they had taken one. What a cool pen.

'We took one. Lauren took one,' he said. Best they should know everything.

'Lauren is your wife?'

'Lauren is my wife.'

'And Lauren is dead because she took the book. Do you understand?' the police officer continued evenly, explaining it all to Shaun. It made such sense now.

'She's dead because she took the book.' The light in the pen did a loop-the-loop. He liked loop-the-loops. They reminded him of roller coasters when he was a kid. He hoped the light would do it again.

'You wouldn't want to die just for a book, would you?'

'No, I wouldn't want that.'

'So, if you knew where the book was, it would be best to tell the police, wouldn't it?'

'Don't want to die just for a book.' Shaun saw the reasoning clearly. He felt much better, calmer.

'You can't even read the language it was written in, so it's useless, isn't it? Where is the book now, Max?'

Max? His name wasn't Max. Why had she called him that? Not that it mattered.

'Oh, I could read it. Lauren read most of it, but I read a little.' The pen stopped moving.

'What?'

'Lauren read most of it in the ambulance. She read it out to me.'

'You read Aramaic, do you, Max?' the woman asked with a different tone in her voice. The pen wasn't so interesting anymore. He started to look up.

'No ... no, it wasn't in Aramaic. It was written in English.'

'You're lying!' the policewoman's voice said suddenly, harshly. 'Where is it? Where did you hide it? You fucking idiot, don't you know they'll kill you for reading it? Where is it?'

Why was she yelling? She had been so nice. 'Max! Max, where is the book now?'

Max? Why was she calling him that ... because he had told her that was his name. Why would he do that?

'*Max!* Look at me you fucking pleb. Where is the book? Where is it *right now*?'

He had told her his name was Max. He had told her because ... because he didn't trust her. He looked at her face again. Her nostrils were flared and her brow was furrowed. She was bright red, and clearly furious about something.

'Where is the book, where is the fucking book?' she spat, the venom no longer hidden.

A cop doesn't swear like that, his brain told him. Shaun shook his head hard and closed his eyes. The instant he did, they stung like detergent had been poured in them. He realised he hadn't blinked in minutes. They watered up quickly and he squeezed them shut as tears formed and flowed down his cheeks. He suddenly felt a sharp slap across his face.

'Where is the codex? Where is the map?' she hissed.

Shaun was stunned. He was now free of whatever influence he had been under, but her new tactic of fear was effective. He recoiled. His brain worked frantically. Where was the diary? The what? Codex? He didn't know that word. Where was it?

It was here. It was right here tucked into the back of his pants. If Shaun knew one thing he knew this: if they found it, they would kill him. Right there, in front of everyone, they would shoot him dead.

'It's in the ambulance,' he stammered. 'It's under the front seat in the passenger's side. I didn't know it was important. We just—'

He was silenced by another slap across the face. 'There is no more "we", Mr Streetlunds. Your wife is dead because she took the diary. Now, where is the ambulance?'

Shaun struggled to think. It had probably been moved by now, probably been taken somewhere for repairs.

'I left it in the driveway of the emergency ward. I swear.'

The woman turned and motioned to the three remaining cops who were standing by the bed where Lauren had been. They turned as one and marched off down the corridor. He watched them go, then looked fearfully back at the young woman. If he knew nothing else, he knew she was no cop.

'You read the codex too,' she said simply, unholstering her side-arm, 'so you have to be terminated, like your wife.'

Shaun knew that his wife was dead. He knew it as surely as it was possible to know something, and when he looked at this woman, this 'cop', and knew that she was involved with those responsible, a new emotion rose from his gut.

Rage.

He went from zero to a hundred in a flash. Within the space of a couple of heartbeats, adrenaline coursed unchecked through his body.

She killed Lauren, she or someone working with her. She killed Lauren. Focus. She killed Lauren. Rage. She killed Lauren. Teeth grinding. She killed her.

Shaun saw red. His vision tunnelled, his cares vanished. In all the world, in all of time, there existed only this woman before him.

She killed Lauren.

She killed her.

The woman was still speaking, her demeanour smug. She thought she had won.

'Now you get the chance to join your wife. Your *dead* wife.'

The bitch. The *bitch*. Shaun wasn't sure where the scream started. It rumbled from somewhere deep in his stomach and burst through his chest. By the time it hit his throat it was like a tsunami reaching shallow waters, unleashing devastating force.

Then it broke.

The woman had her gun out, but she hadn't pulled back the hammer. She was enjoying taunting him, this man who had just lost everything and sat broken before her. It was she who was most surprised then, when before her eyes, he was transformed.

The gun flew from her hand, knocked clear by a smashing, swinging backhand to her wrist. Then, driven by rage, driven by all the pent-up agony, his emotions peaking, Shaun leaped.

He charged straight across at the woman, driving his forehead into her teeth. His body kept going, pushing over hers as she fell backwards out of her chair from the force of the blow. They crashed down to the floor, Shaun landing heavily on her chest, knocking the wind out of her lungs.

The woman's police hat flew off, releasing a wave of shoulder-length black, shiny hair as her head smacked down hard against the tiled floor. Shaun pushed himself up to straddle her, his knees pinning down her arms. Then he started. Driven by blind fury, Shaun's fists rained down on her face. He punched and punched her, smacking her head from side to side, uncaring of who might be watching.

'You ... killed ... Lauren!' Within a few seconds her face was an unrecognisable mess. Teeth were missing from his head-butt, and now her lips were split and jaw broken. Her ability to scream long since silenced, there was now only the repeating dull thud of bone on flesh and her head against the floor.

Gunshot.

The slug took him in the left shoulder, burning as it knocked him sideways off the woman. Blood exploded from his arm, the bullet passing through the rear of his deltoid, missing the bone and exiting cleanly.

Shaun's hand went immediately to the wound, the sudden searing pain snapping him out of his fury. Seeing one of the other 'cops' with his gun pointed directly at him, Shaun scrambled. His feet slid on the tiling as he ducked to avoid the next shot. The zing ran right past his ear, splitting the air.

He dived behind the nearby ward-administration desk as the man with the gun started to run towards him.

If you stay here you're dead, his brain said matter-of-factly. Would that be so bad? Shaun thought in response. Maybe not. What was there to live for now anyway? Lauren's gone, what's left? Then, as always, his brain gave him an answer. *Revenge.*

The splintered explosion of another bullet smacking into the desk just above his head gave Shaun a jolt. He only had a couple of seconds before the cop would be in a clear firing position. There was only one option.

Directly across from him was the stairwell he had run up earlier. There were two flights of stairs between each floor, one folding back on the other. Shaun ran straight across the hall and threw himself into the open space, spreading his arms and legs as if to fly. Instead he crashed down hard and awkwardly on the bottom couple of steps, not quite making the distance needed to reach the halfway landing.

Fortunately for Shaun, and unfortunately for the orderly he had crashed into earlier, the man had been racing up the stairs to see what the problem was. He provided Shaun with just enough cushioning to stop any serious damage.

Before the small Englishman had time to complain, Shaun was up and racing down the next flight of stairs, clearing the last step just as it exploded beneath his feet. Fragments of cement flew everywhere as another shot blasted the rest of the remaining step and he pushed through the door into the stark white corridor.

Running blindly, his only thought was survival. He needed to live to avenge Lauren. As he sprinted down the hallway, leaving bloody footprints behind him, he swore he would make them pay.

He took a corner and looked around him, panting. His bloodied shoulder was still pouring crimson. He needed to lose his pursuer but he didn't have much energy left. He was stopped in a cross passageway connecting one long corridor to another. He had reached the end of one hallway and ran perpendicular to the police impostor chasing him. He came to another T-junction and knew that his choice here would mean life or death. Hard-soled shoes echoed behind, clanging with increasing volume.

When in doubt, turn left, his brain commanded. It was a rule he had lived by most of his life, and one that had rarely failed him – but the stakes had never been quite so high. He turned left and ran, just as the other two 'cops' came around the corner at the opposite end of the corridor. They saw him and drew their guns. Shaun knew there was no time to debate, so he found the first door and turned left again, into the women's restroom.

Oblivious to the commotion outside, a teenage girl looked in the mirror while she applied make-up to her too-young face. She wore a short skirt and tight midriff top, and her ears were filled by small headphones. She didn't notice as Shaun entered and looked about frantically. He ran right through the restroom and out the door on the opposite side. Seeing the reflection behind her, the girl screamed and jumped, sending a smudge of eyeliner across her cheek, down to her jaw.

Shaun found himself back in the original corridor. Having inadvertently run a shortcut, he was now behind the first gunman. Shaun turned right, towards the stairwell, knowing now that all the cops trying to shoot him – the ones he knew about – were on this level. It was then that he saw something else, right at the far end of the hall. A semi-opaque set of double doors with large letters on them: 'Laundry'. Shaun ran the length of the corridor and crashed through the doors at speed. The room was empty, most people having cleared out when they heard the initial gunshots.

He quickly scanned the room and found the big silver panel set waist-height in the wall next to a plastic label that said, 'Chute'. Shaun pulled the handle and the whole top section swung out, pivoting at its base. Grabbing a nearby tarpaulin bin, he fished out a large wad of soiled hospital sheets. He stuffed the sheets into the laundry chute and listened. They bounced down, the passage obviously widening after the initial bottleneck entrance.

About three full seconds passed before he heard the soft thud of fabric on fabric. He quickly stuffed another two bundles of bedding into the narrow chute entrance, a space barely wider than his hips – if he was going to free fall for three seconds, it was going to hurt, but not as much as a bullet in the head. He spun around as he heard footsteps echo from outside the doors. They were looking for him, he thought, probably trying to decide if he had run back down the stairwell or was hiding in one of the rooms on this floor. He grabbed onto the sides of the chute and climbed up – it was tight and difficult to do without making noise.

First one leg, then both into the small opening, then he lowered himself slowly down in a reverse chin-up to find his legs hanging in empty space. His feet searched about for walls to press against, but he could not reach them.

The chute started to close as his body inched lower, the sharp pain in his injured shoulder no longer masked by the adrenaline. Trying to bear his body weight, his arm gave way.

Three seconds later, he landed hard on a pile of hospital bedding as it compressed under his falling body. He hit and rolled off the pile almost in one motion. The roll took most of the sting out of his fall – that, and the large laundry woman who had come over to investigate the sudden, unexpected laundry drop.

He jumped up straight away, thinking only about getting as far away from the hospital as possible. The rotund laundry woman was too stunned to complain when Shaun dashed out through the washing-room doors and into the hospital's delivery bay. It was the most action she had seen in years.

He scanned the delivery bay.

Trucks. Three big trucks with no one around. One was a hospital truck. The next was painted with the picture of a cow and cartons of milk. The third was a DHL delivery truck – and the engine was running.

Shaun's first thought was to jump in the DHL cabin and go. But then, a stolen vehicle as recognisable as this was bound to be reported all over the police scanners, so he reconsidered.

He ran over to the big yellow vehicle. The cabin was small, but the trailer attached was twenty feet long. For a few seconds he contemplated slipping away among all the postage, but there was too big a chance of getting trapped.

The sound of the truck's driver returning broke his train of thought. He ducked down and waited, keeping out of sight of the pot-bellied man in company uniform. It was then that Shaun saw the bars and tray on the underside of the vehicle's trailer. It was a maze of metal, but looked sturdy enough to support his weight.

Worming his way in, Shaun gritted his teeth against the pain in his shoulder as he slid his body between the tray and the support struts. He curled, twisting his limbs around the metal so no part was exposed. He had been there for no more than a second when the driver jumped up into his cabin and crunched the big delivery rig into gear. It jumped to life and started to move backwards, pulling out and around from the delivery dock.

Shaun curled up tighter, acutely aware of the throb in his shoulder. He touched it and winced. A gash of flesh had been taken out. With all his activity, the blood pumping through his body was now seeping through his jacket. He pulled the diary from his pants and put it back in his jacket's large inner pocket. If they – whoever they were – had known they were within arm's reach of it, would he still be alive? He doubted it.

He was now certain that this was all about the book with the strange symbol on the front. He knew that to someone, this diary was important enough to kill for – important enough to kill Lauren.

Lauren. Dear God. Lauren was gone. His brain didn't accept it yet, but he had seen it with his own eyes. No doubt they had shot the hobo too and had disposed of both bodies. Shaun closed his eyes tight as tears started to well again at the thought of what they had done to his wife's body. They would pay.

Shaun had always felt that he was a decent human. But now, with the only person who really mattered to him gone, the rules had changed. All he cared about was revenge. They had taken away the very thing Shaun had lived for, and now he filled the void with thoughts of retribution. If he could summon enough anger he might just be able to keep the heartache at bay.

Right now he had to find out who these people were, and why this book was so important to them. The young woman had been surprised when he told her he had read the book. It had rattled her to the point of breaking character when he had said it was written in English. What had she said? 'You read Aramaic, do you, Max?'

Aramaic? Shaun thought back. The other pile of documents had been in all kinds of languages, none of which he had understood. He supposed some of them could have been Aramaic, but certainly not all. He knew enough about languages to recognise different ones, even if he didn't understand them.

Aramaic, though? To the best of his knowledge, it was an ancient language from somewhere around the Middle East, but no longer spoken, certainly not in North Carolina.

He weighed up the idea that the hobo was a thief; that he had stolen the documents from a museum. But that didn't feel right. Museums didn't usually hire hit squads – at least he didn't think they did – and the bundle had been sealed. Shaun remembered the hiss as Lauren punctured the wrapping, and the smell that had escaped. Old, musty time was concealed in the object. A museum wouldn't have left something so ancient sealed; it would be preserved and out on display. Shaun adjusted his position and looked around in concern as he heard the truck's brakes give off a high-pitched squeal. Then it hit him: they were stopping.

He looked out from his thigh-level vantage point. The night outside was dark, but the lights of the city reflected off every object, giving depth to the blackness. He heard voices.

'Heard about the commotion that's gone on here tonight?' a deep voice spoke in an Italian accent.

'I didn't notice nothin' strange till I got out here and saw you guys everywhere. Why are there so many police around?'

Police? Damn. Shaun didn't trust the police right now.

'We've got reason to believe the people who caused that pile-up on the freeway earlier are in and around the hospital. You don't mind if we have a look at your truck, do you?'

'I got nothing in here but mail,' the driver said, 'but sure, go ahead.'

Damn and double-damn. Real police or not, stealing away in the lower rigging of a courier truck might be classed as 'suspicious behaviour'.

'Thanks, we won't keep you a moment.' The officer's boots crunched on the cold ground as he turned. Shaun froze. He saw the circle of a torch on the ground five feet away. It disappeared for a moment, then flashed again as the policeman walked the circumference of the large delivery trailer.

'Mind popping open the back for me?' he heard the accented voice call. Then, the front door opened and the driver's feet landed on the ground.

'No poppin' nothing with DHL; we do it the old-fashioned way.' He walked around and Shaun heard a lock, then the back roller door rattled up. Moments later the whole trailer dipped a little as it took the weight of the cop climbing up into it.

'Hey, don't you need a warrant or something to go in there?' the driver asked. 'I got a whole lotta deliveries to make tonight and gotta get out onto the road to be in New York by noon tomorrow.'

After a moment of shuffling packages, the trailer bounced back up as the man jumped down. The torch flashed around a little more. Then the light grew brighter as the torch was swung under the trailer, right to where Shaun was hiding.

Shaun's heart hammered in his chest as he held his breath, listening to the slow footsteps barely two feet away. He tucked tightly behind a large axel block hanging down low behind him. The torch's beam moved back and forth, like a snake tasting the air for its prey.

Then it was gone.

The truck heaved under the weight of the driver sitting in his seat again, and the door slammed with a jolt. The cop banged twice on the side of the trailer. Again Shaun heard the gears crunch and felt the lurch of the truck taking him out through the hospital gates. He released the breath he had been holding. He was safe.

CHAPTER 16

Two years ago

David Black was not a stupid man. He was perhaps a little socially awkward, perhaps a little shabby in his grooming, but no one had ever accused him of being stupid. In fact, few minds could process data with the speed of David's. David knew computers. He knew code. He knew the internet, and he knew everything there was to know about digital video. He was not stupid. It had been more than a year since the night his house had been shot up and his boss, Randy Bilis, had been killed in his own home in front of his wife and kids. No one saw who did it. The news blamed a sniper shot from across the street, but David knew better.

David's home had been targeted, but it wasn't just the house that was shot up. If there was an irony to all this, it was that someone *was* killed that night in his home. He could only assume it was a thief. The police said that it must have been a homeless man, because there were no records with which to identify him. That was probably why it hadn't made the news. David knew better. He knew that someone had been in his house searching for something that night and had been shot by mistake.

As a self-confessed geek, David believed stringently in back-up. All his data drives were mirrored RAIDs or: 'Redundant Array of Independent Discs'.

He had doubles of everything. Everything. He had grown paranoid after he lost a short film he created during university due to a storm blackout. The film had taken him three days straight to make, and he lost it all. He had never made another film after that, saying that his first could never be topped. In truth, his technical skills far outweighed his artistic ones, but now, he was vigilant in backing up his data.

David had been on the run for a year, and he had spent the time carefully, working to learn as much as he could about the mysterious situation that had led to his attempted murder. He thought he knew who the game-players were, and he thought he knew who might be able to help. That was why he had agreed to meet this man so late on a Tuesday night, and why he clung so tightly to the small briefcase in his hand. Inside it was the only other unit in the world that could play the small penny-sized disc that had started all the trouble. He had made significant improvements to the unit since that fateful day a year ago when he had screened it to the disappointed Europeans, and they had taken the player as a prize.

He walked along the Paris street with purpose. The cafes were still open and the streets lively. He had deliberately chosen a public place. He felt safe only in the middle of a busy cafe, or holed up in his third-storey loft apartment. The latter had everything he needed: high-speed internet connection, no billing address and a clear view of the surrounding streets. David erred on the side of caution these days.

He approached the cafe, which sat not far from the beautiful Gare du Nord railway station. He was sure he would enjoy Paris if he ever left his apartment, which he was far too cautious to do. His world was built around consuming home-delivery food, collecting royalties from software he had sold, watching downloaded movies, and of course, continuing his research.

David scanned the scene as he approached. A couple of young lovers on the left; a small, elderly woman on the right; a group of late-night businessmen in the back. Then he spotted him, right there in the corner. Through the glass door David saw the man he knew only as Alberto sitting alone scanning the newspaper, which he had folded down horizontally as he read. That was the signal. Checking the area once more, he entered the cafe and 'accidentally' bumped into one of the waitresses, then came and sat in the corner directly across the table from the man reading the paper.

The man continued to read as he began to speak. His accent was Spanish, which made David edgy.

'You have it with you?'

'I do.'

'We have somewhere that we can go. To watch it.'

'We're going nowhere. We watch it here or not at all.' The man lowered his paper and looked at David. He paused. Assessing.

'I see,' he said finally. 'I understand your mistrust, but if you have what you say you have, what I have to show you will convince you of my ...' He left it hanging a moment 'My understanding of your work.'

'First you tell me why this codec is so important.'

The man smiled at David. 'You developed this codec. You must have had a disc to play on the device – and yet you ask me why?' the man was half-surprised, half-amused.

'The disc I had was blank. It just had some text on it,' David said cautiously.

'Blank. Yes, I suppose it would have been.' The Spaniard's eyebrows lifted. He had short black hair and David estimated him to be about fifty.

'What did the text say?' the man asked.

'I don't think I should tell you that.'

'You shouldn't, but you don't have to. I can guess. It read something like: "IDENT: 0012. SUBJECT: Napoleon Bonaparte. OFFICER: X10,"' the man quoted exactly.

David froze. He could not have known that. Not unless he was with the French and Italian men who had taken the first unit away with them.

'How do you know that?' he asked quickly, suspiciously.

'I know,' the older man began, 'because of where the disc was found. It was dug up on an archaeological dig by a university summer student who was later tortured for his efforts. It was found with the skeleton of a fallen soldier from the Battle of Waterloo. I guessed what the disc said, because that is what it should have said. It was intended to have contained a lot more.'

'Should have said?' David asked.

'Look, let me show you what we both came here to see.' He produced a penny-sized disc that looked like the love child of a DVD and a button. 'If we see on this disc what I think is on it, then many of your questions will be answered.' His eyes darted around the cafe. 'Still, I do not feel comfortable doing this here.'

'Then I guess I should go.' David motioned to leave.

'No, no, no. Of course. If it must be here, then it must be. You have the player?'

David placed the small silver-and-black briefcase on the table. His wrist clanked as the handcuffs that connected him to the player contacted the hard table. The Spaniard smiled.

David fiddled with the combination lock on the front and the case popped its latches. Taking a breath, he lifted the lid and revealed a complex interface. On the lower panel a series of dials, lights and buttons were arranged seemingly randomly on the surface. The entire upper section of the lid was a dark rectangular screen.

Along the sides, two pairs of earphones sat in small compartments. David popped them out and handed one pair to Alberto. The older man took the small headphones, which looked like a long string of black cotton with a bulge at each end. There was nothing connecting them to the unit.

'Like this,' David instructed as he placed the earphones in his own ears. The older man did as he was shown.

'Now, tell me when you can hear something.' David began to play with a dial on the unit, then pressed several switches. 'Each set of headphones works on a unique frequency that interacts with your eardrum's naturally vibrating harmonics. It sends a signal, reads the response from your brainwaves and feeds back into the unit. So, once the headset is tuned into your ear, no one else will be able to hear what you are listening to. If anyone else put the headphones on, they would get nothing. At the moment they're both calibrated for me.'

David continued to turn the dial slowly, looking carefully at Alberto. Eventually the older man creased his eyes and gave a curt nod. David set the calibration into memory.

He then pulled out a pair of what looked like sunglasses. Black, sleek and made of flexible material, they sat on Alberto's face as if they were custom built.

'Now,' David continued, 'look at the screen and tell me when you see an image.'

Again he explained the controls. 'This works like the earphones, but calibrates to your unique optics. The lenses are a circular polarisation that screens out anyone from spying.'

'I see something,' Alberto said.

'What?'

Alberto squinted as the image came into focus. 'It says ... "Fuck ... you".'

'Yeah, that's the default in case anyone tries to tamper with the unit. Keep looking.' David adjusted the dial.

'Yes! There! There, it says, "Hello, welcome to the love shack".'

'That's the one,' David smiled and put his glasses on. 'Again, if anyone tries to record the image, or is looking over your shoulder, or has a set of glasses that aren't calibrated specifically for them, all they'll see is a black screen.'

'Very impressive,' the Spanish man said, blinking under the lenses.

Emphasising his point, David continued: 'If anyone tries to steal this unit, they won't be able to get it to work. I'm the only one who knows how to make it sing.'

'Then let us hear its song, Mr Black.' Alberto held out the small shining disc on the end of his fingertip. David took it. He swiped a finger across a small panel in the case and a large tray slid out, about the size of a regular DVD. Sitting in the tray was a disc labelled *Army of Darkness*.

'Hey, if I'm going to build this thing, I may as well be able to watch movies on it,' he said a little defensively. He popped the Blu-Ray out and placed the small disc in the centre of the tray, and the unit sucked it in.

'Hold your breath,' David smiled, and then he hit play.

Black.

Nothing.

Text, white on black:

IDENT: 0011
SUBJECT: Napoleon Bonaparte
OFFICER: X9

Black. Image.

At first it wasn't clear if they had seen something. Then, the orange spot came again. It was a light in the distance. It looked like an adjustment was made as the whole screen suddenly lit up.

The sound cut in just as suddenly. Slowly moving paddles splitting still water. Then, with the image brightening, both David and Alberto gasped as the picture came into focus. The experience was intense, unlike anything they were expecting. They were looking out from a small rowing boat as it approached a cliff face. On the very top of the cliff was an austere stone structure that resembled a barracks. As remarkable as the image itself was, it was nothing compared to the way they viewed it. Right there in the middle of a Paris cafe, the two men were immersed in another world. The picture seemed to protrude from the screen in the very best version of stereoscopic 3-D either of them had ever seen.

The image had an incomparable sense of depth and clarity, as if the cliff jutted out of the screen and the water could splash their faces at any moment.

Alberto Eduardo Florez reached forward with his fingers, convinced he could grab one of the oars from a man in the foreground. His fingers bumped the screen and the whole image jolted a little. He swore under his breath, then quickly made the sign of the cross. David didn't notice; he was stunned by the intricacy of the picture, the realism, the detail.

He had designed this player, he had reverse-engineered the codec, but he had no idea how this was happening.

'When Giovanni sees this ...' murmured Alberto. 'It is more than even he imagined, I'm sure.'

David didn't know who Alberto was talking about, but took a mental note of the name.

Alberto stared at the picture unfolding before his eyes and could almost feel the wind on his face. They were in a boat, heading for what looked like an island. It was night. The only sounds were the lapping of the water and the quiet breathing of several men. David turned his head, thinking that someone sitting directly behind him had whispered, but all he saw was the couple at table three immersed in conversation. He could not believe the quality of the sound. He didn't even know this level of immersion was possible. He stared back at the screen.

A hand wearing an intricately carved gold ring reached forward from the bottom of the screen and rested on the shoulder of the man who was rowing. Something was said in French, but David didn't understand. Then a voice came through loud and clear in English.

'This man is Jean-Paul.' The man rowing turned and nodded his head. The American accent continued, 'He will take the device should anything happen to me. He knows the hide location.'

The voice whispered something harshly as a rifle crack was heard in the distance. The image showed the bow of the boat sliding up on an area of sand no more than six feet wide. It was the smallest of alcoves in the vertical rock wall. The point of view swung around as the man filming the scene jumped from the boat. Another two men jumped out. There were four in total, including Jean-Paul and the man who spoke.

'We have arrived at the prison island of Elba. The courage of these three men should not go unrecorded: Jean-Paul Luvié, Benoit Fontéyne and François Buviour.' The image scanned across the faces of each of the men as he spoke their names. They looked straight into the camera, straight out at David and Alberto. The detail was unbelievable. Every pore was evident.

'These men have risked their lives for our cause, and should I not survive they have instructions on what to do. It begins now. Jean-Paul shall wear the unit.'

The image cut again and showed the men ascending what appeared to be a rope ladder. Their dialogue was French, spoken in hushed commands.

The picture followed the men sneaking up and over a wall, and then peering from a vantage point onto a grassed courtyard. Three guards in white pants and red coats could be seen. The cameraman ducked behind the stone wall once again, then turned to a new face. This man had a modern-day American accent and as his face came forward into full view, Alberto gasped, biting his fist. 'My God! Alex!'

The same voice heard earlier spoke. 'Tell Strickland I owe him a beer, he really is a genius,' the man winked. With that he turned and leaped over the wall, silently, speedily. The camera looked on as the man disposed of the three guards with incredible efficiency.

The images became mixed as the filming stopped and started. Running, hiding, fighting. All close-quarters combat, the likes of which would have made Jackie Chan proud. This man, Alex, displayed skills David had never seen, made all the more intense by the imagery and sounds that totally immersed the two men watching.

Then the men were inside, heading down a dimly lit stairwell that eventually levelled out. They came into a long corridor. Along the left wall were iron doors. Along the right, the rock was jagged and the wall uneven, carved from the natural stone rather than built of manmade blocks.

Only two men could be seen now: the American called Alex and one of the Frenchmen. They trod carefully on a crude, rock-covered floor, their torchlight glistening off the slippery surface underfoot.

After two or three minutes, the men stopped. Jean-Paul, from whose point of view David and Alberto were now experiencing the scene, continued up to an iron door. It was solid, and only a small eye-height flap broke the continuity of the steel. A hand reached out and slid the grille flap to one side. The camera moved closer to peer through the bars.

Perhaps it was pride, perhaps the indignation or perhaps the contempt felt for his captors, but the man inside did not respond to the sound of the grille opening. He sat with his back to the wall on the far side of the cell. There was no window, and the only light streamed in from what appeared to be a thin horizontal vent high on the cell wall. The man was small. He had dark hair and a hooked aristocratic nose. He stared straight ahead, as if he were seeing something in the blackness before him. It was the French greeting that caused him to look up.

'*Salutations, mon seigneur.*' Very slowly the man tilted his head.

'When did the English start educating their jailers?' His tone was mocking, yet curious.

‘My lord, I will ask you a question to which I need your honest reply. If we release you from this prison this night, and return you to France, will you agree to answer our questions?’

‘If you release me from this prison this night, and return me to France, I will grant you the kingdom of Belgium. Tell me, who sits on the throne in Paris?’ the man said as he rose to his feet, moving easily with his eyes accustomed to the darkness.

‘The Congress of Vienna has fully ratified the notion of monarchy in Europe, and has distilled any remnants of democracy. They have installed Louis the eighteenth as king.’

The man in the cell walked towards the door. He was not a tall man, but something about him made him seem large. He had, even in the dim prison cell, true presence. He stood with pride and looked down his nose at the pair of eyes he could see through the six-inch grille in the door.

‘Brother of Louis the sixteenth? That coward?’ the man asked, shocked.

‘Monsieur Bonaparte, you must come with us quickly.’ There were sounds of English voices and yells as the camera swung away to the left. Suddenly the image changed. Hands extended down around the throat of a red-coated man. The English guard struggled for breath, but it was in vain. They were outside, and the grass was wet, glistening in the moonlight. David watched the life leave the man’s eyes. The camera moved again to show the man called Alex displaying incredible martial skill in disabling three more red-coats efficiently.

But one of the Frenchmen was struck. He lay in the wet grass, his body lifeless, his mouth wide. Hiding behind a nearby wall, the prisoner, Napoleon Bonaparte, waited for Alex to dispatch his English attackers.

Within moments, the image jolted sideways and cut to black. They waited.

Black. Waiting. Nothing. Black.

Finally, text appeared on the screen, ‘END DATA STREAM’, and this was soon replaced by, ‘HELLO, WELCOME TO THE LOVE SHACK’.

Gunshot.

CHAPTER 17

The truck came to a stop for the first time in more than twenty minutes. As the traffic light glowed red, Shaun rolled off his metal perch and dropped onto the road. The light flashed green and the truck moved on, leaving its stowaway on the road facing the night sky. There were no other cars around.

Shaun slowly, painfully got up and surveyed his surroundings. The effort of holding his weight on the truck's underside had drained him. He needed to move, but more than that, he needed to sleep.

He was on a bridge, and he saw a large cement canal twenty feet below. He stumbled to where the overpass ended and jumped the fence. He half-slid, half-ran down the long concrete slope to the shadowy cavern below. Somewhere safe to hole up.

The place reminded him of when he was a kid and had seen the car race in the movie *Grease*. Then as he reached the bottom and looked back up his brain chimed in.

No. More like The Terminator.

Any second he expected to see a truck smash through the railings of the overpass and come careering towards him in its relentless pursuit, but it didn't happen. It started to rain, but Shaun walked rather than ran to the shelter. He was sick of running, and all things considered he didn't mind the cool drops hitting his face.

He sank down against the concrete and pulled his knees to his chest. He didn't know where he was, only that he was being hunted. He only had a half-reasoned plan to make it right, for Lauren. He didn't want her death to be in vain.

He pulled the thick book from his jacket and quickly found his place. He sighed, using his palm to wipe the water from his eyes, and by the dim yellow streetlight he started to read.

CHAPTER 18

When I woke, I was blindfolded. My hands were bound behind my back and an acrid smell filled my nose and mouth. The ground was cold and stone. I lay still on my side and the air was silent. I tried to call saliva into my throat, but there was none. It was cracked and raw, and I was hungry. I strained with all my senses to paint a mental picture of my surroundings.

I rolled clumsily up to my knees and swayed from the effort. I was weak from hunger. I had no sense of how much time had passed; no idea how long I'd been out, which was why the next voice I heard was so helpful.

'You're awake.' It was a deep, short voice. The owner spoke Roman, but it was clearly not his native tongue. I tried to reply, but my mouth was too dry to speak. I coughed up phlegm and blood and my chest burned from it.

'Easy,' came the voice again. 'You've been lying there for two days now. I thought you were dead. It is good that you are not.'

I had to agree with him.

'I would help remove your blindfold, but I am chained to a wall,' he said, the rattle of his chains giving testament to his words. I again tried to call moisture into my throat, but I could not.

'You cannot speak because you have been breathing their smoke for many days; it keeps you asleep. I have been awake now for three days and wish I could go back to sleep.'

Again I tried, and again nothing.

'Do not worry. Your voice will return in time. Let me tell you what I know, to save you asking the same questions the last two did.' There was no malice in the voice, but a genuine frankness that comforted me.

'You are in a Roman dungeon,' he began. 'You are a prisoner. Your reasons are your own, although I suspect that you committed the simple crime of being in the wrong place at the wrong time.'

Chains rattled as the speaker adjusted his position. 'My name is Malbool. I am from Africa, many months' travel from here.' The deep-voiced man paused and then said, 'It has been seven years since I was taken from my tribe. Here I was forced to become a slave, but unlike many slaves my master educated me and taught me to speak the Roman tongue. Then he got in trouble with the Roman guard and I found myself here.'

He finished as if that were his story and there was nothing left to say. Again I sought command of my voice, and this time it gave a rasp.

'Where ... is ... here?'

'My friend,' Malbool laughed, 'welcome to the great city of Rome.'

Rome, the centre of the world. I had learned much about it during my short stay in Chorazin, and I could not quite believe that I was here.

I remained blindfolded for the next two days, but my hands were unbound some time during my sleep. I was still tied around my upper arms. I was fed, but not spoken to, and after several meals I was able to speak. I too was chained: a thick iron band securely fastened around my ankle, with a short chain to the dank prison wall.

Malbool was taken out of my cell after the first night, and to the best of my knowledge I was alone. I believed I was going to die. I used the time to think, focusing on what Mishca had said about rediscovering my identity.

I considered what I knew about myself. I spoke at least two languages, but I had only found that out by chance. I wouldn't know if I could speak more unless I was tested. I woke up in the land of Palestine, but I did not look like a typical Israelite. I had physical strength and fighting skills. I did not know how or why I had these skills, but clearly I had been trained. Finally, I now found myself arrested by the great Roman army. Why did they want me?

I had been imprisoned for four days and nights when I received an answer. I was half-crouched next to the wall when I heard the familiar sounds of the feet descending the stairs. The prison door was opened and, still blindfolded, I was yanked roughly to my feet, while another set of hands unshackled the chain around my ankle.

Four rough hands half-led, half-dragged me up the stairs and I was lifted into some sort of carriage. I felt the thing lurch as I landed, and again as the two heavy men climbed in after me, filling the space with the thick stench of sweat. Without vision, and with my upper arms bound, I could only lie helplessly where they had thrown me.

The journey ended about a half hour later as I was pulled from the carriage and made to stand, my captors' arms again gripping me. I heard footsteps, then voices.

'This one as you have commanded, my lord,' a gruff voice announced.

'By Mars! Are you trying to kill him before he can be of any use? Remove his blindfold and bindings. You're not going to go anywhere, are you, friend?' The question was directed at me.

Almost at once, the cords fell away from my arms, cut by a cold blade I felt against my skin. My blindfold was ripped away harshly, and although my eyes remained closed, the light hurt my head. Very slowly I opened my eyes.

'Now, what is your name?' the second voice, the one who had commanded my release, asked with authority. Everything was white. Everything was blurred. My eyes watered and I stared around at the coloured blobs in front of me.

'My name is Saul.' It had been more than a day since I had used my voicebox and the sound that came out wasn't my own.

'My name is Saul,' I repeated more firmly.

'Saul?' the voice asked questioningly. 'Saul. It does have a ring to it. And I am Tiberius. So, they tell me you like to fight, Saul.'

'I do not like to fight,' I said, struggling to focus, but unable to do so through the tears.

'Really? That's not what Marcus tells me.'

'I do not know a man called Marcus,' I replied honestly.

'You don't? Oh, I wouldn't say you know each other in the sense you might drink wine together, but you have *met him.'*

I remained silent.

'You have caused Marcus a deal of trouble. You see, he told me you wounded him and killed several of his guards.'

The penny dropped.

'I defended a boy who was being beaten and dragged from his family. I have no interest in Roman affairs.'

'Oh, but you do. It's the way you defended your little friend that caught Marcus's attention. You see, he and I have a little arrangement. He finds me talent and I reward his hard work with silver. After all, he can only make so much money on a soldier's wage. We both benefit.'

I remained silent, not sure where this was all going.

'Saul, I have a business proposition for you.'

'I decline.'

'I'm afraid you don't have that option,' the voice continued offhandedly. 'Now, I am a businessman, but we all have our vices. Mine just happens to be making money. The way I do that varies, but one of my favourite ways is on the games. Do you know about the games Saul?'

'I have heard of them,' I replied cautiously.

'You have? Excellent. I must say, when Marcus told me how you dispatched so many of his guards so easily, I was expecting someone eight feet tall. You're at least a foot short of that, aren't you? Well maybe a foot-and-a-half,' he laughed flippantly.

'Let me tell you about the games. They are the lifeblood of Rome. They are held weekly and pit the strength and skill of men from all over the known world against each other – and against the occasional lion,' he added. 'I have become a wealthy man by waging on the outcome of particular matches, and owning several successful warriors. But right now I'm in a bit of a predicament,' he continued in a leisurely manner. 'My hero, Spinicus, was going to fight the champion of the western region next week. Unfortunately, he was killed in a preliminary match six days ago, and none of my other warriors stand a chance.'

'I will not fight for you,' I said flatly. His features were coming into view. The tanned, indulged face smiled broadly.

'Oh, come now. Saul, is it? Yes, Saul, you see, you will be put in the arena. If you do not fight you will be killed and I will have to find some other wild animal to take Spinicus's place.'

'Then I shall die.' It could not have been much worse than living as a blindfolded, shackled prisoner.

'Now, now, don't be hasty. There is something in it for you as well. The training will be hard, yes, but you have a chance to win yourself many rewards: women, good food, perhaps freedom.'

My ears pricked up at this. I looked over his still-blurry form. He wore a long robe or cape of some sort and paced slowly. Behind him was a long cushioned chair, which I suspected he spent most of his days lounging in.

'Yes, you like the idea of that, don't you? To be free. That's what they all fight for. But I tell you, if you fight well for me, you'll live well. You can have decent accommodation and my good graces simply by continuing to win. Of course, you only get one chance to lose as that usually involves losing your head in some way.' He chuckled again.

'So, my proposition is this. You fight for me, you win for me, and your life will be tolerable, even comfortable. You refuse to fight, or lose, and your life will be over.'

I looked around the room, which had come into focus gradually as my eyes stopped watering. It was large, opening to the sunset. I knew it was nearly night-time, but it still seemed incredibly bright as the red and orange rays reached into the room. There were rows of columns down the length of the room, and its expanse was dotted with large white statues of draped figures.

This man, Tiberius, stood squarely on a stage. He was chubby and balding, still smiling. He wore long purple robes over a white toga, and although I was new to Rome, I knew enough to know that purple was the colour of royalty. This was the last thing I saw before someone standing behind me roughly blindfolded me again. I thought about fighting right then and there, but I was too weak, and I decided to bide my time.

I spent the next week in a cell about twenty feet square. It was a cell only in the sense of having one wall with iron bars, but otherwise, it was reasonably comfortable. There was a bed in one corner, a toilet with a cover in the other. The floor was stone covered with a large animal skin. At night, my injuries were tended. I was well fed and my strength returned.

During the days, I was allowed out into a courtyard to exercise. I found myself going through a series of pre-rehearsed forms – movements I had no recollection of learning, but seemed as natural as breathing. I found myself flowing, spinning, kicking, striking and leaping into the air. Each sequence was automatic, like I had done it a thousand times, and whenever I did something new, Mishca's words came back to me, 'Surely you can work a lot of it out?'

On the morning of the eighth day I was woken early.

'Time to prove you were worth it,' I heard a voice say. I looked up and saw the thickset, square-jawed centurion who had attacked the village. Marcus. He was flanked by four guards. I was taken to a carriage and I offered no resistance. Now was not the time.

In the time each day that I was not exercising, I meditated, another automatic impulse. I learned nothing new about myself from the two-hour stints, but I was feeling a greater sense of identity, and I healed remarkably quickly. Again, I felt the nagging urge knowing there was something I was supposed to do, but I could not yet place it. As the guards led me away, I hoped that perhaps I was being led towards that destiny now.

The carriage bumped along the road for more than an hour before it was pulled to a halt. I was led into an area that appeared to be in the poorer quarter of Rome. The buildings, while still fine works of stonemasonry, lacked the opulence of the houses I had seen around my cell. There was a small wooden door set into one of the houses, and two large men stood guard outside it. They parted at our approach and, without saying a word, opened the door.

I was surprised to see a stairwell leading down, lit by flaming torches. Marcus led the six of us down, and it was then that I heard the men's cheers.

As we rounded the bottom of the stairwell, deep underground, I was struck by the sight of an enormous pit. It was maybe ten feet deep and thirty square, and surrounded by a ring of at least fifty men who were cheering eagerly at the contest in the centre. Two men were battling with short swords, sweat and blood coating their bodies.

It was an amazing spectacle.

I was led down between the crudely fashioned seats to the very edge of the pit, where I saw Tiberius, again wearing his purple toga. He cheered and jeered along with the rest of the spectators.

'Ah, there you are! Sit, watch. You'll be next.'

'Next?'

'Let me tell you a little history so you can understand what you're watching,' Tiberius continued. I was allowed a seat near him, but not within striking distance, I noticed.

'You see, about two hundred and sixty years ago, as part of an aristocratic funeral ritual, the first gladiatorial contest was held.' He spoke in a grandiose manner, clearly eager to educate and impress. 'It was called a "munus" or funeral gift for the dead. Decimus Junius Brutus put on a gladiatorial combat in honour of his dead father, offering three pairs of slaves as gladiators. Since then, these contests have grown to replace ... OOOOHHHH yes!'

Tiberius paused to cheer for a mighty blow one man had struck the other, then continued to clap and watch the match as he spoke to me.

'Ah, now, it was a replacement for human sacrifice for the tombs of great men. Personally, I think someone just liked the idea of watching men fight for their lives.' I got the feeling that this was precisely the appeal for him as well.

'There are very few among the aristocracy of Rome who know I am a lanista. My troupe is kept secret and I have others who act on my behalf in the public games, but I just cannot stay away from these private affairs. They're a good way to test out my new stock.'

I could feel the passion within him for this 'sport' – he was so addicted that he risked his own reputation to be involved.

'You will face three opponents here today. If you survive, you will be taken to my ludus and trained. Oh, he's not getting up, it's over!'

I turned to look into the pit. One of the fighters was face down, knocked senseless by his opponent's repeated blows. He was out. It was over. The crowd began to chant, baying for blood, and the man standing obliged. He turned his short sword downwards in his hands, and I watched in horror as he plunged the blade deep into the fallen man's back. It was that moment that made me realise that there was no real choice: I would have to kill today, or be killed. There was no way out.

It took just ten minutes for the pit to be cleared; the crowd started to call for the next contest. Coins changed hands and I was led down to the edge of the pit.

'Go!' Marcus said savagely as he shoved me into the pit. Then, across from me, a tall, slim man climbed down the outer lip, hung for a moment, and dropped into the pit at the opposite end. He looked at me with hatred in his eyes. He was primed to fight. Two short swords were dropped into the sand beside each of us. There was no gong; the crowd's yells and cheers gave all the indication needed to let us know the battle was on.

I reached down and grabbed the sword and saw the other man do the same. I felt its weight and twirled it once in my wrist to check its balance. Then I moved. With a large circular motion I brought the blade up in front of me, then stepped forward quickly and completed the circle. Swinging at lightning speed, I let the blade go.

My underhand pitch sent the sword, tip first, shooting across the pit. It covered the twenty or so feet in a split second and slid into the man's sternum up to its hilt. The man took a stumbled step backwards, then dropped, not even having time to drop his own blade before his body hit the ground.

The crowd was silenced, stunned. For several moments nothing could be heard in the underground chamber. Then someone called out their delight and started to clap. Another joined him. They started a chain reaction that had the whole place bellowing and cheering within moments. I turned towards my lanista, my master, and made to exit the pit. But the centurion Marcus stood above me.

'You have two more men to kill today.'

'Unless you move, you will be one of them.'

He smiled. 'I like you, but do not take my kindness as an indication that I would hesitate to cut you down if you cross me. My loyalty to

Tiberius goes only so far.' Our eyes met, and there was direct and unhidden challenge. Not now.

'One day,' I said as I turned back around to see another man approaching the pit. I glanced back over my shoulder to look at Marcus. 'One day you will pay for the way you beat that boy.'

'I beat boys every day,' he returned. Then, pointing to the other end of the pit, he continued: 'You need to save your strength.'

In front of me a very different sort of man entered the pit. This man was huge. His face was split by a long scar that travelled from his forehead across his eye to his cheek.

My new master, Tiberius, stood up in protest.

'You cannot put Samuel in with a non-gladiator!' he protested, but was calmed by Marcus, who looked to be explaining something to him.

Tiberius smiled and reached into his pocket. He pulled out a pouch of coins and gave them to Marcus, who promptly disappeared into the crowd.

Non-gladiator? I thought. Then I realised that this whole thing was nothing more than an illegal fight ring. It had nothing to do with the official games, it was where trainers and owners tested their new stock for extra profit, as Tiberius had boasted.

The big man, Samuel, reached into the dirt and picked up his short sword. I waited for mine to be thrown to me, but it didn't come.

'Where is my sword?' I called up to Tiberius.

'Well, my boy, you gave it away! If you give away your weapon, you do not get it back before you leave the pit. Oh, and be careful – Samuel is a professional gladiator.'

Be careful? Some coach. I looked over at the big man in the ring. He raised his arms to the applause of the crowd, then faced me. Samuel stalked over, moving well for a man so large. His thighs rippled as they bore the weight of his body, and as he came within ten feet I noticed another scar. This one was in the shape of a triangle with a cross through it. It was a brand, the symbol of a gladiator burned into his skin.

Samuel crouched low as the crowd started to chant. Even from the centre of the pit, I could hear the clanking of coins. We were only seven or eight feet apart when he sprang, aiming his thrust straight at my heart. I waited until the last possible moment and then twisted my torso out of the way, raising my knee into his stomach and grabbing his wrist as I continued to turn my body. Then, in harsh contrast to his momentum, I twisted Samuel's wrist back on itself, breaking it. The big man screamed as his body went one way, and his arm the other. His sword fell.

The crowd gasped as Samuel rolled up to his feet, holding his wrist. His sword lay at my feet and he looked down at it, but I did not pick it up. As he lashed out with his other hand I blocked, caught his wrist and rolled inside his blow, bringing us front to back. I drove my elbow into his nose, hearing it break as I stepped out and, twisting with the weight of my body, broke his other wrist.

I was shocked at my own brutality, but I knew that this man would kill me in an instant if he had the chance. Samuel fell to the floor as I walked, picked up the sword and threw it next to his head. This fight was over. I walked to Tiberius.

'I will not kill anyone else today. I have shown you I can fight. Now let me out.' Marcus was nowhere to be seen and Tiberius looked shocked.

'My boy, you can't negotiate these things. There's still plenty of money to be made off your last match, so I'm afraid I can't let you out just yet. You're doing very well, and you'll be rewarded, but you have to take care of him first.'

I turned to see that a third man had entered the pit, not waiting for the signal for a new match. This man was dark-skinned and carried a net in one hand, and an evil-looking trident in the other. He was storming over to me, but when he passed the fallen Samuel in the centre of the pit, he paused. With his eyes glaring at me, he hesitated not a second to turn his trident downward and drive its sharpened spikes into the big man's exposed back.

I was horrified at the callousness of it, and could see that my time to negotiate had run out. Before I had a chance to react the man had thrown his net. It fanned out, weighted at its corners, and covered me. I raised my arms instinctively and barely saw the trident as it was hurtled towards me with incredible force. I dove to the side almost too late. One of the three flat, serrated spikes caught my hip as I dove, slicing deeply and cleanly into the muscle of my upper thigh and buttock.

The evasive action only made my tangle in the roped web worse. The dark man was over at the wall recovering his trident within seconds and the instant it took him to dislodge it from the earthen wall gave me the precious time I needed to scramble loose of the net.

The wound on my hip bit, but I ignored the pain as the attack came again. This time I was ready.

The muscled black man snarled as he yet again thrust out with his deadly, three-pronged staff. I sidestepped, keeping my distance, knowing that his skill far exceeded that of the last two men I had fought. He thrust again, and again I evaded, the sharpened points sailing by my neck. Inching closer as we circled, I goaded him.

He took the bait, and this time when he thrust out the long staff I was close enough to grab it below the spikes. I pulled, dragging the man, whose grip held firm, onto a sharp side kick. Ribs cracked and a yelp of pain escaped the man's lips. His grip on the trident loosened, and I pulled it away, spinning it above my head before sweeping it out down low, slicing at the man's thigh. His leg buckled and he went down. I continued to spin the trident, then aimed its head down at my fallen opponent. I drove the weapon hard. Right next to the man's head. His eyes were wide and through clenched teeth he groaned. 'You see much better with no blindfold.'

I recognised the voice. It was deep, it was familiar. I cocked my head slightly. 'Malbool?' I asked, stunned.

'You must finish it, stranger. You must end it or neither of us will walk out alive.' There was no fear in his voice. He sounded like a man who had expected death for a long time.

'There has been enough death today,' I said, offering the man my hand. He looked up at me, confused.

'Do I have your word that you will not strike me when you stand?' I asked.

Malbool looked more confused. 'What is the word of a slave?' he replied.

'I do not ask for the word of a slave. I ask for the word of a man.' My hand hung in mid-air and the crowd started to jeer and hiss.

Slowly, the injured African reached up and took my wrist, and I gripped his, helping him to his feet. When he stood he looked me straight in the eyes.

'I do not know where you are from, but my life now belongs to you.'

I shook my head. 'Your life is your own.'

With that, Malbool, still gripping my wrist, raised my hand high, proclaiming me victor. The crowd roared with adoration.

Back in my cell, I lay flat. My wound had been dressed, but not stitched. I figured this to be a punishment for my defiance of the rules. The wound would have to heal on its own, a prospect that could take months – time in which I would have to fight several matches. Were they crazy? Did Tiberius want me to die? The whole concept of this punishment escaped me.

I lifted my head and peered under the dressing. It was still slick with blood. And then the strangest thing happened. As the dull torchlight from above shone on the slick red mess, I saw … a gleam? A sparkle of light? Something metallic shone in my wound. I rolled carefully onto my side. I then ripped the dressing clear and pushed my fingers into the wound to pull the flesh apart. The pain was excruciating, but there it was again: a shiny metal glint in the torchlight. My God, there was something inside me.

I pulled on the wound again, breathing in short pants to control the pain. My fingers finally touched something in the deep, bloody hole. It felt like string. I made one final push with my fingertips and caught the string between them. It uncoiled and came out.

The bench was covered in blood from my hip, and a string maybe six inches long and impossibly thin hung out of my wound. I stared in disbelief. The string was silver, like no twine I had ever seen; it looked like tightly wound hairs of metal.

The only thing I could think to do was to pull on the string, so that is what I did. The feeling is not one I can easily describe for you, Shaun. It was—

He almost missed it, he was so engrossed in the story. He stopped. He re-read: '*The feeling is not one I can easily describe for you, Shaun.*'

It was there. It was right there in the book before his eyes. Shaun thought he was going insane. He re-read and re-read the passage. It was still there. The spelling was even the same. 'Shaun', not the more popular 'Sean'.

He was jolted out of the story by the revelation, by what he had just read. What the hell? Could this be coincidence? Could this possibly be coincidence? Shaun Strickland was one of the keenest mathematical brains on the planet, but he did not want to begin to calculate the odds of tonight's strange events.

He looked out from under his sheltered resting place. The rain was pelting hard, the temperature had dropped and the lamplight that streamed down was barely enough to read by. But nothing would stop him reading now. For the first time, he had a strange sense that perhaps, just perhaps, none of this was an accident.

CHAPTER 19

VATICAN CITY, 2001 AD

The old man's face stared straight ahead. He was considering what he had heard. He had seen more of life's battles than many could imagine, but the challenge he had just been presented with was more difficult than any he had faced before. It was not as physically taxing as working in the stone quarries, nor as daring as his escape from Poland during the Second World War, nor as time-consuming as learning the five languages in which he was now fluent. No, this challenge was more difficult because it was a challenge of faith, and faith was the one thing on which he was supposed to be an authority.

The British professor seated across from him stared back. There was something in this man's eyes, something that the old man had not seen before. It was absolute certainty. He struggled with the idea again. Was it possible? But yet again, this man, through the letters, the meetings and the explanations had proven again and again that it was. It was possible. If it was possible, what did this mean for him as a world leader? As an authority on faith? What did this mean? For the thousandth time the question came into his head – did he have a choice?

'If what you have told me is true,' the old man began again slowly, knowing the answer because he had asked the question many times before, 'then I have already agreed? And if I do not agree now?'

The man smiled in that same calm manner he had possessed since their first meeting more than a year ago.

'Your Holiness, I simply do not know. I do not know what would happen. I do not know if things would be changed, or if they simply cannot happen any other way. All I know is this: for all that I have said to become true; for you and I to be sitting here talking, you must agree. The Journalist Project is ... necessary.'

Many nights the old Pope had prayed on this. He was torn between what he had come to believe as the truth, and the prospect of discovering the ultimate, unquestionable, undeniable truth.

What if everything he believed in was wrong?

Dear Heavenly Father, what is your will in this matter?

He was terrified. This was his church, an institution that was relied upon by so many for so much, but what if it was all based on a lie? Dare he risk it? What was the greater sin: to keep the masses, and indeed himself, in safe, blissful ignorance, or to dare to know the truth, even if it meant destroying everything?

The professor sat across from the pontiff patiently with a reassuring smile. The old man's face stared straight ahead. When he spoke, it was a simple phrase that belied the monumental process that had led him to the decision.

'I … I believe.' The Pope reached forward and signed the document on the small oak table before him.

CHAPTER 20

Shaun Strickland was cold. The rain had brought with it a bitter breeze that cut to the bone. The streetlight above him flickered intermittently, making it hard to read, but none of this moved him. He was too engrossed and confused by the line he had just re-read several times: '*The feeling is not one I can easily describe for you, Shaun.*'

There was more truth in that line than the writer could have imagined as he penned the words. The feeling of reading something Shaun knew to be vastly old, something he knew to be important, and seeing his name – the sickness he had suppressed until now manifested itself in the form of a recycled turkey-and-cranberry sandwich, which he vomited on his shirt.

He was utterly exhausted, in pain, and heartbroken. He was sure that his mind was playing tricks on him, and yet he could not stop reading.

I pulled on the string that dangled half-in, half-out of my body. The feeling was like having someone else control your muscles; like having your hamstring cramp halfway but never quite cease up. To try to describe the pain is futile. Needless to say, I blacked out.

When I woke I did not know how much time had passed. The first thing I felt was that same excruciating pain. I looked down to see a small cylinder of shining metal hanging halfway out of the open wound in my hip. The top of the cylinder had a small wire string attached to it, the other end of which was wrapped around the fingers of my right hand. I breathed and remembered.

I pulled some more and the object slid. The blood that had already caked around the opening of the wound peeled away, and as I pulled again fresh blood started to weep out of the cut, providing the lubrication I needed. With one final yank, I pulled the bar of metal clear out of my leg.

I immediately re-dressed my wound, applying pressure to stop the bleeding, then sat back, dizzy. The length of my palm, I turned the metal bar over in my hand. I was examining the cylinder when suddenly my eyelids flickered and I fell back.

I felt an explosion in my head. A bolt of pain shot just behind my right eye, then another down near the base of my skull, accompanied by a flash of white light in my mind. Then again, and again. Explosions went off in my brain like the fireworks of a New Year's celebration.

I screamed the scream of a man in terror, but it was pain, not fear, that forced the sound from me. I thrashed about the cell, holding my head and lashing out at nothingness all around me. I spun and swirled and swung at the air, kicked at the walls, rammed the door, all the while vaguely aware of a biting sensation on the flesh of my palm.

Then it stopped. I fell, exhausted and breathing heavily. Through tears I stared again at my hand, at the object I held, and quite suddenly, I knew what it was. I knew more than this, though. I knew—

'My name is Graeme Fontéyne,' I said.

'My name is Graeme Fontéyne,' I repeated.

'My name is Graeme Fontéyne.' The words came out, as if trying to convince me. I stopped and stared at the object. About five inches long and as thick as my finger, it was covered with indentations and markings, as if it were made of several sections joined together. There were small rectangles along its surface that seemed to glow of their own accord.

'This is a camera,' I said aloud. 'This is a camera,' I repeated. What is a camera? *I heard a distant part of my brain respond.* You are Saul, slave and gladiator.

'No, I am Graeme Fontéyne, Officer X7 in The Journalist Project,' I said aloud. I was confused. Like a dream you think is real but when you wake, the emotions of the dream remain. That is how I felt, stuck inside this lucid dream, unable to wake from either reality.

I was overcome with confusion. For more than a month I had struggled to find a sense of identity. I had searched for information about who I was and where I came from. I had started to develop a new sense of these things based on my experiences, and to now have that all blown away was difficult to accept.

I shall repeat myself: the human mind is not designed to exist in two places in time. I am Saul the gladiator. I am Officer X7. I was born in 1975. I live in a world ruled by Caesar.

I fell, clutching at my head, trying to dig out the images that were flashing through it. Cities, machines, people. Sounds of a world yet to come flooded my mind, memories or hallucinations, I could not tell.

And then I stared once more at my hand. This was tangible, this was real. This thing I had dug out of my body was what I clung to.

As I sat in agony and utter confusion, I heard footsteps. My screams had been heard. I hid the device in my clothing and lowered myself onto the bench. It was the caretaker, the man who saw to my battle wounds. He looked through the barred wall of my cell, concerned.

'Ah, Saul,' he said as he saw the blood weeping from my leg, 'I told them I should have taken care of it properly the first time, that the wound would reopen if you knocked it in your sleep.'

I lay back on the bench. I heard the sounds of the cell door opening as I faded into blackness again.

I awoke some time later. My wound was sutured, held together by thin twine, and dressed. I looked around me and saw that I was not in my cell. There were no bars in this room. Had I been dreaming?

'Again, you are awake. You sleep a lot, white skin.' The voice came from behind me. I sat up and turned. It was the same dark-skinned man who had been with me when I was blindfolded, who had fought me in the pit. I was alert instantly.

'Malbool?' I asked.

'It would seem our master would have us together at every opportunity,' he said in his deep African voice. 'Just yesterday we were fighting to the death, and now we are to sleep in the same room.'

'Our master? *I asked. 'Tiberius is also your owner?'*

'He is.'

'Then why would he have us fight to the death?'

'I do not know, but it was not to the death, was it? Why did you disobey the rules of combat?'

'I did not want to kill you. You were beaten, you were no longer a threat to me, and the fight was over. I do not kill a man who is helpless,' I stated simply. 'What is this place?'

'You have impressed our master,' Malbool said sitting up, groaning as he did, obviously still nursing his injured ribs. 'He has made you a gladiator in full. These are the stables for warriors in his school. Tiberius has a ludus of more than twenty gladiators. Only two of them are auctorati, like the man you fought, Samuel. He was a Thracian and proud, but like all volunteer gladiators he fights only once or twice a year and so is unaccustomed to the level of stamina needed to fight every few weeks. He was not one of our troupe, but men like him are becoming more common.'

'Men like him?'

'Men who fight of their own free will, for the glory or pride or whatever it is they think they will receive in battle. Most of us fight because we have no choice.'

'How long have you been doing this?' I asked.

'I have been a gladiator for one full day! You were my first match, and by your good graces, I shall live to see another.'

He saw the next question in my eyes. 'My old master had a ludus of his own, and when he chose to oversee the games he allowed me to attend. One of my main tasks was to tend to the gladiators and take care of their weapons. I spent a lot of time at the school and learned from them. Obviously not enough,' he said sitting back with his hand to his rib.

'How do I get free?' I asked.

'Free?' Malbool found the question amusing, his big white teeth accentuated by the darkness of his face. 'My friend, there are two ways to be free. The easiest is to fall on someone's spear. But more likely you will fight as a gladiator as long as you survive from one week to the next. Eventually, you may reach your retirement and be accepted as a slave or set free, depending on your master's wishes.'

'We fight every week?'

'No, you train every day, contests are held every week, but you can expect to fight about twice a month. There are games every month or so all around the country, but there are only two main festivals a year in the Coliseum.'

I raised an eyebrow.

'If you are entered in the summer or winter festival you will fight several one-on-one matches. Or you can opt to fight in the Royåle, and if you defeat every man who is before you, then and only then can you earn your freedom. It is then at the behest of the crowd and ultimately Caesar himself.'

'Julius Caesar?'

Malbool's eyes narrowed. 'Not unless he has found some way to return from his grave. No, it is Nero; Tiberius Claudius Nero is called Caesar now. The title is passed down.'

'What is this Royåle?' I asked as I absorbed the information.

'It is a contest of almost-certain death. One hundred men enter the arena all at once, gladiators of every type, from every troupe in the Empire. They all fight. There is no time limit and just one rule: one hundred enter, one survives.'

'All the others die?' I was shocked.

Malbool nodded grimly. 'All the others die. You have to survive a battle with one, two, or ten at a time, then move on. The stream of enemies is endless. The chances of surviving the event are of course remote, but the chances of surviving the event intact enough to make your newfound freedom worthwhile? None. No man has yet survived the Royâle to stand before Caesar and ask for his freedom. Usually men are strewn around the arena, and referees have to walk around for hours waiting for them to die to declare the winner.'

The thought horrified me and added to the multitude of ideas and images swimming in my mind. 'I see,' I said, my hand feeling into my tunic to wrap around the hidden device. 'Is there a place to go to relieve myself here?'

'Ha! It is on the right. In the morning I shall show you the school. We are free to walk around this area. They do not lock these doors at night, but we stay within the confines of the living quarters. There are three other rooms on this level, but the men are asleep, so go quietly.'

I limped along following Malbool's directions. All I could think about was the object now curled in my hand. I snuck past the rooms housing the sleeping men. I guessed that it was late, but after sleeping for hours I needed no more rest. What I needed were answers.

I slid around a corner and sank to the ground. I stared at it, this thing of silver, and like a tidal wave it all hit me. I knew. I knew everything. In my sleep I must have absorbed the information. I knew who I was, I knew when I was, and most importantly of all, I knew what I had to do.

CHAPTER 21

I stared at the device in my hands. Its blue lights softly illuminated the stone walls and earthen floor. It gave my skin an incandescence all its own. Then I saw something on my skin. A marking on my inner forearm. I moved the blue light of the cylinder away and looked at my arm in the dim torchlight. Nothing; my skin was clear and clean. I moved the blue light back and re-examined my forearm. There it was, imprinted faintly but clearly: 'X7'. My mind flashed back to when I had received that mark.

It was at The Facility. A small room. Twelve men. It was the only time I had come face to face with the others all at once. I stretched my right arm out into a small cradle, as did the other men lined up beside me; the other officers. Once my forearm was in, the top of the cradle folded down and I felt a moment's icy chill on my flesh. With a hiss, the cradle opened and I raised my arm out of the unit.

Under the incandescent blue light the mark was clear: X7.

Officer X7 in The Journalist Project. And here I was. It had worked. My God, it had worked and here I was. Numb fingers pressed against my temples as the gravity of it all hit me.

I was part of the most secret and important project ever undertaken by humankind. The details were so closely guarded by those in control that I had only been given enough information to complete my own mission, and I knew relatively little about the project as a whole, save for its main purpose and the extensive training I had to undertake in preparation. The training was intended to prepare me for a life lived out in history, nearly two thousand years before I was born.

I closed my eyes and allowed the memories to flood in. While serving in Iraq, I was recruited into the project. My training had been extensive. It had lasted six years, which, considering what I was hoping to accomplish, was not a lot of time. I was taught to survive and I was taught how to fade into the shadows of the society I was to enter. Fine job I was doing with that! I was schooled in languages and dialects of the time. Aramaic, Hebrew, Roman, Samaritan. Just a few years to learn. How had they done it? The technology.

The Facility took us in and trained our conscious mind while we were awake, but also trained our subconscious mind while we were asleep.

A port had been fixed to my hypothalamus, that most primitive part of the brain, and through this port the seemingly autonomous processes of my body were fine-tuned. My heartbeat, my breathing, my hormonal secretion. All this was tapped into, altered and then re-fed to me, giving my body access to the full potential of its physical capabilities, far beyond what is possible through conscious physical training alone. Other areas of my brain were also amplified, particularly those regulating coordination and information absorption. My ability to learn increased ten-fold, and the short time it took to learn new skills was incomprehensible.

I had my martial skills increased both through traditional methods and image-enhanced learning as I slept. My body trained itself and my reflexes were honed to a point that the time it took me to react to stimuli was imperceptible. I moved as if I could read the future. Mentally I was fed all known information about the time period I was to exist in. I was taught the known customs, the languages, the culture. I was taught history. I was taught more than an unaided brain could assimilate within the time I had. Most importantly, I was taught the one unbreakable rule – The Rule of Knowledge: we could not change something we knew to have happened. Then, I was sent back.

I did not know much about the process itself. The theory was explained to me in terms I could grasp, but all I really knew was that it was a one-way trip, and although I was being sent back with another agent, neither of us knew the other's identity or instructions ... all I knew was my mission.

My mission. Oh God, my mission! We each had our mission. There were eleven others, but I didn't know to whom they had been assigned. All I knew was my own assignment: I was to collect important historical data. Documents, books, items of interest.

I had been given specific targets to track down, but also had to take opportunities and retrieve objects of interest along the way. Then there was something else. The one thing for which I had prepared for six years. I was to conduct the interview.

The interview was deemed by The Facility to be the absolute priority. It was the reason for the whole project, so I had been told, and as I stared at this object in my hands, turning it over and over, I thought about what I had to do. I was to find, wherever he was in the world, whenever he was to appear in time, a man. I had to find and record a video interview with Joshua of Galilee. I was to interview the man they called Jesus.

CHAPTER 22

The rain beat down on cement and formed uncaring pools. The reflection of the dawn gave life to the droplets as they traced their way over Shaun's face. He lay curled in a ball at the bottom of the underpass, the exhaustion of the previous night having finally overtaken him.

The first throngs of morning traffic buzzed overhead, but the sound could not penetrate the world of hazy shadows his mind had receded into – not the traffic, not the rain, not even the sound of a police siren as it blared across the bridge above his head, searching for the fugitive who had escaped from the state hospital late the previous night.

When he woke, Shaun could not tell how long he had been asleep. It was a familiar sound that woke him. His mind created a scenario to cope with what was happening.

In it, he was busy writing at his desk. He was on the verge of something brilliant, his train of thought following through to near its conclusion. Then the phone rang.

'Lauren, can you get that?' he called out from his study. There was no answer. The phone kept ringing.

'Lauren! Can you get that? I'm really busy right now.' She still didn't answer. He was so close, he could not stop his work now. What was she doing?

The phone rang on.

'Lauren, can you get that!' he yelled louder.

Finally she replied. 'Sorry, I can't, baby. I'm dead.'

Shaun sat up. The phone was still ringing. What had she said? The phone rang on. What phone? He was so confused. The phone ring was real. He suddenly became alert. The buzzing was coming from his jacket's outer pocket. His cell. He had forgotten all about it, but now it was ringing. Cold, numb fingers fumbled for the phone, pulling it out just as the sound ceased. Shaun looked at the screen: '1 missed call'.

It was ten to six in the morning.

No caller ID.

Who calls at that time? Shaun's brain asked. But another question invaded his mind before he had a chance to search for possible answers. What had happened in his dream? What excuse had Lauren given for not making it to the phone? Because she was what? Because she was dead.

Then it hit him like a kick to the stomach: she was dead. Like any trauma, the torture of it was not that it had happened once, but that it happened again every time he stopped thinking about it and remembered. Lauren was—

The phone rang again, its shrill pulse cutting into the early morning and pulling Shaun back to the moment. He stared at the screen. No caller ID. Who was calling his phone from a silent number before six in the morning? One way to find out.

BLEEP.

'Hello?' Shaun answered tentatively. Silence.

'Hello?' he repeated with even less certainty. The line was full of static.

'Is this Shaun Strickland?' came a voice. American accent.

'Who wants to know?'

'Where are you?' asked the voice. Shaun hung up. How could he be so stupid? In his daze he had almost forgotten that people were trying to kill him, and he had just given them a signal. The phone rang again.

Shaun stared at it, his thumb moving towards the green 'answer' button. If he answered they might be able to trace him. His brother, Tim, once told him they only needed six seconds to trace a landline, but how long for a cell? But what if it wasn't the bad guys? He thought about throwing the phone or smashing it, but then reasoned that he might need it.

Instead, he flipped the vibrating phone over, his cold fingers searching to find the battery-eject catch. As soon as he popped the battery the ringing stopped dead. He breathed. He had to get out of the area immediately.

He gathered up the diary and tucked it deep inside his inner jacket pocket. He looked straight down the canal. It ran perpendicular to the several roads that crossed it, but it was all exposed ground, and the rain was starting to come down hard. He could not afford to get the diary wet, so he took off his coat, wrapped it tightly, the diary in the middle, and carried it under his arm like a rugby ball.

Shaun ran straight and hard, away from the bridge and the distant blare of police sirens. He didn't trust the police in this town. Maybe at the next overpass he would try to hail a cab. If he could just get away some place, he would have time to think and read.

'Where to?' the taxi driver asked as Shaun, drenched and desperate, bundled into the front seat.

'Hey, man! Shit, this ain't my cab, man!' he protested as Shaun's pockets spilled water onto the upholstery.

'Sorry,' he said, thankful to be sitting down. He had run down the canal for around an hour in the driving rain. Each overpass came and went with his brain giving the same advice: *just one more, not far enough yet.*

'Where to?' the cabbie asked again. He was a gruff-looking man of about forty, with tufts of white hair spilling out from under his cap. Shaun checked his driver ID mounted on the dashboard: Vern.

'I don't care, just go. Just get away,' Shaun said, trying to catch his breath.

'Don't know that street,' Vern said with a straight face.

'Anywhere!' Shaun said. 'Head for DC. I've got money.'

'What? Are you shittin' me?' Vern's brusque reply came.

But Shaun, dazed and weary, and for the moment feeling safe, was already asleep. The cabbie crunched the car into gear and set off north for the interstate, wondering how far he could get before his lucrative fare woke up.

Shaun dreamed he was standing on a stage in front of an auditorium full of people who were looking expectantly up at him. He could not make out the details on the faces, not even the ones in the front row. He was there to deliver his speech. He stood at his pulpit about to preach the good news to his congregation. His theories on the nature of time, and its connection to and dependence on the physical world, were fantastic stuff, he knew.

He had theorised a plausible way to tag a particle and send it back in time. It all had to do with gravity. He was going to blow them away. He looked over the crowd, and they looked back at him. He had come all the way to England for this, and now was his time to shine.

He opened his mouth. A long rasp of air escaped his throat. He tried to speak again, but he didn't know what to say. He knew he was talking about time. He started with the word: 'Time ...' But nothing followed.

He did not know how to explain it; could not find the words. The crowd started to giggle. A ripple of murmurs passed through the auditorium from front to back. Soon they became jeers.

He didn't know what to say. They all wanted him to explain it. What could he say? He could not remember anything. He was an expert on this; why could he not remember anything? He looked into the crowd. The shimmering faces were laughing out loud now, at him, at his incompetence. Then he saw another face. A face that wasn't laughing. This face was looking right at him. Then she smiled. Lauren.

Their eyes met, and although she was way up the back of the room, he spoke only to her.

'I don't know what to do,' he said, his eyes filling with tears. 'I don't know what to say. I'm lost. I'm lost without you. I don't know what to do.'

Lauren smiled again.

'I don't know how to explain it,' he pleaded.

Her eyes softened, then she spoke. Her voice was kind and understanding.

'You have to read.'

'Buddy! I said, is that your phone?' It was the abrupt voice of the taxi driver.

Shaun's eyes tried to focus. He rolled more than turned his head round to face the direction the voice had come from.

'What?' he asked, his tongue feeling furry.

'That, down there. I think your phone just fell out and smashed or somethin'.'

He looked down at his feet. Indeed, while he was asleep his flip-phone and battery had fallen out of his pocket, popping apart. He reached forward and squinted at the dull grey plastic covering. Its screen had a crack in it. He sighed, unsure what to do. He was fairly sure he was safe just so long as he didn't answer any calls, so he decided to put it back together just to make sure it worked then turn it off again.

'You know,' Vern started as he watched Shaun bring the small device back to life, 'I got a kid with one o' those. She's fourteen now and I fink the fing's practically stuck to 'er ear. I can't get it off 'er. She answers calls in the middle of dinner. You know? In the middle of dinner! Now, I'm not saying I'm always around or nothin'—'

'They left a message,' Shaun stated matter-of-factly.

'Huh? You got a message? You know, it was like an extra fifteen bucks a month for my Sally to get message-bank, but she's gotta have it. They always gotta have it. Then it's the added text features this, and ring-tone that. I tells ya ...'

What kind of killer leaves you a message? his brain asked, as Shaun stared at the envelope symbol on the scratched screen.

Vern continued to talk, oblivious to Shaun's lack of response. Shaun was good at colouring sound. His mother had called it 'selective hearing', although she was usually referring to her ignored requests for him to wash the dishes after dinner.

Shaun heard nothing now but the sound of his own thoughts as he debated whether to connect to the network and retrieve the message, or if it was more dangerous to let the information go unheard. He flipped the phone shut.

'... eight or nine times a day! I mean, I know that boys and girls are getting older when they're younger these days, if you know what I mean, but when I was her age I wasn't even allowed to take a girl to the movies on my own. You'd fink I coulda gone to the movies! Not that it stopped me, though ...'

Shaun flipped open the phone. Death might not be such a bad option, relatively speaking. Taking a deep breath, he held down the number 1 on his keypad to speed-dial his voicemail service. Silence followed. Then there was a beep. Finally it rang once, and then switched to the familiar female automated voice recording.

Shaun circumvented the process by skipping ahead, hitting the 1 button twice quickly. *BEEP. BEEP.* Then he heard it. The voice was male.

'Mr Strickland – I believe your life may be in danger—' static. 'This is not a hoax. I need to meet with you.' The voice then recited several short phrases, as if reading from a script:

'We actually move about in time every day.' Pause.

'The space craft would not be able to travel faster than light.' Pause.

'Impossible to hold these worm holes open.' Pause ... shuffling noise.

'Power requirements beyond what we are capable of.' Pause.

'Bethany would be older by a day.' Long pause.

'I may know something about what's going on.'

BEEP. BEEP. BEEP. That was it. The voice was gone.

Shaun sat back. Who was that? What the hell was it about? His life may be in danger? No shit. But then, the other part of the message that had caught his attention: *'I may know something about what's going on.'*

The past twelve hours had been the strangest of his life, the worst of his life, and he had to find a way to figure out why it was happening. He knew, with growing certainty, that the book he carried was important to some very dangerous people. That made it valuable.

And someone out there knew something about what was going on, and was reaching out to Shaun. He tried to recall what he had read last night.

'I had to find and record a video interview with Joshua of Galilee. I was to interview the man they called Jesus.'

Oh, man. He stopped for a moment and thought about it. If, hypothetically, it were possible to travel back in time, with the means to record an interview with a historical figure, who in the whole of history would be the person chosen? Which single person had been the cause of more debate, who had affected the modern world more than this man Jesus?

Shaun was not religious. In fact, he rejected the superstitious nonsense that had been attributed to this man, if indeed there had been such a person. But he knew that enough people in the world believed; that if there *was* an interview with Jesus, it would surely be valuable. Maybe even something worth killing for.

He sank back. His mind reeled. Could it really be all about that? Could it really be about this story in the damp bundle of jacket in his lap? If it were real, it blew everything out of the water. Not only did it talk about a modern-day man on a mission to interview the most influential figure in history, but for that to be true, it meant that somehow, someone had learned how to travel back in time.

As fanciful as that notion was to most people, suggesting it to Shaun was an entirely different prospect. Shaun Strickland was an expert in that field, and he had proved that it was impossible to send anything back in time. He knew the facts so well that he had even documented them in his paper on—

Shaun inhaled sharply. His *paper.*

That was where he had recognised the words from. He could not believe it. He flipped open his phone and hit the speed-dial key again, skipping through the process so he could replay the message:

'We actually move about in time every day.' Pause.

'The space craft would not be able to travel faster than light.' Pause.

'Impossible to hold these worm holes open.' Pause ... shuffling noise.

'Power requirements beyond what we are capable of.' Pause.

'Bethany would be older by a day.' Long pause.

'I may know something about what's going on.'

He replayed the message one last time, listening carefully to a particular line:

'Impossible to hold these worm holes open.' Pause ... shuffling noise.

That was it. The sound of paper being shuffled. Whoever was speaking was turning pages. They were reading the lines from physical pages. Pages of *his* paper. The words the man was saying were Shaun's.

'... You know, now I'm not saying I didn't touch the girl or nothing, know what I'm sayin'?' Vern recounted. 'But when you—'

'Take me to the internet,' Shaun said in a hurry.

'... told me she was ... What?'

'Take me to the internet!' he repeated, suddenly burning with purpose.

'I been driving cabs for a lotta years now, buddy, but I ain't never heard anyone ask for that address. That's a first, for sure.'

'Would you shut up!' Shaun said, suddenly irritated.

Vern stopped short, a little startled. 'I'd take you straight there, buddy, 'cept to be honest, well we've been drivin' north for a while now and we're somewhere on the interstate about to hit Virginia. I'm not exactly sure where the internet is round here.'

Shaun looked out the window, noticing his surroundings for the first time. Vern was right. They were out on a highway somewhere.

He glanced down and saw the meter tick over to five hundred and seventy-eight dollars. He smiled. It was liberating in a perverse way not to care about money. His whole world had just been ripped apart, and he seemingly had come into the possession of the most important book in history. Five hundred and seventy-eight dollars wouldn't make the slightest difference to anything. A day ago he would have been concerned, but everything was relative.

Relative. He sighed. That's how his obsession had started. He was thirteen when his dad gave him a book instead of a basketball for Christmas. He had been upset at the time, but that book, *Einstein and His General Theory of Relativity: The Illustrated Edition* had changed Shaun irrevocably. His dad had told him that an Englishman had struck-up a conversation with him in a bookstore and recommended the book for Shaun, saying that it had changed his own life when he was a boy, and he was certain it would do the same for Shaun. The man had been right; it had sent Shaun down a whole new path.

He saw a sign pass by in a blur. Eighty miles to the next town, where surely there would be some kind of internet cafe. He had written that paper more than six years ago, and barely remembered it, but he always backed up his papers on a secure online server, and he knew he needed to print out that paper. He needed to find the page numbers, then he needed to dial them into a phone. It was the only meaning he could grapple from the seemingly random collection of sentences garbled at him through the message.

He looked down at his lap and saw the insulated bundle. Slowly he unwrapped it and looked over the pages with new eyes.

CHAPTER 23

'There are many types of gladiators,' Malbool told me as we walked through the training yard of the ludus, 'and it is common practice for gladiators of one type to fight gladiators of another type. He is a "secutor",' he said, pointing to a short, stocky man with plating down one arm who was practising with a long, curved shield. 'He will commonly fight a "retiarius",' Malbool finished, gesturing across the yard to where another group of men practised with nets and long, three-pronged spears.

'This is how you fought me,' I said with interest, watching as a tall man showed two others the technique for how to throw a net, swinging it, then twisting his wrist just before letting it go, causing the net to fan out, its weighted edges spreading wide.

'It is,' Malbool replied, pausing alongside me to watch the exercises. 'The net, my friend. The net equals all men. But not you.' He clapped a hand on my shoulder. 'Come, there is more to see.'

He continued to walk, explaining further.

'It is all about the spectacle. If two men came out with no armour, you would have one of two conclusions: they would either massacre one another in an unskilled bloodbath far too quickly, or fight so tentatively as to make the engagement boring. It is for this reason that the men wear armour, but it is measured. A helmet, one arm, perhaps a shield. All this creates the conditions needed for dynamic and skilled combat. When the time comes for you to choose your style of fighting, do so with great care. It could mean the continuation or the end of your life.'

He went on to tell me of many of the other groups of fighters I might encounter, and as I watched groups of men practise with swords, shields and fists, I knew that to gain my freedom, to fulfil my mission, I would have to be part of this rehearsed bloodshed.

'The "eques" and the "provocatuer" usually fight others of the same type, but most disciplines will fight gladiators of other styles. A "murmillo" will usually fight and defeat a "hoplomachus" but if he were to fight a skilled "retiarius" or "Gaul" he would most likely be cut down.'

'Rock, paper, scissors.' I muttered under my breath.

'Still,' finished Malbool, 'it is the skill of the individual that makes the contest most exciting. There are no hard and fast rules for who will win any given battle.' His eyes looked straight into mine.

'You are a man most rare,' he began uneasily. 'You speak in the Roman tongue, yet I have heard you speak in your sleep in many strange tongues I do not understand. You look near enough to a Roman but are more refined, so you could be from any number of lands ...' Malbool left it hanging. I gave no reply, simply returned his gaze. He turned away.

'I was a leader among my people. I had two sons and a daughter. I lost everything when the Romans took me. They killed my wife and my daughter. What fate befell my sons I do not know, and I cannot bear to think about it. I know you are from somewhere far away, but understand this: I too have lost. I do not tell you of the games because I boast of my knowledge, but because I have learned to accept my new life and take from it what I can. My master treated me as well as a master can treat a slave – that is, like a dog, but a dog that he feeds. Not a day went by that I did not dream of slicing his throat in his sleep, though I knew that it would make my situation worse.'

Malbool put his face close to mine then, as if imparting a great secret. 'I took what I could from him. I took the knowledge I needed to improve my station. He had promised me freedom at the end of the year. Then his enemies destroyed him and took his property. I was part of that property. I know you are eager to get away, stranger. I see it in your eyes, but you must learn that the life you had is gone. If you want to stay alive, you must fight for it.' He turned and left me standing in the courtyard, surrounded by the civil practice of an uncivilised sport.

It had been more than two weeks since I fought in the pit, and I was still coming to terms with my situation. When I had known no different, I desired my freedom, but there had been no urgency for it. It was only now that I realised with horror that I was running to a timeframe.

I was miles from my objective, and I was a prisoner. Armed with the knowledge of what I was supposed to do, the gravity of how far I was from achieving that goal became clear. I did not have any real reference to the date as I had known it in my previous life; I could only hope that a man across the sea had not yet been nailed to a cross.

Escape, at least for the moment, was impossible. Years earlier, Spartacus the Thracian had lead a rebellion against Rome with an army of gladiators. He was a man who would accept his station no more – but although his story was legendary, he had seen to it conditions would never allow an event such as that to happen again. We were under heavy guard at all times, so I knew that my ally now, my only hope for survival, was information. I had to play their game long enough to find a way back to Jerusalem.

As I contemplated this, a sudden chill struck me. What if I had arrived too late? Or more than a lifetime too early? There was much debate in the world I had left about when Jesus walked the earth. If he was still alive, then I had to survive and find my way to him. If he had already been killed, then I could not complete my mission. For now, I would have to fight to survive. Little did I know that I would get my chance to do just that the following morning.

It was the horn that woke me. A deep booming bass that shook us awake each morning not long after the sun rose. This in itself was not unusual, but the sound of gravel crunching along the corridor brought me fully alert. Soon a stablehand came into view with four Roman guards beside him. The lock jingled to life and the door to my cell swung open.

'You're coming with us,' the stablehand, a boy not much older than Mishca, said with pomp and arrogance. 'You are fighting today.' With that he turned and the four guards entered the cell. I followed the boy out into the corridor, just in time to hear Malbool's voice call after me.

'May the gods protect you!'

I was taken by carriage for perhaps an hour. When the carriage doors swung open, I was shadowed by the massive structure looming before me. I remembered in my previous life visiting Rome with my parents when I was a boy, and, standing not far from where I was right now, staring up at the tiered structure of repeating arches, at the intricate stone carvings, and at the iron gates that stood with imposing defiance. The last time I saw this monument it was in ruin, but now, larger than life and immaculate, stood the very heart of Roman culture: the Coliseum.

'We are taking you to registration, this afternoon you will fight for Master Tiberius and show him that you are worthy of his graces.'

'I was told I would be given three days' notice before I was to fight.'

The boy turned, shocked that I had dared speak to him.

'You,' he said as if explaining to a child, 'will fight when you are told to do so. When you have earned your way, killed many men, then you will be given the privilege to know ahead of time that you may fight. If

you must know, the master's only invited entry in this tournament was injured yesterday in practice and you are to take his place.'

I was marched into a room with other teams of people, none of them appearing to be gladiators. The boy spoke to someone and then turned to ask me a question.

'What are you?' he asked.

'What am I? What do you mean?' I replied, puzzled.

'What are you? What category do you fight as?' the boy asked impatiently.

'Oh, that? I don't really care.' The ambience in the room dropped off, replaced by silence and stares from every corner.

'What?' the boy spat.

'I don't care what I fight as. With a sword, I suppose.' The room that had thinned its conversation now gave up a few chuckles.

'With a sword, you suppose?' The boy stepped up to me. 'Are you trying to make me look foolish in front of the registrars? Do not forget that it is I who controls your rations at the ludus!' he whispered harshly.

'Boy,' I said evenly, 'I do not care what you register me as. I have had little training in your arts, so it makes no difference to me.'

The boy stepped away, conscious that everyone was now looking at him, and that a slave had called him 'boy'. He spoke to the registrar and then turned back to the troop of guards who were with me.

'Give him a sword and a round shield. He will fill the place of his stablemate and fight as a murmillo! Take him to be branded.'

The boy seemed pleased to show his authority, watching contemptuously as I was taken away to be burned with fire, forever scarred with the smell of my own burning flesh and singed hair. The scent filled my nostrils. To be owned. This is a thing few modern men imagine, a thing over which my country had fought a civil war.

As the glowing steel rod was brought close to my arm, I could feel the heat on my face. It was a mark that stayed with me always, and the scar never let me forget what it means to belong to another.

Six hours later, I stood alone. My left arm had been fitted with a banded golden sleeve of armour, and on the same arm was strapped a round shield. In my other hand my fingers flexed around the hilt of a curved sword, and only sandals and a loincloth covered the rest of my body.

Malbool was right, it really was an intentional deliberation of armour and skin. Naked and shielded at the same time, to add interest to the bloodbath. I had refused their helmet. It was heavy and clumsy and had the crest of a fish-like fin along its top. It cut off my peripheral vision, and I felt safer without it.

As the gate in front of me rose, I saw the stairs leading into the arena. I was to fight a Gaul – a man captured in war who only survived by killing other men. I had been warned about not fighting to kill. I had been told that there were archers poised at all times to end the life of a disobedient participant in the games. Killing now was my only chance of continuing with my true mission.

With purpose, I strode forward. The roar was immense. Jets of perfumed water filled the air with fragrance, accompanied by a fanfare of trumpets and horns. I looked around the massive amphitheatre; in its stately glory, it seemed even larger than it had looked as a ruin and eclipsed all my childhood memories of it. The Coliseum held forty thousand faces, all of whom stared down at me. The energy from every ring of seating, from every bench in the private boxes, made it feel like a full house, pulsing with noise, movement and colour. I only now understood. The people, the crowd, the citizens – they all loved this.

I felt ill. I was part of it. What's more, I would kill this man who now looked across the sand of the arena floor at me. I would kill him because if I did not, he would kill me.

A horn sounded. It had begun.

The Gaul was about my height, a big man by the standards of the day. The straight sword he carried looked as if it weighed nothing in his hand. It was longer than mine, and boasted a double edge and jewelled hilt. His shield was curved but rectangular, maybe half the height of the man himself. I absorbed these details carefully as he advanced.

The crowd's roars grew louder as we drew closer together, circling and sizing each other up until finally, he swung. It was an over-handed blow designed not so much to cause any real damage as to test me, to see how I would react – and react I did, but not in the parrying way he expected. As the blow came down, I raised my left elbow, making as if to meet the blow with my small, circular shield. Instead I spun, guiding more than blocking his blow away. I continued my turn, whipping my back leg up and around my body as I did so. I spun fast and drove my heel hard into the side of his helmet. The blow snapped his head sideways and his body followed, coming forward and down, splaying onto the sand of the arena face first.

Far from a roar, the crowd went quiet, unsure about what they had just seen. A man spinning and kicking another man in the head? It was like nothing ever before witnessed in the arena.

I put my foot on his back, and the tip of my sword to his spine between his shoulder blades.

'Surrender,' I said in Roman.

His reply was to swing back with his sword in a wide arc, nearly taking my leg off at the ankle. I literally hopped over the attack before diving clear. This was a seasoned gladiator, a man of many victories in the arena, and a man who would rather die than live with the dishonour of submission.

So be it.

Drums began to pound. BOOM! BOOM! *A cheer broke out as the Gaul regained his feet. I took a deep breath and resigned myself to the moment. We circled one another. I let go of my abhorrence, my reluctance to be a part of this bloody sport, and I accepted my new reality. Malbool was right. I would fight.*

The Gaul bared his teeth as he rushed forward, swinging his blade in a wide sweeping arc. This blow was intended to cut me in half horizontal to the ground but was in no way a test of my reactions. I folded my knees and leaned back, flattening to the ground in time to watch the blade sail overhead, then bounced back up as quickly as I had dropped. Infuriated, the Gaul swung again, this time cutting down a diagonal. I became the angle. The sword came at the reverse diagonal, and I became that angle too. The man roared in frustration.

Then he surprised me. He motioned to swing again, and, seeing me stay within his range, he changed tact and thrust his shield out. It crashed into my exposed face with force, splitting my lip and momentarily disorienting me. It was then that he swung. The blade whistled towards my head and the roar of the crowd erupted at once as they sensed a kill. They got one.

At that same moment, I dropped to one knee, driving the sharpened tip of my sword straight up, penetrating the soft tissue underneath his jaw. The blade slid easily and quickly, and those watching the Gaul from behind would have seen his helmet raise off his head inexplicably.

The Gaul did not fall. He was held standing by my sword. I stared at his stomach in front of my eyes, and as blood ran down it the warmth of his spent life force showered me and I knew that I was changed forever.

The roar was immense. The crowd cheered like I was a hero as I stayed on one knee.

Then the roar changed almost imperceptibly. It grew louder, and I knew that something was wrong. It was not until I heard another roar that I realised just what it was. This roar was not the roar of the crowd, but the deafening roar of a beast close behind me.

I stood and spun in one action and was met by a huge golden mass crashing into me. I fell back as enormous white teeth were bared. I felt the warm breath of the beast's rage as I stumbled backwards. My sword was knocked clear of my grasp and it was all I could do to grip the animal's mane as I fell, trying with all my strength to hold it away from my head.

I lifted both my feet at the same time and drove my knees up to my chest, tucking into a tight ball. I had never fought a lion before; it was not the sort of thing they trained us for at The Facility. I pulled its head down and kicked out at its body moments before I hit the ground hard.

The leverage I had gained on the animal flipped the shaggy mass over backwards, giving me the time I needed to land and roll to my feet. I turned, seeing that the massive beast had righted itself mid-air and landed on its feet, before skidding to a stop in a cloud of dust.

I bolted, straight for the entrance gate. The sound from the crowd told the story. I had a twenty-metre start, and was being run down by the king of beasts. With each stride, the animal gained. I looked to the portcullis gate that was being lowered even as I ran. They were locking me in. I sprinted on, leaping over the open trapdoor in the arena floor from which the lion had emerged only seconds before.

I could hear the beast behind me now breathing in grunts as its body pounded the ground closer and closer. The gate was closing. Closer, it must be nearly ready to pounce. Closer.

I drove my knees hard and pumped my burning thighs with all the energy I had left. Closer.

The gate was almost down, only fifteen feet away. Closer.

Too late, it has to be too late. Closer.

The pounding steps behind me stopped. The beast had leaped and was airborne. The gate slammed shut in front of me. No gap to dive through. No way out. Waiting for the impact.

I saw the lion's paw slide past my shoulder. I knew jaws were only inches from my neck.

My reaction was automatic. My left foot stepped up on the cross-bar of the gate as I reached it and I kicked out hard. My body was propelled upwards, the full speed of my sprint transferred to the new direction, thrusting me upwards.

I leaned back, throwing my head in an arch with all my might, like an Olympic high jumper. I pulled my feet and knees up to my chest, giving the final rotation needed to complete the flip and sail twelve feet in the air before gliding back to the earth, still facing the gate. The lion leaped into the crosses of iron at full speed, and slammed into the gate with sickening force. The massive cat's paws slid cleanly through the gaps in the gate and the animal took the force of the metal on its open jaws, shattering its gleaming teeth into jagged shards and breaking its face.

I did not wait around to see more. The instant my feet hit the ground, I spun and bolted back towards the centre of the arena, and back to my sword, which was still lodged firmly in the fallen Gaul's head. As I approached I saw that he wasn't fallen at all, but was propped up on his knees in a sad parody of himself. The sword protruded from under his chin and acted like a stilt, holding the man's body up with his arms hanging limply at his side. A large pool of red spread out in a circle around him, and as I approached, not a sound pierced the air.

I had never been more aware of my own footsteps than I was at that moment. The crowd, every one of them, stared in silence. I reached down into the pool of blood and lifted the Gaul's long, double-edged broadsword. Then I turned and walked back towards the giant cat.

It lay crumpled at the base of the buckled metal gate, awful gurgling sounds escaping its fallen body. A horrible sick moan sent feelings of revulsion deep into my stomach. The once mighty animal pitifully slumped at the rim of the arena. I looked up. I saw the master of the games; I saw the aides who stood by his side; and I saw a hooded figure behind them.

The games master, perhaps forty years old, looked at me appraisingly with thin lips and sparse white strings of hair. He watched me keenly as I strode forward. The hooded figure came to whisper in his ear.

I knew then it was he who was responsible for the lion, he who ordered the gate closed. On this altar of sacrifice, the games master was but a puppet – it was the hooded man who was God.

The pathetic, horrible sounds of the fallen animal intensified as I approached. My eyes never left those of the games master as I came up alongside the lion, lifted my sword high and drove it straight down through the animal's head. Instantly the sounds ceased.

I pulled the sword free and as the buckled gate in front of me began to rise slowly, deliberately, I marched back into the darkness.

CHAPTER 24

'How lon you lie?' asked the small Chinese man with a smile.

'Ah, can I print here?' Shaun asked, feeling for his wallet, thankful he still had it on him.

'You prin fifty cen one prin,' the man behind the counter continued to smile and nod. Shaun did the math in his head.

'Yeah, okay. I'll be back in a second,' he turned and dashed out of the store.

The door to the taxi was still open, and the engine was running. Vern leaned against the hood with his arms folded. He liked this guy, but he wasn't going to give him a free ride.

'This the place that's going to do you, then?'

'Yeah, this is fine.' Shaun was nervous. He still could not believe he had talked the cabbie into this.

'Well, lead the way,' Vern held out his hand in an 'after you' gesture. He then turned the engine off and locked the cab. He could not believe that the wet, stinky guy had talked him into this. The meter had read, when all was said and done, a cool nine hundred dollars and thirteen cents. That had to be a record as far as Vern was concerned. He would be a hero, probably get his own car from the company, and maybe get in their records book.

He followed the man into the internet cafe and took a seat next to him. Shaun had told him he could not use the credit card in case he was tracked. Vern was suspicious, of course, thinking that maybe he had just helped a criminal escape or something, but the guy had said that he would pay double the meter fare if Vern agreed to be paid by online transfer. Of course this was only possible if the guy paid the money directly into Vern's personal account, since he didn't know the cab company's bank details.

Convenient.

Vern looked around at the spiky-haired kids and foreign backpackers who populated the internet cafe and felt severely out of place, but he wasn't going to take this guy's word about the payment. He would sit next to him and watch the whole thing go through. All he knew was that if he called his bank once the guy said it was done and the money was in there, then he would be two grand richer. Now, that was worth waiting around for.

Shaun logged on to the bank site and went through the process. Less than twenty minutes later, Vern was sitting in his car on his way back to Charlotte wearing the broadest grin he had had in years. He pulled out his cell phone and dialled the most popular number in America: 911.

After being rudely told that it was a felony to abuse the number without a bona-fide emergency, of which Vern's 'hunch' didn't qualify, he decided to call the operator and ask for the local police. He figured that, hell, he might as well see if there was a reward for finding this guy.

Yep, it was definitely one of his finer moments.

Shaun frantically tapped at the keyboard, scanning the back-ups of his papers online via his private server.

He clicked on a folder called 'Completed' and then on a subfolder called 'Space and Time'. In here were nine papers, all between twenty and thirty pages long.

He thought back to what the voice on the phone had said: 'We actually move about in time every day.' Shaun had used that line in just about all of his papers, so that was no real help.

'The space craft would not be able to travel faster than light.' Space craft? He often talked about space crafts, but usually just to illustrate some hypothetical concept.

'Impossible to hold these worm holes open.' Only three of his papers spoke about these. It was this topic that had caused Shaun to grow so frustrated he eventually abandoned the field of space–time for other areas of interest. The worm holes that *could* be created could only last a moment, and nothing could hold them open.

'Power requirements beyond what we are capable of.' Power requirements. He spoke about power in all of his papers as well, so this didn't help either.

Shaun thought about the last quote in the message, and he stopped typing. 'Bethany would be older by a day.' Bethany? That was it! *Bethany would be older by a day.* He looked up at the screen and saw the paper entitled: 'If I only had a DeLorean – WIS.'

It was a title that referred to the 1980s movie *Back to the Future*, and was one of his oldest. What made this different though was the WIS: Shaun's notation for 'Women in Science'. He had written a version of this paper to send to a 2005 journal celebrating women in science. He had changed his regular Robert-and-Roy twins story to Bethany and Bertha, just to make it a little more girl-friendly. He opened the paper and hit print.

'We clowe in fi minit!' a voice called out to the occupants of the internet cafe. No one looked up, but the speed of finger-tapping increased noticeably. Shaun looked at his watch. Five minutes to four. It was Saturday and he was unlikely to find another place open around here.

He entered his password. After several seconds his inbox opened and he could not help but smile. Of the forty-three new messages, he had been offered: fifteen pre-approved home loans, nine chances for penis enlargement and had apparently joined an adult dating service some time in the past. He clicked on the 'New' button and waited as the blank message window redrew painfully slowly.

Finally he typed in the address of the only person he trusted besides Lauren – his brother, Tim. Nine years older, Tim had been lumped with his younger brother after their parents were killed in a car crash when Shaun was fifteen. Shaun had been sent away to boarding school and for a time the brothers were close. But they hadn't spoken in four years now; not since that argument. Shaun knew, though, that Tim was the one man in the world he could count on if things got serious.

'We are now clowe, you muss all leave now.'

Shaun didn't look up as the voice came from the counter. He tapped away frantically: '*Tim, Long time. Sorry. I need your help. In serious trouble. Lauren's dead.*' He paused. Typing the words, telling someone else, seemed to make it all the more real. He fought back the rising nausea and continued: '*I'm in Virginia I think. Going to get up to DC then call you. I don't want you to try to find me, and I wouldn't normally ask – but I need money. Can you wire me some?*'

'You go home!' the small Chinese man said, standing directly behind Shaun, who ignored him for just a moment longer.

'*Don't call me, I will call you when it's safe. Sorry, big brother, you're the only one I can turn to.*' He clicked send.

The small man began to shut down all the other computers as disgruntled customers, some in the middle of playing the latest 3-D shoot-'em-up game, others just surfing the web, began to complain.

'You go home now! You get ow my shop. We clowe – you go home now!' He was well practised at shooing people from the premises.

Shaun looked up at the printer, where a girl with red-and-white stripy leggings and spiky green hair grabbed at every new leaf coming out of the machine.

'Whose shit is all this?' she asked in an angry Yorkshire accent. No one responded.

'This yours, mate?' she asked, grabbing a handful of the pages and thrusting them out at Shaun. He looked at them. *Yes*. He had beaten the frantic print rush that had begun when the man warned that the cafe would close in five minutes. Unfortunately for everyone else, his job was still going.

'Yeah, thanks,' Shaun said taking the pages.

'Don't fank me, mate. This ain't your personal office, ya know.'

Shaun shoved past her to collect the remaining pages spitting into the tray. 'Actually if you have to know, it's a detailed explanation on the nature of time and why it's impossible to travel back through it, so get your ugly little—' he stopped himself. That's what his paper was about.

Despite everything he had just read in the diary about The Facility and The Journalist Project, Shaun had once argued passionately that time travel was impossible. If anything he had read was true, then this paper was wrong. He was wrong. As the final pages printed, he grabbed a highlighter and left, his papers in one hand, the diary in the other.

He sat against a closed shopfront, shuffling through the unnumbered pages. The spiky-haired girl had messed them all up and he basically had to read through the entire paper to get them in the right order. Reading his earnest words threw him back years in his mind. He remembered how long he had laboured over these ideas, testing and retesting his hypotheses, trying to crack it.

'*We actually move about in time every day.*' Shaun highlighted it and continued to read, losing himself in the world of his own thoughts again. It was so long since he had written the paper, it was as if someone else had written it, thinking exactly the same way he did.

'*... and because time is a tangible thing, it is affected by gravity the same way everything else is. Gravity makes time run slower. There is even a simple formula to measure how much time is slowed down by gravity. It is known as time dilation, and has been measurable for years:* $t' = t/\sqrt{(1-v^2/c^2)}$.

'*So, as gravity is different throughout the universe, it follows that time runs at different speeds throughout the universe as well. Time on a massive star runs far slower than it does in empty space. But what we don't know is how to measure this. To create a virtual field that generates enough artificial gravity so we could actually see these effects with our naked eyes would require an immense amount of power. Power requirements beyond what we are capable of producing today here on earth.'* There was the next line! Shaun again highlighted the paper, and scanned forward.

'To further illustrate this point I shall again turn to our twins Bertha and Bethany, who have put their space suits on. Suppose Bethany stays here on earth and Bertha goes off to an imploded star with the same mass as our sun; each armed with a clock. The star has collapsed in on itself and shrunk inside its Schwarzschild radius, its "event horizon", compressing into a tiny ball of enormous density. So, keeping in mind that a time warp involves "non-local" comparisons of clock rates, you can see looking at the graph below, when Bertha is six kilometres from the centre of the mass, her clock runs at half the speed of Bethany's back here on earth. Supposing Bertha uses her powerful rockets to stay at exactly this distance from the centre of the mass for twenty-four hours (her time), and then goes back to earth (even though the space craft would not be able to travel faster than light, let's assume for the moment that the journey to and from earth takes next to no time at all), she would find that forty-eight hours had passed on Bethany's clock. Bethany would be older by a day, making our identical—'

There they were, the next two lines. Shaun highlighted 'The space craft would not be able to travel faster than light' and 'Bethany would be older by a day'.

Shaun leaned back on the wall. It was getting cold quickly here, but he knew that this was the key to making contact with whoever had called him. He reached the last page; in the penultimate paragraph he found the line he was looking for: *'Impossible to hold these worm holes open.'*

He stared at the line, remembering the frustration it had caused him. After exhaustive research, he had found that the universe contained fleeting worm holes, and that it was theoretically possible to artificially generate these tunnels in space–time – but then he discovered that they were as short-lived in their passing as they were tiny in their physicality. Shaun's grand theory was that it may be possible to transmit radio waves through these worm holes, and therefore, hypothetically, send messages from one point in time to another, but he had found that truly it was 'impossible to hold these worm holes open'.

The irony, he thought when considering all he had read in the diary, was that it was this line of his text that the stranger had chosen to quote.

Shaun looked at the highlighted text on his pages, and then noted the corresponding page numbers: 12, 37, 21, 88.

12372188. That was it. It was a weird sequence for a landline, and there was no area code that started with 123. Not enough digits for a cell phone.

An address? Latitude, longitude?

It's not that complicated, Shaun's brain informed him, knowing that the reason the man quoted the lines was so that he would be able to contact him. The safety of the code wasn't hidden in its complexity, but in the fact that anyone else listening simply wouldn't make any sense out of the random sentences, only Shaun.

He looked down at the lines again. A phone number was the most logical conclusion, and Shaun liked logic. He took the four pages out with the highlighted lines on them and laid them out next to each other. From left to right he placed them in ascending order, fighting the wind to hold them on the spot.

Shaun smiled, suddenly understanding. Counting from the top of the page, he noted the line number on which each quote appeared. Ten digits, the correct number for a cell phone: 34, 21, 29, 13, 22.

Shaun looked at the sequence, thinking back to the man's message. His voice had sounded a little funny, a little distant. Distant in the way that ... Shaun suddenly realised it wasn't a cell number.

Shaun ran to the payphone on the corner, hoping he had enough change in his pockets. Just. He pumped it into the machine and dialled, following his hunch to add the international prefix before the numbers. He waited.

A long silence. A series of beeps. A ring, foreign. Click. 'Took your time,' a voice said after a moment.

'Ah ... hello?' Shaun said hesitantly. 'This is—'

'I know who you are, Dr Strickland. You need to listen to me. You have to come to Madrid right away. I think your life is in danger.'

'Who are you?' Shaun asked, suddenly paranoid and looking about him in the street.

'I really can't talk on the phone, they keep finding me, but I have information I know you'll be interested in.' The voice was stern, but not hostile.

'How do I know this isn't a trap?' Shaun asked. There was a pause.

'You don't.'

'Then I won't come,' he said.

The line went dead. Shaun stared at the payphone, more confused than ever. The guy had hung up. Just like that. Shaun checked his surroundings but could not see anything strange. This could so easily be a trap, but what else was there to do? He thought briefly of going to his brother's house in Washington DC, but he could not endanger Tim. It had been a risk just emailing him but he needed the money, especially after the most expensive cab ride in history. Tim, now a Washington senator, had plenty of money and had often offered to help Shaun financially, but Shaun's pride had never allowed him to accept.

He had no pride now, though. They – whoever they were – had taken everything that he had ever cared about. They had taken Lauren, and now he didn't much care about pride. He had nothing. Nothing but a desire to make them pay.

He looked down at the book in his hands. All he had to go on was this diary. He had always believed that if time travel really were possible, it would have already happened. He would know about it. But there had never been any evidence. Nothing that claimed: 'I am from the future!'

Until now.

There was no longer any doubt in Shaun's mind that this book was old, and valuable. That smell could not be faked, nor the fact that it was sealed airtight in an animal stomach with a collection of other old texts. Then, there was the unusual way Shaun had come by it. Above all, though, he could not imagine that people would want something – want it badly enough to kill for it – if it had no value, if it were a fake.

This phone number he had in his hands was the only clue he had, his only chance to find out what was going on and make those responsible pay. But then … what if? He gave himself a moment to dare to imagine that it was all true. That there *was* a secret facility somewhere that had mastered time travel and had sent people back in time to interview historical figures. This was the single most incredible thing Shaun could imagine, and he had indeed spent most of his life looking at the nature of time. But for a man to travel back through it? If someone had done this, then they had a solution, an answer that had eluded Shaun for nine years. This was someone worth meeting.

He picked up the receiver and punched the numbers again.

CHAPTER 25

Shaun Strickland waited.

'You need to come to Madrid now. Right now,' the voice launched right into it. There was no 'Thanks for calling back' or 'Welome to Mysterious Voices R Us, how may we direct your call?' The voice had known he would call back, he was waiting.

'Why Madrid?'

'Dr Strickland, I don't have time to explain everything, and it's not safe to do so right now. Go to Madrid, catch the train to Plaza del Sol and head to the top of the stairs. You'll find a man with no arms holding a cup in his teeth. When you see him, you ask him where the chicken is. You got it?' The voice was serious.

'Wait! What can you tell me about Graeme Fontéyne?' Shaun blurted out quickly and immediately regretted it. There was a silence on the other end of the line, as if he had thrown a curve ball.

'You have to get to Spain today, do you understand? I'll explain everything then.'

Shaun rolled his eyes at the lunacy of it. A man with no arms? *Where is the chicken?* This guy could not be serious.

'Listen, you've got to give me more than that, I can't—'

The line was already dead. He dialled again. Beeps, then a voice in Spanish: '*Lo siento, el numero de telefono no esta conectado ...*'

Well then. Madrid.

Shaun wasn't even sure which town he was in – somewhere near Richmond, maybe – but he knew that the nearest international airport was still a hike away. Knowing he didn't have enough money for another huge taxi trip, he decided to jump a train.

Half an hour later, he stood on the railway platform. An old analogue clock hung under the iron roof of the station: it was five to six in the evening. It hung next to a dilapidated old sign, 'Salem'. Salem was a town of about twenty-five thousand people, and right now Shaun wanted to make sure he wasn't one of them. He had been told that

Amtrak came through this way just on six every day, the only train service north-east towards Washington DC. The line headed through Richmond, which meant he could get a plane to Madrid. Why Spain? He wondered. Who was this guy?

In the meantime, he had found another payphone and left a message for his brother about where he was going, promising to call again when he got to Madrid. Shaun had hoped to speak to his brother but hadn't been surprised when the call went to voicemail; Tim never answered. Shaun had been furious at first when they stopped talking. He felt like he had lost a good friend.

'He's too important,' he would say to Lauren as he hung up after another beep of the answering machine. 'He's way too big and important for me now.'

Squealing, hissing air broke his train of thought. The huge metal snake that was the Amtrak express seemed to appear from nowhere. The train was long, six full-length passenger cars, with the engine at the front. Each car had two metal antenna that reached up to a cross-bar, which in turn contacted the invisibly charged cables that breathed life from above.

The doors opened, no one got off ... not a single soul. Shaun stepped on and found a seat near the front of the carriage. Within the minute a whistle blew and the doors closed with a hiss. The snake lurched into life, beginning a chugging rhythm as it increased speed. Shaun looked down to his hands, not quite remembering pulling the diary from inside his coat. He opened it to the page he was up to. The trip was a few hours, so he began to read.

CHAPTER 26

Blue light. I saw blue light, felt it wrap around me, penetrate me. Then, piece by piece I felt every molecule of my body begin to break apart. The bonds that held the fabric of my existence were stretched, and I felt every nerve disassemble, every organ dissolve into an organic cloud, and even as I knew I was no longer a physical, solid form, I could still think. I still had my mind. I was still me. Every part of me was sucked into a single point in space. Then I was gone—

I awoke in my cell. I was covered in sweat. I patted my body, confirming that the horror of the dream was not real. I was a solid, yet painfully bruised mass.

But I knew it was no dream. It was a memory, the kind that your brain blocks out from your conscious life because of the trauma, when even the memory of such pain is too extraordinary for the waking world.

My next thought was of escape. My encounter with the lion had changed my mind about waiting to gain information. I decided that I could do that without being torn limb from limb.

I was alone in my room. Malbool was nowhere to be seen. The horror of the day's events returned to me. It seemed so wrong. Why would they lock the pit after I was victorious? If Tiberius had wanted me dead, he would simply have killed me. He did not need to watch me die in the arena. Indeed, it wasn't in his interest for me to die. While I lived I made him money, gained him power and favour in his aristocratic circles. Why would he release a lion on me after I had already won my match?

I reached into my bedding and pulled out the object I had removed from my thigh.

It sat in my hand, a tall thin cylinder of some kind of metal, blue lights glowing faintly, making no sound. My fingers traced along the grooves in its surface until they each found a tiny dip. I held it as a musician might hold a flute, the tips of my fingers resting at odd intervals along the rod. Then I squeezed.

Click! *A faint humming sound started to emanate from the rod. Then, without warning, several small compartments flicked open. I stared at it. So familiar, so much time following this exact routine. I knew that this was the single most important piece of equipment in my mission, not only because of the sound and images it could capture, but also because of the technology it contained. I knew that it could never be found, not for more than two thousand years, and only by those who would know where to look, who knew where I had been told to hide it. I was a long way from that place. I was a long way from where I needed to be.*

I pulled on one of the segments, and it came away from the rest of the unit, a long, imperceptibly thin cord trailing it. I squeezed the segment in the way I had practised and it flattened out. I pressed it to my head just above my ear. I pulled another identical segment and ran it up to just above my other ear. My fingers followed the routine of their own accord. I pulled two more parts of the tube and long, flat cords came out. I wrapped them about my torso as I had been taught, and clipped them in place back on the unit, which was now securely fastened to my hip. Then I tapped the unit twice on one end, and the opposite end sprang up, revealing a small black shape. I took it and placed it in my mouth. The tiny hooked clip attached firmly to the back of my molar, perfectly fitted for me.

Then I stood. That was it. I was now wearing the unit as it had been designed. I turned in the cell, looked at the door and flicked the clip in my mouth with the back of my tongue, a movement that would go unnoticed from the outside. There it was, the slight tingling in my mouth to let me know the camera was recording. I could barely believe it worked.

I closed my eyes and clung to the feeling, the tingling that told me I was not insane, that the world in my head did exist. Even as I stood there, I knew that the sound and vision cameras on either side of my head were capturing images of ancient Rome that had never been experienced by modern man. True depth, multi-sensory images were being sent to the tiny spindle of optical button-sized discs inside the recording unit at my hip. Silently, unnoticeably.

The next morning Malbool came back, dragged between two guards, his feet hanging limply and creating trails in the dirt of the stable's corridor. They threw him roughly onto his bed and left.

I rushed to his side. Bloodied and broken, he smiled up at me, the bruising around his black face looking oddly purple.

'My God, what happened to you?' I knew that he wasn't supposed to fight for another week.

'This, it seems, is what happens when I try to stand in for you, my friend,' he replied, the effort clearly causing him pain.

'Stand in for me? What do you mean? I fought yesterday.' Malbool's eyebrows lifted at this.

'Yes, you did. But not long after you left, Tiberius's guards came down to collect you. When I told them that you had already been taken, the stable master was furious and beat me, accusing me of lying.'

I looked hard into Malbool's eyes. 'These injuries are not from the stable master.'

He smiled again at this. 'No. I fought for you. I was taken in your place, although I was not up to the challenge. Tiberius managed to get a pardon for my life because I was not the true opponent.'

'You fought in place of me? But I was taken to the Coliseum and I fought! After I had defeated my opponent, they locked me in the arena and released a lion. They wanted me to die.'

'You did not fight for Tiberius,' Malbool stated.

'What? Of course I did, who else would I—'

Then I stopped. Tiberius hadn't actually been there. I remembered the hooded man.

'They did say that I was a last-minute replacement,' I said, thinking out loud.

'You were taken to the Coliseum? That is where Augustus was holding his games yesterday.'

'Augustus the Emperor?' I asked.

Malbool paused a moment before answering. 'No, not Augustus Octavian, he died fifteen years ago.' He caught his breath before continuing. 'Augustus Titus. He is the Governor of a province south of Rome. Tiberius and he are not what you would call the best of friends. No one from our troupe would have competed there.' Malbool's deep voice was raspy. He reached across to a broken rib. His breathing was shallow and came in sharp gasps.

'Take it easy. Don't talk. There's time to talk later. You need your rest. Where is the caretaker? Why haven't you been treated?'

'My friend. I am a loser. I have been defeated. I am lucky to escape with my life.'

I shook my head and thought hard. Who would take me out to fight in another contest? Who would have the ability, and access to our stables? I had to escape. It was challenge enough to survive in this game when the game was fair. Now someone was plotting and rigging matches to have me killed. I looked down once more at my battered stablemate. His eyes were closed and his breathing had grown steady. He was asleep.

'You really expect me to believe that you were taken out of my stables without my knowledge?' said Tiberius incredulously as I stood before him a day later, my arms shackled in front of me. 'That you went off and fought in the games of Augustus?'

'All I know is what I have told you and it is the truth.' I was careful with my choice of words, not wishing to offend my master, nor imply any inability on his part to control his affairs.

'If it is the truth, it is something I shall have to deal with most seriously,' he lounged back in his chair with an air of exasperation. 'Not that it matters. The real issue here is how much money you lost me by not defeating Crixus. Your friend, the retiarius, really wasn't much of a match for him. Crixus is the champion of fifty-two matches over the past nine years. He is quite simply the most famous, most feared gladiator in the history of the games. I have waited all my life to find an unknown to pit against him. Do you know the odds on a match like that?'

He rose out of his high-backed chair and walked towards me, circling me closely, slowly.

'Ah, but you ... you were the one. You were the one with a real chance. You have something no one has seen before. When Marcus told me about you, described the way you fought off his guards to save the boy, I knew it was worth my gold to get you. And I did,' he continued circling, looking me up and down.

'Just to set up this fight cost me more than most gladiators make me in a year. So, the question is, what good to me are you now? I suppose you could fight, I suppose you could earn back the money I've spent on you, but now that you've fought in the games the odds are dramatically reduced. Now I cannot claim you as an unknown.'

I stared ahead, unmoving, unspeaking. It seemed that Tiberius had not yet reached a decision about my immediate future.

'If I may speak,' I began finally, my mind working quickly. 'What if I could offer you a way to make more money than you would have on my fight with Crixus?'

Tiberius stopped, tilted his head to the side and looked directly into my eyes. His eyes narrowed, sceptical but curious.

'Short of raiding the royal treasury, how do you propose such a feat? Odds like that are impossible to come by.'

'Not, entirely,' I said, returning his gaze, 'not in the Royåle.'

Tiberius looked at me for a moment, then burst into laughter. 'Ha! Oh, dear boy, for a moment you had me. I thought you had a real plan. You would have done well in the street theatres if you were a citizen.'

He continued to laugh, the tension of the moment broken. I stared at him, stony-faced.

'My lord, how much could you earn if you backed a first-time fighter in the Royåle, and that fighter won?' I asked, my tone and demeanour utterly serious.

His laughter abated and he slowly took in my expression. 'Well, nothing,' he said. 'The Royåle is nothing but a way to get rid of gladiators you don't want anymore, or can't afford to feed. It's a bloodbath.'

'But you do bet on it?' I prompted.

'Of course I do. But only as a parlour game. I usually draw names from a bowl and take my pot luck like everyone else. To actually predict a winner is impossible.'

'What if you could?' I persisted. 'What if you backed a first-time fighter? Surely you wouldn't have to lay much down to make back double what you would have made on my defeat of Crixus?'

'My boy, if I backed a winning first-time fighter, let alone one that I owned, to win the Royåle, and he actually did it ... well, then I'd make a fortune! Not to mention be paid for every fight anyone ever tried to line up with you again.'

'No,' I said simply.

'No? What do you mean by no?' he asked, his white hair reflecting the lamplight. 'I mean no. I mean that if I win the Royåle, I win my freedom.'

If I had thought Tiberius had laughed before, it was nothing compared with the boisterous bellow that escaped him now.

'Your freedom? Really, boy, the only freedom a man who enters the Royåle is guaranteed is the freedom of death. Many champions in the past have thrown their lives away on their quest for freedom.'

'Then the odds must be good,' I said.

'The odds are good, there's no question of that. The odds for a newcomer to win are astronomical, but it's a fool's bet – and besides,

you're not a first-timer anymore.' He looked me up and down, then spoke to the guards behind me. 'Take him back to his cell.'

I had to think quickly. 'I did not fight for you! You said yourself that I was taken without your permission. Who knows what name they entered me under?'

'Enough. Guards!' He turned, heard a snapping sound, an impact, and turned back. His two guards lay on the floor at my feet, each holding various parts of their bodies and groaning.

'I suggest you reconsider,' I said, knowing that I was playing with fire.

Anger flashed across his face. 'You insubordinate pig! Samus, Lonicus!' The doors behind me flew open, and a troop of men filtered into the large room, surrounding me with weapons drawn. I looked around and knew that this was a fight I could not win, at least not without sustaining injuries that would prevent my escape later, although I gave no hint of this acknowledgement to Tiberius.

'My lord, I do not wish to injure or kill your guards. If I must kill twenty men here in your palace, just to prove that I can kill twenty men in the arena, then I will. If I die now, then you have lost your way of making a fortune; if you let me fight, you will be the richest man in Rome.' I held the aristocrat's gaze.

His anger was clear, his ruddy cheeks flushed crimson, but he regained control of himself quickly. I could sense his struggle between the insult of being disobeyed, and his greed at what I was suggesting. Greed won.

'You want to throw your life away?' he asked, as if it were a given.

'I want my freedom,' I responded. 'How many years would it take for me to earn you the money I could make you in one day next week?' I pressed, appealing to that growing lust for gold.

He stared at me, thinking. 'Very well.' He nodded. 'Very well, I shall let you fight. You will either die and I will lose nothing but the expense of keeping you, or I shall become wealthier than Caesar himself. Not even the miracle man of Judea will be able to put your pieces back together!'

With this, he turned and four of the guards moved in to lead me back to the cell. I was limp with shock. They jostled me bodily towards the exit and I gave no resistance. I had heard it. The miracle man of Judea? It was the name the Romans had given the Jewish land of Judah, the land I knew as Israel. If Tiberius spoke of this man, then he must still be alive, and I had discovered it in the most unexpected of places. The countdown had begun.

CHAPTER 27

'Tell me, Malbool,' I said three days later, when my stablemate had recovered somewhat, 'what do you know about the one they call the miracle man from Judea?'

Malbool looked up at me from where he lay on his bunk. I was in the middle of performing a series of exercises, something that had become my ritual since learning the truth about who I was.

'Miracle man? I have heard little. I heard there was a man in Judea who helped lame people walk, some say he could make the blind see again, but I do not think much of it. These claims are just talk. Men talk always of such things.'

'When did you hear about this?'

'Probably more than two years ago. I didn't pay much attention.'

I dropped from where I was hanging on a cross-bar on the wall and went into the first of several sets of push-ups, trying to sound casual. 'Two years? Do you know what happened to him?'

A strange expression crossed Malbool's face.

'No, no I do not. Why are you so curious?'

'No reason. I just thought that if you ever have to fight in the arena again with that giant three-pronged toothpick of yours you might need a miracle!' I said, smiling.

'Ha! You jest, white man, but it is you who will need a miracle should you fight in the Royåle on Saturday.' His tone turned serious. 'Saul, if you fight like the rest of us, one match at a time, you have a good chance to live a long life. And as your reputation grows, Tiberius will give you a better life. You do not need to throw your life away. I tell you, think again.' I heard genuine concern in the African's voice. I stopped midway through a push-up, and lifted my head. Malbool was looking back at me. I dropped my head again and continued with my exercises. When I was done, I sat back, the sweat filming my face and body. I did not rush my next words.

'Malbool, who are you?' I was breathing heavily, and the black man still stared at me.

'What do you mean by this? I am Malbool the gladiator, retiarius for Lord Tiberius—'

'I don't mean what do you do, I mean who are you, the person? What would you do with yourself if you were a free man?' I asked.

He seemed slightly taken aback. 'A free man? I have not been a free man for nearly seven years, so I do not think of such things. In my tribe I was a warrior, but that life is no more.' The pain in his expression gave light to his feelings.

'You were a warrior. Why? Is that something you chose?'

'It was what I did. I did not know anything else. Before the Romans came, all I knew of the world was grass huts and hunting. I knew nothing of iron, nothing of armour, nothing of civilisation and these stone buildings. I was a hunter and a warrior. I defended my people from other tribes, and hunted to provide for—' He stopped, emotion choking his words. 'I hunted to provide for my family. But, as I said, that world is no more.'

'Malbool, what if I told you that the world you know now, this empire of the Romans, is as primitive to me as your grass huts are to the Coliseum? What if I told you that I have to fight in the Royåle because if I do not win my freedom, I cannot complete my mission. The world I come from will be changed forever.' I looked at him with the most serious expression I could muster. Snoring from the other cells penetrated the silence that had blanketed our room.

'I do not understand of what you speak,' he said finally. 'How will throwing your life away change things for your country?'

I shook my head. 'Malbool, if I die before I have completed my mission, the impact would be more than I can describe to you, more than you can understand. Therefore, I will not explain the details to you, not yet.'

'Do not underestimate my ability to understand. I understand much,' he said, defiance and pride creeping into his voice. 'I understand that anything is possible. I understand that the lives we come to accept can be changed in an instant. I understand that things happen for a reason, and no reason at all, and that things we do not understand happen with or without our permission. Just because we do not understand them, it does not make us immune.'

I admit that I had not expected the swell of passion from the man who only days before had been beaten to within an inch of his life. Malbool transformed before me as he began to vent his frustration. 'I understand what it is to come home with a kill on your spear, feeling proud of the hunt and knowing that your family will eat for the next week. Knowing that your daughter will race out to meet you as you near the fire that your wife has kept burning. And I know that when a legion of Romans march over the hill and charge into your village you cannot change that. You can see your daughter screaming as she is run down and trampled in front of you. I understand what it is to hear her bones break and twist and to be powerless to save her. I understand what it is to lose a world in an instant. Do not underestimate me.' His cheeks were wet with tears.

I sat, quiet, heartbroken for this tribesman. His anguish was still vivid. I did not doubt his sincerity.

'I am sorry, Malbool.'

He looked at me with a hint of the fire that I had seen that day in the pit after I had torn away his mask. That burning courage, borne from having nothing to lose.

'I know there is something about you,' he said, quite suddenly changing his tone. 'I sensed something when we met in the pit, and then again after, when I have seen you fight. There has always been something about you, but it seems this past week, that particular something has changed. There is something you have discovered. There is some new secret you carry.'

This surprised me also. I had been careful not to change my behaviour or give any sign of what I had discovered. It seemed my cellmate was more astute than I had given him credit for. I looked at him, and made a decision. This tribesman would either think I was crazy, or he would help me.

I pulled the small unit from around my waist where I kept it hidden under my tunic. I raised it up to his face. Malbool's expression went from one of accusation to one of puzzlement as his brow furrowed imperceptibly. His eyes widened as the iridescent blue light began to pulsate. Holding a series of points on the outer rim of the small silver bar, I tapped the top in a sequence committed to memory at The Facility. The unit buzzed and sampled my DNA, then sang the song that it would sing only for me.

The wall on the far side of the room sprang to life with an image. It was one I had captured the day I first tested the recording unit. The image was now being projected from the underside of the small unit, bringing the rock of the cell wall to life. Malbool stared, unmoving, unspeaking, as I began to explain.

Saturday came quickly. I had done all I could do to prepare, and I had nothing but my physical skill to rely on. I did not know how long it had been since rumours of the miracle man had started to surface, but my mission research told me that, from the first public display, Jesus's ministry lasted just three years before he was tortured and nailed to a wooden cross to die. I did not have much time.

I was taken from my cell early in the morning. Today was the culmination of a week-long spring festival, the largest game of the year. Men, women and children went to the Circus Maximus for chariot races, and to the Coliseum for music, acrobatics and for bloodthirsty games. The week was sponsored by the Emperor, Tiberius Claudius Nero, and the Roman Empire was intent on showing its people the extent of its power.

There was no event in the year that compared with the display of the Royåle. It was the highlight of the season, when more men gathered in the arena than at any other time. It was an event unmatched in history for its sheer bloodlust, with one hundred armed warriors gathering in the dusty pit, all with the knowledge that only one would survive, and barely. It was suicide. Every contestant knew it. I knew it. The result relied on luck more than skill.

Most entrants entered with the knowledge they would not walk out alive, and I entered with the knowledge it was my only chance to escape.

The crowd roared and the beasts roared. Fresh sand covered the arena floor, shimmering in the sun. The atmosphere was electric. There was nothing like it. There had never been a crowd like this in any event in the history of Rome. I smiled – it reminded me of the Super Bowl!

I stood with several others in the holding pen. With this many contestants, we were not afforded the dignity of private preparation rooms. We stood huddled together in groups of five, waiting as a pompous gamesman described the rules of the contest – rules already known to all of us. There were one hundred competitors and there would be only one winner. At certain stages, variables would be introduced. Everyone knew that these variables meant beasts – lions, tigers and the occasional bear – and that they would be introduced at two separate stages of the event. Today, two tigers would be introduced when there were forty combatants left, and a male lion would be introduced when there were twenty combatants left. It was this that I was counting on.

To defeat ninety-nine other men in a free-for-all match was something no one could prepare for. Even though I had every confidence in my ability, with so many men fighting at once, there was no chance of survival. I intended to survive. To do so I knew that I had to stay alive long enough to escape. Escape, not victory, was my plan.

Leather straps were pulled tight as armour snapped into place. The room was full of men fixing and straightening, as if they were going to a formal dinner instead of an all-out war. No one made eye contact, although even within our small group we each sized up the others. The sound of fanfare drifted into the small room where we stood, muffled by the doors of wood and iron that separated us from the surreal world of the arena just beyond. The smell of fear and sweat hung in the air. The men started to move and stamp like animals, their eyes narrowed, ready to pounce.

The doors burst open and the group charged out. The build-up of energy was enormous, and as we entered the centre of this screaming, chanting crowd I saw groups of five and six spring from every door around the arena. It is easy to say 'one hundred men', but to see the sheer volume of meat and muscle, of iron and steel, was overwhelming.

All around were men, imposing, armed, vicious, desperate. Each with only one thing on his mind – to kill everyone else. To kill me.

All at once there was a blare of trumpets and the mass of bodies turned as one to face a balcony at the far end of the arena. The crowd's cheer swelled as we all looked at one of the protruding platforms high in the stands. I squinted to make out the details, and then I saw him. I saw with my own eyes, the living Emperor of Rome. The leaves of his crown could be clearly made out against the thinning white hair and pale skin of the heavyset man's head. Moving forward and waving to an adoring crowd was the stepson of Augustus Caesar – this was Nero.

The trumpets sounded again and all the men in the centre of the arena slammed their weapons into the ground in unison. Then the Emperor raised his arm, palm downwards, and out towards the assembly awaiting their fate. The crowd hushed. The calm came. For the fifty thousand citizens assembled to watch the carnage to come, these few precious and rare words were as much a highlight as the battle itself.

Named Caesar like Julius and Augustus before him, the Emperor spoke: 'Brave warriors, today you lay down your lives for the Holy Empire of Rome. Today your fate is in your own hands, and today you strive for the greatest of prizes, to become a citizen of Holy Rome!'

The crowd roared and cheered. Caesar nodded slightly then called for a hush. It was then that I noticed the cloaked and hooded figure behind the Emperor. I had seen him before. Caesar spoke again: 'Today you will glorify all who have gone before you. Let the Royåle begin!'

In unison the rehearsed response came from the men around me: 'We who are about to die salute you!' I made no such pledge.

I realised that not everyone's voice had the deep bass of the common gladiatorial man, and it struck me that there were women too who were here to fight and die in the name of freedom.

At once, drums began to beat and the group spread out around the arena. There was barely twenty feet between each opponent. Who would fight first when the trumpet sounded? The drums continued to beat and my heart matched the rhythm, then overtook it. I looked around. The sound of the crowd faded and all I heard was my own heartbeat and breath. On either side of me were retiarius, men with nets and tridents. On the outside of them were a Gaul and a Thracian. Already the men were talking to each other, forming their alliances to take them through the early stages of the contest. None of my stablemates were here; Tiberius was not keen on throwing away valuable fighters and had forbidden any other members of his ludus to compete in the Royåle. Other troupe owners were not so protective of their property, and found this kind of contest a good way to get rid of their less profitable stable occupants.

The drums banged louder, faster, thumping the life of the contest into the arena. At that moment, an image came to me unbidden: my mother smiling at my sister and me. She had raised us alone for five years after my father died, and then we lost her too. What would she say if she could see me now? Memories of my childhood came with every new beat of the drums. Then the drums stopped.

Silence. I strode forward. The trumpets blasted. The game was on.

CHAPTER 28

The trumpets blasted. The game was on.

I rolled to my left as a trident sailed towards my head. At the same time the retiarius on my left had turned to face the Gaul opposite him. The spikes caught him in the back of one leg and he screamed with pain. There hadn't even been time to think. The trumpets still blared and already men had fallen. I looked about as I came out of my roll and found two men charging at me. I readied myself for the assault, but before they reached me a third and fourth man charged in from the side to intercept them. They collided heavily and went into a rolling struggle. I didn't have time to watch the melee; all around me pockets of one-on-one, two-on-one and group-on-group fighting were in full swing.

I looked across the arena to see a Thracian hacking viciously at another contestant, raining down blows in over-handed swipes and wearing out his weaker opponent. In an instant a victor from a battle behind the Thracian turned, and without a moment's hesitation he drove his short sword through the bronzed man's spine. The Thracian fell and his assailant moved on before the body hit the ground. It was pandemonium. It was insanity. It was even more chaotic than I had imagined. Everywhere I turned people were dying. Even without having yet engaged I was already within the final seventy still standing. I kept my back to the wall.

All at once, my honeymoon period was over. A tall, thin man turned his attention from a fallen female warrior he had overpowered and marched towards me. I didn't waste time. I knew that in order to survive the opening stages of the contest, while there were too many opponents to keep in my field of view, I had to finish any challengers quickly and focus on self-preservation. I took several quick steps towards him, spun down on one knee and arced my blade around, slicing cleanly through his thighs. The man remained standing for just a moment, until he tried to take another step, and then his severed limbs betrayed him. His lower leg fell away as his upper thigh took a step. Driving my blade into his exposed chest, I made sure he wasn't able to reflect on the horror of his situation for long.

I was up again in moments and immediately found a short, stocky man with dark skin and a curved sabre running towards me, his mouth open in an animalistic scream. He held the sword high to cut me directly in half. Pre-empting the timing of his attack, I slid up to him with my leg tucked up high to my chest; when I released it, I kicked hard and my heel drove into his sternum. I heard a crack as he fell backwards to the ground. His sword fell from his grip and flew within inches of my head before burying into another man behind me. Unfortunately for me, it hit him hilt first, the blade mutely swishing to the ground. Narrowly ducking his quick slash at my throat, I stopped his next thrust for my abdomen with a parry that was barely quick enough. Another man came up behind the first, this one wearing a large helmet with a broad rim and holding a tall shield. Both men struck at me rather than each other, probably in one of the hastily formed alliances made as the competitors sought to prolong their lives. I was being forced backwards towards the man on the ground holding his cracked breast.

Then, employing a different tactic, I broke away suddenly from the group. Sprinting to my left I quickly lost the two who had been attacking me and made for the centre of the arena. The sand kicked up behind me as I scanned the messy floor for one of the trapdoors.

I made it thirty feet before I was cut off by a wall of secutor gladiators – four in a row with their smooth-rimmed helmets and single fin, looking like fish. The small eye holes in the faces of their iron masks seemed particularly apt protection from the trident spikes of the retiarius, their natural opponents.

The four ran towards me, their long shields forming a wall too wide to sidestep. They obviously intended to drive me backwards towards the rim of the arena where all the fighting was taking place. Behind me, two hoplomachus men approached, pausing momentarily to run the man with the cracked sternum through with their blades. This wasn't right; this seemed like a coordinated attack. I knew that this could not be the case, with each fighting troupe having a maximum of two contestants per stable. I would make them fight each other.

I ran hard at the four-man wall approaching me. They baulked, but only for a moment. The two pursuers behind me ignored other challengers in an effort to run me down. I was being sandwiched from in front and behind. I reached the four men, who made no attempt to attack me with their weapons, a tactic that would have meant breaking the integrity of their wall.

I leaped up at the wall, my foot outstretched, and used the leverage from one man's shield to throw myself higher.

I hurdled the wall of men, the rims of their helmets blocking their vision as I flew overhead. I landed still running, and was horrified to see a man on the ground writhing and screaming as a tiger mauled his exposed neck. The wall of men turned, oblivious to the two who had been chasing me. Meanwhile I calculated at a glance the number of gladiators still in the arena. At least sixty. Which meant only one thing: someone had released the cats early. The game was not being run by the rules.

I looked for a trapdoor pit, realising now that I could not rely on the timing of the event. I could not see one, and at that moment I was tackled from the side and slammed into the ground. My sword flew free. I had only been distracted for a split second and cursed myself for the error. I hit the ground hard and pulled my attacker close to me. He had no sword or weapon other than his massively muscled bulk. With one hand I held his chin and the other gripped the back of his helmet. I twisted the man's head, and his body followed, rolling off me. I leaped up, but went down again instantly as he swung his huge hand with force and ankle tapped me hard enough to spin me around before I fell. The big man was on his feet with surprising speed and, once standing, he tore his helmet away from his head. Staring at me was a giant with a smooth, hairless head, a bulky chest and thighs almost as thick as my body. I recognised him from reputation, and a famed scar across his cheek. Crixus.

Now all six pursuers approached. They didn't attack each other and they didn't attack me. They fanned out and circled, forming a ring around the giant and me. Then they waited and watched. It was the confirmation I needed to realise that I had been set up. There was no way that seven men would stand within striking distance of each other in the Royåle and not attempt to hack each other to bits.

I looked up again to see the Emperor cheering a battle happening elsewhere in the arena. There, behind him, was the hooded man. At that moment, seeing me looking at him, he drew back his hood.

My heart skipped a beat. I didn't understand. I knew this man. I knew him from ... from my previous life, from The Facility. Delissio. Louis Delissio. An Italian special-forces soldier who had been recruited, like me, after reports of his Killed-in-Action status circulated. Officer X3.

What was he doing here?

The robed man gave a little smile. His face was mostly hidden by shadow, but there was no mistaking the pitted cheeks and the short crop of thick, black hair.

I forced my attention back to the giant in front of me, wishing that Tiberius had not told me about this man's unequalled track record: fifty-two victories.

Crixus had no sword, and without his helmet, the only armour he wore was on his shins. Two shiny metal plates curved to the shape of his leg. He looked mean. His body was muscled and imposing, but it was nothing compared to the hatred in his eyes. As the ring of men kept other challengers out, I faced the greatest gladiator in history.

The crowd seemed to hush, and if my senses weren't lying, even the sounds of battle from the arena floor seemed to fade as everyone took an interest in the hand-to-hand combat that was about to take place.

My mind raced. Why was Crixus here? There was no reason he would compete in the Royåle; he had earned his freedom long ago and continued to fight by choice, not out of obligation to a master.

Why would this man, the surest bet in the Roman Empire, risk himself to take part in this luck-of-the-draw event – even if that risk was greatly minimised with at least six other competitors protecting him? I glanced up again at Delissio and the realisation dawned on me. Crixus was here because someone had put him up to it. He was here to make certain I didn't leave.

'I have faced and killed a man for every week of the year … and the year is at an end,' he growled with malice unlike any I had seen. He didn't know me, but he hated me with passion, just for daring to face him.

Crixus came at me, intent on punishing me, hurting me, killing me. There was no way I could avoid him. I didn't.

With my back leg I swung forward and planted my foot just above his knee. He was moving forward fast and I used the motion of his leg to step up and spin hard. I spun fast at the shoulders and rubber banded my hips. My leg shot out as I sailed skywards, launched into the air off Crixus's fast-moving thigh. My hips unwound and my heel came round like a sling shot, connecting with the big man's head, just where his jaw met his cheek.

Crixus's head spun so hard the cracking sound was heard throughout the arena. There was instant silence. As if in slow motion, like the tallest tree in the forest being felled, the huge man fell to the ground, his neck broken.

Dead.

I landed. The dust curled up around his body with the impact, but the men around us just stared, disbelieving. I wasted no time and leaped clear over the giant's corpse. There was not a sound in the arena. I shoulder charged one of the tall, curved shields being held by my ring men. He was dumbfounded with shock and simply fell to his backside.

I scooped up my sword and ran hard for the trapdoor nearest the centre of the arena. With a tiger already released into the games, it meant the trapdoor had been opened once already, and the next time it was lifted I needed to be close – close enough that when a beast came out, I could roll into the tunnels below and escape through the corridor that was used to bring the great cats into the arena. It was my only hope to get out of here alive.

I was only thirty or so feet from the trapdoor when the arena erupted with cheering. Their hero, their unconquerable hero, had just fallen to an unknown, and fallen easily.

I didn't stop to bask in the glory, I had to get out. As I moved I looked up to the Emperor's box. Beyond the balcony throne, the Emperor was yelling and gesticulating at the man in black, at Delissio. Officer X3 looked down at me with disdain. Did he know who he was or had he forgotten like me? He looked considerably older than the way I remembered him, so he must have been here in ancient Rome for a great number of years.

Did he know who I was and why I was here? None of us had been told to whom the other officers had been assigned. We knew only that we were going back in pairs, and we knew it was a one-way journey, but we weren't told anything about the other assignments.

Now, here in the centre arena of the largest death match in history, I saw a man I had known in a former life being chastised by Tiberius Nero Caesar. Delissio had to know. How else would he be sitting where he was right now? And if he knew, and if he was at the centre of this conspiracy to destroy me, why all the theatrics? Why not have me killed in my sleep? Why did he want me dead at all?

I reached the trapdoor and found it sealed shut. Damn. I slid to a halt and knelt, willing it to open as the group who had surrounded me recovered from their moment of disbelief and now rushed my way. I slammed my sword down onto the trapdoor, which was still covered with undisturbed sand, searching desperately for the edge, for something to give me leverage.

Suddenly the tip of my blade found the groove I had been looking for. I pressed down on my sword with all my weight, hoping to drive a wedge between the door and the arena floor to lever it up.

A blade caught me in my side; a small, curved dagger thrown by one of the wall of secutors. Not deep, just a glancing blow, but enough to send a burst of fire through my nerves and a stream of blood onto the arena sands. They were here. I was forced to rise from my escape hatch and engage them.

It became apparent quickly that these men had an unusual level of skill for gladiators. I killed two, but in doing so I was being driven backwards away from the trapdoor. They used their weapons in ways familiar to me, but not common in the pits of gladiatorial combat. It occurred to me that these men had been trained differently. The way they moved, the way they reacted ... they had been trained by one of us. I spared a glance at the balcony. Delissio was gone.

Beyond my attackers I could see that the contestants were thinning out. There were perhaps twenty still standing, and the battles were becoming more a test of stamina than of skill. I ducked and weaved and struck and parried, but these men were equal to the task, and while fighting four of them at once it was all I could manage to keep my head on my neck.

Backwards they drove me. I was fighting hard but beginning to tire. Then I got one through – a straight thrust that plunged deep into the Gaul's solar plexus. Three now. More manageable, but I was nearly at the edge of the arena. No one challenged us as we fought; the others seemed to perceive this battle was a no-go zone and let it run its course.

One more down. His head hit the ground before his body, but the other two kept coming. One caught me, a slicing blow across my chest. A line of red appeared as my heart pumped blood from the wound.

Then, the thing I dreaded: a hungry-looking lion emerged through the trapdoor, and I was forced to watch sand from the arena fall into the tunnel entrance as the trapdoor slammed shut, taking with it my last chance of escape. I was too far away.

I paused in shock, barely noticing the lion pounce on a nearby gladiator who knelt wounded and was tending to his injury, and in that moment of distraction my foot slid out from under me. I fell back against the bars of an entrance gate. The first sword came down at me and I barely had time to roll out of the way. I saw it sink into the corpse whose blood and brain matter I had slipped on. I rolled back the opposite way, towards the blade, pulling it from the man's grasp. But the move to disarm my first attacker cost me.

My second attacker, also a Gaul, seized the moment to raise his blade and send it down towards my chest. In the slow motion of that moment I could not avoid, I thought again about Delissio.

Strangely, the sight of him had given me some comfort, reminding me of a world beyond this one of horror, murder and carnage: beyond Rome.

I knew I could not avoid the blow, and it was not until I saw the three protruding spikes from the Gaul's chest that I realised I wouldn't have to. The man fell forward to land beside me, the three spikes digging into the ground and holding him in place.

As he fell I saw the man who had attacked him, a retiarius. The warrior drew a short sabre from his belt and slashed across the unarmed Gaul still at his side. The man's innards spilled onto the arena floor.

Dark-skinned and bathed in sweat, there was no mistaking the voice that boomed out from beneath the bronzed helmet.

'You need to learn to watch where you step!' the African bellowed, breathing hard.

'Malbool! What are you doing?'

'You're welcome, white man!' he said, his panting covering any attempted laughter. I surveyed the arena. Already there were fewer than twenty men still standing. I could not believe how quickly the decimation had taken place. Bodies lay everywhere, the arena floor stained red with the blood of scores of men, and those few women who had braved the insanity. Still there were small battles raging slowly as exhaustion took hold. The tigers lay dead, their glossy coats glimmering wet in the sun. The lion, however, which had not entered the contest till most of the competitors were already limp with fatigue and injury, was faring much better.

As I scanned the scene, the golden beast mauled at the chest of a once-brave Thracian, but this was not what caught my attention. At least twelve of the remaining fighters seemed to have lost interest in each other and were running my way. They were shouting and screaming, and as I glanced up to the Emperor's balcony again, I saw that Delissio had returned. I saw him smile. Bastard! He had somehow given these men incentive. Incentive to kill me, or perhaps they were just his men in the first place. I didn't know, I didn't care. I could feel my chest and shoulders screaming from the wounds they had received. There was no way I could hold off so many fighters alone.

Malbool reached down to help me to my feet. 'Now is not the time to rest; you can do that when you lay your head on a boat to Judea,' he said, this time managing a smile.

I reached up and took his wrist. Warily I staggered to my feet, knowing that losing blood this quickly, I would not be able to maintain my strength for long.

They arrived, fresh-looking and uninjured. They slowed to a walk as they closed the gap, moving as if they were stalking captive prey. At that moment, the truth was undeniable. These men had not engaged in any serious battle; not one of them carried a wound, not one of them was weary. They had fought among themselves in some kind of choreographed, rehearsed manner, turning serious only when an outsider threatened one of their group. In doing so, they had survived, fresh, until they were very nearly the only ones left. I looked out beyond them – no one. The only remaining warriors were engaged in a desperate wrestle with the lion. Two men, one hungry cat, and no chance.

'What are you doing here?' I asked Malbool as we backed up against the gate.

'I thought you might need some help,' he replied, wrenching his trident from the back of the fallen Gaul.

'Malbool, you said yourself it was a fool's battle. I was planning to escape, not to win.' He looked at me, one corner of his mouth curling down as I continued. 'I was planning to escape through the trapdoor when the cats were released.'

'Well,' he considered, 'you might have let me know that before I snuck in here.'

'Snuck in? Jesus, Malbool!'

'Who?'

'Well, I don't know why, but you see that man in black up there?' Malbool followed my gesture. 'He's one of the men I told you about. He's from the future like me. He's trying to make sure I don't get out of here. I think he's got these men working against me.'

The African scrunched his eyes. 'If what you told me is true. If you are from a time yet to come and must meet this miracle man, then you must leave here a victor. I owe you my life, and if I am to pay that debt, then I pay it by helping you win this contest.'

I saw in his eyes the honour and courage missing from so many of the men in my unit, missing from so many men in my time. I knew then that he would die for me, and I knew also that I would not let him.

The twelve were here. They fanned out in a semi-circle around the two of us, all armed. Three of them held nets.

Malbool gripped his trident in one hand and his short sabre in the other. He set himself in the sand, not bothering to replace his helmet. I lowered the tip of my retrieved sword and ignored the pain in my shoulder and across my chest.

The nets came first; two of them in a coordinated attack. I made to roll, but Malbool, being familiar with the weighted ropes, thrust his trident high and caught them both before they landed on us. He flung the nets to the side and caught the first gladiator with the butt of his iron-pronged spear. The squat man's nose spread out across his face and his eyes watered up, giving Malbool enough time to reverse slash his neck. The man fell as two more rushed the tribesman.

I raced forward to intercept them and within seconds three more advanced on us. The bodies and bloodshed became a blur. Like the men who had chased me down, these men moved like Facility-trained fighters, more martial skill than ancient technique. Blades clashed and thrust, and men fell, but outnumbered and against fresh warriors, both Malbool and I took damage. More and more of their blows found us. More kicks, more punches, more glancing nicks that took their toll. Then, with only four of them left, a sword hilt cracked me with force on the jaw and my legs buckled. The world went sideways and I fell. Vaguely I saw Malbool's legs and another body fall just beyond them. But even as I lay there, I knew that he was no match for three of these warriors. I knew he would fall at any moment. There was nothing I could do about it.

No.

I would not let him fall defending me. I fought the dizziness, wondering absently why a sword had not been buried in me already. As clarity returned, the realisation of my impending doom screamed at me. I thought I heard a train. Or was it a plane? It was loud and rumbling, with intermittent shrieks like the brakes of steel wheels on iron tracks. Vaguely I thought that it would be a good idea to move out of the way. It might have been a truck. I certainly didn't want to get run over by a truck. My brain screamed at me: move!

But I was tired, so very tired. I saw Malbool, his legs rushing backwards; he must have been getting out of the way too. I shook my head hard, trying to dispel the fuzziness. Truck? I was in Rome, I was in the arena, there were no trucks here – but there were—

I looked up to see a massive, roaring, heaving beast. A lion of huge and awesome ferocity was tearing at one of the gladiators, and it was the man's shrieks I could hear.

Malbool was fighting the other two when one went down, felled by a second yellow beast.

The man who fought Malbool didn't flinch. He continued to thrust and parry, and each time he gained an advantage, he turned to finish me. Malbool again and again stopped him, engaging in any way he could to keep the large secutor from reaching me. Then he too was down, taken from behind by a third massive lion. Even through my grogginess I could not believe it. Where had they all come from? This wasn't part of the game. Then, looking beyond the screaming victims, not ten feet from us, surrounding us, I saw another five immense, hungry-looking lions enter from three separate trapdoors around the arena floor.

My mind cleared quickly as the beasts began to stalk. The crowd screamed and buzzed with excitement, knowing that we had no way out. We backed up against the gate with our weapons held in front of us.

'When they leap,' I told Malbool, 'drop down and aim for their underbelly. It's the only way to get a quick kill.' Both of us knew, however, that with five lions charging and three more soon to turn their attention to us, the advice was futile.

Closer and closer the great cats came, passing their feasting kin who were tearing limb from warm-bodied limb.

'Malbool, it's been an honour to—'

'Saul! Hurry!' I recognised the voice, although I could not immediately place from where. As the lions charged and leaped over the fallen bodies, I heard the sound of metal clanking behind me. But there was nothing behind me, only the wall and gate. Malbool and I spun as one. The lions crept forward, their nimble bodies low to the ground, jaws open and dripping with anticipation. Fixing their eyes on us, they pounced. We pounced.

Malbool half-dragged me through the gap in the gate as it slammed shut and locked an instant before two of the beasts slammed into it, nearly pushing it off its sturdy steel hinges. The lions roared deafeningly, swiping their razor claws through the gaps in the iron, missing us by inches. Frustrated and insane with hunger, the animals roared again, before turning back to the feast of human corpses littering the sand. I found myself lying next to Malbool in the dirt of a passageway, an iron gate now between us and the arena. We were alive. Just.

'Are you okay?' he asked as we lay flat on the cool earth, catching our breath. I was cut, bleeding, hurting and bruised, but I was alive and nothing was broken. It was more than I had expected.

'I'm okay,' I replied. I squinted in the dark, straining to see who had opened the gate to save our lives. All I could see was a silhouette but it was unmistakable.

'I couldn't let them eat you,' the voice came again. 'After all, you might be rich, remember?' The humour was a brave attempt to cover the fear in the boy's voice. I stood up slowly and looked him in the face as my eyes adjusted. Mishca.

I pulled the boy close in a strong hug. I didn't know how he was here, but right now I didn't care.

'You're bleeding on me,' he said a moment later. I smiled and released him. It was true. His robe was stained with my sweat and blood.

'We have to go,' Mishca said. 'They'll be here any second.' With that he grabbed a burning torch from the wall and headed down the passage leading away from the gate. We passed through the tunnel and into the darkness.

CHAPTER 29

The darkness lasted thirty seconds before the train passed out of the tunnel. It wasn't the change in light that had caused Shaun to look up from the diary in his lap, but more the noise he had just heard. Indeed, he was so engrossed that he had not realised that it was light again. The noise had been sudden and loud. It was several moments before he registered the sound. Gunshot.

He looked up through the doors separating his carriage from the next. He could not see anything. Turning, he realised that no one else in the carriage, which was only sparsely populated, had paid the sound much attention, obviously passing it off as some shunting that was common on the railway. Immediately he shoved the diary back into his jacket and got up, moving towards the back of the carriage. For the first time, he looked out the window. They were up in the mountains. Interchanging trees and rock faces flashed by. How long had he been travelling? Three, maybe four hours? That meant he was still a good couple from the nearest international airport.

He glanced over his shoulder. The constant cornering of the train made a clear line of sight difficult, but each time the windows of his carriage and the next did line up, Shaun saw a shape. A man. Walking towards him, scanning the aisles. It may have been a passenger looking for his seat after a visit to the bathroom, but Shaun didn't think so. The figure moved with purpose.

Quickly, but not so much as to arouse suspicion, Shaun moved along the carriage, coming to the door at the end and opening it. In a rush of wind and noise he stepped out onto the small platform that connected his carriage to the next. He hung to the rail tightly as the rocking motion of the floor shook him with the movement of the carriages.

As the door closed behind him he looked down across the six feet of open bridge that he would need to cross to get to the next carriage door.

This is why they tell you not to move from your seat! Shaun's brain pointed out.

Waiting for the carriages to align, he quickly stepped across the divide and grabbed onto the door at the other end. It was locked. *Shit.* He glanced back through the door of the carriage he had just left. The man, tall and dark, wearing a blue shirt and black jeans, had already entered. *What are you so scared of?*

Shaun answered his own question as his eyes followed the man's arm down past his rolled-up sleeves and tattooed forearm – all the way to his fingers gripping a black, steel colt .45.

He was carrying it casually, and most of the passengers didn't look up at him. He scanned the carriage quickly and continued on his way. Shaun ducked. The man hadn't seen him yet. He tried the door again. It didn't budge. *Damn!* There was nowhere to go. He searched frantically around the small platform for somewhere to hide. Blue-shirt would be here in seconds.

The handle twisted first one way, then the other, before an eventual click gave evidence to the catch opening. The door gave and the sound flooded the tattooed man's ears. The small platform in front of him was empty. Rocking with the motion of the train, blue-shirt stepped out into the uncertainty of the open platform, reaching his free hand out to the chain-link railing for balance. He stretched for the far door's handle and tried to turn it. Nothing. Locked. He tried harder. Nothing. He turned back towards the other door. How could he possibly have missed—

He didn't see the blow coming. Smashing into blue-shirt's back, Shaun leaped from the roof of the passenger car out onto the platform. He had hidden himself flat on the train's roof as the wind rushed by, and it was an approaching tunnel, rather than an act of bravery, that forced Shaun to take blue-shirt by surprise. He had launched himself moments before the world around them went black.

In the darkness the two men swung wildly, and finally there was a sickening thud as one of the frantic blows connected. Bodies fell, chains rattled and when bright daylight flooded the scene once more, Shaun was on his backside with blood in his mouth.

His opponent was not bleeding at all from the blind swinging match, which might have proven to be an advantage but for the fact that blue-shirt now hung onto one end of the broken chain railing, his legs dangling. The ground sped by beneath him and the man fought desperately as his feet bounced and thudded on the ground.

Right there in the open, bouncing with the uneasy rhythm on the tracks, was the gun. Shaun scrambled forward and grabbed it, then turned on his hands and knees and pointed it at the tattooed man.

'Who are you?' Shaun demanded.

Blue-shirt said something in Italian. Knowing how the gun worked in theory, Shaun pulled on the barrel to fill the chamber.

'Who are you and how did you find me?' Shaun screamed louder.

The man looked up at him in fear. Shaun realised that the man was too terrified to answer his questions, so he did something even he didn't expect: he held out his hand.

The man hesitated for a moment, then let go of the chain with one hand and allowed Shaun to grab him by the wrist and pull him up so his elbow could hook over the metal platform. The man still hung, but now his legs were not bouncing off the ground and he was no longer in immediate danger of falling under the back carriage.

'Now, who are you and how did you find me?' Shaun repeated in more measured tones.

In that instant the ground dropped away from beneath the Italian and gave way to a massive drop. Three hundred feet below, through the gaps in the track, was a wide river. They were on an enormous bridge, and the Italian renewed his struggles to climb onto the platform.

'No!' Shaun said, giving a little on his grip. 'Not until you tell me!'

The Italian refocused his gaze. 'Tracking! You are being tracked. A device was planted on you.'

'Device? A tracking device? But when?' Shaun thought back, replaying the events in his mind. Yes, after Lauren had been shot.

The female cop. She had touched him on the shoulder to turn him away from the bed. To comfort him. She had pushed too hard, he remembered.

Instantly he struggled out of his jacket with his free arm, taking a moment before realising he could not take it off and maintain his grip on this man.

'Who are you? Why do you want to kill me? Why did you kill Lauren?' Shaun persisted.

'We want what you have. We want the map. We want—' Suddenly the Italian's face turned ashen white as the chain railing broke away. In an instant Shaun fell forward under the doubling of weight and slid onto his stomach halfway off the platform. Instinctively he dropped the gun and grabbed at the edge. The Italian's free hand pulled at Shaun's jacket, loosening the diary, which had sat precariously in the inner pocket.

'Arrrgghhh!' Shaun screamed under the weight. The Italian dangled freely out over the water below. Shaun hung grimly, his feet hooked around the opposite side of the platform, his free hand wrapped round its edge, his torso hanging off up to his navel.

Then, there was a strange change in the sound of the wind. The rushing whoosh sucked in and sounded like a hollow howl. Shaun knew the sound. It was the sound of an approaching tunnel. The Italian had seen it too, and Shaun fought desperately to pull them both back up.

'Please! Please, let me go. Let me fall into the water!' The Italian begged suddenly. Shaun didn't understand. He turned to see the approaching rock wall of the tunnel and then looked down at the water below. The fall might kill the man, but not as definitively as the wall of stone rushing towards him at sixty miles an hour. *No!* He wanted answers. He could not let the man—

'Please! You must let go now. Now or I don't have time to hit the water.'

Shaun's hand opened.

The Italian disappeared out of sight almost instantly, pulling Shaun's jacket with him just as Shaun plucked the diary from it. Shaun would never know blue-shirt's fate. Without the added weight, he scrambled back onto the platform just as the tunnel wall plunged him back into darkness.

In one hand he gripped the diary. The gun bounced on the platform and Shaun noticed a small lever on the side of the weapon. Above it was the word 'safety' and the lever pointed to 'on'. Shaun flicked the lever and re-entered the carriage.

CHAPTER 30

Cardinal François Le Clerque sat in quiet contemplation. He had not expected the news they had just given him. Losing the school teacher was not part of the plan. Now he had to decide what to do about it. He thumbed again through the pile of papers on his desk. The bundle had been recovered from a motel in south-east America. Hebrew mostly. He had translated these personally.

Much of it was interesting, but not particularly relevant to the task at hand. In any other situation, finding documents of this kind, in this condition, would have been cause for celebration, but there was still no map. He'd had the documents analysed, of course. They were all two thousand years old or more, but ... there was no map. The frustration gnawed at him.

He had been a close friend of Müller for more than a decade and had the old fool's implicit trust. Indeed, it had been Le Clerque's influence over the conclave, including 'suggestions' to certain council members about the way they should vote, that had guaranteed the German's rise to the papacy.

What would the old man think now if he knew what was happening? Ah, it wasn't his concern. Every Pope had their own agenda, a legacy they wished to leave. Why was it that they all cared so much about making their impression on this Church? Le Clerque had grander ambitions, and Müller was running out of time. The cancer eating away at his body would soon force the old German to retire – a move almost unheard of in the papacy, but Le Clerque knew that this was the pontiff's intention. The congregation of cardinals would again vote, and Le Clerque had seen to it that this time when the white smoke rose, he would ascend to the station of Holy See. Of the one hundred and fifteen cardinals who would vote, Le Clerque had 'persuasive information' on eighty-three of them.

Müller had been a close personal friend and confidant of his predecessor, the Polish pontiff Nicholas II, and yet, not even he had known what the old man had really been up to. Müller had not known about The Facility.

It was now Le Clerque's official duty to head up the commission that was investigating the multitude of unanswered questions that the death of Nicholas II, back in 2005, had left. Suddenly it had come to light that the old man had secrets; secrets not shared with even his closest friends, nor any of the other high-ranking members of the cloth. Vatican resources had been used. Vatican connections had been exploited.

There was even a select group of loosely associated Vatican employees whom the cardinal was still ferreting out. He shook his head.

'How did you keep it quiet for so long, Karol?' he said to himself, imagining the old Pope in the room with him. The phone rang, breaking his concentration.

'Bonjour?' It was his private line, and he knew that anyone calling on this number would have news he wanted to hear.

'It's me. We checked all the passenger manifests for the tickets he bought. He's boarding Flight 912 to Madrid this morning.'

'Madrid?' the Frenchman asked, a little surprised.

'Yes, your Eminence, but there's something else. The man who met Alberto in the cafe last year here in Paris – we believe he has been in Madrid for some months now.'

Le Clerque had taken care of Alberto, but the other man had escaped his team.

'They are going to meet?'

'We do not know, but it would seem a logical assumption. Do you want us to move and intercept?'

The cardinal considered. 'No ... two birds. Let him lead us to Mr Black, then get that map.'

'Yes, your Eminence. We have a unit on its way as we speak.'

CHAPTER 31

The airport at Richmond, Virginia, was an interesting hybrid of cultures. Further south, in Raleigh–Durham, or further down to Myrtle Beach, the locals were mostly affluent Caucasians. Up here in Richmond, Shaun was close enough to DC to see the influence of true multiculturalism. Faces of every descent passed him, observed him briefly, then looked away to carry on with their business.

He moved briskly along a silver travelator. He had no luggage and had passed through check-in easily, grateful Lauren had made him carry his passport rather than pack it. The idea of sneaking the gun on the flight had crossed his mind briefly, but the remainder of the train trip had proved uneventful, and Shaun had discarded the gun in a trash can outside the train platform.

After all this time, it had been his jacket. They had planted a bug on it. He had been so paranoid about using his phone. The time and energy he could have saved if he had just used his phone! Still, he had taken seven cabs to get to the airport, swapping at various ill-sited interchange points, making attempts to follow him all but impossible. That is, if they didn't already know he was heading to the airport. But how would they? For all they knew, Shaun was now lying at the bottom of a river somewhere after falling from an Amtrak train.

Using his credit card to buy a plane ticket was not something Shaun had wanted to do. He was getting close to maxing out the card, and he knew that the moment he used it he would give away his location, but he had run out of options. It was not a comforting prospect.

He was going to need money from his brother. He hoped Tim had received that desperate email and wired some across. After buying a plane ticket to Madrid, Tokyo, Sydney and Quito, Shaun felt that if he was going to be tracked, at least he had not made it easy for them.

He arrived at his gate and saw the casual crowd milling in the lounges. Absently his finger traced the looping symbol on the front of the diary, which now hung in a brightly coloured, complimentary airport bag hanging from his shoulder. It stood out in stark contrast to the crumpled, worn and stained clothes he wore, which reflected the way he felt. Lack of sleep and too many jolts of adrenaline entering his body in too short a time span had wrung him out and beaten him flat.

He focused again on the facts at hand. Saul, the author of this account, was a part of a secret organisation which had trained a group of agents at a place called 'The Facility', to travel into the past and interview historical figures. What a wild concept. What a totally, amazingly wild concept. Indeed, the whole idea was one that had intrigued and engaged Shaun for much of his professional life, although he was more concerned with the mechanics of the whole process than what its eventual application might be.

Who would you meet? his brain prompted.

'Da Vinci,' Shaun said aloud.

'Excuse me?' the woman behind the counter asked.

'What?' he said, staring blankly at her.

'I asked you what kind of coffee you'd like,' the woman said, her big white teeth shining a friendly smile out from her smooth dark-brown skin. 'I don't think we got anything called a "Da Vinci", although you might find that at Starbucks. We just stick to your regular old cappuccino, latté or flat white. Unless, that is, you'd like yourself a little short black?' the woman asked with a wink and a giggle.

'Nuh, um, just a ...' he played with what little change he still had in his pocket. 'Just a cappuccino, thanks,' he said ignoring her joke.

So, if you could meet anyone in history and ask them anything, it would be Leonardo Da Vinci?

'Or Isaac Newton, or Einstein,' Shaun said, again lost in his thoughts.

'You sure you don't wanna switch to decaf?'

Shaun took the coffee, paid and walked away, distracted.

Fontéyne had said that there were others: officers assigned to others. For what? To interview them? To ask all the great minds of history, 'Why?' To ask them, 'How?' To ask them all the things we want to know in this world today? Or maybe to tell them what was coming? What a concept!

He looked at the diary as he sat down and pulled it out from his bag. He was about to get on a plane to take him to Spain. Why? Because he believed it all? Because he believed that this book was a diary written by a man from modern-day America sent back two thousand years into the past? No. No, he wasn't doing it because he believed it; he was doing it because he didn't know what else to do. Lauren was gone. Lauren was killed for this. Someone believed it, and someone would kill to get it, and that was enough.

'If you went back to interview someone would you tell them about the future? What would you do if you saw something happening that you didn't like? Would you change it? Would you interfere? *Could* you change it? Or was the fact that it happened one way proof that it could not have happened any other way?' Shaun found himself talking out loud again.

'You're weird, mister,' a voice said from beside him. He looked over at the little girl who had crawled over the seats to the one next to him. 'Who are you talking to?' she asked.

Shaun smiled. 'I'm talking to my brain,' he answered her.

'Your brain?' she asked, screwing her face up in a way that only little girls can.

'Yeah. Sometimes I ask my brain questions and it goes away and works on the answers while I do other things,' Shaun said.

'How can you do other things while your brain is answering questions?' she persisted, curling her top lip to expose the large gap waiting for her front tooth to arrive.

'Well, you see your teeth there?' he said pointing at the girl's mouth.

'Uh huh.'

'Well, it's kind of like that. Your brain is telling your new tooth it's time to come down, but you're off playing with your friends.'

She considered this for a moment, then beamed. 'My friend Jessie has a new doll house!'

'Does she now?' he said, loving the way a child's mind considered all things, cosmic and trivial, equally important.

'Susan, come away and stop bothering that man,' the girl's mother said from a row back after realising her daughter had again gone missing. 'I'm sorry. She just disappears sometimes. I have to watch her like a hawk.'

'It's okay. When I was a kid I ran off on my mom in the museum and sat by the stuffed polar bear in the corner for hours.' The woman smiled, didn't see the relevance, and pulled her daughter back by the arm gently.

He thought back to that moment when his mother came to find him; to her face as she saw him sitting alone, any anger she had far outweighed by the sense of relief she felt. What he wouldn't give to see his mother's face again. What he wouldn't give to go back and tell them not to go to church that morning. He would have played sick; he would have done anything if he had known.

If he had known ... That's what it came down to in life. You think the important things are whether you get your assignment done in time, or whether you'll be late to that boardroom meeting or miss that job you were pitching for. Then the universe comes along and reminds you that the important things in life are the cars in your blind spot that sideswipe you at eight-twenty on a Sunday morning. No, he knew that if he could go back and speak to anyone in history, it would be to his mother and father. It would be to tell them that he had done okay. To tell them that he loved them. Da Vinci could wait.

'This is the first and final boarding call for flight LH912 to Madrid. Your plane is now ready for boarding through gate twelve,' a woman's voice came over the PA system.

Twenty minutes later, he was seated in the middle seat on the far right of the plane, bounded on each side by fellow passengers. The man on his left was enormous. Shaun tried not to get caught staring at the rolls of fat on is neck, but it was mesmerising, reminding him of one of those wrinkled pug dogs.

The older woman on his right sat with her thin spectacles sliding down her nose as she stared intently out the window, willing herself away from the two men on her left, one obese and sweaty, the other unkempt and unwashed.

Shaun didn't care. He didn't even notice when the huge jumbo roared to life and sped down the runway. For his first experience in a plane, Shaun Strickland missed the best part, but it was a good trade, he thought later, considering he was about to read the most important information of his life.

CHAPTER 32

The tunnels were dark and forbidding. The orange light from Mishca's torch filled a circle that danced out only feet in front of us. He had taken us down several sets of stairs and through countless doors seemingly hidden in the stone.

'This way takes us to tunnels that lead under the city,' Mishca said without slowing his pace.

'I left my post at gate four when I saw you on the far side of the arena. I told my supervisor that I had to go to the toilet. He will be looking for me by now.'

'What are you doing here?' I finally brought myself to ask. 'I thought you were dead.'

'No. They beat me pretty good, but then they gave me work to do. I was assigned to the arena straight away. They wanted me to assist in running the fights, you know, setting up the armour and bringing the gladiators to their chambers and everything like that. They make it clear that for a slave, the only way to survive is to do as I am told.' He touched the back of his head absently. 'They make it very clear.'

Just then voices drifted down the tunnel from behind us. How did they know where we were? Obviously Mishca was not the only one who knew these tunnels. The voices were not far.

'Where do these tunnels lead?' I asked him.

'Well,' he began, 'they connect all kinds of things. I know some of them lead out into the city at lots of different places, and some of them lead to where they keep the animals.'

'Where they keep the beasts?' Malbool asked exasperated.

'Do not worry, there are big iron gates that separate us from those chambers.' As if on cue another sound echoed down the tunnel. This sound was not human. This sound was unearthly, deep, tormented. The roar of a beast.

'And they wouldn't open those gates for any reason would they?' I asked Mishca rhetorically. As one, we quickened our pace and drove into the darkness, away from the sound.

It was a labyrinth, a maze unseen by human eyes for decades. The ground changed from dirt to rock and then finally to inch-deep water. The dampness came from everywhere: the walls, the roof, and the very stones themselves. The only thing on my mind, however, was the intermittent guttural sounds that permeated the darkness.

I was terrified. Whether it was the culmination of a day of defending my life, or the eeriness of the atmosphere, all the clichés suddenly held weight: I felt my skin crawl, my hairs stand up and my blood run cold.

'Mishca! What's the quickest way out of the city?' I asked. The boy hesitated. 'I ... I don't' know,' he said.

'The aqueducts,' Malbool said suddenly. 'If we can get to the aqueducts, we can follow them all the way up into the mountains.'

'I don't want to go to the mountains. I want to go to the sea. I need a boat to Israel ... I mean, Judea.'

The roar came again. Then another sound. Not like a lion, but something much, much bigger.

'What is that?' I asked, beginning to visualise all manner of fierce creatures moving relentlessly down the passageway. We were still travelling at a rapid pace, trusting Mishca's decisions when we came to twists and turns in the tunnels.

'What about the river?' I asked. 'Malbool, you said there's a river that runs through the centre of the city. Surely that would be our best way to the ocean?'

'It would, but to get there we would have to leave the Coliseum by one of the gates, which would be heavily guarded by now. I think also that the river might be hard to travel on unnoticed—'

The sound that silenced Malbool was an unnaturally deep growl, felt more than heard, as if from below the range of normal human hearing. It resonated in our stomachs, and we froze. It was right in front of us.

At once the three of us strained our eyes in the darkness, searching out beyond the torchlight. There. A glint. The reflective yellow of eyes.

'Do you—' Malbool began in a whisper.

'I see it,' I whispered back, taking the torch from the terrified boy and pulling him by the arm behind us.

Cats. Cats' eyes glowed yellow. But more disturbing than the thought of a cat standing before us in the darkness, was the distance between the eyes. Too wide. If these were the eyes of a cat, it was the largest cat on earth.

The growl came again, moving towards us. The sound betrayed the creature's proportions. Massive. Heavy. Was this where they kept some monster of an animal long since forgotten in my time? Some great, giant feline saved for those who tried to escape through the bowels of the Coliseum?

We began to back up, very, very slowly.

Another sound. Behind us. Padding paws. Trapped.

'A drink for you, sir?' the stewardess asked.

'Huh?' Shaun looked up.

'A drink? Would you like one?' She beamed a rehearsed smile. For a moment he didn't understand. A drink? Didn't she know he was about to be eaten by a ... something? But no. It wasn't him. The diary had a strange effect. He felt such an empathy with what was happening that he began to truly feel the fear leap out from the page. It weaved around him and only reluctantly released him back into the real world.

'Ah, I want a ... uh ... just a coffee.'

'Sure,' the stewardess said with another smile. She began to pour some steaming liquid from a silver pot.

'Good book?' a voice asked from next to him. He looked over. Didn't these people know? Didn't they know what was happening?

Lauren was dead, people were trying to kill him and he was – no, *Saul* was about to be eaten by something huge.

'Yeah, it's not bad,' Shaun replied, trying not to engage in conversation.

'I don't read much, myself,' the large American man said. 'I prefer movies. Love to sit back and watch movies. Used to have to go out to the video store, but it's downloads now.'

'That's nice.' Shaun commented in as indifferent a way as he could muster.

'Ladies and gentlemen.' The captain's voice came over the in-flight speakers, 'we're now cruising at just over thirty-five thousand feet and travelling at just under six hundred miles an hour.' He paused in the way that only plane captains can do. 'Ahhhh, the weather outside is a sunny minus twenty-nine degrees Fahrenheit, ahhhhh, that's Celsius thirty-four below.'

Good, I'll remember that in case I decide to go for a walk out there later. Shaun's brain was as irritated as he was.

He wriggled back into his reading position, lodged between the obese man and the woman, he could not go anywhere even if he wanted to. Trapped.

CHAPTER 33

Trapped. Mishca was terrified of whatever the creatures were before us and behind us in the darkness. Hunting us. Stalking us. My eyes absorbed our surroundings. The walls were made of rough stone, hewn out of the existing rock. I held the torch high and saw that the tunnels were tall, at least as tall as they were wide. I grabbed Mishca roughly with my spare arm and lifted him onto the wall.

'Climb!' I commanded harshly, to break the paralysis his fear had caused.

'Malbool, can you—'

But the African was already halfway up the other wall, finding hand- and footholds easily.

Then, from behind us, the cats crept forward into the sphere of torchlight. Four of them. Their black fur seemed to suck the light of the torch in, making their forms hard to define against the darkness beyond.

I jammed the torch into a crack in the wall and began to climb. Absently, I flicked the switch to record with my tongue. The panthers saw their prey, but not before something else, something huge, charged.

A massive bulk filled the tunnel, its mouth open wider than seemed possible. Two of the panthers had already launched into the air towards Mishca, and their collision with the massive silver form that slammed them from the air was sickening and welcome all at once. The cats had not seen the hippo as it approached steadily from beyond the torchlight, but they felt it now.

'What the?' I spluttered in amazement. No sooner had the two panthers crunched to the ground than the next two leaped onto the enraged, giant hippopotamus. In other circumstances, I might have been interested to find out the outcome of such a contest, but as it was, I cared only enough to realise that this was our chance.

Heaving its massive bulk, the hippo passed straight under us as it caught and crushed one of the cats in its jaws. The cracking and crunching of cartilage made a sickening sound that echoed through the tunnel.

Malbool was the first to move. He dropped from where he was hanging and landed with a thud on the dirt floor. The torch I had jammed into the side of the arch was knocked clear with the hippo's charge and now lay burning on the ground, right in the middle of the animal fight.

Claws and flesh flew, and the hippo slammed against the tunnel walls, crushing another cat and giving me a chance to grab Mishca and hurl him to the ground behind the grey beast. I looked down and saw the torch being kicked and scuffled near the thrashing hippo's feet. The dust and dirt sprayed up, teasing the flame, but the fire didn't die. Watching the small fire spin and dance in the fray, I realised the horrible truth: we needed that torch – if that light went out, so did our chance of finding our way through these tunnels.

One of the panthers flew into the stone wall, its back breaking with another sickening crunch as the hippo flung its head with surprising force. The torch broke in half as a massive grey foot slammed down, splintering the handle. The flame dipped and died.

For an instant.

The fire struggled to breathe as it bent beneath impacts from every direction. With the final panther clinging to the neck of the furiously thrashing hippo, the violence of the attack was immense. The massive beast fought hard to get the parasite off its neck, but the cat had a death hold and would not let go. Sharp claws disappeared into the hippo's hide. The silken black feline hung to the underside of the hippo's chest, its teeth moving only to readjust their grip on the wound that was rapidly opening and filling with blood. I looked at the animals struggling, and looked at the torch beneath them. There was no way I could reach it.

My fingers began to tremble and I knew that even the simple task of clinging to the wall would soon be beyond me. My shoulder ached and I became aware of my injuries once again, unable to keep the pain at bay much longer. I was slipping.

From beneath the hippo, a hand emerged holding the torch. Mishca's hand. Then I saw both the bravest and stupidest thing I had yet witnessed.

The boy had scrambled between the dancing feet of the hippo and now had the broken but still burning torch in his hand. Then, instead of scrambling out, he paused and thrust the flame up under the panther's back as it hung from the flailing beast it was attacking.

As if the great cat were doused in a flammable liquid, its fur ignited with a WHOOP! *and Mishca rolled clear. At once the light from the new source of flame illuminated the passageway. The thick smoke and smell of burning animal flesh drifted up to where I was losing my hold on the wall. I fell.*

I hit the back of the hippo and bounced off its rear end, but the animal didn't notice. It now sank to its knees, losing consciousness from lack of blood. The flaming panther roared and hissed in agony. It was an ungodly sound. Gagging from the smoke, I fell into the dust behind the two animals and felt a hand grip underneath my arm and drag me clear.

'No time to rest,' came the heavily accented African voice. 'A couple of these other panthers are not quite dead. We have to get clear of the tunnels.'

Mishca appeared with what little remained of the torch. I felt as if I was going to pass out from the exertion, but I pressed on into the darkness. My body refused, but my mind insisted.

'Mishca,' I said, still reeling from the boy's amazing bravery, 'take us to the aqueducts.'

Shaun exhaled.

CHAPTER 34

Shaun Strickland's first experience outside the United States was like being thrust into the twilight zone. As he wandered through the airport baggage claim in Madrid international airport, he was horrified to see people smoking everywhere. In America, you just simply didn't smoke inside – the foul smell added to his sense of disorientation.

Everyone around him rattled off sounds, but he had no idea what they were saying. He felt lost, confused and very alone.

Shaun went straight to the information counter and waited in the queue. At last an exotic-looking, dark-haired girl looked up at him and said, '*Hola! Como está usted?*'

Shaun stared at the girl. 'Ah, do you speak English?'

'Of course,' the information girl responded with a British slant to her accent.

'Ah, I need to get to ... Sol?' Shaun stammered, expecting this request to throw the young woman into a panic. Without missing a beat, however, she drew a pamphlet from the counter-stand next to her and began to write on it.

'Choo are here,' she said, circling the white block representing the airport. Shaun was relieved to see that the map was in English. 'If choo go outside to the left choo will see the subway trains, mmm ... yes, and then choo go to the man in the box and ask for a ticket to Sol, and take the train from Platform Three.'

'Oh, okay then. That's very helpful. Thank you,' he said, looking at the map.

'Do choo have Euro?' she asked, as if predicting all the problems this American, one off the production line, would have in the next few moments.

'Ah, no. How do I?'

'There is a machine outside on the right. And here,' the woman said as she produced another, slightly thicker pamphlet that read 'Useful

Phrases' in big bold writing on the cover just under a red title 'Welcome to Madrid'.

'Ah, thanks,' Shaun said, amazed he hadn't given this stuff a thought until now. Like so many things in life, getting around was something he had taken for granted.

He bustled through the airport until he came to the ATM the girl had spoken about, and realised that he would have to chance using his card to get some cash. If they were indeed tracking him, they would take a while to get to Spain, by which point he hoped to have met with the man on the phone.

If they're not already here, his brain cut in.

He withdrew one hundred Euro and waited for the printout of his receipt. The money spat out followed by the receipt: Available balance: €60,245.

Shaun looked again. There had to be some mistake. Sixty thousand Euro? That equated to about eighty thousand American dollars. He had asked his brother for some cash, but Tim wasn't exactly the generous type – not eighty-grand generous. By his last recollection Shaun was overdrawn on his account, so this sudden injection of funds made him very nervous.

Someone had accessed his account and put money in. That meant that someone might just as easily be able to take it out. He thought for a moment, then decided to shove his card in again. He punched in €1000, and was greeted with a message saying that the maximum daily limit was €500. He took the additional €400 and headed for the train.

Paranoia kept Shaun company in the standing-room-only rail carriage. The train was packed with commuters and he stood not too far from the double sliding doors, holding a hand strap dangling from the roof to stop him from careening into other passengers as they swayed and lurched in time. The coloured key showed that he was only two stops from the station marked 'Sol'. According to his pamphlet, Sol was the very centre of downtown Madrid, with great nightlife and a reputation as a tourist mecca. Excellent. Great. Perhaps he could go for a dance after he escaped the villainous killers.

Right after you discover whether there is a video recording of an interview with Jesus in a remote cave somewhere, his brain reminded him.

That's what this was really all about. It wasn't about the diary – but then again, no one had read the diary. When it came to Shaun it had been sealed airtight, so no one could know what he knew. No one knew about Graeme Fontéyne, so maybe no one knew about the interview.

'*Próxima estación – Sol*,' a voice came over the train's internal speaker system. Sure enough, before two minutes were up, the doors opened and people spilled out onto the underground platform at Madrid's Plaza del Sol train station, and Shaun tumbled out with them. He watched the train pull away into the tunnel before he followed the crowd up the stairs and could hear the sounds of the street spilling down from above.

The bright sunlight and the oppressive heat struck him at once. He looked around blinking, and started to absorb how life looked outside the United States.

To Shaun, it was like a fairytale. All the buildings were old in their style, but not in their decor. And, if this was downtown Madrid, where were the skyscrapers? Where were the huge steel-and-glass structures that dominated every major city in America? The tallest building here was what looked like a department store called Corte de Ingles. At four storeys, it was hardly worthy of its own observation deck.

The streets were narrow and the people hurried about in their individual, busy lives. Shaun found himself standing in the middle of a small plaza, a triangular pinnacle where four roads converged at strange angles. Over on the right were a couple of open-topped tourist buses.

'*Limosnas para sin brazos! Limosnas para sin brazos!*' The sound came from his left. '*Limosnas para sin brazos! Limosnas para sin brazos!*' The voice came from the other side of the stairs and was punctuated by the sound of coins jingling in a metal cup. He could not quite see who was talking through the crowd coming up out of the subway. '*Limosnas para sin brazos! Limosnas para sin brazos!*' *CHINK! CHINK! CHINK!* The voice came again, and Shaun thought it sounded like someone talking with a mouth full of food. Over and over: '*Limosnas para sin brazos!*'

And then, as a break in the crowd came, he saw why. In the heat, a man stood alone at the top of the subway stairs in a sweaty white singlet and old black tracksuit pants. His black curls were the universal greasy unwashed hair of a beggar, and he held a metal cup in his mouth. He spoke again, with the cup still between his teeth. '*Limosnas para sin brazos! Limosnas para sin brazos!*' Then he shook the cup making a small chinking sound as the few coins it possessed rattled. Shaun looked at the man, but the man paid no attention. The busy Madridians passed by him without so much as a second glance, and then Shaun saw why the man held the cup in his mouth. He had no arms. His contact.

Small bulbs swelled where his arms should have been, and he waved the little stumps as he spoke. Shaun pushed his way through the throng coming up from the station as yet another subway carriage emptied its load onto the Spanish street.

Standing right next to the man, he saw the milkiness of the beggar's eyes. How the hell did someone survive in this life with no arms, let alone blind? He felt suddenly very guilty and ashamed of himself, simply for being able to look around and see what this man could not. He reached into his pocket and pulled out a twenty-euro note, and placed it in the cup in between shakes. Then he looked into the man's face and asked, 'Where is the chicken?'

'*Limosnas para sin brazos! Limosnas para sin brazos!*' the man blared back at Shaun, not realising that he had just put money into the tin without the rattle of coins.

Shaun tried again. 'Where is the chicken?' he asked more insistently. The man shook his can and continued his calls, rocking from side to side like Ray Charles. Shaun began to feel frustrated. He did not come to Spain for this.

'Answer the fucking question!' he growled. 'Where is that stupid fucking chicken?'

The man appeared to slow in his rocking motion for a moment, staring with his milky white irises, obviously detecting that someone was getting angry at him, but then he shook his can and called again.

'Okay ... there had to be some reason to this,' Shaun mused. Then he looked down at his pamphlet.

'In the restaurant' it read. He followed the heading down to the list of phrases below it. 'Where are the toilets?' then next to it was a phonetic version of the Spanish for the same phrase. '*Don-de estan los servisios.*'

Shaun stared at it. For a smart man, he was truly an idiot sometimes, Lauren used to chide him. He wasn't in Masonville now, he was in Sol, Madrid. Shaun scanned the section further.

'Ordering: I would like the chicken, please,' and then across from it '*Yo qui-ero tener el pollo (poy-yo).*'

He studied the translation, then looked back at the man. He was beginning to draw stares from the passers-by, it wasn't often someone hassled a blind armless guy on the street. But Shaun didn't care. He had come this far. He wanted to make those people who killed Lauren pay, and the mysterious voice that had summoned him here was his only lead.

He took a breath to calm himself, then said slowly and clearly, '*Donde ésta el pollo?*'

'*Limosnas para sin ...*' the man stopped.

His rhythmic swaying came to a slow halt and then, through the milky whiteness of his eyes, Shaun swore he saw something move. 'You can hear me!' he exclaimed. '*Donde ésta el pollo?*' he then repeated. '*Donde ésta el pollo?*'

All of a sudden, the man began to sway back and forth again and shook his can, but in between shakes his chant changed – but just once.

'*El pollo ésta en Roma! Limosnas para sin brazos!*'

'What? What did you say?' Shaun asked. The beggar, though, was back to rocking to and fro, calling his mantra once again to the world. Shaun watched him for a minute then turned away. He looked up and saw, of all things, a McDonald's on the corner. At least that creepy, smiling clown was a constant.

'*El pollo ésta en Roma*,' Shaun repeated to himself, not quite grasping the meaning of the words straight away. He walked into the restaurant and grabbed a pile of napkins, then slumped into a seat. He scribbled the phonetic sounds he had heard the man say, and then sat back to try to make sense of it all.

He looked at the napkin. 'Roma? Roma?'

Rome, you idiot! Finally, his brain kicked in.

'The chicken is in Rome? Are you kidding me?'

'Not at all. You haven't had your passport stolen yet, have you?'

Shaun spun quickly. Sitting next to him, eating a burger with some kind of white sauce spilling between his fingers, was a pudgy man with a slicked-back ponytail of mottled, dark-coloured hair. The man wore a long black coat and thin, black-rimmed glasses, and looked to be about forty, although it was difficult to tell.

'Excuse me?' Shaun said, then, basically because he could not think of anything else to say, he asked: 'Are you the chicken?'

'Well,' the man said, swallowing the last of the fillet burger he was devouring, 'let's just say, the chicken is within me.' The man smiled and licked his lips.

The joke was lost on Shaun. He looked at this man, trying to make sense of what this was all about.

The man held out his hand in an offer of a handshake. 'David Black,' he said.

Shaun looked at the hand. He wasn't sure how to feel. In one sense he was relieved beyond belief that he had finally made contact with the man he assumed had called him and instructed him to come to Madrid. In another sense, he was enraged at this man's casual demeanour. Slowly, tentatively, Shaun reached out and shook David's outstretched hand. To Shaun's great surprise, the man pulled him into an embrace and held him tight. It was the hold of a long-lost friend, but as innocent as it may have been, it caught Shaun off guard and he pulled out of David's grasp.

'I'm sorry,' David said quickly. 'It's just that, well, it's *you*! It's really you. You're here, right here in front of me. It's just a bit hard to believe.'

'Okay, I'm talking to you because you're the only one who speaks English around here, but this conversation won't last very long unless you stop weirding me out and start giving me some answers,' Shaun said, looking over the other man, who was now standing. He was about three inches shorter than Shaun, but looked a good deal heavier. He had the look of a man who spent a lot of time indoors. Even in the bright sunshine and heat of Madrid, David Black had managed to stay pasty white.

'Okay, okay. It's really you. Okay, look, we can't talk here, let's take a walk.'

David led the way out of the little restaurant and diagonally up a cobblestone side street. Not seen from the main road, it appeared to be one of the many walk-only streets around the place. It was a metropolis for shoppers, with stores ranging in wares from silks to Toledo swords. It was a busy mid morning in the Spanish capital and the businesses had kicked into full swing. Shaun could not even remember which day it was. A man who didn't know what day it was, was either drunk, an idiot or rich, Shaun's father used to say. Shaun knew he wasn't drunk or rich – well, not until this morning.

The narrow street led up a hill for several blocks before opening out onto one of the most beautiful places Shaun had ever seen in a city.

It was a large paved square about the size of a football field, enclosed by a solid wall of three-storey buildings on all sides. Most of the lower levels held cafes snuggled among the arches, but Shaun guessed that the thin windows of the upper levels belonged to backpackers' accommodation and the like. There was a sign on a wall saying 'Plaza Mayor'.

Shaun watched curiously as David Black followed a crisscrossing grid of stonework on the floor. He turned sharply and then turned again at right angles.

'Okay,' Shaun said as he walked, grabbing his new tour guide by the arm, 'this is far enough. Who are you, how do you know me, and what do you want?'

'Wow, that really sums it all up, doesn't it?' David replied, still walking.

'Look, just on the other side of this square is the Palacio Real. There's a large park, and it'll be safe to talk there.'

'What's with all the crisscrossing crap?' Shaun asked sternly, his patience beginning to fray.

'It's nothing, just protocol ... I have a friend watching. If I walk in a certain pattern, he knows I've found you; if I walk in another, then I am with someone, ah, not friendly,' David continued, starting for the other end of the plaza.

'Who says I'm friendly?' Shaun countered, not sounding threatening at all. 'Is this friend of yours blind as well?' he added, referring to the beggar.

'Ah, Jeorge? He's not blind. He wears white contacts because he doesn't like it when people stare at him.'

'Contacts? How does he get them out? Or in, for that matter?'

'Mostly his wife helps him, or one of his kids.'

Shaun shook his head and let it go. They passed through the crowd and crossed another busy street, coming to a fence of tall iron spikes. Beyond the fence was a large, lush and heavily wooded park.

Shaun glanced around nervously. He was beginning to think that coming to Spain was a bad idea. The instant they passed the threshold of the iron-spiked gate and moved into the cover of the trees, however, David's manner changed entirely.

'Okay, listen to me: the trees keep us safe for a while; they can't see us here,' David said, the chirpy tone gone from his voice, replaced by a new seriousness. 'I've spent the best part of the last two years trying to find you,' he continued, walking more slowly. 'I have reason to believe that you're in danger.'

'In danger!' Shaun almost laughed. 'Listen, I've been on the run for the last three days. My wife has been murdered, there are some crazy Mafia cops after me, and I've read some stuff that'll keep you up at night.'

'They've found you? They killed your—' David looked to the ground.

'Found me is an understatement! You have no idea.' Shaun paused. 'Who's "they"?'

David stopped.

'I'm working on it. About six years ago I used to be a researcher for a company called Newcom Technologies. We were a big research and development house and I was on some project they were paying a truckload for. I was the only researcher though. They had this ... disc. This disc that they'd found in France somewhere. It was weird, really weird. It was tiny, like the size of a button, but apparently someone had hired Newcom to find out what was on this disc. Now, it was about three years worth of work just to come up with the idea that it was some kind of digital video. The data was encoded on the disc in a way no one had ever seen before. That's when they brought me in.'

'Why you?'

'Well,' David said a little modestly, 'I'm the best video engineer in the world.' He paused to no applause. 'So, the stuff on this disc, it was like ... Let me put it this way: I was the best in the world, and it was a full-time job for me six days a week to crack this code, to work out the format it was recorded in. It became my obsession.'

'Well, surely there aren't that many options,' Shaun said, showing his ignorance on the subject. David shot him a look that politely told him to shut up.

'The thing is, this data wasn't in a codec that existed yet. Nothing like it existed. It was so far ahead of anything else in the world that it was like finding an F18 in ancient Rome.'

Funny you should mention Ancient Rome, Shaun's brain said, squinting its mental eyes.

'Anyway, I finally cracked it, but I was under strict instructions not to watch any of it. So, my boss, Randy, calls in the guys who had been paying us so much and they come in and sit and watch.'

'And what did they see?'

'Nothing. Well, nothing really, it was just some text. The rest of the disc was just black. I didn't really realise the significance of what the text said at the time, I was just all hyped up because I had got an image. The fact that there was anything at all there meant that I had been successful, and that we were going to take this new codec to the market and make a mint off it.'

'And what did it say? Do you remember?'

'Do I remember!? I know every pixel. It said: "IDENT: 0012. SUBJECT: Napoleon Bonaparte. OFFICER: X10."'

Shaun nearly tripped where he stood. 'Officer X10? Are you sure?' he asked, though he knew it was not the sort of thing someone randomly made up.

'That means something to you, doesn't it? I knew it would!' David's enthusiasm built and he started to walk again, prompting Shaun to do the same.

'Right after that, the Europeans took the player I had built, and Randy fired me. I looked up on the TV in a bar that night to find that my house had been shot up and Randy had been killed. So, I went into hiding. Stayed off the grid, and tried to find out what the hell was going on.'

'And did you?'

'Yeah. Well, sort of. The biggest thing is that I was determined that my work wouldn't go to waste, so I used some contacts I had on the net to put the word out that I had a player for this disc, which was true – and also that I had found another disc, which I hadn't. I established a certain contact protocol to protect my identity, which led me to a meeting with someone who did have another disc. We met at a cafe in Paris. He brought the disc, I brought the player, and it worked.'

'Who was he?'

'His name was Alberto. He was Spanish. But he mentioned the name of an Italian before he died.'

'Before he died?'

'They shot him then and there. I think they had been after him for a long time. I don't know if they used me to get to him. At the time I thought they didn't know where I was. I had been living in the attic of a crazy woman's house in Paris, and I hadn't seen them for months so I thought I'd finally lost them. But I hadn't lost them at all. They were waiting. They were waiting for him and they shot him through the back of the head in the middle of the cafe. I ran, and took the unit with me, with the disc still inside.'

'Why didn't they shoot you?'

'I think they thought they could use me.'

'Use you for what?'

'To find you.'

Shaun's blood stopped where it was in his veins. Suddenly he saw it, clearly. He had been set up.

CHAPTER 35

Shaun had flown all the way to Madrid, avoiding detection the entire time, and keeping the diary safe, and now he had walked straight into their trap. He was about to bolt when David saw the look on his face.

'No, no, no, don't worry!' he said, trying to be reassuring. 'They don't know you're here. There's a web-cam on the Plaza Mayor that I have monitored. When I walk a certain pattern along the grid of the paving, it sends a signal to disrupt the satellite feed they use to monitor me.'

'Satellite? They monitor you with a satellite? Who are these people? Government? Military?'

'Ah, there's a bit more to it than that. Look, there's something I want you to see.'

David veered off onto the grass among the trees. He came to an obscure bunch of bushes and reached in to them. After scratching around for a moment, he pulled on something, and heard a gratifying click. David's smile was like that of a child, anticipation dancing in his spectacle-enlarged eyes.

He pulled his hand out of the bushes and walked around to a nearby tree. When he cleared away the dirt at the base of the tree he uncovered a small metal plate. He pulled on a handle and the plate slid to the side.

'This is what made me come looking for you. You see, when I met with Alberto, he had a disc, but no player. They didn't have the codec yet.'

'I don't follow,' Shaun said, watching as David pulled a small plastic briefcase out of the hole in the ground.

'This is what's so valuable to everyone. It's why they killed Randy and why they shot up my house, because they didn't want anyone else around who knew how to develop a player that would play back the video codec on the disc they had.'

Shaun still didn't look convinced.

'Okay, every video in the digital age has a particular codec or format. DVD for example has an Mpeg2 codec. A standard DVD player will play any disc, any DVD video that is, encoded with the correct header information and which contains the correct Mpeg2 codec. That's what I developed at Newcom. I didn't just crack the codec on the disc, I developed a player, like a DVD player, that would play back these discs. But Alberto's disc had contained something I didn't understand at the time.'

David led Shaun over to a nearby bench and sat next to him. He opened the combination locks on the black case that now sat on his lap and revealed a black monitor built into the lid. He pulled out two pairs of black sunglasses from compartments in the briefcase's base.

'Here,' David said, also handing Shaun some earphones.

'Won't it be hard to watch with sunglasses on?' he asked.

'They're specially calibrated for each viewer. Here, play with this knob until you see an image on the screen.'

Shaun went through the process of calibrating his glasses and earphones until he was greeted with the words: 'Welcome to the Love Shack'.

'Okay, now, I'm hoping you can make some sense of this.' David Black pushed play.

Black. Nothing.

Text, white on black:

IDENT: 0011
SUBJECT: Napoleon Bonaparte
OFFICER: X9

Black. Image.

At first Shaun could not make out what was happening. He was staring at blackness, but he wasn't staring at a screen. He was staring into the screen. Then there was a light. As the image unfolded, he refused to accept what he was seeing. One moment he was sitting in a park in the middle of bustling Madrid, the next he was in a boat. He was in a boat on a lake, or was it the ocean? He could not be sure, but he was there, totally immersed in the vision.

The scene had immense depth to it. There was very real distance in what he was looking at. The sound of the boat cutting through the water came from all around him; and there were men. There was a man sitting right behind him, breathing hard from the effort of rhythmic exertion.

Shaun forced himself to look up and beyond the screen inside the briefcase. Yes, there was the tree, and there was the bush from which

David had pulled the player they were now watching. He was still in the park, still in Madrid, but this was incredible. He returned his gaze to the screen.

A hand wearing an intricately carved gold ring, with the symbol of an eagle, reached forward from the bottom of the screen and rested on the shoulder of the man who was rowing. Something was said in French, but Shaun didn't understand. Then a voice said in English: 'This man is Jean-Paul.' The man rowing turned and nodded his head. 'He will take the device should anything happen to me. He knows the hide location.'

The voice then whispered something harshly as a rifle crack was heard in the distance. The image suddenly cut to a new scene.

The boat slid up onto the sand beneath him, the voice speaking about the bravery of his three companions, and slowly Shaun began to understand what was happening. A shudder went through him when he heard the name Fontéyne. Was this the same man who had written the journal? Shaun clutched the diary in his hands more tightly, feeling its shape through the cloth of the bag. And then something happened that made his heart skip a beat.

One of the men crouched behind a rock as they hid at the top of a cliff face. The man looked directly out at David and Shaun as they watched on. In an excited American accent, the man spoke. 'Tell Strickland I owe him a beer, he really is a genius.' With that he turned and leaped over the wall, silently, speedily.

The camera looked on as the man disposed of the three guards with professional efficiency. David's glance darted sideways, gauging Shaun's reaction. He had spent his days and nights for the last two years looking for the man called Strickland.

Shaun watched on in silence. He didn't move, didn't speak. He just watched – taking it all in. He examined every detail, every nuance. A few short minutes later the screen cut to black, and the words 'Welcome to the Love Shack' reappeared.

For a long while, Shaun just sat there. It was all he could do to breathe. What he had just seen had all but confirmed the diary's validity. If what he had seen was genuine, if it really was the rescue of Napoleon Bonaparte from his island prison on Elba, then it meant that the chances of him holding a diary written two thousand years ago were much higher. It meant that, somehow, beyond all his scientific conclusions to the contrary, time travel was possible. Someone had done it.

'How—' Shaun began but then stopped as his brain worked faster than his mouth. He could all but qualify what he had seen by the *way* he had seen it. The viewing experience in which he had just engaged was unlike anything he had experienced before; it was ahead of its time. The complete immersion, the depth of vision, the unbelievable hyper-reality of the sound – all contained not in the latest state-of-the-art cinema, but in a relatively small, plastic-looking briefcase. A briefcase that sat here on his companion's lap.

It was now clear to Shaun that this could not be an elaborate hoax. The death of his wife, the pile-up on the freeway and the man falling from the train were all far too real.

Then, there was that moment. 'Tell Strickland I owe him a beer, he really is a genius.' The man had said it loud and clear. Slowly Shaun took off his glasses and handed them back to David who was looking back at him like an expectant child. Finally David spoke.

'This makes sense to you, doesn't it?'

Shaun didn't respond.

'I mean, it's you. You're the Strickland he was talking about? You know that guy in the video, right?'

'No,' Shaun said flatly.

'No? But I'm sure it was ... I mean, they *have* been after you?'

'No, I don't know that man,' Shaun clarified.

David furrowed his brow then sat back. 'But some of it makes sense to you, though?'

'Some of it makes sense,' Shaun confirmed.

David closed the briefcase and glanced at his watch. 'We've got to go.'

'Go?' Shaun slid back into the present, his mind still reeling from what he had seen. 'I just got here. Where do we have to go?'

'The chicken is in Roma!' David said with a smile, then was suddenly serious. 'We have to go to Rome. I'm sorry, I know you must be totally exhausted, but there's a man I have to meet there. The Italian that my contact mentioned before he died; and I know he will definitely want to meet you.'

'What's in the briefcase, sir?' the security guard asked David.

'It's a DVD player. I always take it on board with me, don't trust those guys in the luggage handling. You know, last year I went to Sweden and—'

'*Basta!* Move along,' the guard said, moving quickly to the next piece of luggage coming through the X-ray machine, clearly not wanting to engage in idle chitchat.

David closed the case and moved forward with purpose. Shaun came into stride next to him.

'So, the crazy zigzagging in the plaza? It disrupts a satellite?' Shaun asked. It was the first thing he had said since they left the park. He had been going over and over what he had heard and seen, desperately trying to make sense of it all.

'The zigzagging is a little something I devised to protect myself,' David said proudly. 'See, there's this web-cam set up on the plaza. So, I hacked into the satellite coordination systems for all the birds that—'

'You hacked into the satellite coordination systems?' Shaun echoed with more than a hint of scepticism.

'Yeah, well, actually it's not so much the satellite itself as the feed monitored back to earth,' he admitted, as if this made it easier to swallow. 'I have my little terminal sitting in an attic near the Palace and it's set to display the feed from the web-cam on the plaza. I have it programmed like a DVD menu, with hot spots on the screen. When the pixels on my screen turn from white to black at those hot spots in a certain order, and at a certain time, it starts running a program that disrupts the feed from the twelve satellites that pass over Madrid in any given year.'

'What does that achieve exactly?' Shaun asked, wondering if this guy was nuts.

'Well, it means that they get some screwed-up vision from twelve of their birds. Those twelve can be anywhere in the world at any given time, but it means that the chance of them seeing me doing something important is next to none. I walk the pattern whenever I don't want them to see what I'm doing. Somehow I don't think they'd want me meeting you.'

'Thank you. Seat 15B,' the stewardess said as she took David's boarding pass. The two men shuffled down the aisle to find their seats and Shaun again resigned himself to sitting still and cramped for another few hours.

'You expect me to believe that? That you can hack into government satellite feeds?'

'Are you crazy? Everyone does it! Every spy agency on the planet is stealing the feeds from every other government. Hell, it's even relied upon these days, so they throw out misinformation through the feeds to screw up their counterpart agencies.'

Shaun raised his eyebrows. Considering everything that had been going on, he felt he had no choice but to trust this guy. He clicked his seatbelt in and breathed deeply, then, he turned to David. 'Okay, again. Who are "they"?'

'Let me come back to that. There's a chronology to this that I'm hoping you can help me with. I think I know who the players are here, but there are some gaps.'

'Help you? I want the answers, here. It's my wife they killed!' Shaun struggled to stay calm.

'I'm truly sorry to hear that,' David began earnestly. He paused, then continued. 'I fear there may be a lot more people in danger of being killed. Firstly, we need to talk about the disc. It made sense to you, yeah? I was sort of hoping you would know who the man was who said your name.'

'No. No, I don't know him. But I think I know what he was.'

'*What* he was?'

'He's part of something called The Journalist Project. The whole Officer X11 thing. It's a group who work to gather interviews of important historical figures. What I think you have there is an interview disc.'

'Yeah, except with no interview,' said David as he shuffled his feet. 'After they shot up my house, I moved around a lot. I mean, a lot. I moved all over Europe, lived in Germany, France, Holland and settled about three months ago in Madrid. The whole time really I was searching for you. Searching for information on this Strickland guy. Funny, I started looking for historical references to the name in the time of Napoleon; I didn't even think about the present. But then I had the idea of speaking to a modern-day descendant and asking them about their ancestors.'

He drifted off, remembering his long search with a vague smile on his face. 'I found a chicken farmer in Kentucky and he thought I was someone he'd met on an internet dating site, and a guy in France who said he was going to be a famous soccer player one day – he was sixty-four. But nothing else looked promising.'

'So, how did you find me?' Shaun asked.

'Chance, really. I received an email about a month ago about an upcoming conference being held at Cambridge. You were advertised as a leading expert on the field of time travel.'

'What?' Shaun asked, exasperated. 'I only found out about that conference three days ago! In fact, that's what started this whole thing. That's why we were heading to the airport when we hit that guy.'

'What guy?' David asked, and Shaun knew he had said too much. He squeezed the cloth bag in his hands tightly and felt the bulk of the diary through the material. His head began to pound. What if this guy was part of it all? But then why would he share the whole Napoleon thing?

Because he wants information from you, his brain answered. *Like the cop in the hospital. They want information from you.*

Shaun suddenly felt trapped. 'Okay,' he said, changing the subject. 'I had been sending out papers for years, and I hadn't heard back from anyone – not a single university, a single professor or a single journal. I figured no one was taking me seriously.'

'I think if they had read your papers they would have. I called the university to find out about you, but of course they wouldn't give out any contact information. I later got an email back from the university professor running the conference. He said that if I was interested in your work I should look at a particular site, which he sent me a link to. It was more an FTP site than a website, but it had loads of your papers. I read them and I knew you were the guy. More than just because of your name, but because that guy Alex had said you were a genius. It was a genius who wrote the papers I read.'

Despite himself, Shaun felt the faintest pangs of pride at David's comment, but he did not lower his guard. 'Who's Alex?' he asked to keep him talking.

'You really don't know him?' David replied. 'Ah, Alex is the man with the American accent in the video you saw. The contact I met last year in Paris – Alberto, the one who gave me the disc – recognised him. It was right before his head exploded in front of me.'

Shaun swallowed.

'Who was this Alberto, then? Police?'

'No,' David Black looked serious. 'He was a priest.'

CHAPTER 36

On a plane ninety minutes later Shaun downed a shot of much needed scotch and sucked on the ice left in the glass. It was cool on his tongue, and he wondered why he felt so thirsty. Their conversation came in spurts, each one giving a little information, then pausing as the other digested it and fit it into their own context of events. Then suddenly, Shaun had a thought. 'Does the name Graeme Fontéyne mean anything to you?'

David thought for a minute. 'No it doesn't, but give me a second. There was a Fontéyne on the disc. Might be a relative? But should it?'

'Well, not if it doesn't, if that makes sense.'

David pulled out a credit card and swiped it through the panel of the seatback in front of him. Shaun could not help but notice that it wasn't the name David Black on the card.

'What is he? A scientist? Politician?' David asked, pushing the touch screen.

'No, at least I don't think so.' Shaun remembered the diary: '*While serving in Iraq, I was recruited into the project.*'

'Something military I think – not sure what else. I'm not up to that bit yet.'

David stopped tapping. 'You're not up to that bit yet?'

Shaun realised what he'd said.

'Come on, man, what aren't you telling me?'

'I think that maybe if we find him, he might be able to help us,' Shaun said, wondering why the thought hadn't occurred to him sooner.

David was again focused on the screen. 'Ah, there's going to be a bit of a problem with that, if he *was* military, that is.' David leaned aside so Shaun could see the screen.

Staring back at him was an online newspaper article dated 14 March 2003, and the headline read: 'SPECIAL-FORCES HERO GIVES LIFE TO SAVE FAMILY'.

The story described the premature death of a special-forces captain who single-handedly fought off two special guard units in Iraq to save a terrified Muslim family. The crack commando was gunned down by Iraqi forces as he tried to escape. This wasn't what caught Shaun's attention, though. What caught his attention was the smiling, dark-haired man who stared out from a full colour photo, right back into Shaun's eyes. Shaun realised with a start that he was looking at the face of Graeme Fontéyne; the face of Saul the gladiator.

CHAPTER 37

My blood mixed with the water as it stung and cleaned my wounds all at once. I lay on my front in the small stream, Malbool and Mishca ahead of me. We pulled our bodies forward with our hands, feet floating behind us. The stream of the aqueduct's water flowed gently. We drank heavily before climbing into the water, and our strength had been somewhat replenished. Now we moved slowly, but necessarily so, staying low so as not to alert anyone who happened to glance up. The aqueducts were an engineering marvel, and kept the people of Rome plentiful in the ancient world's most precious resource: fresh water. The stonework consisted of arches upon arches. These tall structures, some of the highest in Rome, housed long, narrow, rivers that used gravity to transport the natural water supply from the mountains down through the city. It was through this network of open tunnels that we now escaped from the Empire's capital.

It had been an hour since we had seen the light of day, and our progress was painfully slow. Below I could hear the bustle of the city, and then the occasional gallop of horses as soldiers searched the streets for the defiant gladiators.

We had moved in virtual silence the entire time. Stealth, rather than speed, was our weapon. Malbool led the way decisively, knowing that we had to head ever upwards, against the gentle flow of the running water. The gradient was slight, but it was present, and the effort of climbing upstream took its toll on our tired, damaged bodies.

At intervals we came to filtering points, where the water stream was cleaned of impurities through small enclosed structures that blocked our progress, and we had to leap up and scamper over or around without being seen. The grille in front of me now forced just such an action. I poked my head up over the side of the aqueduct wall to look down on the streets of an outer suburb in Rome. It was mostly residential villas here, simple and small, but with enough pomp to justify their place in the capital. The streets were bare of soldiers. We climbed up and over the sandstone structure that housed both a filtering system and a major junction point. Within moments we were back in the long, straight duct.

The mountains were not too far; at our current rate we could reach them in another hour or two, but I intended to leave the water system once we were out of the city and continue overland. I didn't know this region in detail. It was not part of my assignment. I knew that the next major city south was Capua. I planned to head out of the district and get as far from the city as possible before turning south and heading for a port. We needed a boat to take us to Jerusalem. I had to complete my mission, and Mishca needed to return home.

Time was short. I didn't know how short, but if there were reports of a miracle man reaching Rome already, it meant that Jesus had started to teach. It was three years from the first sermon to death on a cross – there was a chance I was already too late.

We continued the slow trek and I thought about another lifetime. I had no wife or children. I joined the Marines when I was seventeen, and learned the meaning of hell.

The training we endured was on the boundary of human endurance, but it was nothing compared to the real thing. My first combat mission was reconnaissance in the first Gulf War. It showed me that no matter how well you plan and prepare for something, no matter what your technological advantage, a single bullet can kill a man. A single bullet can rob you of your friends, your decision-makers and your politics. War is hell.

Then I died. The unfortunate part was not being able to tell my sister. Although we didn't see each other much because she lived in Europe, we had the unbreakable bond of siblings who have shared the tragedy of losing their parents. I loved her dearly, and still do, and I hope that one day she will understand what I was trying to do when I was killed in Iraq.

'Killed in Iraq?' David commented as he turned the page.

'Yeah, although it goes on to say that it was faked so he could be recruited to the program at The Facility,' Shaun answered, leaning back in his seat. It was the first time he had relaxed in days, and he no longer had the strength to fight the urge to sleep. He had read ahead in the diary, and now let David catch up. He was amazed at how quickly that had happened, David obviously reading much faster than Shaun originally had.

At first he was hesitant to let David see the diary, but he gave permission on the condition that David did not read any further than the last page Shaun had marked.

Shaun lifted his complimentary sleeping mask and looked over at the computer engineer bent low over the book in his hands. David Black was not the sort of guy Shaun would have normally associated with. David was the guy who lived for gadgets, for pulling them apart and seeing how they worked, and then improving on them. But something was starting to feel right, like they were supposed to try to figure this out together. Their brains seemed to work with a certain synergy.

David flipped pages faster than three a minute. Every so often he would comment on something he had just read, and make connections with other information he had not yet shared with Shaun.

'Okay,' he said finally, leaving the diary open on the page Shaun had marked. 'I'm there.'

'Well?' he asked David.

'Well?'

'Do you think it's real?'

'Real? Of course it's real! You know it's real too, otherwise you wouldn't be here.'

Was that true? Shaun thought about his motivation for getting on the plane to Rome. He could not decide if it was simply because he didn't know what else to do, or because he really believed this might be his only lead to finding the people responsible for Lauren's death. If he had not received the call from David, Shaun would have headed to his brother's home in Washington DC, but now his path seemed set. Tim would wait.

'What else can you remember about that cop?' David asked then. 'The woman who tried to hypnotise you?'

'Ah, besides the fact that she got really pissed when I told her the diary was in English, not a lot. I wasn't thinking too clearly just then.'

'Did she mention why the diary was so important?'

Shaun paused. There was something else she said. 'Actually, yeah. She said something about a map. She asked me where the map was.'

'The map?'

'Yeah, she slapped me and said, "Where is the codex? Where is the map?"'

'Do you know what she was talking about?' David asked, his mind already starting to draw conclusions.

Shaun's eyebrows raised as one, and his lower lip jutted out in that upside-down smile that universally meant 'I haven't the foggiest idea!'

'Did she say that the map was *in* the diary, or that they were different things? This is important, Shaun.'

Suddenly, Shaun's blood boiled. The words escaped his mouth before he had a chance to rein them in: 'I know it's fucking important. Don't tell me what's important, my wife is dead!'

David sat still. A moment passed.

'Sorry,' Shaun said.

'No, I'm sorry. I know, man, I know this sucks for you. I know it does. My house was shot up and I've been on the run for years. I guess I'm kinda used to it. I can't imagine what you've been through already. I'm sorry I didn't find you sooner, before it all started.'

Shaun shook his head. *Before it all started?* Those words gave him an awful sense of inevitability, like he did not have a choice. Up until this point he had been sure that if he had left that hobo on the road to die, Lauren would be with him now, and none of this would have happened. But then, was that really the case? David had been looking for him long before Lauren had hit the hobo, and that was something Shaun did not like at all. He had never believed in fate. He had never believed in destiny. But now, everything was different, and he was unsure of the new rules. Life before was simple. Science. Science made sense. Cause and effect. But with this, with the fact that this man next to him had seemingly known that all this was coming, the boundaries had shifted.

'Okay, what's this map?' Shaun asked.

'I don't know, man. I really don't. Maybe this is it?' David motioned to the book now on his tray table.

'Ladies and gentlemen, the captain has switched on the fasten-seatbelts sign and we have started our descent into Rome. Please make sure all seats are in the upright position and all tray tables are put away.' This was said in Spanish, but Shaun got the idea when everyone else began to shuffle. David closed the diary and handed it to Shaun without a moment's hesitation.

'So, what's this guy's name? The guy we're meeting?' Shaun asked as he tucked the diary away.

'Vincenso Giovanni. He found me right after Alberto was shot, and I recognised the name. He claims to have information about another disc.'

'A disc like the one you found? Like the one we saw?' Shaun queried as he felt the plane drop in altitude.

'I don't really know. He said he knows where a disc is. He said that if I am who I said I am, then I would know what that meant.'

'Could be a trap?' Shaun posed the obvious question.

'Could be,' was all that David said in response.

'But it isn't, right? I mean, you did a whole bunch of security checks on the guy?'

'I ran social security, criminal records, visas, passports and other stuff. Oh, and I Googled him.'

'And?' Shaun prompted.

'Well, it's kinda hard. I didn't have much information to go on.'

'So, how can you say that he passed everything?'

'Well, because I didn't find much.'

'What do you mean? Isn't that a bad thing?'

'Not necessarily. You see, if he were using an alias, then there would be a lot of information out there, and it would be easy to find. That's the whole point of creating an alias: you generate information so people can look it up and verify who you are.'

Shaun thought about this for a moment as the plane neared the runway.

'Okay, I get that. But the reverse, not being easy to verify, doesn't prove otherwise. It hardly proves you are who you say you are.'

'True,' David conceded, 'but the one thing I did find out about him makes it worth meeting him. He works for the most secretive organisation in the world.'

'The CIA?' Shaun asked, surprised.

'Ha!' David laughed. 'No, not the CIA, not Mossad and not MI5.' He leaned back in his seat as the plane bounced violently on landing before settling its full weight onto the safety of the tarmac.

'No,' David said again. 'Vincenso Raul Giovanni is a Jesuit priest, and he works at the Vatican.'

The hotel air was stuffy. The room was on the third floor, and smelled of stale smoke. Shaun lay on the bed, diary spread open, next to another man. David was heavier than Shaun and the science teacher kept rolling down onto him on the bed. It must have been a comical sight. Shaun had never imagined his first European adventure would be sharing a room with another man, but David had confirmed the arrangements long before they arrived.

David was frustrated. He would read the pages twice as fast as Shaun and then wait. Like a child who is bored at a parents' dinner party, he would grunt and fidget and make an exaggerated show of being ready to move on.

He had pleaded with Shaun early on – 'just let me finish it and tell you what happens', but Shaun's look had silenced him.

The meeting with Giovanni was not for another hour or so, and Shaun had decided to use the time to get as much information as he could about what had happened two thousand years ago. The book was like a drug; he didn't want to put it down. It was his key, his connection and, moreover, for an autobiography, it was a damn good read.

CHAPTER 38

I fell more than climbed to the ground. My fingers were weak and I found it hard to grip the rough holds provided by the aqueduct walls. Malbool and Mishca were already down and helped me to my feet. We had travelled through the waterways all day without incident, and only now, when we were out of the throng of the city, did I feel that it was safe to leave the stonework rivers.

The amber light of the setting sun covered the stones. The blanket of night would soon envelop the city, giving us the cover we needed to slip through the Romans' net.

'You have lost a lot of blood, my friend,' Malbool commented as he slung my arm over his shoulder. I winced from the movement. 'If you were white before, now I think you cast your own glow!'

'Do you know where we are?' I asked as we shuffled to a nearby building for cover.

It was Mishca who answered. 'We're near my master's neighbourhood,' the boy said, looking around. 'There, that building; I recognise the shape of its roof. It's where they brought me when I was first taken from my village.' The boy pointed to a silhouette on the near horizon, where a sharply pointed roof broke the monotony of the city's skyline.

'That house looks like a Moorish temple,' Malbool said, following the boy's gaze. 'Who was your master?'

Mishca looked a little awkward. 'I ... I don't really know. They brought us to him, me and about twenty other boys, and then they put us in a large room. He sold us off. Every few days they would take us out of the city to some place where people came to buy us. I think I was luckier than a lot of the boys. A games man bought me. I was taken to live in the cells at the Circus Maximus, ready to tend to chariot races before I was moved to the new Coliseum. Many of the boys were sold to other types of places.' He didn't have to elaborate. I felt sick and angry at the same time.

'There's a stable on the other side somewhere,' Mishca continued. 'We used to hear horses in the mornings.'

I smiled at the boy. If only I had been so resourceful at his age. I realised how totally foreign to him this place must be, how displaced he must feel. He didn't speak the language, and had been torn from the simple village life he had led; the only life he knew. Perhaps it was because of his youth that he had been able to adapt and accept his new reality. I, however, was struggling with mine.

Just then, a voice cut through the darkness.

'You really should try not to bleed so much,' it said from behind Malbool. Malbool and Mishca spun as one as I watched the voice's owner walk from an alcove in the wall.

My jaw dropped. In a loose tunic and centurion's leather skirt, the man stared at the three of us with amusement in his eyes. His thick black hair was flecked with grey, and his face bore a scar across the left cheek; cheeks that were pitted and discoloured. Hanging loosely on his hip was the short sword of the Roman guard.

It took me a moment to realise that the words he spoke, although with a thick accent, were in English.

'Louis?' I breathed.

Malbool pushed Mishca behind him and looked at me, not understanding what was being said.

'Ah! So, I'm right. You do know me! The blood, Graeme. The blood gave you away. It's not every day the city's water supplies are contaminated with blood and oil. Slips right through the filtration systems here.'

'What is this?' Malbool asked.

'I'm not sure yet,' I answered him in Roman. My eyes never left the Italian standing in front of me, but I slowly pulled Mishca in closer behind me.

'I'm surprised how long you stayed in there, really, although I was guessing you'd pop up around sunset.' Delissio stepped forward.

Malbool blocked his way.

'Tell your monkey to move or I will make him move,' the Italian said.

'First tell me what's going on. Who is your assignment? Why have you been trying to orchestrate my death?'

'Yes, you really have put on quite a show, haven't you? Crixus! Now, that was impressive. Didn't even give the poor man a chance. Of course, you always were too flowery with your technique.'

Malbool became increasingly nervous, feeling the tension. He flexed his fingers instinctively.

Delissio looked me up and down, smiling as he saw me struggling to stand from blood loss and exhaustion. 'You can't stop it, Fontéyne.'

'Stop it? Who's your assignment?' I pressed. The Italian squinted, as if deciding something. He was much older than when I had known him at The Facility, and was now a man well into his fifties.

'It's a funny thing. As I'm sure you realise, the process has some unanticipated results. I've been here for a quarter-century already, and if it wasn't for your arrival, I might have lived out my life in blissful ignorance. I suppose I have to thank you for that. You turned up just in time.'

Louis Delissio stopped for a moment and looked at Malbool, who was still nervously blocking the man's path. In a blur so fast I didn't see the move until after it happened, Malbool was lifted bodily off the ground and sent backwards. The uppercut knocked the African out. When he hit the ground he lay in a folded heap at my feet. Delissio held up his hand and spoke calmly, as if his blow had never been delivered: 'I just can't have him listening in to this conversation.'

'He can't speak English; you didn't have to knock him out,' I spat through clenched teeth. I crouched, checking Malbool's pulse. 'What do you mean that I arrived just in time? In time for what? And how long did you say you've been here?'

'Well, let me answer your last question first. I woke up twenty-five years ago in the middle of ancient Rome with no idea who I was. At first I was confused. It didn't take me long, however, to realise that I had certain skills that set me apart from those around me. I was able to work my way up through the ranks of the military, and then into a position of considerable political power.

'My vice was betting on the games. I like going to the pits and watching the amateurs rip each other to shreds. Call it a weakness.

'Then one day at an underground fight I see someone come in and annihilate his opponents without breaking a sweat, and my head starts to explode with images. Images of your face, images of buildings, lights, planes, guns and time machines. Twenty-five years. Actually, in hindsight, it really wasn't such a bad life, but then I remembered my purpose.'

'Your assignment. Who was it? Caesar?'

Delissio smiled again.

'Why, yes,' he said slowly. 'Yes, Caesar was my assignment. Augustus Caesar, not Julius. But I guess I'm too late for that now. He was banished for a time, did you know? I don't think that's recorded

anywhere in the history books. No, the assignment they gave me was Caesar, but my purpose is quite different, and if it wasn't for you arriving as you did, I may never have remembered it.'

'Get to the point.'

'Actually, now it's time for you to answer my question. I would ask you how you got here, but I can guess at that. What I want to know, though, is what made you remember?'

I looked back at Mishca, who was now standing far enough away to get a good start on Delissio should he be made to run. Mishca too didn't understand what was being said, but clearly he sensed that it was not friendly.

'The camera,' I said simply.

'How did you find it?' Delissio asked, intrigued.

'I was cut. I found it.'

'Cut on the hip? How convenient for you. Ah, you know, I don't think I could be bothered cutting into my leg for the historical gratification of The Society, my camera can stay just where it is. So, you want to stop me? Well, now is your chance, but you should know that Barishnikov is not the only one.'

I had no idea what he was talking about, but I feigned surprise.

'Well, not anymore. You being here can mean only one thing: you discovered Barishnikov and he told you about me.'

I remained silent and clenched my jaw as if I had just been discovered, my mind reeling at the mention of a third Facility agent – Barishnikov.

'The moment I saw you and remembered what I was sent here to do, I sent my two best agents into Judea to finish the job. With you dead, there will be no one to stop them. I'm afraid you'll never get your interview with Christ.'

It was all too much. My mind raced to piece together what I was hearing. How did he know my assignment? None of the agents knew which historical figures the others were assigned to interview. The very fact that Delissio had this information, knew that I was assigned to interview Jesus, meant that he had gotten it from somewhere other than the officials at The Facility. It meant that—

'You're a plant?' I asked. I saw the look of confusion on his face pass momentarily. He assumed I knew this. I quickly sought to cover my slip. 'Barishnikov said he turned you after *you'd arrived.'*

Delissio considered the lie.

'Ah, well, I suppose he was smarter than he looked. No matter, you won't be around long enough to tell anyone the truth, and after my

agents have carried out their assassination, the world, our world, will be a much better place. It's for the greater good.'

With that he loosened his sword. This told me two things: Jesus was still alive, and Delissio meant to cure me of being the same way.

'If you want a job done, do it yourself,' he said as he slid the blade out of its scabbard and arced it at my neck in one lightning movement. I very nearly didn't get out of the way, only managing to evade the strike by flailing backwards at the last moment, causing me to crash clumsily over Malbool's unconscious body.

The blade came down hard in a dagger motion, and only by thrusting my legs apart was I able to avoid the sword's point as it slammed into the dirt. I crossed my legs in a scissor action as I spun onto my side, catching the blade and flipping it free of Delissio's grasp. The instant that it was, I knocked the blade clear and then kicked hard up into Delissio's stomach, but he was too fast. Riding the blow backwards, he grabbed my foot and twisted. The pain was instant and forced me to roll my entire body so my knee wasn't torn from its ligaments. As I did, I swung my other foot around, catching him on the side of the head. He stumbled and I rolled clear, coming to my feet.

I was moving on adrenaline alone, and I knew that it would give out at any moment. Delissio was unlike anyone I had yet faced. He was an agent, an X officer, with all the same training and skill I possessed, but he was fresh and I was on the verge of collapse. It was a fight I could not win.

A scream of rage cut the air between us as Mishca charged Delissio, Delissio's sword now raised above his head. His battle cry alerted the Italian with too much time to be taken by surprise. My heart sank as I saw Delissio drop, spin and sweep the boy as he got within range. The advantage I had gained by ridding the Italian of his weapon was nullified as his hand reached out and snatched the blade back from the boy as he fell.

Mishca dropped, unmoving.

I circled, feinting and baulking attacks as I led Delissio away from the fallen bodies of my friends.

'You come alone?' I taunted. 'Why no legions? Are you so sure of yourself, Louis?'

'I need no legions to finish you, Fontéyne. You think you can kill me? Well, here I am! I was always better than you.' With that, Delissio thrust forward, the tip of his eighteen-inch gladius sword speeding for my heart. Weariness clouded my reactions. I made to avoid the blow

but too late realised that I had fallen for his feint. As Delissio thrust the sword with his right hand, he spun his torso all the way around, pulling his stabbing motion short, but forcing me to move. He continued his rotation and brought his elbow up, travelling fast in the spin. In an effort to evade his thrust, I moved right into the blow. It broke my nose and sent me sprawling backwards. I was dazed, unable to move and water filled my eyes. I was beaten.

Too exhausted to be sharp, too fatigued to anticipate his trick, I looked up and knew that the end was here. Blood poured from my nose and mixed with the tears as my eyes spilled over. My head lolled to the side and I saw Malbool and Mishca lying on the street in the darkness.

Jesus would be killed before I could speak with him, and my disc would never reach its resting place.

'I hope you're recording,' Delissio said as he raised his short sword with both hands.

CHAPTER 39

'Okay,' Shaun said, slamming his hand down on the book as he reached the bottom of the page.

'What?' David said like a petulant child. 'Come on, let me turn the page! I've been waiting for, like, five minutes.' In fact he had been waiting for closer to one minute for Shaun to catch up, and had been making noises of frustration the entire time. His running commentary of 'Wow!' and 'Oh no!' as he raced ahead was driving Shaun insane. But that was not why Shaun had stopped reading.

'Okay, this is it,' he said. 'There's no possible way he can get out of this.'

'But there's more book!' David retorted.

'I know! That's what bugs me. It's like when you watch a TV show and they leave it with the hero in some totally un-get-out-able situation, and then return next week for some random freak thing to happen to save their ass at the last moment. It pisses me off!'

'So, what are you waiting for? Let's find out!' David rocked back and forth on the bed next to him, like a child so filled with anticipation he was going to burst.

Shaun breathed. 'It's a fake,' he said.

'What? Why?' David blurted, not following.

'Well, for Fontéyne to get out of this situation something totally ridiculous would have to happen. Malbool and Mishca are unconscious, and he's totally exhausted and lying there with a super-agent ready to stab him. There's no way out. If he gets out of this, then it's some bullshit and the whole story is a freakin' wannabe Matthew Reilly novel, not a diary. There would have to be someone hiding in the shadows who shoots Delissio with an arrow in the back. It's just fake.'

'We've got twenty minutes before we have to leave and I'm going insane, man. Please. *Please* turn the page.'

Shaun sighed. 'Fine. Whatever.'

He turned the page and they both continued to read.

Through watery eyes I looked up at the man who would deliver my death. I had survived the hordes of Roman gladiators only to be killed by one of my own agents. Delissio smiled, and then his eyes widened.

He stared down at his chest to see an arrow head protruding from—

'Ha!' Shaun got up off the bed.

'Shit, man, you've been reading ahead. That's not fair!' David protested.

'Ha! I told you! I told you this thing was freakin' ridiculous!' Shaun pointed an accusatory finger at the diary. 'All this time I've been hanging on its every word when I should have been looking for the people who killed Lauren. It's crap. It's impossible.'

David didn't know how to respond. It was Shaun who had brought the diary to him, and they both knew that the whole time-travel thing was legitimate – they had seen the disc.

'Maybe it was just lucky. Come on, read the rest of it, it might make sense. Maybe Fontéyne was exaggerating a little?'

'Okay,' replied Shaun with a heavy dose of sarcasm. 'So, even if he survives the fight with Delissio, he's fucked. He's been cut to shreds in the Royåle and all the other fights, and has lost tons of blood. He'd need specialist medical attention to survive. Probably a truckload of antibiotics from all that crawling through sludge with open wounds, and a good tetanus shot.'

David saw that the stress of the past few days was taking its toll on Shaun. The guy had lost his wife. He was being hunted. He had been on the run and hadn't had time to grieve. David didn't take the outburst personally. Instead, he breathed calmly and continued to read while Shaun paced about the room.

Delissio stared down at his chest to see an arrow head protruding from where his heart would have been. His knees buckled as another arrow severed his spinal column at the neck and burst through his windpipe.

I lay back and breathed. I didn't understand, but at that moment, I didn't care. I just breathed. Then I passed out.

I woke to smelling salts, their acrid scent causing me to gag. I stared up at a man's face. He was old. Much older than the age most people lived to in this era. He must have been eighty, but his eyes were clear and when he spoke it was with the life and vibrance of youthful vigour.

'Ah, Graeme. My God, boy, are you okay? No, no of course you're not okay. But you're alive and that's the way we like it. Come on, you

bag of bones, I'm too old now to carry you. Get that saggy ass of yours up and follow me.'

The man spoke quickly in English. With an effort, I sat up on my elbows and looked around. I could just make out the forms of Malbool and Mishca being carried on crudely fashioned stretchers.

'Who are you?' I asked as I struggled to my feet.

The old man ignored the question and continued to speak. 'Just round the corner and down the street. Fifty years I've been waiting for tonight. An old man starts to question his sanity after a while. But then I would look down again at my arm and I would remember. Still, it seems so long ago. The bastards sent me back too far – fifty years too far! I don't think they'd worked it out as an exact science yet, if you know what I mean? Professor indeed! The bastard! Still, I've put the time to good use. Just because you were my assignment doesn't mean that I couldn't make a little profit out of the specialist medical knowledge I just happened to have, does it?'

I grabbed the old man by the arm to stop his rambling.

'Who are you?' I asked again. The old man turned and looked into my eyes.

'Really, Graeme. Have I changed so much?' he asked with amusement.

Then I saw it. The small mole above his left eyebrow, the defining dimple in the end of his nose ... I recognised a man I had known once.

'Miles?' I asked, barely believing my eyes.

The old man smiled. 'It's not been more than a month or so for you, has it? But it's been more than fifty years for me. The bastards sent me back too far. "Just need to make sure you don't arrive late," he said. "Gotta make sure of it; might give you an extra year." Extra year my ass – try fifty of the bastards!

'Five decades I've been waiting to put an arrow in that treacherous bastard's back. Not a bad bit of shooting for an old boy, if I don't say so myself. The Marines would be proud of me. Of course, I did *know he was coming and he* did *have his back to me. Still, there would have been trouble if I'd missed. The bastard would have beaten the old shit outta me. And then he would have screwed you for good measure. Then we'd all be in the drink, wouldn't we? Ah, here we are.'*

Walking briskly while he rambled, Miles showed me a small wooden door through which his aides had already carried Malbool and Mishca. Gesturing to what looked like an ancient doctor's waiting room, he said, 'I even built the bastard out here just to make sure I wouldn't be too far away when the day came. Not too good for business, I'll tell ya, but I got 'im! Right through the breather! Not to mention the wagers I've won from my staff who all bet me you wouldn't be there. It took me a while to work out the spot, mind you, and I was about to go and take a piss when you finally showed up. Think of that! Fifty years of waiting to save your ass and I miss the chance because I had to take a piss. That would've been a good one. Now ...'

He walked through to a back room and came to a padded bench in the middle. He tapped it with his old, bony hand and said, 'Let's have a look at that nose of yours and stop you pissing out all that blood. But first, take this.' He held his hand out and revealed a small white capsule.

'What is it?'

'Just a potent little cocktail of antibiotics. You're going to need a tetanus shot too, so I hope you're not scared of needles.'

'Needles? What are you talking about?'

The old man seemed to be enjoying this. He shuffled over to a drawer and unlocked it. When he returned he carried several vials and a syringe. When I looked at him blankly he laughed again.

'Well, we're not all cameramen, you know! They only told me what I needed to know, but when I arrived I had no clue who I was or what I was doing. All I had to go on was this.'

He pulled up his sleeve to reveal an old, bony arm. The sagging skin on his forearm was speckled with sunspots, but that's not what caught my attention. On the underside, a faded scar was visible. It was a single word: VOMIT.

'It was fresh when I arrived – still bleeding and stung like a bitch. I guess that was so I would notice it. None of these dull bastards believed me,' he continued, nodding towards his assistants. 'I tried telling a couple of them once, but they think I'm senile. Still, it was all I had to go on, so that's what I did ... vomit. Fingers down the throat and a big hurl. Bile and all – and there it was. A little piece of home. A little capsule of metal with instructions inside it. As soon as I touched it my head exploded with images and sounds and all the crap you would have been through as well.

'So, there I was, every bloody year for fifty years waiting for you to show up in the Royåle. The bloody thing didn't even exist when I got here, so I had to suggest the idea to an old games master when I treated him one time. Can you believe that? No one gave old Miles any credit for inventing the bloody Royåle, did they? No siree! But I did,

you know; told them what a bloody good idea it would be to have a hundred of those poor bastards in there at once hacking away at each other. And I only did that 'cause I got sick of waiting for someone else to invent the bloody thing while I was waiting for you to arrive. Can't show up in a Royåle if the bloody thing doesn't exist yet, can you? Bastards. Fifty years. Fifty bloody years too early, the bastards!'

David stopped reading. This time it was he who didn't want to turn the page.

Shaun was still pacing, talking to himself.

'Shaun,' David said from the bed, but Shaun continued to mutter to himself. 'Shaun,' he said again. More muttering.

'Strickland!' he shouted.

Shaun stopped. 'What?'

'You, ah, had better come and look at this,' David said.

'I don't want to look at it. It's crap. I even said, he'd have to get an arrow through his back and that's *exactly* what happened! It's like a bad action movie!'

'Um ... Yeah, and you also said that he should take some antibiotics and get a tetanus shot, your words ... guess what happens next.'

Shaun finally stopped and looked at David. 'What?'

'Just like you said.'

Shaun raised an eyebrow, but his heart started to beat a little faster.

'Come and read it,' said David. 'There's something strange going on here.'

Shaun grumbled, then did so.

CHAPTER 40

Vincenso Raul Giovanni sat with his back to the sun. The man was late. He did not like it when people were late – in his line of work, it usually meant they were dead. He worked his fingers around the small paper tubes of sugar that sat on the table. Finally he gave in, tore one and added it to his coffee.

Giovanni did not wear anything to give away his position as a high-ranking cardinal at the Vatican. In the Jesuit order, he was second only to 'the black Pope', the term given to the head of the Jesuits, named for the robes he wore rather than any sinister connotations.

Forty-one degrees, fifty-four minutes north; twelve degrees, twenty-seven minutes east, Vatican City State. A completely independent, self-governed country in the heart of Rome.

He looked out across the city towards the world's smallest nation. The Vatican sat on a small rise in the old part of Rome, guarded by three thousand *Corpo della Guardia Svizzera Pontificia*, the pontificial Swiss Guard. Although theoretically only for show – responsibility for the defence of the State fell to Italy – the Guard provided an excellent means of incorporating highly skilled agents within the grounds. Ah, if the people knew what went on there. If the priests who worked and worshipped there knew what went on there.

Although small, the Vatican was powerful. Resources, influence; so much more than the outside world would ever know about. Even the officials at the Vatican didn't know the secrets within its walls – and there was an immense secret that even the Holy Father himself was not privy to.

Giovanni enjoyed thinking especially about the Vatican's unique place in the world. Three treaties signed with Italy on 11 February 1929 acknowledged the full sovereignty of the Vatican, among other things. The origin of papal states, however, could be traced back to the eighth century. But soon things would never be the same; Giovanni was certain of that. The world was on the brink of change, on the brink of war, though they didn't know it.

Vincenso Giovanni was born in the south of Italy sixty-three years ago. He had shown extraordinary ability at school and was offered scholarships to three of Italy's top universities, all of which he declined, opting instead to give his life to the service of the people. He had been fifteen when he had received 'the calling'. Unlike most vocational priests, however, this was no intangible feeling. This was a very direct, very real calling.

The teenage Vincenso had just come in from his weekly football match, very disappointed that his team had failed to qualify for the semi-final. He had taken the defeat very personally and did not want to tell his father, but his parents were out when he arrived home. He had walked out to the back garden to fetch his clean shirt, and there he had seen a man sitting on the sandstone bench next to the clothes line.

Vincenso had stopped dead, his heart in his mouth. In trousers and a loose shirt, the man wore the fashion of the day. His skin was olive and his brown hair fell loosely around his face. And when Vincenso saw that face, that face he would never forget – he was changed.

Such a simple, kind face. Light brown eyes had looked out at the boy as the man stood up.

'Who are you? How did you get in here?' Vincenso had asked, trying to sound brave. He laughed now at the memory.

The man had smiled at him and said simply: 'Bring me to my people.'

He had then walked around the corner of the house. Vincenso had raced around after him, but the man was nowhere. He was gone.

Later, people would try to tell him that he had imagined it. They would say all kinds of things and try to rationalise. But he knew straight away. Vincenso knew what he saw.

Now Vincenso Giovanni was a Jesuit. He had always endeavoured to do what he felt was right, but knew he was far from a saint. Life had been challenging. Because of his childhood experience, he had something that he found lacking in many who walked around the Vatican. He had knowledge. Many had faith, but there was *no* doubt in his mind.

At least there hadn't been until the chance arose that he might be proved wrong.

'How are the omelets today?' he heard a voice ask him in broken Italian.

Giovanni didn't look up, but answered in English. 'The eggs are a little runny, but they taste as good as always.'

There was a moment's silence before the owner of the question pulled up a seat at the small table. It was a cafe situated in the old part of town, and one of Giovanni's favourites. The smells from the kitchen always made him hungry, and he often felt a little guilty when he ordered a second or third helping. Right now, however, his stomach was the last thing on his mind.

The man who sat in front of him was the man from the surveillance photos Giovanni's team had provided. Good. But a moment later a second chair was pulled back and a third man sat at the table. Giovanni instantly grew angry. After all the trust and crosschecking they had done on each other, to bring another person to this meeting was beyond bad manners, it was dangerous. He started to speak a moment before he saw the second man's face.

'How dare you—' His heart skipped a beat. 'Oh, I'm sorry. I didn't realise it was ... that you would be joining us today. I ...' Giovanni stammered.

David and Shaun both froze. Shaun was certain he had never seen this man before. The Italian priest wore a dark suit that fitted snugly. He was not overweight, but he knew that his heavyset shoulders often gave the impression he was not quite as physically fit as he really was. Giovanni didn't mind. His life in recent years had been all about deception and subterfuge. He was relieved there was not an eleventh commandment saying, 'Thou shalt not lie under any circumstances.'

'Have we met?' Shaun asked the man, knowing the answer. The Italian stared at him long and hard through his thick spectacles.

On closer inspection Giovanni began to doubt himself. This man was much younger. His hair was not the silvery grey of the man he thought it was, and there was no scar on his forehead. No, it was maybe not the same man, but still, they could have passed as brothers.

'I'm sorry. Forgive me, I thought you were someone else.' Giovanni turned his attention to the other man, the one he had had followed for more than two years now. 'It is highly unorthodox to bring another party to our meeting; this is not what we had arranged.'

'You said you had information. Do you want to speak or are you wasting my time?' Shaun was taken aback at David's abrupt tone. Giovanni, however, didn't flinch.

'I may have information, yes. But first, coffee.' The old man signalled to a nearby waiter, who came and took their orders. Giovanni noticed that the second man was extremely pale, his face showed the strain of ongoing stress and little sleep.

'You know about me, I assume. You are a clever man, Mr Black. I assume you have run background checks on me, no?'

'I have,' David replied shortly.

'And what is it that you found?' the Italian asked with interest in his voice.

'I saw you were a Jesuit priest who worked at the Vatican.'

'Anything else?' the Italian pressed.

David paused. This was no time for games. If this man was going to help them, he had to play straight.

'Nothing.'

'Nothing,' the priest repeated. 'Good. Good.' He pulled a manila envelope out of a small black briefcase. He slid it forward on the table, allowing a pile of photographs to spill out. David picked up the first of them, then skimmed the rest. They were all of him: in Spain, in France, in Germany and in Holland. His every move had been monitored.

'This is ...' the Italian priest began, rubbing his temple with his index finger, 'proof for you that I know about you, who you are, where you have been. Proof for you too that if I meant you harm, I could have inflicted it at any time. It is proof that you can trust me and what I have to say.' The Italian sat back and waited for a response.

Shaun looked over at David, who in turn looked through the photographs, feeling fear, anger and shame. He was furious with himself for allowing this to happen, for not knowing it had happened. He was a smart guy, and he had been so careful.

'Don't be upset. Your skill is commendable considering you had few resources. There is not a human being on this planet the Vatican cannot find, follow, and if necessary, terminate.' Again the Italian spoke with no hint of emotion.

Shaun sat and listened. This man was a priest, so what was this talk of 'terminate'? He knew he was naive to the worlds of religion and espionage, but there were some things he had hoped were a given.

'Okay,' David said. 'Why do you want to help me?'

The Jesuit stroked the small white goatee on his chin. At that moment the waiter returned and placed a cappuccino in front of Shaun and a long black in front of David. When he was out of earshot the Italian continued.

'I want to help you, naturally, because you can help me,' Giovanni said as he fixed on David's eyes. Shaun remained silent.

'What do you know about The Journalist Project?' Giovanni asked David.

'I've heard of it.'

'Do you know what it is?'

'Do *you* know what it is?' David shot back.

Giovanni smiled. 'Mr Black. Let me be, how you say? Fred with you?'

'Frank,' Shaun piped up, then immediately fell silent. Giovanni smiled.

'Yes, let me be frank with you. I did not come here to fuck around.'

Shaun swallowed.

'I did not come here to waste your time, and I would appreciate it if you didn't waste mine. As I have said to you, and as I have proven, I mean you no harm. I have the ability to help you. You can start by answering my questions truthfully. I will do the same. It is my hope that at the end of our conversation we are both a lot closer to reaching our goals.'

David felt like a chastised school boy. He had come to this intending to play hard ball, but deep down he knew he was not a negotiator. He was a computer geek, and he had just been schooled by a professional.

'Okay,' he conceded.

'Good. Now, what do you know about the project?'

'I know it was created to send people back through time to record interviews with historical figures,' David spat out. Saying it out loud would have sounded ridiculous in any other situation, but Giovanni didn't laugh.

'Good. Yes, that is correct. Do you know why?'

'Why?' David baulked. He had not really thought about why. 'I didn't think that sort of question needed an answer. Money? Who wouldn't want to see an interview with Da Vinci, or Mozart, or Hitler or ... Jesus?'

'Perhaps,' the Italian sat back. 'I used to think it was money, but you are right, an interview with Jesus is not something you could sell, you could not keep it quiet. I think it's some other reason.' Giovanni paused and took a long sip of his coffee.

'The late Holy Father, Nicholas II, commissioned me to be his chief liaison officer with an organisation we knew as The Society for World Historical Accuracy. I reported to the Holy Father directly and no one, I mean *no one*, knew about this commission. A person in my position is not questioned about their use of funds and resources and so for several years I facilitated many of the Vatican's dealings with The Society.'

'Facilitated?' Shaun cut in. 'Past tense? You don't do that anymore?'

'I don't do that anymore,' he echoed. 'When I say no one knew, I mean it. Cardinal Joseph Müller, the current Pope, was one of Nicholas's closest aides, but even he had no idea. When the Holy Father passed away in 2005, I was cut off. Müller found some files relating to the project and commissioned an inquiry. The cardinal in charge of this inquiry is a Frenchman named Le Clerque.' Giovanni took another sip of his coffee before he continued. 'This man followed the trail and uncovered some of what was happening. Ultimately this led him to me. I spoke with him and, well ...' He trailed off.

'What?' David pressed.

'Le Clerque is a fanatic who dishonours our faith. He has – other agendas. He has deceived the Holy Father; he told Müller that The Society was nothing more than a sermon the late Holy Father had been working on.'

'So, why didn't you tell Müller what was going on?'

'Why didn't I? Our Holy Father Müller, Pope Pius as you know him, is a great man of unshakable faith and passionate conviction. But Pius is not the same person Nicholas was; he is a scholar. If I were to go against his official inquiry, saying that Le Clerque is a liar, that he is plotting to misuse Vatican resources for his own political gain, and that for years I had been working on building a time machine to interview Christ on the behest of our dead Pope ... If I were to say all these things, bring these accusations, all without proof? Without infallible, undeniable proof, proof that would shake the Pope of his convictions? Well, I would be ...' again, the priest let the sentence trail off.

David and Shaun both slowly began to get the picture. Even with the diary, combined with the run of strange events and the disc from France, they both still doubted. If they told anyone, people would think them mad. If Giovanni had told anyone this absurd story, especially in the Vatican, he would not only lose credibility, but he would offend many powerful people to their core. Shaun could almost hear the echoing cries of 'blasphemy' being shouted down the halls.

'And if you'd pursued your allegations,' Shaun speculated, 'you would have had to prove them, which would mean revealing all the secret work you'd been doing, which would mean defeating the purpose of keeping it secret, which would mean revealing the technology ...'

'Which would lead to time-travel chaos,' David finished.

Giovanni sat back again, impressed. 'So, you at least understand a little of where I am coming from.' He finished his coffee and waved the waiter down for another.

'Now, as I was saying. I find myself in a delicate situation. I no longer speak on behalf of the Vatican in this matter, and have lost access to my liaison at The Society, although I'm working on that. I still control a Vatican intelligence team, but none of the contacts I dealt with regarding the work for The Society knows who I am. They knew me only by my code name, a code name and identity assumed now by Le Clerque.

'He has changed all the passwords and access codes that I established. I was a fool for not doing so the instant the Holy Father passed on from us.'

Shaun and David both absorbed what they were hearing as the incredible truth finally hit home. The Vatican. The Vatican knew about, and for all they knew, had instigated, The Journalist Project. And now, they had lost control. With the death of Pope Nicholas II in 2005, control had been wrested from its master's grasp.

'Okay,' David said slowly. 'What do I have to do with this?'

'Tell me, Mr Black,' Giovanni said with an amused smile, 'how did you get involved in this in the first place?'

'You want the player,' Shaun said matter-of-factly. 'You want the player to take to the Pope to prove your allegations without revealing your sources.'

'Very good, Mr ...?'

'Strickland,' Shaun said, not seeing any point in lying. Giovanni paused for a moment as if he had heard the name before. 'My name is Shaun Strickland.'

'Mr Strickland, you are very astute. I need to convince the Holy Father not only that The Journalist Project exists, but also that Le Clerque has plans to control it for his own gain. I have intelligence that suggests he has planted at least two agents into the program, although we don't know who yet.'

'Delissio and Barishnikov,' Shaun said flatly. David winced, uncomfortable about giving away all their cards, but Shaun was simply amazed as the pieces fit into place.

Giovanni's bushy eyebrows shot up. He fixed Shaun with a look that didn't falter even as he thanked the waiter for his fourth coffee that morning.

When they were again alone he said, 'Well, Mr Strickland. It seems you have some knowledge about our situation. I don't suppose you would care to share where you got the names of Journalist Project agents?'

'No, not really,' Shaun replied.

'Mr Strickland, I have to admit, I don't know anything about you. I do not know where you have come from, or what your role in this is, but for you to have such information means that you have access to something that we do not. What is it that you want, Mr Strickland? What is your part in this?'

'What do I want?' Shaun asked, leaning forward. 'I'll tell you what I want: I want my wife back. I want to catch the assholes responsible for her death and squeeze their nuts in a vice, then I want to tie them to a stump in the desert, tear their eyelids off and watch the sun boil their eyeballs.'

Giovanni raised his hand. David cowered at Shaun's apparent lack of respect for a man of the cloth. When the old Italian priest spoke, however, it was not with malice.

'I am sorry for your loss. May her soul rest with God.'

'Don't talk to me about God,' Shaun spat.

'I'm sorry you feel that way, but I'm afraid it's what I do. I talk about God. What I am interested in, however, is how you knew the names of two of the agents.'

Shaun said nothing, again a little heated from his outburst, his emotions at breaking point. The priest changed tact.

'What about you, Mr Black? What is it that you want? You travelled here on the promise of information about another disc. Why is it that you want one of these discs?'

David thought for a moment. 'I was commissioned to crack an encryption. Something so advanced it was like finding a television in the middle of a caveman's house,' he said, getting proud of his analogies. 'The minute I cracked the algorithm, I was fired. They fired me just like that and tried to kill me. I guess I want two things. I want to stop fearing for my life, to stop running and hiding; and I want to meet the person who invented that encryption. I want to meet the genius who makes me feel like I'm in kindergarten. If you have another disc, I thought you might know something about where that algorithm came from.'

'Aliens,' Giovanni said with a stern face. For a long moment no one spoke. Then, like a balloon bursting, he exploded with laughter.

'Ha! My friends, I jest!' The priest's mouth sprang wide as his eyes wrinkled. 'Aliens! Ha! You should see your faces! Ha haaa!' His hysterics began to infect Shaun as he started to chuckle. Giovanni continued to laugh as David stared ahead with a look of confusion and horror. He turned to stare as Shaun who had now fully opened the floodgates joined in with Giovanni's boisterous howls.

'That's not funny,' David said as he realised he was the brunt of the joke. 'That's not funny!' he repeated. 'How can that be funny!??'

'Aliens!' was all Shaun could say as he laughed uncontrollably slapping David on the back. People began to stare, but they could not stop. Before long, he too was beginning to chuckle and then broke out into an embarrassing snort-laugh that made the other two laugh even harder.

PART 2

SAILING UPWIND

'Brother can you spare me food, and give me a drink of wine?
I've been travelling on this road, for such a long, long time.
I have seen the wonders, but most amazing of them all,
I believe I've seen the face of the risen Lord.'

'The Risen Lord', Christopher Davison

CHAPTER 41

For the first time in minutes it seemed, he breathed. When he did, it was only short, sharp intakes as each new moment amazed him more than the last. Vincenso Giovanni removed the 3-D optical glasses in silence. He had not realised he was holding his breath. He folded the glasses and placed them on the table, then looked around. He was still in the hotel room. The two men who were staying here sat around the circular wooden table, watching him expectantly.

When Giovanni spoke, it wasn't what either of the Americans had expected to hear.

'I will give you five million dollars for this device,' the priest said, as if making an announcement.

Shaun and David didn't know how to respond.

'Five million,' the priest repeated. 'American, of course.'

Shaun and David paused a moment to make sure they had heard correctly. Then Shaun spoke up.

'The player is not for sale.'

There was a long pause.

'Ten million,' the Italian said, then sat back, waiting. After another lengthy silence, he smiled. 'Gentlemen, I jest!' he said, letting out a short laugh. The two other men in the room released a collective sigh.

'Fifteen,' he said then, with a deadly serious face.

Shaun and David looked at each other in confusion.

'Ah, you're still joking, right?'

The Italian waited a moment, then laughed again. To break the uncomfortably long silence that followed, Shaun got to the point.

'So, what do you make of it?' he asked as the Italian got up and helped himself to the room's mini-bar.

'What do I make of it? Ha! What do I make of it?' The priest sat back down and took a long pull on the cocktail of brandy, whisky and Baileys he had poured into a single glass. Then, without warning, he began to cry.

Shaun's head didn't move as his eyes slid sideways to David. The cardinal was visibly shaken, but Shaun soon realised that the tears were not those of someone who was upset.

'What do I make of it?' Giovanni repeated again. 'You say you invented this?' he turned to David.

'I … ah, did,' he stammered. All at once Giovanni leaped out of his seat and threw his arms around the software engineer, embracing him in a joyful bear hug that took David completely off guard. It was all David could do to return an awkward squeeze. With tears streaming down his face, Giovanni kissed David on the cheek.

'Okay! That's about enough of that!' David said.

'My dear boy,' Giovanni spoke through sniffles, 'do you have any idea what you've done? Do you know what you have created?' The priest released his hold and sat back, gripping David by both shoulders. 'You have completed the path. You have made it possible. They told me it would come, but to be honest, I didn't believe it. I have had the best scientists in the world working on that encryption for the better part of nine years, and no one has even come close. Almost all of them said there was no data on the disc. I knew that couldn't be true, not with what The Society has helped us achieve. You have given us a chance.'

'You've got a disc?' Shaun asked, suddenly realising that there was a very real possibility the whole thing was a trap.

'Got a disc?' Vincenso Giovanni echoed, turning to face him. 'Mr Strickland, I am the man responsible for their manufacture.'

Shaun's pupils dilated to let in more light. It was the only response his body could give while he tried to take in what he had just heard. Before he could ask his first question, however, David launched into a stream of his own.

'You make them? How can you make them and not know what's on them? Where do you make them? Who knows about this? Who's the man in charge? Who invented them?'

Giovanni, still beaming with delight, held up his hand. 'One at a time, my boy. One at a time. The how is not important, because what you have given us here today is the ability to see the why!' Giovanni sat back in his chair and took a deep breath.

'As I have told you, I had much responsibility over the organisation and facilitation of this project on behalf of the Holy Father, may God rest his soul. I designated tasks, many seemingly random to those involved, and brought the components of the operation together – well, from the Vatican's end anyway.

'The manufacture of the discs was outsourced to a company in Syria, a small group of men who were able to access the materials needed without arousing suspicion. I told them that we were trying to develop a new type of hard drive; an optical medium to be used in mobile phones. They did an excellent job and didn't ask questions, which is why they were paid so well and have all since retired.'

'Okay, but how did they know how to build these things?' asked David. 'I mean, the data is encrypted on these discs in a completely new way. It's nothing that could have been stored in any other compound, nothing save this exact molecular structure. Where did you get the spec?'

'The "spec"?' the intelligence officer asked, not quite understanding.

'The specifications? The requirements?'

'Oh, yes, well ... all the technology was provided by The Society. They sent the plans to me and I passed them on to these men. It was all, how you say? Gobbled-gook? Yes, it was all gobbled-gook to me. They were very secretive in how they released the information, making sure no one had enough to understand the whole picture.'

It was Shaun's turn to break in with the question he had been burning to ask for the entire afternoon.

'The Society? Who exactly are The Society?' he asked, staring straight into Giovanni's eyes.

'Who are they? Yes. That is something I would like to know myself. "The Society for World Historical Accuracy." It is nothing more than a name to me. All I know is that The Society ... well, they are the ones who seem to have the controlling hand in all this. Limitless funds, unparalleled technology. They started all this, although why they did so I do not know, save that perhaps they really wanted an accurate historical record.'

'I thought it was Nicholas II who commissioned all of this?' Shaun put in.

'Ah, yes, well ...' the Italian waved his hand. 'It depends on your point of view, doesn't it? It was the Holy Father, may God rest his soul, who approached me personally, but through my liaison I have come to understand that it is The Society who pulls the strings. It is they who provide the instructions; I simply use the resources at my disposal to make things happen. No one can pull more favours than the Pope, and I believe that The Society somehow convinced him to become involved. He was their "Angel investor", as you Americans put it.'

'Then, where are they? Where is this Society? How do I contact them?'

'How indeed!' Giovanni laughed his full belly laugh. 'Until my dealings with The Society, I would have said that the Vatican had perhaps the most professional, resourceful and secretive intelligence operation in the world. But now ... well ... I still don't know anything about The Society. All I could ever find was a phone number that diverts to an answering machine for a video store. It is a cover, of course, but when The Society wishes to make contact, they do. I have only ever met one of their junior agents, who does nothing more than silently deliver messages to me. I have tried to trace him but have never been successful. This Society seems to possess a technology greater than our own. Indeed, it was a blueprint handed to me one day that allowed the construction of The Facility.'

Shaun and David both pricked up at the mention of the word, recognising the reference from the diary. Shaun's eyes reflectively darted to his stomach, where he had the diary tucked into his belt, adding the look of a few extra pounds to his stature.

'Then it is The Society that is responsible for Lauren's death?' Shaun asked, again fixing Giovanni's gaze. The old Italian man drew a deep breath and sighed.

'I ... I do not know. If I am honest with you, I do not know, although I think not, but I could not rule it out. There is nothing in my experience to suggest that The Society would kill an innocent. I think that perhaps these people you say chased you and your wife were from somewhere else.'

'How do I know that *you* didn't send them?' Shaun said, accusation creeping into his tone.

'You do not. You do not know this. All you have is my word, and the fact is that if I had wanted to kill you, I could have done so one hundred times over by now. Mr Strickland, in my world, trust is a very important thing. It is the ultimate accolade to attain someone's trust. It is the one thing that you can never be certain of, but very often you have no choice but to give it. It is a little something that my life revolves around, a little something called faith. You have to trust me when I say that I did not kill your wife, and that I do not know who did.'

Shaun held his gaze a moment longer, then looked away. 'Fine.'

'The Society have been involved in this project for more years than the Vatican. When I was approached, I had very clear instructions from the Holy Father, but—'

'May God rest his soul,' David cut in.

'Yes,' Giovanni smiled, 'exactly. It was when I heard about what we were trying to achieve that I realised there was nothing worth more. And now, finally, thanks to you, we have the ability to see what all the fuss was about. We have the ability to watch an interview with Christ himself.' A tear threatened to burst free from Giovanni's eye. 'Now all we need is to find the disc! And before Le Clerque does. His motives, as I have mentioned, do not comfort me.'

'Then you're sure it exists?' David asked.

'Ah, my dear boy, again we run on faith, but I believe it exists,' Giovanni replied. He watched Shaun, who was deathly quiet and looked pained. 'There is something troubling you?' he asked quietly.

Slowly Shaun began to shake his head, as if struggling with something. Finally he spoke. 'I'm sorry, Father, it's just ... I don't believe like you believe. I just don't believe in Jesus, in God, in any of that stuff. I know it's your whole life and everything, but I just don't believe in a God that can be so cruel, that can let so many bad things happen. I just can't understand that.'

Giovanni nodded slowly, as if accepting an argument he had heard a thousand times before. He knew not to push the point.

'I understand what you are saying,' he said. 'I too do not always understand the way in which the Almighty works, but I know that the limitation is mine. It is I who do not understand in the same way a dog does not understand where or why its master goes away every day, needing to work to pay for the food he comes home to provide. Understanding changes. Knowledge changes, but things are the way they are. The world was always round, but men were killed for claiming so because the people did not understand. It is the understanding that changes, not the thing. I cannot answer that for you; it is not my place to. Each of us must come to our own conclusion.'

This did not make Shaun feel any better. Lauren was dead, and it was all because of some shared superstition. Shaun could not accept it. He would not accept it. He hated Giovanni then. He hated all of his kind. Their pompous knowing smiles, their gentle understanding nods, he hated all of them, all the religions, all their followers. Because of them, he was alone and Lauren was dead. If there were a God, why didn't he do something for Shaun for once? Why didn't he bring back Lauren ...

'Things are not always what they seem.' Giovanni was still speaking. 'We arranged for the discs to be laid in certain places in which they could survive the centuries and remain undiscovered. The Society chose those locations, but for the Christ interview, for the disc of our Lord, we were told there would be a map.'

Shaun sank down in his seat. He was tired of all this. He was tired of running and tired of the stress and he missed his wife – their nightly conversations, the feel of her hand in his as she gently fell into sleep. It hurt him like a bodily bruise. Even the thought of Masonville High provided some comfort. How far away that seemed right now.

Still, even if he did not believe in God and faith and religion, there were millions who did, and so he knew that there were many who would kill for this, as he had seen on the freeway and at the motel.

'Gentlemen,' Giovanni said after a moment, looking at his watch, 'I have an appointment at three o'clock with the Holy Father and I must hurry back.' He rubbed his face, running his fingers down his nose. 'But I will be done by four. I hope I might visit you again at that time?'

Shaun nodded, and David sat back like a kid who had to wait until he got home from church on Christmas morning before he was allowed to open his presents.

'When I return I will bring with me some things that will be of interest to you, I'm sure,' the priest said as he rose and walked to the door. He turned and gripped each of the men by the shoulders, planting a kiss on both cheeks. Then he paused and stood in the open doorway.

'I do not suppose I might take the unit to my meeting with the Holy Father now?' he asked. David was taken aback, but Shaun spoke before he had a chance to respond.

'I'm sorry, Father, the unit stays with us at all times. I'm sure you understand.'

'Yes ... yes I do,' the Italian sighed and nodded. 'And you understand that I had to ask.'

'We understand. We'll see you back here just after four, then?'

'Yes, four o'clock, gentlemen.'

With that, Vincenso Giovanni, the man in charge of one of the world's foremost secret intelligence agencies, turned and walked down the long hotel corridor. Shaun closed the door behind him.

For many moments the two men did not speak. Then with a sigh they sat, each alone with his thoughts. A considerable amount of time passed, and Shaun grew more and more nervous, but it was David who spoke first.

'You didn't tell him about the diary,' he started.

'We have to get out of here,' Shaun replied.

'Get out? What do you mean? He's coming back here,' David countered.

'We have to get out of this room. I have a bad feeling about this. I'm not sure our friend is all he seems to be; there's something he wasn't telling us. Did you see how he brushed his finger across his nose when he said he was meeting the Pope? That means he's lying.'

'How do you know that?'

'I watch a lot of TV. C'mon David, just get out of this room is all I'm saying. We can tell him where to find us. I've just got the feeling that this thing is a whole lot bigger than we thought.'

'Well, time machines, interviews with Napoleon and Jesus – it's pretty much the biggest thing that's ever happened,' David said.

'Yeah, but I just don't think we're safe in this—'

An enormous explosion cut into Shaun's comment and the men instinctively ducked at the sound. Glass sprayed the room.

'That came from the hotel car park!' David said, racing to the shattered window. He looked out from their third-storey window onto a mass of black smoke where a once-white Alfa Romeo spewed flames into the air. Shaun joined him as, in horror, they watched Giovanni roll out of the car onto the tarmac in death throes, his body a writhing mass of bubbling skin and fire.

'Shit!' Shaun yelled, then bolted for the door. David quickly packed the glasses back in with the player, then followed, suitcase in hand.

By the time David arrived at the burning car, sirens were already wailing. Shaun was crouched down next to the disfigured but still breathing figure of Giovanni. Smoke still rose from his clothing and his red-raw skin weeped fluid from its burst blisters. He made no sound. His pain looked absolute, the air seeming to sting every sensation as it whispered past. Shaun tried to reassure him, to calm him but felt incredibly helpless.

As an ambulance came screaming around the corner and the milling crowd parted, David watched. In an extreme surge of will and strength, the dying man lifted his hand and grabbed Shaun by the collar, pulling him down. David was having trouble getting through the thickening crowd to where the flaming wreckage was, but he could see that the old man was trying to say something to Shaun. It was only a few short moments before Shaun was being ushered away from the burning car and the Jesuit priest was covered in a special plastic wrap and loaded into the back of the ambulance.

When Shaun finally walked over to David, his eyes were hard and aggressive.

'What did he say?' David asked. For a moment Shaun didn't answer.

'We have to leave Rome,' he replied, and walked away.

'He knew about the diary,' Shaun said once he was sure there was no one in the nearby seats who may have taken an interest. He had bought first-class tickets this time, thanks to his newly overflowing bank account. He knew they would be followed – whoever had attacked Giovanni wouldn't waste time. Shaun and David only hoped that the fact that they hadn't decided where they were heading meant their moves could not easily be anticipated.

'You told him about the diary?' David asked.

'No, I didn't tell him. He knew. When he was lying there, he pulled me down to him and said: "Read. Read till the end." We both understood what he was talking about.'

'Then, do you mind telling me why you bought ten open tickets all over Europe and the Middle East?' David continued.

'Because that's exactly what we're going to do. We need to move, but there's no telling where we should go. That is, until we track down this Society for World Historical Accuracy or this mysterious Facility.' Shaun held up the diary, wound the binding string, and laid it on the tray table in front of them both. 'The answers are in here, I'm certain. Giovanni knew we had it, but he didn't say a word. What does that tell you?'

David stared at him blankly.

'He didn't want us to know,' Shaun answered himself. 'He probably assumed that if we knew that he had information about the diary, it would have caused problems for our negotiation. He knew that Lauren was killed by people looking for that same diary. He probably had some inkling as to who they were.'

'So, you think Giovanni had a connection to the people who are chasing you?'

'That's what I think. But maybe not a happy connection. I think he really was trying to help us and they found out about it. Right now, the only way we can solve this is by getting through the rest of what's written. Maybe we'll find the map. This little tour we're taking will give us the chance to do that.' Shaun flipped the book open and buried his head. David reached forward to his first-class 'environment' panel and switched on his reading light. He squeezed his eyes shut for a moment, then opened them and looked down.

CHAPTER 42

We travelled south for a week. Miles's guide, not much more than a boy, steered us clear of the likely places the Romans would search for us. Malbool thought they would not search for more than a few days, but I suspected otherwise. Miles had given us horses and food, while describing how he had been given instructions to be at this place, at this time, the night after he saw me fight in the Royåle. It was a huge victory for him, after living so long to complete the mission, that it had happened exactly as he was told it would.

Leaving him, I carried a strange sense of inevitability as we rode through the night, our guide and me on our own horses and Malbool balancing Mishca asleep in front of him. When we finally came over a rise to look down on a shipping port, our guide spoke.

'There is a merchant vessel here that you can take to Jerusalem. If they ask for a bounty, pay them with this,' the guide said, pulling a large leather pouch from his saddlebag. I loosened the drawstring and nearly fell off my mount as the gold twinkled in the moonlight.

'What's this?' I asked in amazement.

'My master has been keeping this fortune for you for a long time. He says it's to guarantee your safe passage. He says that you are on a mission to change the course of the world.'

These past few days our guide had treated us with what I took for mistrust but now realised was actually a nervous fear.

'Exactly what has your master said about us?' I asked.

The boy's eyes quivered a little, then he looked away. 'He said you would come. No one believed him. They all thought he was going mad in his age, but he said that it was prophecy, that you were the chosen one.'

'Ha!' I laughed. 'Chosen one indeed!' Then I stopped, realising my boisterous laughter did nothing to bolster the boy's confidence. I took the pouch and shook the guide's delicate hand.

'Tell your master that he has helped to save the world. Tell him that every year he waited for me was not a waste, that I won't let him down, and that I will return for him before his years are through.'

The guide nodded. 'He says that you must, for there is more he has to tell you. The merchant's name is Zachariah. He has chartered a boat already, and it sails at first light today. If you'd come last year, you would have been waiting a week!'

'It's all about timing, isn't it?' I said, motioning for Malbool to wake Mishca. It amazed me how readily the boy was willing to accept the extraordinary events that were taking place. Children, it seems, are still discovering everything, so the boundaries of their worlds are not set. They can still believe.

The guide spun his horse and began the long return journey north. Malbool, Mishca and I stood atop the hill, bathed in moonlight, staring down at the sea. The last frontier before Jerusalem.

'We are looking for Zachariah,' I said in a hushed voice to a man setting up a stall for the morning's market. He eyed me up and down, then shook his head. It had been the same story for the past hour, and I was getting nervous. No one seemed to know who we were talking about, and we had exhausted every vessel along the dock.

'What I don't get,' Shaun whispered to David as they hunched over the text while the rest of the cabin slept, 'is why, if this whole mission is so important, The Society didn't send more people back to help him out.'

David looked up at Shaun. He had already finished the page and was busy scrunching a cloth napkin with his left hand. He studied Shaun for a second silently, then motioned down to the diary with his eyes. Shaun continued to read.

'Graeme.'

The voice came from behind me. I turned, to look into the familiar eyes of a man I had once known, though he was easily ten years older than when I had seen him last.

'Hamza?' I stared in disbelief.

The man, shorter than me and with the warm olive skin of his Jordanian lineage, smiled back.

'Zachariah,' the Arab corrected me. 'I'm an Israelite now – you'd be amazed what passes for a Jew these days!' Again he smiled his broad

smile, exaggerated now by a small goatee of gold and grey. His teeth showed a decade of neglect, but still beamed the same warmth they always had. Back in The Facility, Hamza, Officer X2, was my closest friend. I could not hold back from an embrace.

'What are you doing here?' I asked, bewildered. Hamza did not say anything, but he held out his forearm. Small, but clearly visible, was a scar that took the shape of a word: VOMIT.

'I don't understand,' I said, shaking my head. 'Who is your assignment?'

Hamza smiled again. 'You.'

He pointed to a moderate boat just down the port from us. 'Come, we have a long journey ahead of us, and not much time. You can ask all your questions on the way.'

'Why not much time? I'm fairly sure the Romans would have stopped looking for us by now, and Delissio is dead.'

'Ah! Then somebody got his shot in?'

'How did you know that?'

Ignoring the question, Hamza looked again at me, his forehead crinkling with concern. 'Graeme, I'm not talking about the Romans. I'm talking about your assignment. It's a three-day journey to Jerusalem, and two nights from now Joshua Ben Jacob will sit down to dinner with twelve of his most esteemed colleagues and break bread. I don't need to tell you what happens the next day. We must hurry.'

Shaun moved to turn the page, but David held his hand down. 'Are you telling me everything?' he asked.

'What are you talking about? You're the only person I've been able to tell anything.'

'Level with me, man, c'mon. Have you read this thing already?'

'David, what? You know I haven't.'

'Well, you just seem to know an awful lot about what's coming: the arrow through the back, the antibiotics, sending more people back to help him. Right after you say it, it happens. I don't want to be taken for a ride here. Just tell me if you're after the unit; I'm sick of all this deception.'

'If I knew what was coming, would I tell you? Would I give you a running commentary? Seriously. I know that we're in the middle of something huge and that we both have something everyone else seems to want – this diary and your video device. I know that Lauren died for this, and I'm not going to let that be for nothing. I don't want your player.'

David slowly removed his hand from the book, and the two men eyed each other warily. David started, 'Look, to be honest, this is frustrating as hell. No offence, man, but my grandmother reads faster than you. Why don't you keep going for a bit, then I'll catch up?'

Shaun didn't understand. 'What? You don't want to know what happens?'

'Of course I do, but there's something I have to do. I should have done it a while ago.' With that, David pulled out a pen and the complimentary airline notebook, and began to write. After a couple of seconds, he looked back up at Shaun. 'Seriously, go ahead, I'll catch up.'

Shaun shrugged and returned to Graeme Fontéyne on the boat to Jerusalem.

CHAPTER 43

The first two days of the voyage passed without incident, save for Malbool's bout of seasickness and Mishca's excitement at learning to climb the mast. The seas were calm and the crew, all four of them, seemed content to do their bit and leave us alone. The vessel was called The Jewel of the Sea *and carried a variety of goods bound for Jerusalem, mostly silk and weapons. I was deep in conversation and finally enjoying the company of a familiar and friendly face.*

'So, the whole time your mission was to collect me at that port?' I asked.

'Well, I was given a few subsidiary tasks, of course. I took a bunch of scrolls from the Essenes and hid them away near the Dead Sea, but basically that was all just to pass the time. I had a few years to wait – they sent me back a little earlier than I expected.'

'So, the mark on your arm?' I pressed.

'Yeah, funny, just before I was about to go back, literally as I stood on the transporter platform naked, the professor himself approached me, handed me a capsule and told me to swallow it. He said that you must *get your interview or millions will die. I had to make sure of it. Then the guards came and held out my arm and cut me. Can you believe that? They cut me right there on the platform. I guess they wanted the pain to be fresh when I arrived, because when I did ... well, I'm sure you know how it feels.'*

'Millions will die?'

Hamza held his hands out and shrugged.

'So, the first thing you did was to look at your bleeding arm and saw the word VOMIT?'

'The very first thing. Of course, I think I was the last of us to be sent back, it was three years after you'd gone! Ah, who can say why they do anything they do? We each only know our little bit, don't we?'

'So, what did you do when you arrived?' I asked.

'Well, unlike you and the other primary agents, I didn't have any implants. All I had was this massive pain in my arm and an instruction to vomit. Funny really, it's like they knew that you'd forget everything, but that was never mentioned. Did they say that to you?'

'No. No, I went for more than a month and had no idea. I was cut in a fight and found the filament that led to the camera inside my leg. I would have never known otherwise.'

'Hm, strange. If they knew it makes you forget, I don't know why they wouldn't have done the same thing for everyone.'

'I don't know either. But we have another problem,' I then told him.

'Oh, really? Besides the fact that once we dock in port we may already be too late for you to complete your mission?' Hamza sat back in his small cabin. These merchant ships were not designed for comfort.

'It was Delissio. Something he told me. I think there's another agent in Jerusalem.'

'Ah, well, yes there would be, wouldn't there? Two for each assignment and all that – your pair would have been there.'

'Yes, but Delissio wasn't part of the project. I mean he was, but he had another agenda. He said Barishnikov was in Jerusalem, and was going to kill Jesus.'

'What?' Hamza sat up.

'He thought that I had discovered Barishnikov's intention, and that the Russian had spilled the beans on Delissio's own involvement, and that's why I was in Rome. He thought I was there to stop him. He must have thought I'd killed Barishnikov, so he sent agents back to Jerusalem to "finish the job" as he put it.'

'How did Delissio know? Was he really a spy for someone? And if he was, then who? Who would want Jesus killed prematurely? And how could they possibly infiltrate The Facility? It's in the middle of the Afghan caves in the middle of an Allied war; it's not exactly something you'd stumble across.'

'David!' Shaun yelled, grabbing the engineer by the arm. Groans from around the plane's cabin indicated how little the other passengers appreciated his outburst. He shrank back in his seat, but shook his new friend vigorously. David looked up from where he was filling pages with notes, diagrams and code.

'What? Man, you know I'm really in the zone here, it's hard to break this train of thought.'

'It's in Afghanistan,' Shaun whispered excitedly.

'What is?'

'The Facility. It's in the caves in Afghanistan!'

'The diary says that?'

'The diary says that. We've got to get there.'

'Okay, okay. In case you didn't know, the US has a major military operation going on there. I don't think it's as easy as "Let's get there."'

For the first time Shaun looked down at the masses of information David was pouring out onto the paper. 'What are you doing?' he asked.

'Ah, I'm writing down the spec. I studied that damned disc for years, and next to all my research was wiped when I left Newcom. The rest was at my apartment in Spain, and I zeroed all the data just before I left to meet you. I'm trying to figure out how they could create a recording device to encode the video data without knowing how to play it back.'

David looked up at Shaun. He sometimes forgot that this was the same guy who had written those papers he had read online, the most ingenious works he had ever come across. He was so used to treating people like idiots, that when he came across someone of Shaun's intellect he forgot that the guy might actually understand what he was talking about.

'Look man, just read. Keep it to yourself for now, I'll catch up, but I have to get this down while I've got the time.'

Shaun nodded.

'It's in the middle of the Afghan caves in the middle of an Allied war; it's not exactly something you'd stumble across. It would have to be someone who's involved with the program, wouldn't it.'

'I don't know. For all we know, Barishnikov may still be blissfully unaware of the fact he was born two thousand years in the future. Delissio said that he only remembered who he was when he saw me – and that was twenty-five years after he arrived in Rome. Seeing me caused the recall. What if Barishnikov hasn't remembered his mission? When Delissio remembered, he sent his own men to Jerusalem to make sure the job was done properly. I may have caused the very thing I am now trying to prevent.' The thought struck home.

'It's possible,' Hamza said, sinking back down onto his bunk. 'This could change history immeasurably; create effects that would ripple out across time and have untold ramifications. If there were no crucifixion, there would be no Christianity, at least not the way we know it. Millions of people would never be born.' Hamza's eyes stared into the distance as possibilities and consequences filtered through his mind.

'There would be no need for your mission. The whole Facility may not exist, and you and I may never be sent back here.'

'But we are *here,' I protested.*

'We are now. *But who's to say what will happen if we change things that we know have happened? The world we come from may never exist. Graeme, we can't let this happen. If even one thing is changed now, the course of history will be altered and we may not exist! And as I said, you* must *get your interview.'*

The constant thing drilled into us during our training at The Facility was The Rule of Knowledge: knowledge is absolute; if there was something we knew to have happened, then we must not interfere. This still allowed me a lot of freedom in the sense that there was very little from this time period that was known for certain, and so I was taught to work with the philosophy that if I didn't know for certain that something had not happened, then the fact that I was here doing it meant that it did. Of course, you would know all this better than me.

Shaun read the last line again. 'Of course, you would know all this better than me.'

Who was he talking to?

Puzzled, he continued.

CHAPTER 44

We could not have been more than half a day out when it happened. It was Mishca who alerted us to the ship heading towards us from our port bow. Immediately one of the crew boys, a lean, wispy figure not yet twenty, scaled the mast to check what Mishca was calling about. The word he called down sent the crew into a frenzy. 'Raiders!' he screamed.

There was instant panic all over the boat. Hamza bolted out of the cabin and scrambled onto the deck.

'What is it?' I called from below.

'Sea raiders. Pirates. They've started getting game beyond their years, attacking boats along the merchant channels. They want their bounty, and they'll kill us all for it.'

'Pirates?' I repeated. 'We're being attacked by pirates?' I would have laughed if the situation were not so serious.

'Can we defend this ship? Can we outrun them?' I asked, coming up on to the deck to see for myself.

The ship's captain, a broad man of nearly fifty, came down and barked at his crew in Hebrew. He paused a moment to stare out over the ship's port side.

'They'll not catch us without a fight!' The salty old sea dog growled as he stalked past me.

The Jewel*'s single mast was held tight by a forestay, a line running from the top of the mast to the ship's bow. It creaked with the unfurling of the sail. Mishca ran up to the front of the ship, and Malbool sat near the stern, the wooden barrels on the deck providing him something to grip as he battled his nausea.*

'What's he doing?' I asked Hamza as he stared at the frothing whitewash parting before our pursuer.

'The captain is going to tack upwind. They'll chase us, and catch us too – they're far more manoeuvrable than we are.'

'Well, ah, what's the point in letting ourselves get caught?' I queried, not understanding the tactic.

'The point,' he said, watching the skilled crew at work, 'is that if we tried to pass them now, they would intercept us. If we head away from them upwind they will tack and jibe and follow us. It will take them an hour or so to catch us like that.'

'I still don't follow,' I conceded.

'Well, we're much lighter. Our sail is almost the same size as theirs and we have little cargo. When they get too close to us to cut any angle, our captain will come about and head directly downwind with an open sail. We'll shoot away from them, and once we're downwind of them, they'll never be able to catch us.' He sounded almost excited at the prospect of the chase. 'That's why they approach from downwind like that. They scare the vessels into making a straight bolt diagonally downwind, but the big raider ship just cuts a slightly shallower angle and catches them.'

I was thrown forward as the boat tilted dangerously, and boxes and crew were sent scuttling across the deck. From the front of the boat I heard a squeal of delight as Mishca clung to the figurehead. Unbelievable! I looked up from my hands and knees and saw Hamza regain his footing.

'Can't he tell us when he's going to do that?' I spat.

'You better find something to hang onto,' he replied. 'That's going to be happening for the next hour or so.'

'Isn't it obvious what he's doing?'

'I'm sure it is.'

'Then why are they following us?' I asked, looking out at the large foreboding silhouette that seemed to grow noticeably larger before my eyes.

'What choice do they have?' Hamza countered. 'They have to make a run for us or we really would put too much distance on them heading into the wind. We'll be zigzagging across each other's path soon, so I hope our captain doesn't misjudge his line. We'll have a couple of close crosses before it's safe to try and come full about.'

I sat back and grumbled, wrapping my arm in some loose rigging as Hamza kept watch on the ship, which seemed to gain far too quickly.

Malbool was having serious issues with the sharp turns and was now a peculiar grey colour. Mishca, on the other hand, was being flung about and, despite knowing the danger of the situation, he giggled with glee.

The raiders gained rapidly, and I was amazed at how the large vessel sliced through the water. The Jewel *came about again and cut an angle into the wind. The rope bit into my arm as the deck tilted violently, and many of the smaller objects were flung into the water.*

The hull righted itself and we lurched forward. Each turn took half a mile off our lead as the details of our pursuer's vessel began to come into focus. Still we pressed on.

'They're gaining too fast!' I heard one of the crew call back to the captain. The old seaman ignored the call and prepared to jibe. This run would take us across the path of the oncoming vessel, and the captain knew it.

'Now!' he barked. Again it felt as if a great weight suddenly attached itself to our speeding vessel as we dug into the water. As the sea level rose all around our starboard side, it became clear that we weren't going to make it. The raiders' ship was much faster on the straight than Hamza or the captain had given her credit for. As we continued on the only course we could take, the reality began to sink in: they were going to catch us.

'Up two!' the captain called. One of the crew sprinted the length of the deck, hurdling the wooden boxes of silk along the way. When he reached the front of the boat, he pulled on a rope that sent a sail, about half the size of the main sail, springing in to the air. As it filled with air and funnelled it back into the main sail, the effect was instant: the Jewel *shot forward. At the back of the boat, the remaining two crew struggled to hold the steering oar against the pull of the wind.*

Like losing control of a car on a wet road, we slid towards the inevitable, and as we approached I watched the raiders adjust their line to compensate for our new speed. They wouldn't get close enough to board us on this pass, but perhaps on the next.

The air moved in gusts, rocking and tilting both boats as they cut through the water. I counted down to the moment we would cross their line. Eight, seven, six ...

'Mishca!' I called out, 'get down from there!' The boy was no longer having fun as he came to understand what was happening. He scrambled down from the bulkhead and came to rest near where I was crouched halfway along the deck. The Jewel *groaned with the effort. Four, three ...*

I looked out at the vessel, which was now larger than life and speeding straight towards us. We would clear it – just.

Two, one ...

We shot across the raiders' line and I saw clearly six men standing on the bow with their swords drawn. I looked into their dark faces as our eyes met; close enough to make out their sneers. I locked eyes with a man caressing his long, straight blade with menace. The men just behind him were holding coiled lengths of rope with grappling hooks tied to one end. My head turned slowly as we held each other's gaze. The large wooden ship crossed behind us. It was mesmerising, so close and yet unable to do anything. Our entire crew was seized with terror. Then, the moment was gone, and the frenzy began again.

'Full ahead!' the captain called, but was distracted by one of his crew calling up to him from the stern. All on deck turned in time to see, to our horror, the raiders' vessel coming about. They were turning to chase us.

This was not supposed to happen. We were hoping for another diagonal pass, but the raiders were backing their own upwind speed to chase us down directly, without giving us the room to cut and run.

The captain sprang into action. 'Prepare full about!' he called. He was going to try to start the run downwind early, a dangerous ploy.

I looked to Hamza as he stood nervously at the rear of the boat, his fingers curled around the wooden railing, splinters biting into his flesh.

'It's our only chance,' he said before I could ask. 'They're much faster than us upwind, and for us to outrun them, we must run true and straight. They're still downwind of us, and if they match our turn they'll catch us before we can get clear.'

'Everyone grab onto something!' the captain called, while twisting his forearm in a lashing from one of the cargo boxes.

'Now!' he barked, and immediately the world tilted on its side. Anything loose on the deck was catapulted into the water. Malbool's feet slipped out from under him. Landing flat on his back, he slid the width of the deck and planted his feet on the railing, narrowly avoiding being sent into the water himself. Barely holding his lunch from the constant tacking, the slide across the deck gave him no reason to keep his food any longer: bile and bread exploded across the wooden surface. Rolling away from the pile of vomit, he wrapped his arms around the rope webbing that bound the crate of swords.

Within moments the ship straightened, and the wind that had been wisping across the main sail now filled it completely. The wooden hull split the ocean, and the Jewel *seemed to sing as she ran. We all looked out over the port stern, watching as the raiders' ship turned to match our course.*

'They're coming with us,' Hamza said. 'They're going to try to intercept.'

Our trading vessel shot like an arrow, its large, lightweight sail paying off. But the raiders matched our pace, and with their ship already a little further downwind, we were bound for collision.

'They're going to hit us!' Mishca called from beside me, fear in his voice. 'They're going to ram right into us!'

The boy was right.

The captain shrieked more instructions to his crew, who began to protest, but they were silenced by his reprimand. Grudgingly one of the oarsmen rushed over to the crates where Malbool was lying entangled in the webbing. He unwound the binding rope and lifted the top of the box, frantically pulling out swords and throwing them into the ocean to ease the weight of our boat. I had serious doubts as to whether it would make any difference to our speed, but the next box gave up its quarry, and then the next.

Malbool, still queasy, struggled to his feet and began to help the crewman throw the swords over the side. He paused just long enough to grab a sword for each of us before disposing of the last of the metal.

Both ships raced for that inevitable point of intersection, and I could hear the raiders' brutal cries as they anticipated the lunge. If we made it first we would be clear; they would not have the legs to run us down. If they got close enough to hook us with their ropes, it would be a very different story.

Malbool handed each of us a sword, unable to do anything but wait. Mishca was sent below. Eighty feet now ... seventy ...

We gripped our swords and came to stand at the port bow of the Jewel *as the raiders approached, four or five men with ropes standing on their boat's starboard side. Sixty feet ...*

We sped on as the first of the hooks came sailing towards us. They fell short and splashed into the water. Forty feet ...

The raiders cried out savagely as two more of the grappling hooks sailed out towards our deck. They were going to get us. I ran back along the side of the boat and timed the hook as it arced and fell. Like a batter sending leather to the bleachers, I swung my sword at the falling hook and batted it away from the ship.

The second hook, however, breached the side of our boat and fell onto the deck, quickly dragging backwards to bite into the decking. Malbool leaped, his sword outstretched in front of him. In an overhead swoop he brought his blade down below the hook, severing its umbilical cord to the ship as he crashed onto his stomach. Twenty feet ...

We sliced in front of the raiders' vessel as the final two hooks landed on our stern. Hamza and one of the oarsmen responded instantly; the hooks were cut and thrown back into the water. Thirty feet ...

That was it. We were clear. In a moment of exultation Hamza ran to the stern and called out with his middle finger raised. 'Fuck you!' he screamed back at the pirate ship.

I shook my head and allowed a smile, knowing the insult was wasted on the sea raiders. Hamza cheered, but the elation was premature. In a moment his smile changed to a look of inquisition, and then concern, as he followed my wide-eyed glare skywards.

It flew straight. From the rear of the boat, twenty-five feet up, a long wooden spear flew from their vessel to ours. It would not hit anyone on deck, but then, it was not intended to. A mass of burning cloth was wrapped about its shaft, leaving a trail of black smoke. Its steel tip pierced the material of our main sail easily, and the eruption of flame engulfed the fabric.

The tongues of orange spread about the sail as the fire ate with feverish hunger. Buckets were immediately lowered over the side in an effort to collect precious water to douse the flames, but the damage was done: the main sail was useless, and within a minute the raiders' vessel would pull up alongside our own. I tightened my grip around my sword. While the crew fought to control the flames, the raiders' ship came within touching distance. The raiders had lined up along their port side in anticipation of boarding our now crippled vessel, and I knew they would slaughter us without exception.

I remembered Mishca downstairs, hiding in the cabin as the flames licked at the wood of the mast. I knew that if the crew were busy fighting pirates, they would lose in their plight to douse the fires before the ship became a blazing inferno. With that thought, I ran towards the stern. Malbool and Hamza called after me, but I didn't stop.

The box that contained the support for the steering oar gave me just enough foothold to spring into the air. I hit it running and leaped off the back of the boat, hanging for an eternity out over the open ocean.

I hit the raiders' deck and rolled as I landed. The sound caught the sea pirates off guard as I retook my feet and drove my sword forward. Two of the pirates fell before they realised what was happening. The last thing they had expected was for us to bring the fight to them. As I stood and spun, I counted nine on the deck but knew there would be more. Each was armed with a variety of weapons, obviously collected from their various bounties.

A tall, willowy man slashed downwards, but I cut in close to him and took his arms off at the wrists before he could deliver his blow. Shooting my heel out, I kicked the man off the deck and into the water, streams of blood pulsing from the stumps where his hands used to be.

Calls went up as the raiders tried to decide whether to leap to the flaming merchant vessel or deal with the attacker on their own ship. Their hesitation gave me enough of an advantage to spin and decapitate two raiders as they stood next to each other dumbfounded. Thrown rather than swung, a heavy wooden club caught me in the back, causing my fingers to open reflexively and drop my sword. I didn't reach for the weapon but rather shot my foot out at the nearest raider's knee. The tearing ligaments sounded like the branch of a tree breaking. The knee bent the wrong way. A full row of yellow rotted teeth greeted me as the man screamed in pain. His sword fell into my waiting hand and I smashed his teeth out with the hilt.

I had now lost the element of surprise. The next attacks came two at a time, one from the front and one from the rear. Having the sword gripped like an enormous dagger, I pushed the blade backwards, assisting the thrust with both my hands. Simultaneously I tucked my knee high and shot the sole of my foot out at the attacker rushing towards my chest. His jaw broke on both sides. I barely noticed the sound of the body behind me sliding off my new broadsword.

Three more of the raiders battled Malbool and Hamza in an attempt to board our ship as flames began to take hold. Mishca was still hiding in the cabin – between the flames and the raiders, he did not have long. I refocused on a new attacker in front of me.

He swung at my ankle as I leaped forward from a box in a twisting somersault above his head. I struck before I landed, my blade skewering the crown on his head. His brain blended as his body danced like a possessed marionette. By the time he fell to the deck I was moving back towards the Jewel.

Malbool fought with determination, and felled one of the attackers brutally, but he was unused to fighting at sea and found it difficult to balance on the burning, tilting ship. Hamza, on the other hand, was in his element. Trained at The Facility and living on trading vessels between Jerusalem and Rome, he punished any who dared to engage him.

As I jumped back to the Jewel, *the main mast, weakened by the onslaught of flame, fell back onto the cargo netting at the rear of the deck, setting the ropes and boxes ablaze. The silks took to the flame, producing a pungent black smoke. I sprinted for the cabin, but before I could get there, a raider kicked the cabin door off its hinges with a crack. I heard Mishca's terrified scream as the raider grabbed him by the shirt and dragged him onto the deck.*

Without time to close the distance, I did the only thing I could. Underhand like a softball pitch I swung my sword and released it. The blade tip bit into Mishca's shoulder, drawing both blood and a yell of pain from the boy, but not before it passed through the lung of the pirate who held him. Mishca kicked free as the man's grasp went limp and his body fell back onto the cabin floor. I raced to Mishca, who reached up to his shoulder where blood had started to seep.

'I'm sorry,' I said as I knelt beside the boy to inspect his injury. Before I could get a good look at it, he threw his arms around my neck and began to sob. I hugged him back, but pulled away to look at his face.

'You have to get off this ship, do you understand? It's going to sink, the fire is too far gone.' The boy nodded and looked about, for the first time seeing the flames and their destruction.

'Mishca, listen,' I said, refocusing the boy's attention. 'You need to make it home. Stay away from the fighting. Head for the bulkhead.'

The boy looked at me, confused.

'The front of the boat. Like where you were playing earlier. Stay up there and hide if you can, there're some boxes up there. Do you understand?'

Mishca nodded and ran for the front of the ship, steering clear of the spot where Malbool had opened the belly of another of his attackers.

Hamza had dispatched two of the pirates and boarded the larger vessel to engage the few remaining mercenaries. Two of the Jewel's *crew lay face down in pools of their own blood, beyond help.*

It was useless. The flames had caused too much structural damage and we were taking on water quickly. I hustled the remaining crew along the length of the ship.

'This is my ship! I'll not leave her!' It was the guttural voice of the Jewel's *captain. He stood alone with a single bucket, futility his only companion as he tried to douse the roaring flames. As he turned to protest my anticipated negotiation for him to leave, I thumped the side of his skull with the hilt of my sword, knocking him unconscious. With the old man in a shoulder carry, I drove along the ever-increasing slope of the deck and made for the raiders' vessel. When I got to the border between our ships, I saw that the fight had spilled entirely onto*

our attackers' boat. Mishca too had slipped from the bulkhead onto the attackers' boat.

The Jewel *was sinking fast, her deck now at least six feet lower than that of the raiders' large vessel – and the gap increased every second. I dropped my sword and brought the old captain onto my chest, then used every bit of strength I had left to throw him up to the deck.*

The boat tilted as it sank. The stern disappeared below the rolling ocean, forcing the pointed nose of the ship to rise, water streaming from its barnacled underbelly. It was to this last bastion of hope that I now ran, in a race against fire, gravity and friction as my legs pumped quickly just to stay in the same spot above the water. Slipping and sliding, I struggled upwards. When at last I scrambled on all fours to scale the ship's figurehead, it was vertical.

With a final leap, even as the last of the wood fell away from beneath my feet, I launched myself at the rim of the raiders' ship.

One arm.

Fully stretched. Fingers.

I hung. For the briefest of moments I caught my breath, then reached up with my other hand just as a blade came down on it. My fingers were sliced in two, severed at the second knuckle, and my hand fell away. Once again I hung by one arm.

I didn't scream. I didn't even realise what had happened, just wondered how I'd lost my grip. I looked up to see Malbool pounding his fist into the raider who had severed my fingers. He was punching him repeatedly in the face, his nostrils flared, rage in his eyes. He continued long after the raider's face had caved in beyond repair. With a final shove, Malbool tossed the body over the lip of the railing and sent it splashing into the frothing water. I looked down and saw the trail of blood fanning out below me, and dark shapes moving curiously around the scene.

'Saul!' I heard a voice as my wrist was gripped from above. 'Reach up!'

Malbool caught my other arm by the wrist and hauled me over the railing and onto the deck. Bodies were strewn around me, spilling their life force onto the rough wooden boards. His chest heaving, the African grinned.

'Well, nice to see that you can break too, man from the future!' With a thud he flopped onto the deck beside me and recovered his breathing. After a moment, he became serious. 'Do you have any other magic to put those back on?'

I stared at the stumps on my left hand. The slice was diagonal, and ran just above my middle knuckles, leaving only a thumb and forefinger intact. Malbool took his blade and sliced into his tunic, tearing a strip. He wrapped it around the offending stumps as I winced at the contact.

Looking about, I saw that the captain was conscious and giving commands to the remainder of his crew. Hamza and one of the other men threw bodies over the side of the vessel, fuelling the feeding frenzy that had begun off the port bow. The time we had lost was precious, as were the men, but we were alive and Mishca still had a chance to get home.

Shaun flicked the page, and as he did so he noticed the intricacies of his hand. He looked at his fingers, and wondered what he would do without them.

CHAPTER 45

'So, tell me again,' Mishca said. Hamza stood behind the boy and stretched his arm out.

'Now, hold up your thumb.' Mishca did as he was told.

'That's two, right?'

'Yes, good, that's two. Now a fist. Good. Look beyond the fist at the stars. The width of your fist is ten arc minutes. That's right. Good.'

'And when I spread my hand it's twenty?'

'Very good. Yes, twenty. That's how sailors for thousands of years will measure the distance of stars, but they won't understand what they're doing.'

'And where did you learn it, Zachariah?' Mishca asked the Jordanian who posed as a Jew.

'Well, you know that friend of yours? The one you call Saul?'

'Saul knows about the stars too? He taught you?'

'He knows about the stars, but he didn't teach me exactly. We learned at the same place. We sort of went to school together.'

'You did?' Mishca asked, then said, 'What's school?' looking at the grey-and-gold-haired man. Hamza laughed.

'It's where you learn together with children your own age.'

'But you're old. He wouldn't have been born when you went to school.'

My friend threw his head back and laughed at this, clasping the boy's shoulder.

'You're right. But I was not so old once, and there was a time when we were about the same age, if you can believe that,' Hamza said offhandedly.

'Yeah, the time machine.'

Hamza stopped laughing. 'What did you say?'

'The time machine. The doctor who fixed us told me about it. He kept saying that they sent him back too far. He kept saying they were bas … bar-tards?'

'Bastards?' Hamza asked, and then roared again. 'They are bastards! They are! They sent me back too far as well.'

Mishca started to laugh at seeing Hamza so jovial. Hamza came over to me and sat down. We looked at Malbool sleeping and the captain manning the steering oar. We had all settled to gather our strength before our arrival in Jerusalem. The captain wanted to dock a little south to avoid arriving at the port in a pirate vessel, but all being equal he was happy with his new acquisition. Underneath the silver full moon, the ship was like a ghost.

'Who was it?' Hamza asked me.

'Who was who?' I replied.

'Who was it that fixed you up? The boy said that you were cut up pretty bad in the arena.'

I let my head fall back against the wood. 'It was Miles, as an old man. It was a shock to the system to see him, but it was ... nice.'

'Miles? He wasn't an agent ...' Hamza let it hang.

'No, I know. He said that he had been given a special mission. He wouldn't tell me how he knew where to be, but he saved my life.'

'I knew that someone was going to shoot someone, but I didn't know who. We haven't really talked about this.'

'I know,' I said. 'We haven't talked properly for months.'

'Over a decade,' Hamza put in. I smiled. Although I had seen my friend recently, he had not seen me for years. It was still a little hard to comprehend.

'Like I said, Delissio thought I was in Rome to kill him. But, Hamza, it's all too convenient. I was exhausted and injured from the Royåle, and Delissio was about to kill me – then Miles conveniently popped one through his back. He said that he had been waiting for fifty years. Every year he went to the games and waited to see me fight. His whole mission was purely to put an arrow in Delissio's back. Hamza, how could he have known?'

'I don't know,' Hamza lied as he sat back.

I began to get a little suspicious.

'So, how did you *know I would be at the port in Italy?'*

'I knew you would be there the same way you know what your mission is. It was programmed into my mission log. I have no other assignment, Graeme. You are it. This journey is it. I have no camera implant like you do. I have to make sure you get your interview.'

'Yeah. But that's just it. I wasn't supposed to go to Rome. I arrived a hundred miles from Jerusalem. Getting in that fight in the village

was a mistake, it wasn't part of my mission. At the time I didn't remember anything. I didn't even know who I was. I didn't have your, ah, inscription.' I motioned to the scar on Hamza's forearm.

He nodded slowly. 'Perhaps there is more going on here than we're supposed to know.'

'I don't understand!' I protested.

'The Rule of Knowledge, Graeme. What do you really know about your mission? You have to interview Jesus, right? You were supposed to ask him all those questions so the guys would have the answers. Scientific questions, philosophical questions, the questions people would ask him if he'd have lived in our time.' Hamza scoffed and looked around. 'Our time. What does that even mean? I had myself convinced that I imagined the whole thing. I never expected to see you, although I always had this.' He held out his arm where the word VOMIT was formed by thin scars. 'The fact that I could read it, that it was in English, meant that I wasn't insane. It was always with me, I couldn't drop it or lose it. Graeme, what you're doing, what you've got to do, well, you know what happens if you don't, but imagine, just imagine what's going to happen when they find that disc with all the answers! Brother, you know that I follow the way of the prophet, but I am here six hundred years before him. My whole religion hasn't been invented yet. Does that mean it doesn't apply? No, the teachings are in my red-time, my past ... they still apply to me.'

'But what if we're too late? What if Delissio's men have already got to Jesus? What if he's dead already?'

'Graeme, for ten years I wondered if you would ever show up. All I could go on was faith. I had inquired about you, searched, tried to find you, but no. I didn't know when you would appear; I certainly didn't expect to have to wait that long! Faith. I have faith in Allah, and I have faith in what you're doing. It all comes from the same place, this faith. You have to have faith that you will not be too late, that the professor knows what he's doing. I have faith that we can get to Jerusalem and that Jesus will be alive,' he said with reflection. 'Ah, of course, if what you say is true, we must come up with a plan to discover these men who would rob you of your moment.'

'Land!' the captain called.

Scrambling to our feet, we turned to look out. There, burning not more than a mile away, were the lights of Jerusalem.

CHAPTER 46

'Done!' David Black announced as he slammed his pen down onto the airline tray table. Shaun looked up.

'I don't know what you're talking about, but I'm happy for you.'

'That's what my mother used to say.'

'Did she buy you first-class tickets too?'

David smiled. 'You're not going to rob me of this.'

'Rob you of what?'

'My moment of glory.'

'Wouldn't dream of it. You want a drink? I've got a lot to tell you.'

'I'll get a drink, sure, but keep your story to yourself. I've got another hour on this flight, and I'm ready to catch up. You should get some sleep.'

Shaun hated to admit it, but he was exhausted, and although he wanted nothing more than to keep reading, he knew he needed to give his body a chance if they were going to make it to Afghanistan. He pressed the call button and slid the diary over to David. But before the flight attendant arrived to take his order, Shaun Strickland had fallen back and landed gently on a padded sofa in the middle of a field. The sun shone and birds chirped, and as he lifted the remote to change the channel on the small wooden television about ten feet in front of him, Lauren lay her head down in his lap and curled her knees up to her chest.

'I don't know how you can watch it sideways,' Shaun said to her.

'My brain flips it up the right way for me,' came her contented response. 'Anyway, I only have one eye open. So my brain's only got half the work to do.'

He growled in irritation as another cow walked across in front of the screen. There was some type of gladiator movie on, but the lead character was wearing a wristwatch. Didn't he know watches were from the future? Mistakes like this really irritated Shaun. He wished film-makers would do their research before bungling up movies like this.

Shaun gently stroked Lauren's hair. It was so soft. Strawberry blonde and like the smoothest silk, every fibre of his being relaxed as he touched it. A rabbit jumped up on the sofa next to him.

'What's on?' it asked.

'Some crazy thing with men in leather skirts,' he responded.

'Look, baby, robots!' he then said, seeing a line of silvery metallic men marching a little beyond the television.

'It's okay, they're from the future, they aren't allowed to do anything bad. If they change anything they might never get built,' Lauren said.

'Really? You sure?'

'Sure she's sure,' said the rabbit. 'Can't kill your own grandfather then expect to be born in order to go back and kill him. Just can't happen.' With that, the rabbit wriggled its bottom and hopped forward, leaving balls of soft, rounded turd on the sofa.

'Anyway, looks like I'd better go. A lot of fibre in this new diet they've got me on at The Facility.'

'Wait! Where is that again?' Shaun asked after the white creature as it hopped away, but he got no response.

'Look in the TV guide,' Lauren said. 'I think it's on Channel Three.' He hit the remote, which was sitting in his hand. Funny, he hadn't noticed it before.

The screen crackled into white static for a fraction of a second before showing a very different picture. It was a cave full of massive structures of metal and lights all around. There were gangways of metal and men in grey uniforms walking the perimeters. In the middle of the whole complex was a platform, a large disc of metal that stood on a pedestal of rock was surrounded by arches of silver. There were lights all over the arches and masses of cables running above it.

'Now, that looks cool!' Shaun said, but Lauren was asleep.

Technology bored her, and she was so happy lying in the sun of the peaceful meadow. Another cow walked across the screen, and he waved his free hand to shoo it, but it walked right up to him. It was holding something in its mouth and looked as excited as a bovine can.

'Holy shit, man, have you seen this?' it said, the smell of bourbon on its breath.

Shaun tried to look around it, but the cow wouldn't get out of the way.

'No, really! Have you read this, man?' David said, pointing excitedly to one of the pages in the diary.

Shaun opened one eye and looked sideways at him. The book was open on the tray table and the light illuminating it was the brightest thing in the first-class cabin. He reached down to wake Lauren, who would also probably want to see what they had found. But she didn't want to wake up. She didn't move. She wasn't there. All at once, everything came back to him. She was dead. The moment condensed and had an instant and dramatic effect. He threw up.

'Aw, *shiiiit*!' David said wiping his arm. The call button lit up and a flight attendant came gliding over. She stared down at the vomit on Shaun's legs.

'Oh, I am so sorry! Let me help you there,' the tall brunette said with a thick German accent. 'We have started our descent, so you need to pop that away now,' she said after she finished wiping down his legs and the back of the seat in front of him.

She walked back to the front of the cabin and strapped herself in for landing.

'Are you drunk?' Shaun asked, smelling his friend.

'I maaaay have taken advantage of a certain unlimited consumption policy.' David lifted his chin. 'When you read what I've just read, you may want to have a drink too. I'm finished.'

'What?' Shaun protested. 'You read past my page? We agreed—'

'Ah, blah blah ...' David lifted up his hand. 'You can read it at the airport. I think I'm going to have a lie down.'

Seething, Shaun took the diary and shoved it under his shirt.

CHAPTER 47

With a promise to return, I shook hands with the ship's captain. Malbool, Hamza and Mishca followed as I walked away from the dock.

'You're sure you know your way around?' I asked as Hamza came up alongside me.

'I've spent many years selling my wares here, Graeme, so I know every street of Jerusalem. The only thing is, I'm not sure where we are now. I think we're about ten miles south of the city, and I'm guessing it's about four hours till dawn. That doesn't leave us much time to track down your friend and save his life so ... uh ... he can be killed ... um ... properly.'

If Delissio had indeed sent men ahead, they may have struck already.

'Okay, there are three men that we know of who could be a risk,' I told the others. 'Barishnikov is about my height but stockier. He's got a big dimple in his chin, kind of like Kirk Douglas,' I said, winking at Hamza.

'And the others?' Malbool asked.

'The others I don't know. I can only assume they are Romans, part of the troupe Delissio trained. I don't know any more than that.' I shook my head. 'Hamza, you're sure we have somewhere Mishca can stay?'

'My business partner lives in the outskirts of the city. I would trust him with my life, although maybe not my wife,' he added in a mutter. 'The boy will be safe there, and should anything happen to us, he will see that the child gets back to Chorazin.'

I nodded.

After half an hour of brisk walking we came to the crest of a hill. Then: the lights of a city. It could have been a modern town, and it took my breath away.

'Ah, and what a night for you to lay eyes on this city for the first time,' Hamza said.

'Do you think it's real? Do you think it really happens?' I turned to Hamza, doubt creeping over me as I faced my final destination.

'That, I don't know,' he replied solemnly. 'What I can tell you is that the Nazarene is real. He's been causing quite a stir, especially this last year. I haven't seen him, as you know, because my mission was to help you and I was instructed to stay away from him. But I've heard about him. "Miracle man" they call him – but then again, this lot call just about anything a miracle and think any illness is a demonic possession. Sometimes I want to introduce the concept of germs, or accidentally leave a drawing of an aerodynamically correct wing somewhere, just to see how they would respond.'

'Fifteen hundred years before da Vinci's drawing of a plane? Imagine that.'

'The Rule of Knowledge. Who's to say we can really change anything anyway?'

'Care to take the risk?' I asked with a smile, knowing the answer. 'Okay, first things first: let's get Mishca safe.'

Jerusalem. The holiest of cities. It would be fought over, owned, won, lost and shared by three of the world's major faiths ... only one of which existed in this time. There were not yet any Christians or Muslims.

The streets in the outer city were lit with dimly burning oil lamps. The ambience was like a mist, laughter and revelry coming from nowhere in particular but filling the night.

The dirt and gravel crunched under our feet, and my body was electric with anticipation. I thought that we must be in the very early hours of Thursday and that tomorrow morning, Jerusalem would play the most crucial role in modern history. This time tomorrow, Jesus would march to his death. Before that happened, I had to find him and get my interview. He needed to survive the trial and be nailed to a cross on Friday.

Following a gravel path into the city, dotted with stone houses, we came to a small wooden door nestled into a humble sandstone wall. Hamza paused a moment.

'Ah, Jacob is rarely alone. He likes the company of women, several at a time to be precise.'

I rolled my eyes. 'You want to leave Mishca with this man?' I asked, but he held up his hand.

'Just let me go in first. The boy could be in no safer hands.' Taking a breath, he knocked loudly on the door. Nothing. Hamza knocked again and called, seemingly unconcerned about the neighbours.

'Jacob! Levinson, you devil, get up, it's me Zachariah!'

There was again a moment's silence, and then a groan. From deep inside the house, clanking and shuffling could be heard. Some voices followed.

Eventually, the lock on the door was lifted and the face of a sleep-dishevelled man emerged, peering suspiciously outside.

'Zachariah! What do you want? Don't you know I have company? It must be hours before sun-up!'

'Get rid of the women, I have urgent need of your help,' Hamza said in Hebrew.

'Ha, you and I both know what you have urgent need of. Perhaps you should come in and join us?' Then, for the first time, the leathery-skinned Jew noticed the rest of us standing outside. 'Who are they?' he asked, eyeing Hamza with renewed suspicion.

'You know the package I have spoken of often since we met?'

Jacob nodded, not taking his eyes from the rest of us.

'Well, they are the package. I need for you to take care of the boy for a day or two.'

Jacob looked up and down each of us, his eyes narrowing particularly when he saw the muscled figure of Malbool. After another moment, Jacob spoke again. 'Okay. Give me a minute or two.' The door closed, and we stood in the street looking expectantly at Hamza. A cat meowed in the silence as our weary group stood in the dark.

'He's okay, I promise,' assured Zachariah, sensing our anxiety. Just then, the door opened once more and three pretty young girls came out with embarrassed faces and their robes wrapped loosely about them. They didn't look at us as they passed, but continued up the road, sounds of their giggles floating back to us as they moved into the distance. A good night's work, no doubt.

'Be quiet when you come in,' Jacob said as he reappeared and opened the door wider. 'I don't want you to wake Alisha.'

'You have your daughter staying with you?' Hamza said a little too loudly.

'Shh! It's only for the week. She is visiting from Capernaum.'

'And still you have your whores? Seriously, I have told my friends that they can trust you!' he whispered harshly.

'Ah, we were quiet. Alisha understands how hard it is to grow old alone ... and since the death of her poor mother—'

'Don't give me that. Her mother's been dead twenty years and it's never been about that. Now, go and put a pot on the fire.'

With that we all filed into the house. Half an hour later, we were seated in the living area of the trader's home.

'... and so the boy must stay with you while we carry out our search for the Romans,' Hamza finished. He was selective in his storytelling, but it was obvious that he trusted his friend, telling him that we knew of a planned assassination attempt on Jesus.

'I see. Yes, this man, the "miracle man" as you call him, arrived in the city last Sunday, and what a reception! You would think Caesar himself had arrived. I was selling in the lower city, when a mass of people went rushing to the gates. The Romans didn't know what to do, and they thought we were being attacked by a zealot army, but there came a man riding on a donkey. A donkey! Can you believe it? Needless to say, everyone was in a good mood and business has been booming all week, which is something I wanted to talk to you about. I don't see a lot of silk in your possession.'

'It was burned. I, ah, forgot to mention that we were attacked by raiders in the gulf.'

'What?' Jacob cried in dismay. 'No, you certainly didn't mention that! My silk!?' Then he added, 'How did you survive?'

'My friends here are rather handy with a sword,' Hamza said, motioning to me and then to Malbool, who was sitting with his broad limbs arranged comfortably, not understanding a word of the Hebrew conversation.

'Papa, what's all this yelling—' The girl's voice paused mid-sentence. We turned to see a sleepy girl rubbing her eyes, standing in the light of the flames. With long, flowing brown curls and almond eyes, she took my breath away. It was then that I first met Alisha.

'Ah, Alisha, my child, come and join us. We have guests.'

She looked around the room and blushed. She was dressed only in a sleeping robe that hung loosely about her shoulders, exposing her elegant, pale neck. Instinctively she pulled it tighter around her and came forward. Jacob jumped to his feet and guided his daughter into the circle.

'Gentlemen, this is my lovely daughter, Alisha, the most spirited and independent child a father could ever hope to have. Refuses to marry or go into my trade. She's twenty-one already and I tell her no one will want her before too long!' The girl flashed him an angry glance, then turned to us and nodded to each of us in turn as we were introduced, before sitting next to her father.

'Alisha, Mishca is going to stay with us for a few days while my friends are in town.'

'Sorry, Jacob, but can you tell me more about the Nazarene? What has he been up to? Do you know where he stays?'

'Ah, where he stays, no, although I think he and his followers have been mostly over on the city's north near the mountain of olives. What has he been doing? Well, that's a different story. He has been in the temple every day, teaching and preaching. People come away changed; some are calling him the Messiah. Naturally I was curious, so I went to the temple one morning to hear him for myself.'

'You heard him speak?' I asked, my heart suddenly racing.

'No. I was too late, the temple was full. I couldn't get in, but from the gates I did catch a glimpse of him. And the strangest thing happened. Even though he was hundreds of feet away in the middle of a crowd, I swear he looked right at me and smiled. It was the most curious thing.'

'You saw him?'

'I just told you I saw him.'

'What did he look like?' I pressed.

'What do you mean? He looked like a man.'

'Yes, but, what did he look like? You have to understand that these people are going to try and kill him, so we need a clear description of him.'

'Well,' Jacob thought for a second. 'He's a Jew. He looks like a Jew. Very good looking, like all Jewish men.' He winked at Hamza. 'Long brown hair, short beard, light brown eyes.'

'You saw his eyes?' I asked. 'I thought you were far away?'

Jacob paused for a second. 'Hm, yes, I was a long way off. But ...' he looked up and squinted as if looking reflectively into the past, 'he ... well, I think he had light brown eyes. I guess I could have imagined it. But he looked right at me. I can see that smile still. Funny, he was a long way, but ... I'm certain of it ...' he trailed off.

A moment later his attention snapped towards me. 'Now, how are your bandages?' he asked, referring to the wrapped hand I nursed. He had given me fresh bandages for the injury, but the pain was constant although the bleeding had stopped.

'They're fine,' I said.

Just then we all heard shouts from outside. Then, at the sound of screams and the clashing clang of weapons, we jumped up as one.

'Alisha, go to your room!' Jacob commanded, but the girl ignored her father and ran to the front window with the rest of us. He swung the wooden panel open to reveal a street – empty and lifeless an hour ago – now packed with men fighting.

'Zealots!' Hamza said as we watched a crowd of men on foot and on horseback being met by Roman centuries. Hopelessly outnumbered by the surprise attack, the Romans' leather armour prevented not one of them dying.

'What is going on?' Malbool asked me, speaking for the first time in an hour.

'I don't know,' I told him. 'Zealots, religious fanatics, seem to be attacking the city.'

'Why would they do that?' the African asked in his Roman tongue.

'Rome. The Romans occupy Jerusalem, and the zealots don't like it. There looks to be at least fifty of them. This is no scuffle, this is a coordinated attack.'

Looking out the window, glancing beyond the melee immediately in front of me, I saw lights come to life as the commotion woke the city.

Built into the hills and rock of the mountains, Jerusalem was a maze of bridges and walkways. The streets were hilly and sloped, the entire town built on levels.

'Something big is happening,' I said to Hamza. 'We have to find him now, we have to go.'

He didn't argue.

'You want to go out there?' Jacob asked, perplexed.

'I have to find him now; this could all be part of the assassination attempt. This goes further than I can explain.' I turned and made for the door, but stopped when I felt arms around my waist. I looked down into Mishca's pleading eyes.

'Don't go. Don't go, Saul,' he pleaded.

I knelt before the boy. 'You have to stay here. Jacob and Alisha will take care of you until we return.' I gently pushed the boy away and looked up at Jacob, fixing him with an earnest glance.

'As Jacob, son of Levin, you have my word the boy will be safe.'

'I thank you. And ... I will be back for him.' Without further thought I also turned to look at the man's daughter and smiled. She had no look of fear in her eyes.

'We will take care of him,' she said to me, coming over to rest her hand gently on Mishca's shoulder.

I nodded, and then with Malbool and Hamza at my side, I left the house.

CHAPTER 48

David groaned and rolled a little. The puddle of drool that had formed under his cheek stuck his face to the leather couch. Sitting next to him, Shaun could smell the alcohol seeping through his skin. Glancing at his watch, he sighed; David would hardly be fit to travel in an hour when the next flight to Pakistan was due to leave.

There were now only a few pages left until the end of the diary. With a deep breath, he journeyed back into Jerusalem for the last time.

All over the city, people were awake. It was no more than two hours before dawn when we reached the city walls. The Roman guards fought with the zealots. We took advantage of the fray and slipped through the gates unnoticed, entering the city proper. I knew that in about a hundred years from now, the zealots would incite a massive Jewish uprising and the Romans would put it down in the most definitive way. I knew this from my history lessons, but I also wondered if that history could be changing right now. If this assassination was successful, the history I knew might not exist at all.

'Where to?' Hamza asked.

'The north. Jesus and his followers stayed in the hills to the north.' I only hoped that Barishnikov or Delissio's agents hadn't got there first.

At that moment a mob of people, jeering and screaming, exploded around the corner. They came from one of the narrow city streets to our right. These were not zealots, but Jews and Romans alike. Citizens of Jerusalem. We moved back into a side street to let the rabble past when the most curious thing struck me. Women and men were crying.

'What's going on?' Malbool asked. The crowd was thick in the narrow streets and growing steadily all the time. I could not see what was happening through the impenetrable throng.

Hamza and Malbool stayed close behind me as we were engulfed by the mass of people.

'Hamza, what day is it?'

'What do you mean? It's Friday morning.'

'Are you sure? Are you sure!'

'Of course I'm sure.'

A flash of horror waved through me. Friday? I had lost track, and was a day behind myself. Not in the same way you were, Shaun, but it was already happening. A woman screamed off to my left, then started to wail hysterically.

'Look! They've got him! They've got him!' she cried. It could not be. I reached my tongue to the back of my mouth and flicked the small switch to start the camera.

I reached out to a woman close to me. 'What's happening?'

With tears in her eyes she gripped my robe as if begging me to help. 'They have him. They've arrested him.' No sooner had she spoken the words than I was torn from her grip and carried along with the growing mass.

I grabbed a man next to me as we moved and jostled down the street. He looked panicked, and struggled in my grip.

'What's happening? Do you know?'

The man fought free of my grip. 'I tell you, I don't know him! I do not know him!' He pushed his way through the crowd, insane with grief. In the distance, a rooster signalled the coming of the new day. The man stopped and turned back to me, wide-eyed and staring. Then a strange look crossed his face as understanding dawned. His head hung low as the crowd bustled and carried him further on. I froze, realising I had just met the first Pope – Peter, apostle of Christ.

I turned back and tried to see further up the rising path into the crowd, now illuminated by torchlight. Too fast, it was happening too fast. We were supposed to have a whole day. It could not be.

'Get to the temple!' I called to Hamza, who was quickly being squeezed away from me as I was jostled along. 'Get to the temple and look for Barishnikov. Get ahead of the crowd.' He was swallowed by the noise and mass of people and forced out of my sight. I turned once again and gripped Malbool by the arms as we were both swept along.

'Stay with me,' I said in Roman. 'The man I told you about, the one I have to interview, it's him they are talking about. He's been arrested. They're taking him to trial now. We have to find Barishnikov and the Romans who want to kill him. I have to get to him before he goes to trial.'

Malbool nodded and kept his eye on me as we moved. Eventually, the crowd fanned out into a larger street and I worked my way forward. I could not get near the source. The most influential figure in the modern world was being led to a defining moment in history. I had to speak to him before that. I had to keep him from being killed prematurely. I was going to be too late. Just a day; but a day that would change everything.

All around me people called out, some crying, some cursing, but all filled with emotion. The rocks and sand beneath my feet were kicked along by the shuffling crowd until finally, after moving slowly in the mass through the city we came to the courtyard of the high priest. Some of those who had joined the throng filtered inside, and the rest of us jostled for position by the gates. It was still dark and the only lights were those cast by burning torches. I called to Malbool and he knelt down. I sat on his shoulders. The big African then stood to his full height and I was raised above the masses.

I still could not see Jesus, but in the distance stood a ring of men in robes and headdresses of brown and yellow. There must have been twenty of them, standing in an organised court. There was no doubt that this was premeditated. Malbool continued to push his way forward, people growling as his wide frame shoved them out of the way. I listened hard and reached down to my side, adjusting the knob on the camera to boost the sound amplification. At last, we came to a ring of soldiers who would let us go no further. They pulled me roughly down from Malbool's shoulders. I did not resist them, and I could finally see into the courtyard.

Then, it began. There before my eyes I saw the sight no modern man had seen, but millions imagined: the ring of priests, the soldiers and a crowd of followers and accusers alike, all crammed into the high priest's courtyard. There had been stories, films and stage plays – but this was the real thing. Right here, right now.

All around were elders, scribes and chief priests. Standing in front of them, with his back to me, was a hunched man. One shoulder was dropped slightly, and a mass of hair, matted from blood and sweat, hung about his shoulders. His hands and feet were bound and he did not move, the weight of the chains pulling on him.

Finally, one of the men spoke in a deep baritone voice and the crowd hushed. 'Who is this beggar? Who is this man bound before me? Why is he chained?' the man said in a show of ignorance, as if he had no prior knowledge of the events taking place.

'He is the trouble-maker they call Jesus!' one of the other priests replied. Instantly cries of fear and anger erupted from the crowd once more. The smell of the crowd filled my nostrils, the unwashed morning sweat of what looked like thousands of bodies.

The deep-voiced man spoke again, continuing his rehearsed charade. 'Ah! So this is Jesus of Nazareth! This is the man causing so much trouble for the people?'

As he said this, one of the guards holding Jesus drove an elbow deep into the prisoner's stomach. I winced, seeing him double over in pain.

'Look at Master Caiaphas when he addresses you, dog!' The high priest smiled a little, and held up his hand; the show of nobility was barely attempted. I could not believe how blatantly they abused this man. My blood ran cold.

'They say you're a king?' the deep-voiced man continued. 'So tell me, where is your kingdom?'

Then, before the prisoner had a chance to answer, a second priest spoke. 'Which line of kings is it that you descend from?' the man asked, smiling and playing to the crowd.

The chained man did not answer. The jeers rose again. Yet another of the priests called out. 'Speak up!'

'Are you not a Galilean? Are you not the son of a carpenter? Yet you say you are a king? Some say you are Elijah. How do you answer?'

Still the man said nothing.

'Why do you not speak? You have been brought here as a blasphemer, how do you respond?'

Yet another of the priests said, 'Defend yourself!'

The crowd again began to raise its collective voice as the man stayed silent. I tried to push my way past a guard who seemed to have been distracted by the proceedings, but he moved to block my step. Almost on cue, the crowd hushed, and I looked past the guard to see the man raise his head. He straightened and stood at his full height, perhaps a little less than six feet. Then, he spoke.

'I have spoken openly. I have spoken for all to hear. I have taught in the temple where we all gathered. Ask those who have heard what I have had to say.'

The high priest looked around uncomfortably. Then one of the guards responsible for the prisoner's injuries, spoke.

'Is this how you speak to the high priest? You speak with such arrogance?' He accented his point by smacking the prisoner across the face. The blow sent the man to the ground, and those assembled voiced their anger. When the man rose, it was slowly. He breathed deeply, then spoke again.

'If it is ...' He groaned, then continued. 'If it is evil that I have spoken, tell me what evil. What evil have I said? But if you cannot,

then why is it that you hit me?' It was said plainly, highlighting the abuse without a hint of aggression.

As the priests surveyed the crowd I scanned their faces, my eyes coming to rest on a stocky, broad-nosed priest. One hand clutched a staff, the other hung loosely by his side. He looked around at the gathering with a crooked smile, pleased with himself, proud of his piece in the show. Then something twigged. I looked hard at the man. He was dressed in the same manner as the others, long robes of ornate brown and yellow stripes, and a headdress that stood high and fanned out, falling down past his waist at the back. He looked across those gathered, and our eyes met for an instant.

Then it happened. The man's smile vanished. His face dropped, and his eyes widened.

Suddenly he threw his head back and screamed, clutching his temples. The high priest had begun to speak again, and the crowd yelled. The noise was so loud that the man now curled over on his knees in agony drew no attention.

'Then we will listen to those who have heard you. Bring those who have witness against this man,' said Caiaphas, the high priest of the Pharisees. But I was not watching him. My eyes were locked firmly on the kneeling priest, a man who was clawing at his head with his fingers. Then suddenly, he vomited.

Those around him stepped back but paid the man little attention. In another circumstance it would have been a cause for alarm, but everyone here was filled with emotion, absorbed by the trial. The priest wiped his mouth and looked up, his eyes wide, comprehension dawning on his face. He looked first at the prisoner, who was now being accused of using devils to drive out devils. Then up the hill beyond the courtyard walls, over to the Roman district. Finally his eyes came to settle on me. Recognition.

Beneath the dark-bearded face and headdress, there was no doubt whose eyes they were. Vladimir Barishnikov. For a brief moment our eyes locked, and then, with the speed of a snake, he shot up and ran back through the crowd.

I knew that what I had just seen was an awakening, a dawning of understanding and a barrier being broken in the brain. By my presence I had woken the dormant memories within the Russian agent. By jostling through the crowd, by showing my face, I had set his plan in motion. I had caused the very thing I was here to stop. I cursed myself and then turned to Malbool.

'The Russian. That priest who ran off, that's him. That's Barishnikov.'

Malbool shook his head, indicating that he hadn't seen the man. 'We must stop this!' he then said to me as yet another guard open-handedly slapped Jesus across his already beaten face.

'We cannot. We cannot change this.'

'What do you mean? They are beating this man for no reason. He's chained up and they are beating him in front of a crowd. They are humiliating and knocking him senseless. What has he done?'

I tried to separate the scene in front of us from my knowledge of the event, and I saw how it looked. 'You must stay with him,' I said. 'You have to make sure they don't kill him. There are two Roman agents here who don't want him to survive till morning. Stay with him and watch. Intervene only if they are going to kill him. He will be beaten savagely, but do nothing unless it looks like death. You have to trust me. Do you understand? He has to die on a cross, no other way.'

Malbool stared at me, not comprehending. But then slowly he nodded. I gave a curt nod in return and set off after Barishnikov.

Freeing myself from the crowd, I looked around desperately. The courtyard was surrounded by high walls, and I assumed it was from here that Barishnikov would strike. The crossbow would not be invented for a thousand years, but from the top of these walls it would be no trouble to launch a spear into the centre of the prisoner's back.

After circling the perimeter of the sandstone structure I still had not caught a glance of the Russian. Where was he? He had nowhere to go.

It was then, almost by chance, that I glanced towards the western road. Like a man possessed, Barishnikov sprinted. I took off after him, hearing the howls from within the courtyard – cries of, 'These proceedings are a mockery!' and, 'Where are the other councillors?'

My heart pounded as I steadily gained on the Russian, knowing that I had always been faster than him. But a disconcerting thought crossed my mind: he was the only agent who had beaten me in combat. Recruited from Spetsnaz, the Russian SAS, Barishnikov was an expert in unarmed combat. So, what would I do when I caught him?

Where was he going? I examined the path we were taking and concentrated. Instantly I was transported to my subconscious, planted with every element about this place during my training at The Facility. Imprinted as I slept. He was heading west. I suddenly knew to where: the Governor's house. The trial of Jesus would move there soon. He was getting ahead of the crowd.

I drew closer to the stocky Russian with every step.

'Vladimir! Stop!' I called in English. He looked back but did not reply as he continued to huff and puff up the winding stone pathways of the city. Who knows how long he had been here, living the life of a priest? His age was hard to guess, but he was clearly not in the same physical shape as when he left The Facility. Behind me, torchlights started to snake a path away from the temple. They too were on their way to the house of the Roman Governor.

The road wound back on itself and dropped a level as we started to descend the mountain. As soon as Barishnikov rounded the bend, I leaped towards him from above, crashing down on him. We rolled off the path and tumbled down hard on the stone another level below. The fall knocked the breath out of me as I landed, and streams of blood pulsed from my finger stumps like water out of a severed hose.

Barishnikov began to scramble to his feet, but I reached out and pulled him down. He lashed out with his leg and caught me square in the face, knocking two teeth from my mouth. My grip loosened on the Russian's robes and he slid out, but he did not run. He knew he had to deal with me here and now.

'You came along just in time. I have been in a dream, and you have wakened me,' he said, still in Hebrew.

'Even your Hebrew has a Russian accent,' I replied in English. 'You can't do this, Vladimir. Delissio is dead. You have failed.'

'Failed?' Barishnikov raised an eyebrow. 'On the contrary, if it were not for you, I may well have failed. But now you have come along and saved me. You have saved Our Lord.'

'Saved Our Lor—'

His boot raised straight up into my groin, and I dropped to my knees, my eyes bulging in that sickening agony known by all men. Intense nausea shot into my stomach, and I barely noticed the blade being pulled from under Barishnikov's robes as it flashed in the moonlight. Incapacitated, I waited for the blow. When it came, it decapitated Barishnikov cleanly.

His head bounced twice before his body fell.

Hamza stood behind him, his blade coated in Soviet blood. I did not understand, nor did I complain. I smiled up at my friend, but the smile he returned was full of sadness.

'Hamza?' I asked, not bothering to thank him, a gesture and its gratitude immediately understood.

The Jordanian who had been my friend and confidant let the tears well in his eyes even as his smile broadened. I did not understand how he knew to be here. He answered before I could ask.

'My mission was you. It was always you, my brother. And now it is done.'

'What? What are you talking about? Barishnikov said something. He said that I had saved Our Lord. Do you know what that means?'

'I know,' Hamza said, the tears now freely flowing down his face. 'I have a message for you from the professor,' he said, referring to our project leader at The Facility who had taken a particular liking to me for a reason I could not fathom at the time.

'The professor? What? What message?'

'He said to remind you: "Write it down. Everything you have seen here; everything you have done."' I stood for a moment, I did not understand. Obviously now I do. But Hamza had not finished.

'And I have a message from me: I love you, my brother. As salamu aleiykum. Thank you.'

In that instant, a spear slammed into Hamza's chest. The force of the blow drove his body backwards and off the path. It was gone. Hamza was gone. It had all happened too quickly. Far too quickly. I was not ready for it. I had not had a chance to prepare, not even a chance to register surprise before I heard the voices of guards from the street above me.

'They have killed a priest! They have killed a priest!' The second spear flew, giving me barely enough time to roll out of the way. What was happening? Still suffering from the agonising pain in my groin, I half-fell, half-leaped to the next street level down. I landed next to the body of my friend. He lay with an accepting face and a wooden shaft growing from the centre of his chest. He was dead. Just like that. I did not have time to contemplate the insanity that had just taken place as I set off running into the darkness.

I ran blindly, heading west. To kill a priest in Jerusalem earned an instant death penalty. I did not understand what was happening. One minute my friend saved my life, the next he was dead. And the thing that disturbed me the most was that he knew it was going to happen.

I rounded a bend and ducked into an alcove. The sounds of the rabble further back along the street began to intrude on my sanctuary. There was too much happening that didn't make sense.

Barishnikov had told me I had 'saved Our Lord', and I did not understand what he meant by it. In my mind I replayed the moment before Delissio was killed. It was a moment of uncanny resemblance to the one that had just taken place. Just seconds before he was shot with the arrow he had said: 'And with you dead, there will be no one to stop them. I'm afraid you'll never get your interview with Christ.' I had taken it to mean that I would never get my interview because they were going to kill Jesus, but he had meant I would not get it because he was going to kill me. *Realisation dawned. They had never meant to kill Jesus; they had meant to save him from crucifixion. Then, who? Who were they going to—*

The thought struck me like a blow. Pilate. They were going to kill Pontius Pilate. They would 'save our Lord' by killing Pilate.

The sweat on my brow turned cold as it ran down my face. The implications began to branch out in my brain like ice crystallising in water. They were not here to kill Jesus, which was why it had not happened already – they were here to save him. They were here to kill the man who ultimately was responsible for putting Jesus to death. Pontius Pilate, the Governor of Jerusalem. And Barishnikov had been running towards Pilate's house. If they were here to stop the crucifixion, they would have to do it before the trial just after dawn. Which meant—

I leaped from my hiding spot and bounded forward with new vigour. Delissio's agents were still on the loose, and one question burned in me as I ran – who were they? How would they get close to the Governor?

I raced through the streets until I came to the tall columns of the Governor's residence. I stopped outside the gate. There was already movement in the courtyard, and the guards were alert. I would have to get in another way.

The crowd was only a few hundred feet behind me and the guards who followed were being distracted by the mass of people pouring onto the streets to see what was happening. Then it occurred to me: I need not sneak at all. My nose had been broken, and my fingers were severed and bleeding, but my confidence was intact, as was the knowledge implanted in my mission. With that, I walked right up to the front gate of the Governor of Jerusalem.

I was met by a centurion who looked me up and down. 'What do you want?'

'I have an urgent message for the Governor,' I replied with all the bravado I could muster.

'The Governor is asleep. He doesn't take visitors at this hour. Come back after breakfast.'

'Tell Pilate that Caiaphas has arrested the Jew named Jesus,' I turned and pointed down the road to where the mob from the trial appeared on cue from around a corner. 'You see that tumult?' I asked. 'They are about to break down these gates and start screaming for the Governor.

I suggest you let me see him first and explain what this is all about before he faces that angry mob.'

The man paused, unsure of what to do. Finally he said, 'Wait here.' He turned, leaving only one other guard at the gates. This second man had seen the crowd and shuffled nervously. A moment later, the first man returned and asked, 'Who is it who wants an audience with the Governor?'

Who indeed? I thought. I had hoped to have bluffed my way through by now.

'Listen to me. Tell Pilate that I know his wife has woken this night with nightmares. Tell him that the man she has dreamed of is being dragged to this house, and I am the only one who can prepare him for what is to come.' The man looked at me suspiciously.

'Tell him!' I said in a commanding tone. It had been recorded that Pilate's wife had awoken and warned him about her dream. I only hoped this was not one of the many embellishments sure to have taken place between the events and their chronicling.

The man disappeared as the crowd drew nearer, and by the time the centurion returned, they were only fifty feet from the gates. Uncomfortable, the centurion grew nervous when he looked beyond me at the approaching mob.

'The Governor asks that you come,' he said, making as if to lead me, but then uncertainly he faltered, pointing up the stairs.

'Up there. He's expecting you.' The man ran back to the gates where the soldiers were demanding entrance to the courtyard.

Relieved and somewhat incredulous, I ran up the stairs, which led from the courtyard up to the balcony and doors in full view of the gates. Rather than knocking on the door, I darted off to the left behind the massive columns and searched for another way into the house. I figured that the living quarters would be too well guarded for the agents to make their move, and that they would wait until Pilate was called out into the open. I found a small stairwell that led up to the mezzanine level of the balcony, almost on the roof ringing the massive stone courtyard. The vantage point would provide me the best opportunity to discover the agents, but how would I tell who they were?

I made it to the roof and looked down upon the scene. It was more enormous than I could have imagined. There were ten times the number of people I had expected, and the crowd was much more heated. They were all but brawling among themselves – those who were calling for blood, and those who were crying at the travesty.

Then guards came forward and led Jesus, bound, blindfolded and bleeding, up the stairs. They dragged him, and when he fell, they did not stop. When they reached the top of the stairs, the doors opened and they took him inside.

In the courtyard at the front of the crowd, I saw the bare and glistening black shoulders of Malbool. He was looking around desperately, not wanting to let Jesus out of his sight; so unaware of his role in all this, yet willing to give it everything he had because he trusted me. I scanned the guards who had seemingly appeared from nowhere to fill each space between the columns. It was impossible to tell who the agents might be.

Grudgingly, I turned and crept over to the house's roof. It seemed that all the guards had been ordered outside to control the crowd. There were none posted here. I glided across and found the door that gave access to the upper rooms. The explosion of splintering wood barely made a noise above the crowd.

The hallway was deserted so I quickly made my way up the stairs. From the third floor above the open chamber, I could see a small crowd of scribes, guards and priests were gathered. When I recognised what was going on, it took my breath away.

At the front of the proceedings stood a broad man dressed in a fine, gold-trimmed sleeping robe. He had thick forearms and a smooth, bald head. He looked to be about forty, but the kind of forty forged by years in the military. It could only be Pontius Pilate. Presently he walked over to where Jesus stood and then looked around at the others in the room.

'Leave us,' he said with authority. The others retreated through the door.

Pilate held up a cup for the prisoner, whose face was obscured by angle, shadows and hair, but at least the guards had removed his blindfold. 'Drink,' Pilate said. I could not tell whether it was an offer or a command.

The man in the once-white robe did not respond, and so Pilate lowered the cup and walked a full circle around him.

'Tell me,' he said, 'are you, as they say, a king?' This time, he waited for a response, and when none came, he grew irritated. 'Are you the king of the Jews?' Again he waited as I crept forward, unable to take my eyes from the two men standing in the room.

After a moment, the taller man took a pained breath through a dry and cracked throat, a breath that in itself spoke of how he suffered. 'Is it you who asks me this question? Or do you ask because others have told you it is so?' came a rasping and broken voice, although its timbre told of it once being rich and musical.

'Is it me? You have been brought to me by your own people. By the high priest. The very people of whom you say you are king!' Pilate spoke with a genuine and keen interest, more surprise than accusation in his voice.

'My kingdom,' the man began again, 'is not a kingdom as you imagine. It has no fences, nor walls, nor boundaries. It is not a kingdom of this world.'

'And yet you are a king?' Pilate pressed, then sighed. 'And they want me to execute you, you understand?'

Jesus said nothing.

'Why do they want this? What have you done? Why ...' Pilate spread his hand around the room, 'are you here?'

Again Jesus drew a slow breath. 'I am here, I was born, to bear witness to the truth.'

'Truth? But what is truth?'

'All who seek to hear truth, hear my voice,' the prisoner said, and then spoke no more.

Pilate turned and walked to a table on which his breastplate and armour lay. He placed his cup on the table, then lifted the moulded metal torso up over his head and lowered it, immediately transforming from man to soldier. He tightened the straps and motioned for his guards to take the prisoner back outside. The doors remained open and as they shuffled out onto the top of the tall palace stairs, I could hear the crowd raise its voice once again. Pilate followed and addressed the masses from his balcony.

'I can find nothing that this man has done wrong. I have questioned him and found no fault,' he said to the crowd. Immediately there were jeers and it was only when Pilate held up his hands for silence that he was able to speak again.

'Is this man not a Galilean?' the Roman Governor asked. From my spot crouched two floors up I could not see the priests as they responded, but I heard them hiss when Pilate said, 'Then he is King Herod's subject. Take him to Herod to be judged, Galilee is his jurisdiction. Hand him over.'

And with that, a yank on the prisoner's chains thrust him forward and he stumbled down the stairs to be led off by the mob. From a window at the far end of the room, Pilate's wife, Claudia, stood and watched. When her husband came back inside he sat in a small curtained-off chamber and she went to him.

If the accounts were accurate, I had perhaps half an hour during which time Jesus would be presented to King Herod and then brought back here for the sentence.

I did not know if it had been recorded, but King Herod just happened to be visiting from his coastal villa and was in town for just a few days. I knew that he would demand to see a miracle, and when he did not get one he would send Jesus back to Pilate.

Still I could see no agents – although I did not know how to recognise them if I did see them – but I reasoned that if they were going to strike, they had to strike now, before the mob returned. Until they struck they would not reveal themselves, so I had no choice but to stay close to Pilate. Any kind of disturbance here might well cause Pilate to act outside the true course. Who knows how easily the balance is tipped, how easily The Rule of Knowledge is broken?

I slid a ceremonial sword from its wall mounting and took it with me as I descended the stairs.

'Is it the truth? Will I know it when I hear it?' I heard the Governor say as I approached the room. 'Do you know it?'

'I know it, but if you do not, how can I tell you?' his wife replied. My eyes scanned the room. Guards were stationed at the outer door, Pilate's personal escort stood just inside the entrance chamber. All the others were outside.

'Do you want to know my truth?' Pilate spat. 'I have been putting down rebellions in this town for eleven years. Eleven! If I do not condemn this man, Caiaphas will start an uprising. There will be rebellion. If I do condemn him, the man's followers will do the same. I fear that there will be bloodshed this day that I cannot avoid. Caesar has promised me that if I cannot control this city, the next blood shed will be mine. That is my truth, Claudia.'

I could not see it, but I knew then that they embraced, shrouded in silence. I hid behind a stone bowl of fruit, each piece carved with incredible workmanship, and I marvelled at how much we did not know about the talents of this age. As I crouched, a servant girl came down the stairs carrying a pitcher of water. I sat back and breathed. The girl stopped and spoke briefly with one of the guards, who seemed reluctant to let her pass, but after a word from his partner the girl was waved through. The guards then went outside to remove those who were still jeering in the courtyard.

The guard who had motioned the girl through returned and closed the outer doors behind him. The man's thickset jaw and black hair gave him a distinctive and unique authority, and it was with horror that I realised I had seen this face before.

The centurion who had first brought me to Rome. Marcus.

I spun and stood in one motion to look through the window above my head. In the room the girl poured water into an earthenware cup held by Pilate. I searched desperately and my hand settled on a stone apple in the nearby fruit bowl.

'No! Do not drink!' I screamed, even as the stone fruit sailed through the air, shattering the pitcher and exploding water all over the floor. Pilate and Claudia looked up in astonishment and did not see the woman snarl and draw a curved dagger from beneath her cloak. This time I was too far away. The knife came down with frightening speed, right into the steel breastplate of the Roman Governor who spun at the last possible moment.

The blade glanced off and the woman drew it back for another attempt at the bald man's neck, but Pilate responded instinctively and lashed out at the woman's face with a vicious backhand. His blow caught the assassin on the temple and sent her sprawling to the floor, unconscious. Pilate looked around in disbelief and called for his aide.

'Guards!'

But there was only one guard still alive inside. The outer door rattled with the noise of the others trying to answer their summons, but it was locked from the inside. As Pilate and Claudia came out of their room into the open chamber they were greeted by one centurion, sword sliding from his scabbard and eyes locked firmly on his prize.

Pilate threw his wife behind him as the soldier closed.

Marcus swung his blade as I came out of my roll and raised my sword to meet his.

For a moment in time we were frozen, Marcus not realising where I had come from, Pilate bewildered by what was happening.

The centurion's eyes locked on mine, his face showing dawning recognition. 'You,' he breathed.

I answered by turning my body to knock him on the side of the head with my hilt, but the mercenary rolled with my move and evaded the blow. There was neither time nor need for talk: he was here to kill Pilate and I was here to stop him.

Marcus swung several times, forcing me back. I blocked, parried, ducked and weaved and at the end of the exchange we were no different to when we had started. Still the doors rattled and the calls of the guards outside came through in alarm.

'Sir! Sir, are you all right?' Then to another soldier, 'You, go to the roof, get in that way!'

I smiled at Marcus; his time was running out. He slashed again and the ceremonial sword I carried shattered in my hands. The centurion pressed his advantage and let fly a flurry of blows, but each time I became the angle and the blade sailed by. We moved in a deadly dance with the Governor and his terrified wife looking on. I fought hard to keep myself between Pilate and Marcus. I had to end this.

Marcus swung down towards my back, and I waited long enough to make him commit to the strike. The sword cut through the air and I dropped and spun, my rear leg circling around, my hands touching the ground. My speeding heel caught him on the side of the head, and as I continued my rotation I leaped up with the other leg and drove the instep of my foot across his jaw. The move looked like a ballet dancer leaping and spinning across a stage but it had a far more devastating effect. Marcus stumbled, and I slammed him with my fist, completing the trifecta of blows to the side of his head. Yet still he stood.

He swung again, but this time with less accuracy and I evaded easily. As soon as the blade had passed me, I switched my stance and skipped up to connect my front foot to his face, like a boxer executing a jab. Yet still he stood.

'You tough bastard,' I whispered, seeing the tenacity that had assisted his rise to the rank of centurion. My instinct was to follow up with a stomach shot, but the metal breastplate made me think again.

Still, Marcus swung; again, I evaded and punished, and again and again. I stepped in to grab his wrist, ducking under his arm and disarming the Roman as his sword became mine.

He dropped to his knees in front of me and I stood with the sword raised, ready to plunge it deep into his chest. Pilate looked on in horror and astonishment, finally beginning to comprehend that he had escaped assassination by a very narrow margin.

'This,' I said, as I stood there, 'is for Mishca.' Then, as he stared up at the sword, I kicked his face hard with the ball of my foot, breaking his jaw and sending him sliding across the marble floor on his back.

The Governor and his wife stared wide-eyed at me. I nodded then sprinted for the window.

'Wait!' Pilate called, but I was already gone, knowing as the guards filtered into the room that Marcus's fate would be worse than the death I could have delivered him.

CHAPTER 49

I ran back up the road and stopped as I saw the crowd heading back into the Governor's palace. I mingled with them, looking for Malbool. The crowd had grown thicker, and searching for the African proved difficult. I was back inside the gates once more jostling for position before I found him.

'Malbool! Malbool, it's done. Pilate is safe.' The tribesman stared at me angrily.

'What?' I asked.

'How can you allow this?' he growled at me. 'How can you stand back and let this happen when you have the power to stop it?' He waved his hand out angrily at the scene in front of us.

I looked into his eyes and saw that they were reddened, his face filled with emotion. He had witnessed the entire procession.

'You say this man has done nothing wrong? Well, criminal or not, no human should be treated like this. Even in Rome, this public beating would not be tolerated, even for a criminal.'

He had done as I asked. He had stayed close to Jesus and had seen every taunt, every spit, every blow. I looked back at my friend. How could I explain to him? How could I explain that The Rule of Knowledge forbade me from intervening in what I knew had taken place?

'Malbool, I don't know how to say this to you—'

'Saul, this man is beaten worse than a slave. He is dragged through the streets and no one can find anything he has done wrong. Do you not need to interview this man? Is this not the very reason you are here? And right now you have power to stop this and get your inter—'

'Silence!' came the call. At that moment another fifty or so guards arrived, reinforcements called in case of an uprising. Looking somewhat shaken, on a throne at the top of the stairs, sat Pontius Pilate. A servant poured what I suspected was wine. The crowd was boisterous, filled with every class of citizen: Jewish men in their headdresses, women in their veils, Romans, children, slaves, tax collectors, fishermen. I

doubted that there was a trade or a race currently in Jerusalem that was not represented here.

At the front of the crowd, still in chains and surrounded by a circle of soldiers, the prisoner Jesus stood in a robe stained with blood and dirt. His head fell forward.

'Herod can find no fault with this man, and neither can I,' Pilate said in a loud but quivering voice. Immediately the roar started up again. This time Caiaphas walked up several steps and turned to quiet the crowd.

'Have you no respect for our Roman procurer?' he asked, with sarcasm in his voice. The crowd lowered its collective rumble once again.

Caiaphas turned and looked up at Pilate. 'This man claims to be the Messiah. He claims to be the Son of God. This is blasphemy by our law. He must be punished!'

He motioned, and soldiers dragged the prisoner Jesus up the steps to be level with Caiaphas. They turned him to face the crowd. I gasped, for the first time seeing the man's face. He was beaten horribly, one eye swollen in a purple bulge, his lips split and fat, the rest of his face disfigured by welts and blood. Welts upon bruises upon bruises. His hair hung around his face and his eyes were cast down.

'You see!' Malbool cursed at me. I could not believe the passion in his voice, so moved by what he had seen. 'Do not tell me that you knew this was going to happen. I do not believe that you would let this happen! What kind of man are you to let this go on?'

I shook my head. Maybe he was right. Maybe I should save Jesus now; I could get my interview. Would his answers not be the same today as they would have been a day ago? Hamza had warned me that if I failed, millions in our time would die, that the interview must take place. I banished the thought from my mind. No. The Rule of Knowledge. It had to happen, Malbool just could not understand.

Shaun smiled at the irony of his own question just a day before, and Giovanni's reasoning. The priest had told him that it was perception, not reality, that changed. The thing remained, no matter what you thought about it. This thing had happened, and Malbool not understanding did not change that.

'It is custom,' Pilate said, 'on this day of the festival, to release to you a prisoner. I can release this man Jesus to you.'

Again the crowd started to shout, most in approval, but Caiaphas held out his hands.

'No!' he cried to the people. 'This man must be punished!'

'No,' Pilate said defiantly, 'there has been enough bloodshed in recent times. Shall I release this man to you? It is your right.'

Again it was Caiaphas who tried to quiet the crowd. The priests shouted up, 'No!' But Pilate had begun to make motions. Then it struck me: it was really going to happen. Had I changed Pilate's mind by saving his life? They were going to release Jesus. The crucifixion would not take place.

I studied the prisoner's face. My heart ached to see someone look so completely dejected, so beaten, so—

Jesus looked up at me.

Time stood still.

Through a swollen, blood-filled eye, from beneath a mass of sweat-drenched hair, and from the full distance of the courtyard, he stared right at me. Right into my eyes. Right into my soul. A chill spread through my body. It was as if he knew why I was here, and in that moment I had to make a decision.

I had been sent back in time to interview this man. To ask the questions the people in my time – a time of science, a time of doubt – would have given anything to ask. But now this man was beaten, broken, and suddenly it looked like I may not be too late after all. It looked like Jesus might go free. He looked at me, his eyes penetrating through the crowd. If they released him, I could complete my mission. I would get my interview, I would save the lives of millions.

But.

The Rule of Knowledge.

No, Jesus must die.

'Barabbas!' I screamed. 'Free Barabbas!' I screamed louder. Around me the crowd quieted, and Caiaphas, who was desperately trying to control the throng, looked up to the back of the crowd.

'Free Barabbas!' I called again. 'Give us Barabbas!' The priest's face lit up, and he nodded vigorously. 'Yes, yes!'

He turned up to Pilate. 'Yes. Free Barabbas! That is our wish. Give us Barabbas!' he started to chant, like some absurd football mascot trying to rally support for his team. 'Barabbas! Barabbas! Barabbas!'

Jesus lowered his eyes.

Pilate stopped, turned and looked stunned. Then he looked out over the crowd. The chant was growing. Slowly he began to shake his head. 'No ... no ...'

The high priest spun back to him with a broad grin. 'But you must. You must! It is the will of the people. Give us Barabbas.'

Pilate motioned, and a guard moved inside. Several minutes later he reappeared, dragging behind him a pitifully dirty, grotesque-looking man with wild black hair and scars all over his face. The two prisoners were dragged higher, to the top of the stairs.

'Again I ask you,' Pilate boomed, becoming angry, 'whom do you want released: this man Barabbas, who is a murderer, or this man Jesus, who is called your Messiah?'

'He is no Messiah,' Caiaphas spat. 'He is a blasphemer and should be put to death. Free Barabbas!'

Yet again the crowd took their cue and began to chant the name of the murderous criminal.

Pilate closed his eyes, and when he opened them again, he raised his head in a curt upwards nod. The soldiers released Barabbas from his neck iron and stood back.

The man, confused at first, screamed wildly and danced around like an animal, and then spat at the feet of the other prisoner whose fate he would not share and whose freedom he had been granted. I hung my head. I was responsible, and for the first time for as long as I could remember, I cried.

'Holy shit!' Shaun burst out far too loudly.

'Holy *shit!*' he said again. The other passengers in the airport lounge looked up from their various international newspapers and mundane airport conversations. What they saw were two loud Americans: one obnoxiously yelling at the top of his lungs, the other drunkenly drooling on his seat. After a few seconds, all of them returned to what they had been doing.

Shaun could not hold back; he needed to tell someone. He leaned over and shook David roughly. The big man had been asleep for a couple of hours.

'Huh? It's only a five-to-one compression, it's not even a transport stream ...'

'David!' Shaun whispered harshly.

With unfocused eyes, David Black stared at his friend. 'What? Is it time to go?'

'He killed him! He fucking killed him!' Shaun said, exasperated, 'Saul killed Jesus!'

'Oh? Yeah, I know. Keep going; it gets better. Wake me up when we have to get on the plane.'

'Better?' Shaun said. His eyes darted around; he needed to share the experience, but he knew he could not.

Almost before he could do anything, his hand acted of its own accord and pulled the book back to his face.

Read! his brain screamed.

CHAPTER 50

There would be no interview. There would be no answers. I had failed my mission. But as I stood watching the flesh fall from his back, I barely cared about my mission anymore. I had become one of the crowd; I was witnessing something so abhorrent that I could not look away. The horror compelled me. The lashes continued.

Twenty-one ... barely a spot on his back was not covered in blood ... twenty-two ... it was so much more brutal than I could have imagined ... twenty-three ... the crowd had demanded his death ... twenty-four ... but Pilate had refused ... twenty-five ... saying instead that he would flog the man and let him live ... twenty-six ... now he could not even stand, his hands were bound to a stump, shackled ... twenty-seven ... even Caiaphas dropped his head, unable to watch the Roman guards whip the bloodied pulp any longer ... twenty-eight ... Jesus no longer cried out ... twenty-nine ... I was one of the crowd ... thirty ... I had never believed ... thirty-one ... but as I stood watching ... thirty-two ... I could not understand man's inhumanity to man ... thirty-three ... I had been in the arena ... thirty-four ... and the military, but had never seen someone so defenceless take such a beating ... thirty-five ... Malbool stood next to me, with tears streaming down his cheeks ... releasing one hand, they turned Jesus over to expose his front ... thirty-six ... although I wanted more than anything to turn my head, I knew my obligation now was to record ... thirty-seven ... and when they saw this, they would cry as we had ... thirty-eight ... and it was happening because of me ... thirty-nine ... I felt ashamed.

'Enough!' the overseer said, raising a hand to the soldiers holding the whips. They stopped, exhausted by the effort.

It was as they dragged him away from the stump, leaving a trail of blood on the stones, that I looked at this man's broken body and marvelled. How could they expect him to walk? But they did.

We followed the soldiers as they took Jesus into an alcove. There they dressed him in a cape and put a ring of thorns on his head, pressing down deeply to keep the crown in place. Thorns punctured his scalp and pockets of blood exploded, creating streams that quickly became lost in the river already cascading down his face.

When once again they presented Jesus to Pilate, the Governor chastised his guards for allowing this to happen. Gently he took the pathetic figure by the arm and angrily addressed the crowd.

'You see what has been done to this man?'

'Crucify him!' one priest spat back.

'Is this not enough? Look at him! He is beaten! He has been humiliated and has suffered, and yet still you call for blood?'

'If you do not crucify him, you are no friend to the people!' called another of the men, this one a scribe.

'Do your duty, Governor: crucify him!'

Then Pilate spoke quietly to Jesus. I could not hear his words, but again I adjusted the amplification on the recording unit to try to pick up the signal. Pilate bowed and shook his head.

'Why? Is this not enough?' he called out once again to the multitude.

And then, with emotions heightened, the surrounding crowd began to break out in scuffles with the soldiers. They were going to riot. Pilate had to do something.

The Governor held a pitcher of water out and had a guard pour the liquid down over his hands. Curiously this detail struck me at the time, having always believed that Pilate had used a bowl for this famously symbolic act. But just knowing it had actually taken place was something of a relief in this surreal moment. The emotional Governor called out that the blood was on the hands of the crowd, and he wished not to take responsibility. Yet he had passed the final sentence.

And now we stood and watched. The soft buzz at my temples recorded every moment. The crucifixion would be televised.

The sun rose on the most fateful of mornings in Jerusalem, giving life to the dusty streets. So quiet at this time yesterday, now they were lined with people.

First I shall set one thing straight: what Jesus was made to drag through the streets was an entire cross. It was fashioned with the cross-bar attached and would have weighed more than two hundred pounds.

I saw amid a group of women weeping for him one who was inconsolable. I looked at the woman's face as she watched the man shuffle with painfully small steps along the stone path. With each step he received new abuse, the crowd throwing both rocks and insults at the man who now wore nothing but a cloth tied carelessly around his waist. The procession, led by men on horses, contained another four men heading to their fate, not just two as accounts indicated.

I walked among the crowd, trying hard to keep my camera on the subject. He was being motivated by constant lashings from a guard's whip, and it took all my strength not to rush in and decapitate the cruel punisher with his own sword.

The first fall was the most dramatic. A member of the crowd, trying to rush into the line of travel, charged bodily into a guard, who in turn stumbled backwards and knocked into Jesus. The condemned man, already close to death from injury and exhaustion, lost his balance and dropped the massive wooden cross, his slight body following. As the cross-bar lodged in the stone and rolled, it pole-vaulted Jesus into a full flip, so that he came down hard on his face, landing awkwardly with his legs behind him. I pushed my way forward as jeers broke out. He did not move. The only thing that had kept him going was the momentum of not being able to stop, and now that rest had been forced upon him, his body shut down.

Stones were thrown at the fallen prisoner, and a soldier lashed his unmoving body. Still Jesus did not move.

Malbool pushed his way up to me and spoke harshly in my ear. 'Do you not see this!' For the first time since I had met him, I heard hatred in his voice. 'What sort of man are you that you can simply stand by?' he demanded of me as he moved forward, meaning to intervene. I grabbed Malbool's arm and held firmly.

I looked at the guard who again swung his leather into the mass of blood that was Jesus's back. At that moment, all I wanted to do was kill that guard. I think I would have if it were not for the woman – the one I had seen earlier in the crowd – who suddenly knelt beside the motionless body. She carried a white cloth and brought her face close to the man's face. She stroked his hair, and slowly pressed the cloth to his forehead, soaking up the blood. Her cheek moved to the man's cheek and she whispered in his ear. 'I'm here, Joshua. I'm here,' she said gently.

Her words did what the soldier's whip could not: they brought hope. In what seemed slow motion, Jesus lifted his head and turned it to the side. The woman continued to wipe his face with the cloth, which was already saturated. Through his swollen eyes he looked at her, and whispered back something I could not make out.

'Who is that?' Malbool asked me, looking at the amazing scene.

'That,' I replied, 'is his mother.'

With what must have been a supreme will, Jesus clawed his way to his feet once more. He stood, bent at the waist, and reached for his cross. As the party once again moved forward, the faintest hint of a smile twitched in the man's mouth as his mother reached for him, only to be pulled back into the crowd. The procession moved on.

We came to a curve in the narrow street and the road ramped upwards. I fought for position in the streets, trying always to see, to record. The horses broke through the crowd ahead of the criminals marching up the hill in shuffling, uneven steps. Several times Jesus looked like he was falling. His breathing was cracked and worn, coming in the desperate gasps of a man past his limit. The men driving the movement ever upwards were relentless, taking pleasure in being able to lash all four prisoners at will.

With banded leather straps that curled around his shoulders, and a curved plume on the head of his dented and bronzed helmet, the soldier behind Jesus lashed again and again. The leather bit into exposed skin. The bloodied prisoner cried out with each new blow. Pure hatred burned within me. Finally, as yet another blow slammed into the raw flesh, I could take it no longer. I pushed past Malbool and threw those in front of me out of my way. I would kill the man with his own sword.

As I broke the line, another blow sent the Galilean stumbling forward. He dropped his cross and its heavy trunk slammed and bounced to the ground. Following after it, without even the strength to stretch out his hands to protect himself, Jesus fell forward.

His face slammed uncushioned into the stones and I saw an explosion of blood splash onto the dirt as part of his swollen face burst.

I stood in the middle of a jeering, cheering, hysterical crowd, Roman soldiers in front of me, behind me and mounted on their horses all around me. Lying fallen at my feet was a bloodied figure, covered in sweat and purple bruises. I looked up at the guard who stood behind him. Our eyes met, every fibre of my being wanting to punish this man for what he had done and continued to do.

But I did not. Instead I looked down at the fallen Nazarene and his burden. I walked to him and reached down to pick up the cross, my own blood flowing from where my fingers should have been.

I watched distantly as it ran down the wood and mixed with that of the man destined to die that day. The colour of our blood was the same. It mixed together and formed a single river flowing down the grain, travelling a distance before falling to freedom from a notch in the wood. With both hands I hoisted, feeling the weight, so much heavier than I had expected. Shifting the load to one arm, with my other hand I reached down to the man at my feet, and helped him in his feeble attempts to rise. I held him gently but firmly under the armpit and lifted him up. His hands reached for the wood, which he had embraced in this macabre dance through the city streets for far too long.

He half-held, half-hung when he finally found the cross-bar. As I supported his weight, and that of his cross, his hand rested on mine. Time seemed to stand still as, for the most fleeting of moments, the man lifted his head and turned his face towards mine. As they had moments earlier with the guard, my eyes locked with the Galilean, and my heart missed a beat. Just as quickly as it had arrived, the moment passed and the man turned his head and shouldered the full weight of the wood once more. Purposefully, he began to shuffle off.

The guard shoved me roughly to the side and began to whip at Jesus again, but I felt no desire to return the aggression. My fury was gone. The crowd closed in around me and the procession moved further up the hill, but I stood motionless. For a long time I did not move at all, while the jostling and shoving masses streamed around me without so much as a bump. I knew I should have been following, recording, documenting, but I could not move.

Eventually Malbool forced his way against the flow of the people and came to stand in front of me. His eyes were red rimmed from sadness and rage, but now there was something else in them. Wonder. When at last he spoke it was a simple statement. 'Your hand.'

Without moving, I looked down at my hand, then brought it up in front of my face. My simple hand. My simple, complete, whole hand. My hand with five full fingers. My hand that had touched the man with the cross. A wave washed over me and I sank to my knees. As never before in my life, I cried tears from the depths of my soul.

Shaun turned the page. It took him a few moments before he registered that he could not read the words written on it. He stared at it for a second, and then his brain told him ... *It's not in English.*

CHAPTER 51

'What?' Shaun asked aloud. '*What!?*' he yelled.

Business-class travellers from around the world now stared uncomfortably at Shaun. He did not notice. He stared at the pages, trying to make sense of it. There were still five pages in the diary, but not in any language that he could understand. What was it? Hebrew? Roman?

What had he just read? He was still sitting in the plane cabin surrounded by modern technology, but just a minute ago he had been walking through Jerusalem more than two thousand years before. The roadblock he had just encountered had forced him to sit back for a moment, to remember where he was and what he was doing. What had he just read? A miracle. It could not be true ... could it? It was the same question Shaun had asked himself again and again about the diary, and yet its very existence vouched for its authenticity. The possibility that the whole thing was an elaborate set-up was even less plausible than the chance, however bizarre, that this whole thing was real. Then, there was the disc. He had seen with his own eyes the amazing footage on it. How could that have been anything but genuine? He had seen the video in the most amazing way, a living image of unparalleled depth and detail, clarity and substance. It was unlike anything he – or anyone, he suspected – had seen before.

So, what about the disc? Could it be a fake, some kind of Hollywood movie magic? He looked over at David, now sleeping soundly. Was he for real, or was he part of the conspiracy? On cue, David belched in his sleep.

No. If Shaun felt certain about anything, it was about David. Simply, he believed in his new friend. The man was too flawed to be an evil genius.

Then, he really had seen the escape of Napoleon from the isle of Elba more than two hundred years ago. Which meant that someone, somehow, had succeeded where Shaun had failed. Someone had figured out how to travel through time.

Shaun was a scientist, a very good scientist. He could believe in the process of creating the means to travel back in time. But for Saul to have captured video of Jesus Christ performing a miracle? In all his experience and all his study he had never seen anything that he thought could not be explained by science. Religion? Superstition; stories created to explain life to the masses because they could not understand the science behind it. Stories created to maintain control of people, to keep their behaviour in check. No, Shaun did not see any need for religion. So, how could he believe this? How could he believe that this time-travelling journalist with stumps instead of fingers was miraculously healed by a man beaten to within an inch of his life? How could he believe in this miracle?

No matter how Shaun refitted the situation, trying to force and squeeze it into his current system of belief, he could not deny the logic of it all. Science was a system of hypothesis, testing, results and conclusion.

The boundaries of Shaun's beliefs squeezed outwards under the pressure of the new information. Why was it so hard to believe? Did he want there to be nothing beyond what he could understand? Did he *want* there to not be some sort of God? He examined himself and realised that he had shut himself off to even the possibility for one simple reason; it meant that he was wrong.

Like many men on the planet, he did not want to be wrong. If he *was* wrong, then maybe there was a chance there was a God of some sort. Maybe Jesus was some sort of divinely inspired, connected, all-knowing deity, and if all that were possible, then that meant that maybe death was not the end Shaun had always asserted it to be. And if that were the case, then maybe Lauren still ... maybe Lauren ... Lauren ... Tears welled at the thought.

Say it! his brain urged.

'I can't!' he shot back.

Say it! Why can't you just say it? It doesn't mean you believe it, it just means that you've said it.

'I won't!'

Why?

'Because ...'

Because why?

'Because ... then I would have been wrong all this time!'

About everything?

'No, just about this, but this is everything.'

Then say it! his brain commanded.

Shaun had always listened to his brain. His internal dialogue had provided him with startling insights in the past. It had given him breakthroughs when he had been able to reason his way no further. So, why did he not listen to it now? Why?

Why?

'Because if I have been wrong all this time, then somehow, somewhere, Lauren might still exist.'

Yes. Say it again.

'Lauren might still exist.'

Again.

'Lauren might still exist. She might not be gone. She might be here. She might know how I feel. She might know how much I miss her. She might know how sorry I am for every time I hurt her, for every time I made her cry or didn't pay her enough attention. She might be with me right now, right here with me. She might not be gone.'

Yes.

'She might not be gone.'

Is that so bad?

The tears that had welled spilled over and streamed down his face. Suddenly something changed. The energy that had kept him going, the driving energy borne of anger, of hate, of revenge, released its hold just a little. The possibility that he had been wrong all his life, and that perhaps there was something more, folded around him like a blanket and enveloped him in a warmth he had never felt. As he released his breath, he sank deep into the chair and relaxed a little for the first time in what seemed like days.

As he started to drift off to sleep with his fingers curled around the small brown book, he took comfort in the thought that just maybe, he was wrong.

PART 3

GRAND PLANS

'On a night like this there came a stranger on the road,
I saw him stumble, heard him fall, I helped him with his load.
The further that we walked, well the heavier it became,
And I believe I've felt the weight from another world.'

'The Risen Lord', Christopher Davison

CHAPTER 52

VATICAN CITY, 2014 AD

Cardinal François Le Clerque bit into his steak. He chewed the meat thoroughly while he considered the information. He liked his steak well done. It tasted exquisite with the merlot he had selected. As he mashed the meat in his jaws, he contemplated the poor judgement exercised by the man sitting across from him, fixing him with a steely stare. Had Le Clerque been in this man's situation, he would not have chosen to deliver the news to a man holding a steak knife. Le Clerque sipped at the wine and savoured the taste. Good length. It was a dry red that left him puckering his lips, and with a deep richness – the colour of blood.

A second man sat across from Le Clerque, several years younger than the cardinal. With the delicacy of the information involved, there were few others who could have delivered it. He had no choice.

'You have checked all the manifests for each of the ticketed flights?' Le Clerque inquired in a thick French accent.

'Yes, Your Eminence, all that we could gain access to. We had agents at each of the airports where they should have landed, but they bought more than fifty tickets, each with different airlines, different destinations with multiple arrival times. Our agents are spread very thin.'

Le Clerque raised an eyebrow. The second man immediately went silent. He knew better than to phrase anything in a way that might sound like an excuse. He scrambled to change topic.

'The documents we recovered at the motel in America are of extraordinary value. The ones you could not translate are being translated now by The Society.'

'You gave them to The Society?' Le Clerque snapped, suddenly serious.

'Ah, we have no one with the expertise in our inner fold, Your Eminence. We did not give The Society all the documents, only five. We are using the find to act as a contingency should there be no other discoveries in the expected timeframe. We can filter the documents out and make it appear that we have recovered them from several sources.'

Le Clerque nodded. It was a sound enough decision, and was not of great importance.

'Do not tell the professor about the remaining documents. Have an independent expert brought in to translate them.'

'And then?'

'And then see to it that our expert has an accident on his trip home.'

The Italian sitting across from Le Clerque nodded once. He relaxed a little now that he had been given a task; it meant the cardinal was not going to kill him on the spot. He was Le Clerque's most trusted aide – and had accompanied him when they had confiscated the player from Newcom years earlier. It now sat idly in the cardinal's safe, waiting for the time it would show the cardinal the disc that no one else would ever see.

'And what of the others?'

'Ah, we are having some trouble keeping up with them. We lost them at the hospital in Charlotte. He seems to know where we are going to be before we get there.'

'*Oui, oui*. He would. He is a traveller. This is why he beat us to the diary in the first place.'

'We assume that the map could be within the diary itself. It is not among the rest of the discovery. None of the other documents from the motel appear to be anything like a map.'

'In the diary? It is possible, although when the school teacher was questioned at the hospital under influence he did not reveal this to be the case. He did not know about the map, that much is certain. We should have killed him there and then.' Le Clerque threw down his napkin in disgust. His meal was not finished, but he had lost his appetite.

'Should I have teams continue to investigate the known hide locations for the other discs?'

The cardinal, rosy-cheeked from the wine and running scenarios quickly through his mind, shook his head. 'No. Louis Delissio was extremely cautious getting the list to us, and we do not want our friends at The Society to know we have it, or that we infiltrated The Journalist Project. We must have patience. The matter at hand is the important one.'

Le Clerque leaned forward a little and his eyes narrowed. 'I do not need to tell you how important it is that we find this disc. It is the only thing that can stop my rise to the papacy. Müller will announce his retirement within days, and the conclave will gather. We find the school teacher and his friend and we will have the diary. The map and the diary shall be together, as it is written, and the map will lead us to the disc. When I have the disc they will have no choice but to elect me ...' his words trailed off. 'Concentrate everything on finding the school teacher, he is the one with the diary now,' the cardinal said as he sat back, satisfied with his command.

François Le Clerque was a man of intense intellect who could process information rapidly, reaching decisions quickly and concisely. He had been immensely frustrated when his people reported that the signal they were receiving had been traced to a jacket in the bottom of a ravine, but then, quite unexpectedly, the man turned up again.

An officer reporting back upon his daily surveillance of Giovanni had raised the alarm. The description of the two men with whom Giovanni had met was unmistakable, but Le Clerque had not expected them to move this quickly.

To allow them too much time with Giovanni would have proven dangerous. It had given him the excuse to do something decisive about his predecessor on The Journalist Project. But now the two men had run scared; the car bomb had frightened off the prize they were after in the first place. The team should have chosen a different method – the diary was, after all, highly flammable. He could not afford to lose it now.

Few knew of Müller's ill health and his plans to retire. Le Clerque had spent considerable resources researching members of the one hundred and fifteen cardinals who would vote when the time came, and he had gathered enough evidence of their habits, vices and failings to ensure he would be elected. In the Church, reputation was everything – and blackmail was more powerful than bullets. It had been a plan in the works for decades, but then Pope Nicholas had died, and he had learned of Giovanni's project – he had learned of The Facility.

If someone presented the conclave with a disc showing an interview with Christ, all bets were off, which was why Le Clerque had created a contingency – a chance that the disc proved that Jesus had not, in fact, died on the cross; that he was nothing more than a mortal man. If this plan succeeded, Giovanni would not dare present such a disc to the council and destroy the Church he loved.

Le Clerque considered the two options: the disc showed Christ's interview and would never be seen by anyone, or it showed that Christ did not die on the cross. Either way, Le Clerque would be the next Pope, and when he was, his plans would far surpass holding a Mass for the faithful. He would change the world in a very real, very decisive way. He licked his lips in anticipation.

CHAPTER 53

WASHINGTON DC, 2014

The President of the United States sat at his desk in the Oval Office. He stared at the sheet of paper in front of him, but his mind was on other things. He had just received a phone call from a university professor in England. He had expected the call but had still been disturbed by it. It was not the first time he had spoken with Professor Landus, but he knew this would be the last, at least for the rest of his term in office. To say that the President owed much of his success to the professor would be an understatement. Indeed, many of the key decisions he had made during his term relied on important information provided by the professor on this very telephone.

The professor had an uncanny knowledge of what was going to happen. He had forewarned the President of disasters before they occurred so the government could properly prepare. He had told him of the motivation of key allies or enemies, and what actions they would take. He had even casually phoned one day and told the President, before he came into office, that he should lay a few dollars on the Patriots when they faced the Carolina Panthers in the 2004 Super Bowl.

The cost of all this knowledge? On the single occasion President Samuels had met the professor, Landus had made him promise something. To be honest. To be honest and stay honest. It was something the President at the time found curious. He was, after all, as honest as a politician could be, but it was only later when he held the weight of world-changing decisions in his hands that he came to know the true weight of his promise. But he had kept it. How could he not?

'You will become President in early 2013,' Landus had said simply, and he had, after the untimely resignation of the former leader midway through his second term.

But honesty was not the only cost. Ongoing support for The Society for World Historical Accuracy was something else the President had authorised. Not specifically financial, but it meant that The Society and its activities were not to be questioned or challenged. The third, and most immediate matter, however, was the one Landus had just mentioned. It was a favour. Landus had said that when this favour was completed, their communications would cease.

Samuels owed the professor at least that much, and a lot more. He was the first Hispanic American to become leader of the free world. The whole political landscape of US politics had changed thanks to the assistance of the professor. President Samuels owed much of that to Landus and was a man of his word. So be it.

The intercom buzzed and Samuels gave the all clear for his guest to be admitted. The Oval Office door swung inwards and an army general, dressed in full ceremonial uniform, strode purposefully into the room.

'You asked to see me sir.' It was a statement, not a question.

'Yes. Jack, I need a favour in Afghanistan.'

CHAPTER 54

David's head hurt. His brain pulsed and seemed to want to escape his skull about once every two seconds. He looked over at Shaun sitting in the rickety old car behind him. It bounced and bumped along the road, threatening to collapse with each new corrugation. Shaun looked well, David thought, all things considered. He had slept for nearly the entire flight from Paris to Pakistan. David had not shared the pleasure. It was the smell. The smell of the aircraft resembled the odour of recycled Indian food, and had not made for easy napping.

Shaun was nervous. He was nervous because of the third man in the car, the man who drove. Shaun had not thought much beyond the flight. He did not know how he was going to get to the Afghan border, but he knew it would not be as simple as jumping in a taxi. That the problem had been taken out of his hands was more than disconcerting. Shaun did not like it one bit.

After landing in Islamabad, the Pakistani capital, and shuffling their way through the chaos of an overcrowded baggage claim, Shaun and David had headed towards an information booth hoping to formulate a first step when David saw the sign. It read 'Black, Strickland' and was held by a man who had somehow fought his way to the front of the crowd at the arrivals gate. The man's face was familiar. They had both seen it on CNN many times over the past few years as the front-line journalist had reported on the latest developments in the Allied war against Al Qaeda and the Taliban. Craig Schwartz. Why he was waiting for them at the airport was a mystery.

'I have instructions to get you to the border,' the journalist replied when Shaun had questioned him. 'The only people they're letting through the checkpoints are news crews and reporters. Just can't get up there without credentials.'

David had freaked out. How had this man known they would be there? Craig's explanation just didn't satisfy David's well-developed sense of paranoia.

'I got a call from my editor saying that it's essential to get you two across the border. Didn't tell me why. I was hoping you'd be able to answer that.'

Schwartz did not mention that he had readily agreed, sniffing a story, though he did not understand why he was instructed not to use the company vehicle.

And so began the five-hour ride of dancing around the truth. It had become apparent that Craig knew nothing about the diary, nor The Facility, and Shaun was not about to broadcast the information to CNN. But Schwartz was a journalist, and if there was one thing he was good at, it was getting information.

After two hours of subtle and not-so-subtle interrogation, the foreign correspondent quieted, realising that the two were not going to tell him what they were up to. Still, he was determined to figure it out.

The landscape grew sparser of vegetation as they travelled, the earth seeming to force its way through the covering of greenery to expose its grey, jagged rock.

Neither Shaun nor David really had a plan, but Shaun had a feeling that if they just got here, somehow he would be able to work something out. David did not care – his whole life was mixed up in this venture now and the only way he could ever feel safe again was to face it head on. Besides, he wanted to meet the guy who developed that codec. He had reverse-engineered it and had been astounded by its sophistication every step of the way. It was the mind that had actually conceived of it that David wanted to experience – there was a big difference between understanding something that had been created, and conceiving the idea in the first place.

Eventually signs of life appeared again and Shaun studied the map. He reasoned that they were entering the town of Peshawar, in the far west of Pakistan. According to his guidebook, the city's origins were lost into antiquity, but many of its buildings were erected over two thousand years ago.

Shaun had decided, even before they arrived in the town, that this was where they would stop, get their bearings, and formulate some kind of plan.

David had not said much. With the hangover wearing off, he was beginning to process what he had read before he had drunk himself into oblivion. He did not feel like speaking to this reporter any more than Shaun did, and his mere presence led to David's growing sense of conspiracy.

'You heard of the Pathans?' Craig asked, trying a new approach on the bigger man.

'No. Should I have?' David replied sombrely.

'Not really. Just that they sort of rule the roost in this area. Government law only really extends as far as the city suburbs, then it mostly becomes tribal.'

'Well, we knew this would be a shit of a place,' David said uncharacteristically.

'You okay?' Shaun mouthed to his friend.

'Sure,' David replied, meaning not at all.

'Well, you seem a little upset.'

'Ah, I'm not. I just keep thinking about that …' He lowered his voice. 'You know. What we read.'

Shaun had not spoken a word about the diary since they had landed.

David turned and looked Shaun square in the eye. 'You read it. Man, you read it. We're in Pakistan! How the hell did we get here?' His voice began to rise just a little. 'I mean, look around you. We're really doing this, and I believed it totally, I really did, but that last stuff? I mean, that's a lot to swallow. It just makes me question the whole thing. Miracles?'

Shaun gave his friend a look that told him to keep his voice down, but David only grew louder. Craig stayed silent and strained to listen above the noisy vehicle. David gave up trying to be quiet.

'I mean come on … time travel? Really? Is that really possible? You're the expert, and you said no. I mean, do you really think that someone has found a way to do it? Or is this whole thing some elaborate hoax?'

Craig's reflexes sprang into action. 'Hoax? You guys in some kind of mess? Time travel? Been watching some good sci-fi on the plane, have you?'

Shaun glared at David, then shook his head slowly and pursed his lips. If this reporter wanted information, Shaun would flood him with it. At least it might throw him off their scent.

'You see, time's a funny thing,' he started, launching into his teacher voice. Craig listened, thinking this was the start of what he had been waiting for.

'I guess the most important change is the realisation that time is not what we thought it was.'

David turned and looked out the window, aware of Shaun's tactic.

'It's natural for us to think of time as a separate, constant thing, completely outside our physical world. It turns out, that's not quite true.'

'It's not?' Craig prompted, finally getting something out of these two.

'It is wrapped up in our world very physically – it even has shape and is affected by things such as gravity, which is really just a curve in what we call space–time.'

'Time is affected by gravity? But it doesn't have any weight, how can gravity have an effect on it?'

'Tell me, do you think light has weight?' Shaun asked, warming to the challenge.

'Ah, I don't really know. I don't think so,' Craig stammered.

'But gravity affects it.'

'It does?'

'Sure, what do you think a black hole is?'

'It's what my mother told me I had instead of a stomach,' David put in, hinting that he was coming out of his grump. He had read Shaun's papers online, so many of these concepts were familiar to him.

He could not help but smile as he listened to Shaun explain time, gravity, black holes and the rest. And it worked: Craig seemed content to improve his scientific knowledge without realising he was being fobbed off. ✕

Before Shaun could finish his explanation of the twins paradox, his concentration was shattered by an exploding window next to him. The shock sent a cold jolt of adrenaline through his body, and only a second passed before he saw Craig in front of him slumped forward, his head making a dull thud on the steering wheel. Immediately the car sped up and began to drift off the road.

David grabbed the wheel frantically, trying to keep the car straight, but the wheel was slick and slippery with blood.

'He's been shot!' David cried as Shaun grabbed the journalist by the shoulders and pulled him off the wheel. David fought for control, but Craig's foot had become stuck on the pedal and the car continued to accelerate. In desperation, Shaun released Craig, revealing a large, dark hole near his temple, bubbling thick red blood. He grabbed the handbrake sitting in between the driver's and passenger's seats and pulled it hard. The effect was immediate.

David slammed forward, inadvertently pulling on the wheel. Shaun was also thrown forward, and with no seatbelt to hold him in place, he flew through the centre of the seats and smashed into the front windscreen. The car spun with David's hand fixed to the wheel. The sudden jolt freed the car's accelerator, and it sat for an eternity up on its two driver's-side wheels, before bouncing to sit still in a cloud of dust, sideways across the road.

Traffic had stopped and the pair sat for a moment, ripped from the depths of intellectual theory into the harsh, practical light of day. With a dead body in the car.

Gradually the cars started to part and move about their business, beeping their horns at the unwelcome roadblock. Within seconds the source of the shot revealed itself as a jeep sped up behind them and screamed to a halt. David glanced in the rear-view mirror, then turned. There stood eight men, all with their faces covered in long black material, like some hideous impersonation of wild west stagecoach robbers.

Without pause for thought, Shaun grabbed the inert driver by his loose-fitting clothing. David scrambled to help, and within moments the dead reporter was in the back seat and Shaun was in the front, spinning the wheel and gunning the engine hard. The blue smoke of burned rubber spewed from the tyres. The car fishtailed away as the black-clad men jumped back into their vehicle and took off in pursuit.

There was no need for words. Both men knew that when someone shot at you and hit the guy next to you in the head, it was either a very bad shot, or a very good one. Either way, it was not something you wanted to stick around to find out.

CHAPTER 55

Shaun floored the pedal, glancing back through the rear-vision mirror while trying to navigate a way out of the city. Even with its load of eight men, the jeep seemed to gain on them as it swerved through the sparse traffic. Then there was gunfire – it was all the inspiration Shaun needed to spin the wheel and get off the main road.

The back windscreen exploded with a *BOOM!* David and Shaun both ducked instinctively, and with the front, side and now back windows blown out, the rush of wind brought the smells of the city streaming through the cabin. Peshawar was a frontier town, and a maze.

As they dodged a horse-drawn cart and came over a rise, the full majesty of the mountains in front of them dwarfed the outline of the city.

Again, gunfire ripped through the air and Shaun spun the wheel once more, turning down a side street into the old city. If it were a different day, the Americans would have marvelled at the beauty and rugged strength of the place. Two- and three-storey houses made of unbaked bricks and set against wooden frames lined the streets. Cobblestones replaced bitumen as the car hurtled through twenty-five centuries of history. They spun and weaved and braked and skidded through winding streets too narrow and too old for motor vehicles. Ten minutes of inner-city close calls passed before David finally urinated in his pants, his body reacting on its own to the constant production of terror-induced adrenaline.

Bullets tore into the ancient walls of a gate of the old city as the pair sped under the bridge spanning the road. And all of a sudden, they were out of the city's winding bends, out of the strange narrow streets. Just as quickly as they had entered the old city, they shot out now onto a road that seemed to fly clear of it.

Shaun looked up, and in front of him the massive mountains loomed with impossible drama. Their grey, jagged crags and snow-lined peaks gave foreboding a whole new definition, but as the howling of the wind was punctured again by cracks of gunfire from behind them, neither

Shaun nor David had time to marvel at the awesome beauty of the Khyber Pass.

'What the hell do they want? Why are they trying to kill us?' Shaun yelled at David. Sometimes David wondered if he existed purely as a focus for Shaun's rhetorical questions.

'I pissed in my pants,' was all David could think to say by way of reply. Shaun did not notice. His side mirror had just been shot off and he knew that without the refuge of sandstone buildings and narrow streets to shield their way, it would be only a minute or so before the jeep would run them down and be within an accurate firing range.

And then, a strange thing happened. In the rear-vision mirror Shaun saw the jeep slow and turn off the main road.

'What are they doing?' David asked as he followed Shaun's gaze.

'They're giving up!' Shaun said, more hopefully than triumphantly.

'Who were they?' David asked.

'I don't know. Taliban? Apparently it's just one giant male-only tribe up here.'

'Did you see those people?' David persisted. 'The people on the street? They were walking round with full belts of ammo slung across their chests as if it were Halloween. I mean, shiny bullets are really in this season,' David joked, insane with fear.

'I know. It's frontier country here, but I really didn't expect ...' he looked out at the enormous mountains in front of them, '... that,' he finished.

The peaks rose up like something from a Tolkien fantasy novel. For a country which boasted the Himalayas, not a lot was mentioned about the enormity of the sister ranges to the north.

The landscape was unearthly, and gunmen could chase them through city streets and go all but unnoticed. The idea of normal was not one they were accustomed to in this very foreign land.

'You okay?' Shaun asked. David was white. His response, a weak smile. He shook his head slightly, looking at the body in the back seat.

Shaun looked down to crunch the gears, then his eyes returned to the road only to see the jeep reappear from a hidden driveway fifty feet ahead. David could do nothing but scream, and Shaun looked forward in terror.

This time there would be no chase, no evasion, no city-street manoeuvres. This time, the jeep was parked right in front of Shaun and David, and its occupants had their weapons trained at their windscreen. They were too close to miss. Shaun slammed on the brakes.

The men yelled orders and fired into the air. Three men jumped from the vehicle and one pointed at Shaun, shouting demands he did not understand. He took it to mean that he was to get out of the car. He turned to David as his hands came up off the wheel.

'Just stay calm. I think they want us to get out. Just stay cool.'

'The player,' was all David had to say. The silver briefcase housing the portable disc player sat on the back seat next to the dead newsman.

'Leave it. If you reach back there, they'll kill you. Just leave it and get out slowly.'

Hating every second of it, David did as Shaun suggested, and no sooner was he out of the passenger door than he met a rifle butt across his temple. The blow knocked him to the ground and left him bleeding. David struggled to stay conscious as he pressed his face into the dirt and felt a boot sink repeatedly into his soft middle. The Pakistani men continued to shout, giving orders or making demands – David could not tell, nor did he care; all he wanted was to stop being kicked.

Shaun did not fare any better. An almost-identical action had knocked him to the ground, the rifle butt slicing into his forehead and releasing a torrent of blood. Although able to protect himself from some of the attacks, he dared not fight back. The men grabbed and blindfolded him, driving the butts of their weapons into his sternum, face and groin. His forehead still bled, quickly staining the blindfold.

He let himself be dragged towards the back of a truck, trying to decipher the stream of commands. His hands were tied, as were his legs, and he was shoved roughly onto the hard metal tray. Soon after, he felt David thud down next to him, a whimper coming through his rattled breathing. Shaun could tell that David was hurt, worse than he was. What the hell was going on?

The militants did not seem interested in trying to communicate beyond what could be prescribed with the contact of a rifle butt, but Shaun knew that the attack could not be totally random. Shortly, the truck moved off.

CHAPTER 56

Lieutenant Dan McCabe stared at the hand-held monitor. The image it showed was that of a mountainside rushing past, as the reconnaissance bug flew bare centimetres from the rock face. He took off his backpack and undid the clasps. It was so cold up here that his gloved fingers did not seem to follow his commands properly, but it was still only a matter of seconds before the pack was open and the second bug was pulled from its pouch. When it was folded up, the bug was not much bigger than a cat, but it represented the latest in reconnaissance technology. It was essentially a tiny helicopter, capable of speeds upwards of two hundred and fifty kilometres an hour. Small enough for a soldier to carry on his back and deploy within a minute, it gave him the ability to see what was over the next hill, or indeed the next twenty miles' worth of hills, without complex controls.

McCabe had marvelled when the bugs were first explained to him. The key to their success was the fact that they were self-navigating. They had the ability to fly along under radar, close to the ground, and yet follow the landscape beneath them. They could intelligently avoid obstacles and items that were not on any maps. The previous form of the bugs still relied on the inbuilt three-dimensional mappings of their GPS system to navigate the terrain. This was all well and good until someone parked a van in the bug's flight path. Because this obstacle wasn't there when the mapping had been done, the bug would not know about it until it was too late ... usually at the expense of being smashed into a thousand of its intricate pieces. The model before that was even less effective, requiring a soldier to be specially trained in the flight and navigation of the unit. This meant the controller had to take his valuable concentration and divert it to a radio control unit and try to fly around terrain he could not see, using only the bug's inbuilt camera for a guidance system.

They had tried lasers and even sonar, but these systems proved expensive and drained power quickly, giving the bug only a few minutes of flying time. Not anymore. The new system was based, of all things, on a bug. It was research into the optics of the humble bumble bee that had given the US military this now highly self-sufficient technology.

It had to do with the way bees saw the world McCabe had been told. A bee's view of the world was three-dimensional, but not based on the same system as humans' idea of three dimensions. In humans, eyes were far enough apart to view a different enough perspective to give depth perception. In a bee, this was not the case. But the system they used was quite ingenious. A bee measured the velocity of objects moving past its eyes and was able to judge distance based on this motion. This gave an amazing take-off and landing ability. They had used the analogy of driving in a car. Objects that were closer rushed by at a fast speed, while the mountains in the distance seemed to barely move at all. So, like a bee landing delicately on the lip of a teacup, the discovery had been made that if the velocity was kept constant as the bug flew closer to the ground it was almost like using an auto pilot; allowing the recon bug to navigate and touch down on the most precarious terrain.

Dan McCabe now hit the button that released the springs that locked the eight rotors into place. He hit another button and threw the bug into the air. It immediately took off and followed in the path of its predecessor.

From where he was, the trek down to the road running into the Khyber Pass was all but impossible. But making that trek was not his job.

His job was to locate and relay information back to his commander on the ground. Beyond that, he had no idea what this mission was about, except that his commander had said it had come directly from the President.

CHAPTER 57

It was freezing, and both men were starving. Shaun muttered to David that 'everything would be all right' as the computer engineer lay bundled beside him. The militants had kept them bound overnight. They had been held in separate tents for no apparent reason, before being woken today, beaten a little more, blindfolded and thrown back in the truck. David whimpered from the pain of his bruised body bouncing on the truck's metal tray. The militants had not spoken a word of English, and Shaun wondered if they had simply seen two Westerners who might be worth a ransom. Not that Shaun thought anyone would pay much for him. He supposed by now that Lauren's father was frantic, and probably blamed him for her disappearance, and he would be right.

It was his fault, after all; he had let her come when he knew he should have taken the trip to England alone. He cursed himself again, but then felt that strange sense of calm he had experienced after reading the diary.

He had let Masonville High School know that he was taking leave, so they would not be overly concerned. Other than that, who would miss him? Certainly no one with enough money to pay any sort of ransom.

David, he suspected, was in a similar boat. The man had been in hiding for two years, and had been extremely careful about making contact with anyone. Shaun doubted that anyone would have noticed his absence.

They had been travelling for about an hour when Shaun heard sudden yells and felt the truck stop abruptly. Shaun heard the men jump down from the back of the truck amid gunfire. Then, more gunfire, and then an earth-shattering explosion as something very close to them blew sky high – possibly the gun jeep that he knew was travelling with them. Screams, guns and the impact of bullets. None hitting the vehicle holding Shaun and David, but close. There was a firefight going on around them, and they were helpless, lying bound and blindfolded in the middle of it.

'What's happening?' Shaun heard David say through gurgled breath.

'I don't know. Turn to face away from me.' He heard the big man wriggle and roll in front of him.

'Okay, I'm going to move my face down to your hands. Do you think you can take off my blindfold?' Shaun asked.

'Yeah. I'll try,' David answered.

He moved his head down to David's hands, running his face down his friend's back in an effort to guide his movements. David's stubby fingers fidgeted with the material, and soon the cloth came free. The move opened the cut on Shaun's scalp once again, unsticking the cloth from the spot where the dried blood had held it in place.

Shaun growled.

'Sorry! Okay? Can you see anything?'

Shaun looked about. They were alone in the back of a utility vehicle, a metal tray covered by canvas on a frame. Out behind them the road stretched back, winding away around a bend. The mountains were harsh and cold. The first hints of snow were lining pockets and drifts along the side of the road. Then all at once his view was blocked by three men in uniforms. US military uniforms.

'Well, fellas, I think it's time you got out of bed for the day, don't you?'

Shaun was stunned. He had never been happier to see a man with a gun.

'US Marines,' the bald man who sat in the front seat said a short while later. He wore large reflective glasses and blue camouflage fatigues. Shaun and David sat in the rear of the personnel carrier with two other soldiers who looked straight ahead without a word.

'It seems you are very important, gentlemen,' the man continued in what Shaun guessed was a Texan accent.

'I still don't understand,' he said. 'How did you know where we were, and what do US Marines want with us, and who were those men?' The stream of questions flowed out, his mind still reeling from what had happened.

'To be honest, son, I really can't tell you much. What I can tell you is that the President himself diverted an entire unit of military personnel to rescue you from your assailants. He gave us all the information and orders directly. I can't tell you just how unheard of that is. He also told us where to find the body of that journalist.'

Shaun was silent for a moment thinking about Craig Schwartz. He could not help feeling that the man had been used as a pawn in some sick game. He forced himself to refocus on the present.

'Okay, let's get this clear. The President of the United States sent a division of US Marines to rescue us. Are you sure you got the right guys? Not that I'm complaining, but I'm fairly sure I've never been invited to the White House. I didn't think he kept that close an eye on things.'

The bald man turned.

'He doesn't. You are Shaun Strickland. Your friend here is David Black, and the dead man is CNN journalist Craig Schwartz.' It was a statement, not a question.

'Yeah, that's right. Okay, I'm going to ignore the fact that the President knows who I am for a second. Where are we?'

'You're just over the Afghanistan–Pakistan border heading west to an undisclosed location. You have passed through the Khyber Pass and are now in the Afghan mountains, probably the most lawless place on earth at the moment.'

'And how did you know where we were?'

'We were given information about the general area and then our recon scouts found you. It's what we do, son.'

'Okay ...' Shaun realised that this man, who had identified himself as Captain Allan Johnston, would only respond to direct questions, and if he wanted to get the information he needed he had to ask the right questions and in the right way.

'Why are we important to the President?' he asked slowly.

'I don't know, son. Not my department.'

'Who were those—'

'Did you get my briefcase?' David cut in. 'Did anyone get my briefcase?'

Captain Johnston smiled.

'I was told you'd ask about that. Someone has been sent to retrieve the item. We are expecting to receive some reports within the next few minutes. I have to tell you, though, that car was shot up pretty bad. No guarantees it wasn't looted.'

David looked both relieved and worried all at once.

'As for who your friends back there were, well, they were Pathans, but we don't know much beyond that. There are militant groups within the tribe, as well as mercenaries who act for the Taliban. We don't know any more than you do as to why they grabbed you.'

'Okay. Okay ...' Shaun looked straight ahead. He felt down to his empty stomach. The diary was still tucked safely into his belt. It had become so much a part of him that he hardly noticed it anymore. 'Tell me this, then: what were your orders? Where are you taking us?'

'My orders, son? My orders are to take you to a certain spot in the mountains and leave you there.'

'What?' Shaun thought he had misheard. '*Leave us there?* In the middle of the mountains? You're not taking us to your base? To a hospital?'

'No, son. No hospital, no base. In fact, we'll be there in about ten minutes,' he said as their vehicle turned off the track onto an even less defined path. Shaun's sense of relief quickly vanished.

'You can't just leave us here!'

'I'm sorry, I have my orders, son. That's what the President instructed.'

Shaun started to panic. He looked at David, whose face was bruised, his right eye swollen.

'What are we supposed to do?' he said to Captain Johnston.

'That's not my area.'

'Not your area?' Shaun screamed. He made to lean forward but the Marine at his side grabbed him by the shoulder and pulled him back into his seat. He could not believe it. This was not a rescue. He spent the remaining minutes in seething silence until the all-terrain vehicle pulled to a stop.

'Looks like this is where you get off,' Captain Johnston said, turning. Without a word, one of the other men slid the door open.

'No,' Shaun said defiantly.

'I'm afraid no is not an option for you, Mr Strickland. Don't worry, you will be provided with food. Now, please get out of the vehicle.'

Shaun sat for another moment and looked out the door. He could not imagine a less friendly or more isolated environment. He looked into the faces of the men in the truck, but none of them looked back at him.

They waited patiently in silence. Finally Shaun looked at David who was strangely quiet again. Slowly, grudgingly, he stepped out of his seat. The rocks crunched under his feet, and the cold bit into his skin. He felt sick. Exiting the military vehicle was like head-butting the air. Unbelievable. He promised himself he would not vote for President Samuels come the next election. A second later, David stood next to him holding a backpack one of the Marines had given him. It contained food and water.

'One more thing,' Captain Johnston said, stepping out. A Marine stood next to him with another backpack. He opened the pack and pulled out what looked like a futuristic helicopter hit with a shrink ray. It was painted with the same camouflage design as the Marine uniforms and as it was unfolded, Shaun could see several cameras at its front.

'This is a bug. It's your guide. Follow it.'

'Where's it taking us?' Shaun asked as David looked at the unit with interest.

'Sorry, son, that's not my area,' the captain said as he climbed back in the cabin. 'Godspeed and good luck to you both, gentlemen,' he said, and with that, he closed the door and the truck pulled away.

Shaun turned and looked at David, who still said nothing. The personnel carrier disappeared around a bend and was soon out of earshot. There they stood. Alone in the middle of nowhere. Pockets of snow dotted the uneven ground all about them. Rocks broke the sparsely covered surface and a chill wind bit into their flesh. Shaun looked down at the bug sitting at David's feet. It had not moved. David reached into the pack he had been given and pulled out a foil package. 'Sandwich?' he said.

Almost an hour had passed and snow had begun to gently fall. Shaun had been through all the emotions he had energy for, frustration not the least among them. They had drunk a good deal of the water and eaten most of the food, including a slice of carrot cake, which Shaun had wolfed down and nearly choked on as an unusually large chunk of walnut got caught in his throat. To make it this far only to be killed by a giant walnut from the survival pack? A fitting end, Shaun thought.

Still the bug sat there. David had passed the time by examining it as closely as possible, without getting in the way of the evil-looking rotor blades that sat on the top of the tiny unit, trying to work out just how the bug was built.

It was while his head was mere inches from the tiny helicopter that a beep alerted him to the fact that it was not as lifeless as he had thought. The beep was closely followed by life singing itself into the rotors, which whirred within seconds of their first twitch. More smoothly than seemed possible, the bug lifted into the air and started to move away to the left of them at a steady pace.

'Ah, Shaun?' David said as the unit paused for a moment, turning to face them as if waiting for them to follow. Shaun moved quickly to stand beside his friend – the beginning of some action was a welcome change from the fruitless speculation that had occupied them for the past hour. The bug moved off again, leading Shaun and David on a trek for which they were neither dressed nor prepared.

The bug kept its distance for most of the day as the two men, more accustomed to the lab or classroom than the great outdoors, followed as best they could through the rocky, unfriendly terrain. When it began to grow dark around five hours later, David's hands were so cold they no longer felt like part of his body. It had taken all of their energy and skill simply to not fall off the many narrow ledges to their death. When at last the bug entered a small opening in the rock, the fear of the unknown was washed away by the relief of getting inside to shelter. No sooner were they out of the howling wind than the bug's front light came on, casting a red glow around the tight passageway.

The next hour consisted of inching along dark passageways and bumping shins and elbows on rock. David marvelled at how the bug was able to fly in the confined space without hitting the walls or ceiling. It hovered and moved and darted all without bumping into a single stone, which was more than could be said for Shaun or David. The maze of passageways the pair followed had been disorienting, but the bug never moved too far ahead.

The eerie silence was suddenly punctuated by a sound echoing through the cave. Distant but distinct, it was a high-pitched yelp of pain.

Shaun stopped dead, listening, waiting. David stumbled into the back of him in the darkness and fell against the wall. Exhausted, he sat where he dropped. The beating he had endured at the hands of the Pakistani militants had robbed him of the will to push on further.

'You heard that, right?' Shaun asked.

'I think I did,' David said.

Shaun waited, but no sound came again. His mind was playing tricks.

'Come on, if that thing gets ahead of us, we'll be left here in the dark. We'd never get out. We have to keep going,' Shaun said, but as he spoke he noticed that the bug had stopped, waiting patiently as David drew his breath. The thought of getting lost in the caves caused David's mind to fill with images of panthers and hippos. It was all the motivation he needed to get to his feet and press on, but the bug did not move.

'Well?' Shaun asked, looking up at the drone. It hovered, unmoving except for the rotors. Again Shaun called to it: 'Okay, we can go now, we're ready.' Still the bug did not move.

It's waiting for something, Shaun's brain warned. For another ten minutes it hovered, before once again turning into the maze of cave passages and leading the men further into the mountain.

David struggled to keep up, and Shaun slung his friend's arm over his shoulder and helped him walk for the next hour. It was just when he was also about to drop from exhaustion that the bug touched down in front of them and faced a wall. Shaun and David limped up to the robot and looked into the beam of its red light. Nothing. Rock. It had been flying nonstop for the past eight hours, so why had it stopped now?

The sound came first: something heavy, like hydraulics moving. The sound was followed almost immediately by a blue light, as an outline appeared in the wall that both men now faced. The outline framed an area the width of a bus, and twice as high, before it split in the middle. The hydraulic sound came again, and then the hum. Finally, the rock began to move outwards.

Apart. Opening. The bug's light went out; it was no longer needed. Now the men were bathed in the blue light that came through an ever-increasing gap in the stone. Wide-eyed and exhausted, Shaun and David stared through the opening, which they now saw was, in fact, a set of doors.

CHAPTER 58

Light from the other side of the doors bathed Shaun and David in an eerie blue wash. Silently, they stared through the massive doorway, then they strode through.

Nothing could have prepared them for what they saw. Nothing. After hours in darkness, in tiny twisting passages and a maze of tunnels, they now stared out into a monstrous cavern that was altogether too enormous to be inside a mountain. Even more spectacular was what the cavern contained.

It was a city; a mass of grey steel domes and passageways connected in every direction. They found themselves on a ledge three storeys above the ground level on which most of the buildings sat. Each level was ringed around the cavern walls with a metal walkway.

Without thinking, David walked forward. Shaun followed and they both stood at the very lip of the railing gazing in awe at the impossible structures. Everything was bathed in a blue light that seemed to permeate from everywhere at once. Off to one end of the city was a large area of grass, on which ran lines and markings, almost like a football field.

It was, however, the middle of the whole mass of structures that drew Shaun's immediate gaze. Rising up above the level of the surrounding buildings, like a centrepiece for the whole world around it, was a large circular platform. It was around one hundred and fifty feet off the ground and had all manner of cables running to it. He stared at the scene and his blood ran cold.

'David,' he said. 'I've seen this before.'

'You've what?'

'I've seen it. I've seen it in my dreams.'

David did not respond but merely looked at Shaun. Neither man doubted where they were, but neither had imagined that it would look – so beautiful.

Blank monitors hung everywhere. The technology mingled with the rock as cables and pipes disappeared into and reappeared from the walls and floor. But there was something that made the whole place even stranger: it was deserted. They could not see a single sign of life, only the blue light that shone steadily throughout.

'How do we get down?' came David's question.

Shaun looked about for some kind of stairwell but could not see one. Each ring of catwalks seemed to be a full, unbroken circle.

'Where is everyone?' David asked.

'I don't know. I suspect we'll find out something if we can get to ground level.'

As soon as he said 'ground level' the section of the platform on which they stood began to move downwards. The small jolt caused Shaun to grab onto the railing for support, and as he looked down he saw the railing levels parting beneath them. Within seconds, they were at ground level, their platform becoming an elevator for their wishes.

'Look at this tech!' David enthused, through his swollen eye. They walked forward off the gangway and set foot on the rock and dirt that made up the floor of The Facility. From down here it was hard to get perspective, but one thing they could always see was the raised dais in the centre of the cavern.

'Do you think that's—'

'Yes,' Shaun replied before David could finish. 'I have to see it.'

'I don't know, man, this is really creeping me out. Where is everyone? I feel like ...'

'Like you're being watched?' Shaun said, mimicking Yoda's voice.

'Exactly.'

'I'm almost sure we are.' Shaun looked up to a dark windowed observation deck jutting out of the rock at the far side of the cavern. 'But what can we do about it? We may as well have a look around till someone talks to us.'

They continued to explore the domes, the squares and the bridges that surrounded them. The doors were all locked, and their knocks gained no response from any of the buildings. Only the dull hum that Shaun suspected came from the plethora of large monitors gave a hint to any life at all.

The longer they walked and searched, the more they were drawn to the central platform. It loomed, waiting, as if everything here existed only to serve its purpose.

'How can someone build this in the middle of a mountain? I mean, there's grass growing over there!' David said.

Shaun almost laughed. 'These are the guys who invented time travel, remember? I'm sure they've mastered the art of gardening.'

David didn't argue; he was too amazed by everything. There was nothing that could pull him out of a slump like the stimulation of his inner nerd.

'Yeah, you never did get to finish telling me how that all works.'

'What, time travel?' Shaun asked.

'Time travel.'

'I never thought it did. I'd been working on it for years, but I hit a brick wall. It comes back to black holes. A black hole is the ultimate test of Einstein's ideas.' Shaun paused, transfixed by sights.

'The existence of gravitational time warps, even on earth, has been confirmed by experiments. The effects are tiny, but still enough to have real effect on things like satellite GPS navigation systems,' Shaun said as he continued towards the tall spire that contained the central platform.

'They've got super-accurate atomic clocks on board, and because the satellites are in orbits, where gravity is less, the clocks run faster. But they're also travelling fast relative to someone on earth, so that makes them run slower. We get a combination of these two effects; the clocks on-board tick faster by about thirty-eight microseconds per day. This sounds small, but if these effects were not properly taken into account, errors in global positions would continue to accumulate at a rate of about ten kilometres each day.'

David began to get the perspective. 'So, that's just on earth? It must get even bigger when things get cosmic?'

'Sure. Time at the surface of a typical neutron star runs at about twenty per cent the speed of time on earth.'

David did some calculations in his head. 'So, if you were on a neutron star looking out, earth would be only about three and a half billion years old, instead of the five times that they think it is today?'

He never ceased to impress Shaun.

'Time runs at all sorts of different speeds all over the universe, but wherever you are, you wouldn't notice anything weird because your brain would operate at a proportional speed.'

'I get it. That's a cool idea.'

'Well, here's the thing: there are points in the universe where the timewarp becomes infinite.'

'You mean nearly infinite?'

'No, I mean infinite. If you were to take something with the mass of say, our sun, and you started shrinking its size, you get to a point where the warp shoots off the top of the chart. It's a critical radius. For something with the mass of our sun, that radius is around three kilometres. At this critical radius, the warp becomes infinite.'

'And this was all Einstein?'

'Well, not entirely. Einstein came up with a set of equations, but it was a German who provided the first complete solution; just before he went off to fight on the Russian front in World War One.'

'World War One!' David blurted, looking up from the small blank screen he was examining. 'You mean people have known about all this since then?'

'That's right. Schwarzschild was the guy's name. It corrected Newton's laws of gravity at large distances. It was a revolution!' Shaun said, examining a doorway that was sealed shut.

'You see, they basically allow you to determine the time dilation at any distance from an object's surface. Let's say that you are six kilometres from the centre of an object as heavy as our sun, but the size of a basketball. Then your watch will run at around half the speed of mine in open space. When we see each other, to me your speech will be slow and stretched out, and your watch ticks only one second for my two. To you, however, nothing is unusual about your speech at all. It's me that you can see who is running and yabbering at double speed.'

'I think if you yabbered at double speed it might negate that Southern drawl of yours!' David said with a laugh. Shaun's eyes rolled.

'The runaway time warp bugged Einstein in a big way. The existence of this Schwarzschild radius would mean that if something ever collapsed inside its own Schwarzschild radius, then light would become infinitely red shifted and lose all its energy. It could not escape. The sun is thousands of times larger than the size of its Schwarzschild radius, though, so we don't need to worry.' Shaun smiled, seeing David's look of increased concern.

'But when something *does* collapse inside its Schwarzschild radius ...'

'Black hole,' David finished.

'Black hole,' Shaun confirmed.

'So what's inside a black hole?' David asked.

'Well, that's just it, isn't it? We can never know. Theoretically, there's some tiny ball of incredibly dense matter that continuously sucks things in. But we can never get there to have a look. As soon as you get to the Schwarzschild radius, time slows to a halt.'

'This was your impasse?' David asked.

'No, actually, not at all. You see I was wondering, what's in the space between that three kilometres and the centre? Nothing. There can be no static matter inside the Schwarzschild radius. If you were actually at the radius; you wouldn't notice any distortion at all. To an outside observer time stops, but not to the person travelling there.'

'Hang on, I thought you said that we could never get there?' He now poked at the black screen with his finger.

'Well, as you got closer, you would eventually get so slow you'd freeze. You would look redder and dimmer until I eventually couldn't see you at all, your light couldn't escape.'

'So, I would stop? Become frozen still in time?'

'For me yes, but for you, you would fall quite happily past the radius until you were obliterated in the singularity at the hole's centre. Get it?'

David stopped for a second as his brain churned away.

'Well,' he said, 'you say that these things are created by a star collapsing inside its Schwartzschild radius. So, like our sun, it would have to shrink down under three kilometres?'

'Yep.'

'Well then, wouldn't it *never* do that? I mean, wouldn't it start to collapse and then as its surface reached the three kilometre radius, it would seem to freeze?'

This guy was the brightest button Shaun had come across in a long time.

'Good question. Perfect question. You're right again. To someone looking from the outside, yes, but of course the light would no longer reach us, so it would simply seem to disappear into the blackness. Locally nothing would seem weird except for the fact that you would be squished to death.' Shaun winked.

'Okay, well, then if it takes forever, your forever, for me to cross the radius, then once I am inside the radius I'm beyond the end of time.'

'That's about it.'

'But only for you, not for me.'

'Yeah, what happens inside the radius can never be observed from the outside. No events can be seen. That's why it's called the event horizon.'

Shaun had abandoned the door and had started to climb the long spiralling staircase that led up to the central spire in the room.

'At the exact geometrical centre of the black hole that would be a point where the gravitational field becomes infinite,' he called back down as he climbed higher. 'It's a space–time singularity. If the singularity exists, then it is a boundary to time itself, and an edge of infinity where time ceases to exist and there is no beyond. It's a one-way trip to nowhere, and nowhen.'

'Okay. Well, you know that spaceship ticket I bought? You can have it back.'

'Thanks. But you know, that's not what I think happens.'

'No? What happens then?'

'Well, I've told you that gravity is just a space–time curve, yeah?'

'Sure.'

'Well, the general theory of relativity allows for it to be curved round so far that it may intersect with itself. It's possible that you could "leap" to these points through something called a worm hole. Look, it gets a bit more complicated, but for now, I think I worked out a way that you could simulate the singularity you find in the centre of a black hole, but at an atomic level. The point is not static like Schwarzschild's equations account for; it's spinning. In essence you could send a particle through this worm hole from one point in space–time to another. You could theoretically have the particle arrive before you sent it. Faster-than-light travel is forbidden by physics locally, but globally on a universal scale, it's possible. If you could send a particle travelling faster than light through a singularity, it may arrive before you sent it.'

'I assume you can show me the math?'

'I can.'

'Then what's your impasse? Why did you give up on the theory?' David had to yell up to Shaun, who was now on the top of the spire. It was a flat metal platform about half the size of a tennis court. It was covered with blue strips like a strange helipad.

'Well, it's a physical more than a theoretical problem,' Shaun called back.

He was examining the strange markings on the platform, and looking up at the metal arches that intersected above him. On one side of the platform there was a long pointed tube, one end of which was thick, but then it segmented like an extendable telescope into successively smaller tubes until, by the time it reached ten feet into the platform, it was no thicker than a human hair.

'To hold these microscopic worm holes open, even for an instant in time, would require the energy of a black hole. So, imagine trying to do it for long enough to send say, a person through. There's just not enough energy to hold the hole open. You could never generate it. The matter is squished.'

'Well, what about—'

'WELCOME, DR BLACK.'

CHAPTER 59

David leaped back at the sound.

The voice was feminine, but it didn't come from a female. It came from all around the room.

'What the?'

The screen that David had been poking around on now flashed and sprang to life.

'David, what did you do?' Shaun asked in his school-teacher tone.

'Nothing, I didn't do anything,' David said defensively.

'SEQUENCE INITIATED,' the voice spoke again.

'David!' Shaun called down. 'What's happening on that screen?' David looked down at the screen to see a multitude of figures and graphics flashing by. Then, the beeps started.

'Ah ... I, um, I just touched the screen,' David said, starting to panic as the lighting in the room suddenly changed from blue to red.

'Shit! What's happening?' Shaun said as a low hum began in the arches above his head.

'COORDINATES CONFIRMED. SECONDARY CONFIRMATION AUTHORISED,' the woman's voice spoke again.

Shaun was not taking any chances; he made to leave the platform and get down to his friend. He started to move, but his limbs felt heavy. 'Whoa ... queasy,' he said to himself, trying to shake off the effect.

David looked down at the screen, which now displayed a series of numbers. Then the sound of hydraulics filled the room, and he looked up to see several doors open. Men began to spill out from the buildings and recesses in the walls.

'David!' Shaun screamed as he saw what was happening. He went to move but again he felt too heavy.

The men wore grey-and-blue uniforms and carried nasty-looking guns. A group of them formed a circle around David, but none raised their weapons.

'Shit, Shaun, get down from there! What are you doing?'

David looked up at the central spire and saw Shaun making an effort to run for the stairwell, but before his very eyes, he noticed Shaun move slower and slower. Then the alarm sirens sounded and the entire Facility was filled with a shrieking 'Whoop! Whoop!' David covered his ears and looked around in fear.

'*Shaun!*' he shrieked, trying to be heard above the din, but he may as well have been miming.

'THIRTY SECONDS TO TRANSMIT,' came the absurdly calm computerised woman over the massive sound system. Shaun tried harder to move, but with each moment he became heavier. He now stood almost in the middle of the platform. He could hear both the siren and the woman's voice, and both seemed to be speeding up.

'COMPRESSION SCAN COMPLETE,' she said, then almost without a pause she began to count.

'TWENTY ... NINETEEN ... EIGHTEEN ... SEVENTEEN ... SIXTEEN ...'

Why was she speeding up? Why could he not move? David was screaming something. He was surrounded by men. There were suddenly people everywhere. Everywhere he looked there were people running and moving. Moving fast.

'ELEVEN ... TEN ... NINE ... EIGHT ... SEVEN ... SIX ...'

David watched in confused horror. Why was Shaun not moving? Why was he not running? 'Move, you idiot! *Run! Get down!*'

Shaun's attention was caught by the doorway through which he and David had entered. He saw a silhouette; no, two. A man who wore baggy clothes, and – Shaun squinted in the red light – was that a woman?

The woman who was speaking? He wanted to tell her to slow down. In his peripheral vision he saw another movement. This was from somewhere up in the observation deck he had noticed earlier. The office overlooked the whole Facility, but it had dim windows. There was someone up there watching him, looking down. Observing.

'FIVE, FOUR, THREE, TWO ...' The woman's countdown blurred into a stream.

'*David!*' Shaun screamed again, looking down at the terrified expression on his friend's face.

'ONEZEROINITIATECOMPRESSIONTRANSMIT,' came the chipmunk-like sound.

Then something amazing happened. Shaun could not move. He was being held by some invisible force in every direction, like walking in wet cement that had suddenly dried. He wanted to scream out to David again, but he could not.

Systematically, each particle of his being began to separate. There was no description for the pain. The very fabric that held him together was split in every possible direction at once. The electrical bonds that held his atoms together now repelled each other. Shaun Strickland became a cloud of himself, and then he became nothing.

CHAPTER 60

Pain.

Searing, unbearable pain.

Nothing.

Light. Brilliant and white.

Nothing.

Is that my heartbeat? What is that? Stop that sound, it hurts. Too loud.

Nothing.

How much time has passed? Why am I cold?

Nothing.

When is it? How old am I?

Nothing.

God, I'm so thirsty. I have to ... what? What do I have to do? What do I ... I ... who ...

Pain.

Who *am* I?

Shaun Strickland was naked. He was cold, and he was naked. He knew this before he opened his eyes. Though he did not know anything else.

The sounds around him slowly disrupted his sleep. They were the sounds of traffic. Horns and engines and the smells of exhaust. A plane roared overhead. No, he wasn't naked, it had been a dream. He moved the newspapers up to cover him a little better, but they were painfully inadequate. He had the same dream again: that he was lying here naked and thirsty.

That was how he had found himself three weeks ago in this park. It had taken him most of the day to steal clothes from a dumpster on 5th Street, all while having no idea where his clothes had gone.

He had slept in this park for three weeks. He did not want to leave it because he felt ... something. He felt that if he stayed here long enough, something might click. People thought he was crazy. It was amazing how quickly he had come to look grubby and smell awful, but he did not care.

Had he been here in this city long? He did not know. He guessed that he had. He spent most of the morning as he usually did: he looked through the garbage for any discarded newspapers, reading what he could, looking for something, anything, that might jog his memory.

'Dems wanna hit?' It was Ernie, who shared the park with him and lived on the far bench. He was mad after years of alcohol abuse.

'No thanks, Ernie.'

Ernie smiled his toothless grin and took a long pull on the bottle he held within the paper bag. Shaun never accepted, but Ernie always offered. If that were the extent of it, things would be fine, but now the homeless man had made contact for the day, Shaun would be bombarded with at least an hour of inane babble. Not that he really minded; Ernie was the only person who would talk to Shaun.

Shaun suspected that it was because of years of his own alcohol abuse that he could not remember anything before a couple of weeks ago. Consequently, he had decided to kick the sauce. He could not afford it anyway, and he often wondered how Ernie financed his habit. Although, the man did work hard. From dawn till nearly dusk, by which time he was incapacitated, Ernie worked the streets. It must be something in his technique, Shaun decided, because he had a lot more success than Shaun ever did. What a depressing thought. If depression had a physical form, he was it. He did not even know what he had to be depressed about. He had nothing; no money, no home, no memory. He just was. He suspected he would be fine about it too if he did not have this nagging feeling. There was something he had to do.

'.... and tha fife off em didn't know why, or who, or when, or fife!' Ernie was still talking.

'You know what, Ernie? I will have a hit,' Shaun decided. He had run out of reasons not to.

He took the small bottle from the man next to him and looked down at it. The rim was covered with brown-stained saliva and what Shaun suspected was vomit. He did not care. He took a big swig of the liquid inside and swallowed.

He reacted almost straight away. Whatever it was in there, it was a hell of a lot stronger than he had anticipated, and no sooner had it hit the back of his throat and flowed into his stomach than he began to cough violently. He spluttered and gagged, and Ernie laughed at his park-mate.

'Weeeee! Oh, dems dem and dats tha one ey!' he said as Shaun promptly threw up in a puddle next to his feet and a little bit on them.

Shaun's eyes watered. Vomit strings fell from both his mouth and nose. He looked down at the puddle as Ernie laughed at him. Bile contrasted harshly with the green grass. But as he looked, he saw something else. There was something there. He looked harder, his brain laughing at him for examining his own vomit. What was that? Was it a ... a walnut? A giant walnut? He had not eaten a walnut, had he? No. He was quite certain he had not eaten a walnut, let alone one this big. It was the length of his finger, and double the width.

Slowly, uncaring about the world around him or the passers-by who had seen his display and cringed in disgust, he reached down to pick it up.

'Dats dem! Secondsies! Weee!!! Ha ha!' Ernie squealed with delight.

Shaun turned the object over in his hand. It had a seam down one side and was made of something hard and metallic. Who knew how long it had sat in his stomach undigested. He dug his dirty fingernail into the crack and tried to pull it apart. Then, without warning, his head exploded in a violent flash of white and immediately his hands went to his temples. Images. Pain, *BAM! BAM BAM!* The explosions were accompanied by sound, and the images cracked through his consciousness. Shaun fell to the ground clutching his head. People on the footpath stopped, some showing genuine concern, others simply laughing. Others still recoiled and moved on their way.

The episode lasted for nearly a minute, and when it stopped, Shaun sat up, his weight back on his hands.

'Shit,' he said to himself quietly. 'Shit,' he said again. 'Shit, shit, *shit*!' he yelled. His eyes danced wide with shock and realisation. He looked up at Ernie, who seemed to be enjoying the show, then down at himself, and then at the walnut on the grass next to him. He picked it up and again dug his fingernail into the seam. It snapped apart on a hinge and a roll of tightly packed paper fell out.

He picked it up, but before he unrolled it, he said aloud, 'My name is Shaun Strickland. My name is *Shaun Strickland*!' With that he unrolled the paper in his hands and looked at the type it contained:

FOLLOWING IS A TRANSCRIPT OF THE FINAL PAGES OF THE FONTÉYNE DIARY – TRANSCRIPT BASED ON DOCUMENT 351-6.

Found 1954, Cave 9, Khirbet Qumran, Dead Sea.
ORIGINAL DIARY TEXT LANGUAGE: Aramaic.
ORIGINAL DOCUMENT LANGUAGE: Italian.
TRANSLATION AUTHORITY: Vincenso Giovanni.

TRANSCRIPT OF DOCUMENT 351-6:

The final pages of the text acquired for Essene Research translated here:

'In accordance with the wishes of Saul, I, Mishca, son of Mycha, of the Village of Chorazin, have accounted for the final instructions leading to the disc of Officer X7.'

Shaun shook his head. Diary? The diary. Where was it? So much information. So much all at once. The final pages, the final pages not in English ... He sat back on the park bench, and read.

CHAPTER 61

In the days after our arrival in Jerusalem, I stayed for a little over a week with the man named Jacob. He was a trader and a good man. He lived alone in the city's outskirts, although at the time I was visiting him, his daughter was staying in his house. His daughter, Alisha, caught the eye of the man whom I had come to regard as my older brother, my friend and my hero – the man who wrote this book in a language I do not understand. He is the strangest man, and the most incredible man I ever met, and he saved my life – now I will honour his. I will finish his story.

For almost a week I didn't see Saul or his African friend Malbool, nor did I see Zachariah. The whole time I was questioned again and again by Alisha about our adventures, but I realise now that she was seeking information about Saul. It was Tuesday when Malbool and Saul returned. They told me Zachariah had been killed and we mourned his death and attended his funeral.

Saul had changed. For a start, his fingers that had been severed on the journey from Rome to Jerusalem were now whole. His nose was healed too, and all his cuts were gone. He assured me that the explanation would be made clear, and that one day he would be able to show all of mankind.

He spoke of something called a disc and said that it would be hidden and would be found at the right time; that there would be a map leading to this disc, and the map would be with this diary.

We stayed in Jerusalem for another few days, and then left for my village. It was curious to me then, but now I understand why Alisha came with us on our journey. I look at my own children and know that somewhere Saul from the future has a line of his own, and may even be his own ancestor!

When I walked into Chorazin it was perhaps an hour after nightfall and the people were just sitting down to their evening meal. I came upon my house and paused outside the window. The shutters were open a little, and I could see my mother and father sitting together eating. There was a third place at the table. A third candle had been lit and a third bowl set. My place.

My heart broke at the sight of them – a sight I never thought to see again. It took all of my will to not cry out at that moment, but instead I nodded to Saul and Malbool and smiled at Alisha. Then I walked up to the door and knocked.

The door swung open, and my father stood before me. He looked first above me, expecting an adult, but when he looked down into my face he stopped. I think I counted five or six breaths before anything else happened. It was enough time for my mother to call out and ask who was disturbing them at this late hour.

There was no explosion of joy in my father's face, he simply nodded and a tear streamed down his cheek. Then another. He sank to his knees, his hand still on the door, but his face now level with mine. I could resist no longer and I threw my arms around his neck.

By this time my mother had stopped eating and looked up from her food. She ran over to us and also fell to her knees, embracing me with all her strength. For the longest time we stayed there, in the doorway of my house.

In the years that followed I saw Saul many times. He told me that he still had work to do, and had taken many long journeys to collect things from distant lands, but it was not until he had been absent for many seasons, and I now worked in my father's fields, that he returned one day with an object he called a book. It was a scroll bound up in small square parchments and would become the way scrolls are read. It was the story of his time here in our lands. He said it contained important information that would ultimately lead to a change in his world, and could save the lives of many. He looked into my eyes and charged me with its safekeeping. He told me that it was my part to take the book, and through my lineage, ensure its final hiding place, where it would be discovered two thousand years from now in a faraway land. This land Saul spoke of was not yet known to the people of my time. He told me it would rest there, undisturbed in a cave on the mountain of Caroline's grandfather, until the bluebird falls from the sky.

He returned again many years later, as an old man. He gave me many parchments and scrolls and asked that they be taken together with his diary. He also told me more things he learned from his doctor friend Miles.

It was always a celebration when my children were visited by 'Uncle Saul'. When it was time for my children to leave home, my son went to Jerusalem and worked as a trader with Malbool, who had taken up permanent residence in Jerusalem trading the rare and exotic goods of his African homeland, and as I write this I am an old man myself.

Saul never spoke of how he got his fingers back, but he said that one day the world would see and that it was not for me to know. To whosoever finds this diary, the story of Saul the gladiator, the man who saved my life and freed the slave Malbool, I have one final message given to me before Saul closed his eyes forever with one hand in mine, the other in those of his wife, Alisha. His message is this: 'The Rule of Knowledge is unbroken, but this may not always be so. You cannot sit by because of what has happened, you must act. You must remember and act right now. Leave the park.'

Shaun stared at the paper. *Leave the park?* What had he been doing? He recognised the names but, yes ... the diary. Did he still have the diary? He checked his stomach where he felt it should be. Nothing. Oh God! Had he lost it? Where, when? He was walking in the caves with ... with David. He was following the bug. The doors, the lights ... shit! What had happened then? Looking around. No one there. Men in uniforms. Lights, sirens. Someone at the door, a woman who was talking ... someone in the office, looking down.

So heavy.

Shaun shuddered as he suddenly remembered the pain. The very thought of it caused him to scream again and start to panic. He shut it out. The pain he never ever wanted to remember again. Never ever.

He looked back down at the paper. 'TRANSLATION AUTHORITY: Vincenso Giovanni.' Vincenso Giovanni? The priest! It was on his authority that the document had been translated into English. But there had been another translation, an earlier one. One from the original language into Italian. This meant what? It meant that the Church – the Vatican – was in possession of this document, or at least an Italian version of it. But what was it about Giovanni? There was something about him. Shaun found it hard to remember, hard to concentrate. His head was still playing tricks on him and causing intermittent explosions of pain. There were gaps in what he could remember. There was something about him. Yes, they had met him and, oh, he was dead.

He was a nice guy, Shaun recalled. No, there was something else. Giovanni had said something. What did he do? He, ah, he was taken off The Journalist Project. Someone else was in charge now. Someone else was investigating. Someone ...

Le Clerque! Shaun heard his brain tell him, a voice that had been silent until now. That's right. Le Clerque. Giovanni had said he would kill for the disc. Le Clerque would know about this translation, about this document.

'Oh my God!' he said aloud. Le Clerque would be looking for the diary.

'Ohmaygod, ohmaygod! Dems that wanna gives the fives ey! Eh heh heh!' Ernie said with a knowing smile.

'But I've already found the diary,' Shaun said, a little confused. He looked down at his feet as a newspaper swirled among the mess that lay there. He reached down to pick it up.

'NATIONAL LOTTO JACKPOT GOES OFF!!!' the headline read.

Shaun knew that headline. He had read it before; he was sure he had. He remembered it because of the odd sequence of numbers the winner had chosen – they happened to be Shaun's birthday. He remembered that headline. From when? How could he remember it?

Below the story was another headline that caught his attention: 'Haven in Pakistan – CNN Investigates 7.30 Eastern'. It was not the headline that caught Shaun's attention, however, but the name underneath. Craig Schwartz.

The weight, the immense weight of his limbs, right before ... no, he didn't want to think of it again. The sirens. David. Shit, David! What had happened to him? A few minutes ago Shaun thought he was an alcoholic who had lived in a park for years. This paradigm shift was hard to absorb. The sirens. The Facility. They were at The Facility. The one Graeme had spoken about in the diary. The one where they ... sent you back in time.

Shaun stopped. Was it possible?

Why don't you believe? his brain asked.

I just, I just find it ...

Find it what? How can you not *believe? Don't be a total idiot! Everything makes sense, everything fits together.*

'I've been sent back in time?' Shaun asked his brain, but it did not answer.

'I've been sent back in time,' Shaun said, this time out loud. He searched the fine print of the newspaper: Friday, 13 June 2014.

'Today! That's today!' Shaun shouted, instantly struck by panic. He would never forget it: '*This diary will be found on the 13th of June*

*2014*AD*, more than two thousand years from now. My name is Graeme Fontéyne, and I remember everything.*'

The diary was going to be found today! But what if the fact of him being sent back in time had changed all that?

Shit. He looked again at the last line of the paper he had vomited up in the walnut: *His message is this: 'The Rule of Knowledge is unbroken, but this may not always be so. You cannot sit by because of what has happened, you must act. You must remember and act right now. Leave the park.'*

It was speaking to him; this translation. This message passed through the ages – it was speaking to him right now. '*You must remember and act right now.*' He could almost hear the words, and again he was overcome with panic.

The Rule of Knowledge? What did he know? He knew that the diary's first lines predicted that it would be found today. It did not say anything about by whom. What if he was not the one to find the diary? What if Le Clerque found it? And the map? It was supposed to be hidden with the diary – if Le Clerque found the map, then he would find his way to the disc.

Shaun looked at Ernie, smiled, put his hand on the man's shoulder and said, 'It's been swell.' Then he bolted down the street.

After about a hundred yards he began to wonder where he was running to, so he stopped. He was breathing hard and his head throbbed. He pulled the paper up in front of his face and scanned it: '*He told me it would rest there, undisturbed in a cave on the mountain of Caroline's grandfather, until the bluebird falls from the sky.*'

In a cave on the mountain of Caroline's grandfather? What did that mean? Grandfather's cave?

Then a realisation hit him. He was in America, and had been for the past three weeks.

This was the first time he had left the park, but as he stood on the street, being ignored by passers-by, he looked up to a shopfront: 'Dr Drains: We Fix Drains. Charlotte's 24-hour plumbing service.'

He knew where he was; he had known all along, he just had not realised it.

Charlotte. North Carolina. Home. He was home ... relatively. It was bizarre, because it suddenly made perfect sense: Grandfather Mountain, North Carolina. It was a clue only Shaun would understand. It was something that was so perfectly designed for his own style of thinking that he could not imagine it to be any other possibility.

Grandfather Mountain was the highest peak in North Carolina's Blue Ridge Mountains, and it was a place Shaun used to visit with his brother Tim as a child. They stayed near Boone at the campground and often took day trips up to the mountain, to hike and explore the caves.

Without another thought, Shaun ran again, this time in the direction of the airport. His bare feet started to blister on the concrete, but he kept going. Pain exploded in his head again and he fell as he ran, sprawling and rolling. His clothing ripped, but he was up and moving again without pause. A taxi pulled around the corner and Shaun flagged it, but it sped past him, the driver barely glancing his way. Did they not see? Did they not see past the rags now? *BAM!* Another explosion of pain in his head. Should this still be happening? He had not really gleaned how long it had taken Graeme to get over the headaches, nor any of the others the diary mentioned, but he was sure it was not supposed to go on and on like this. But this felt different.

Cars passed as Shaun rounded another corner, following the large blue road signs to the airport. He tried to think things through as he ran, but his feet were killing him. He needed shoes.

It was about this time that a shard of broken glass punctured his heel. He dropped immediately as the pain again made him stumble and fall. He pulled the shard from his foot and forced himself to stand. Looking around, he saw a red scooter, whose owner had happened to leave the keys in the ignition and the motor running while he made his pizza delivery next door. Without the luxury of time to regret what he was doing, Shaun kicked up the stand and placed both feet in front of him.

The *nig-nig, nig-nig* of the tiny engine as he sped away from the pimply-faced teen was the sweetest sound Shaun had heard for a long time. The wind stung his eyes and blew his considerable beard apart into tufts. He did not care; he was on his way.

He had not formed a plan of how to get to Grandfather Mountain, but he knew that he had to be there today before Le Clerque's men could find the diary – and it *would* be found today. He knew also that the hundred-and-fifty-plus miles to the mountain through immense terrain could not be covered by road in the time he had. He had to fly.

He rode on faith. He knew only that he had to act, that what he knew had happened, must happen, otherwise ... none of this would begin in the first place for him to be sent back to where he was right now, and, what? He would cease to exist? He did not know and agreed with his brain that these were awfully big thoughts for a homeless man on a stolen pizza delivery scooter to have.

CHAPTER 62

Ron Shaw ran through his checklist one final time. The replies of 'Check, check, check' gave him the buzz he always felt when he knew that the next thing he would hear was, 'Azulejo, you are cleared for take-off on the south-west runway.'

He sat with his earphones on in the small four-seat Cessna, content and ready to fly his plane solo for his first day off in six months. It was with surprise, then, that he heard the next words from the domestic control tower: 'Ah, just sit tight there, Azulejo, we've got a disturbance on the tarmac.'

What? A disturbance on the tarmac?! He sat back and closed his eyes, trying to hold onto his holiday frame of mind. He was not successful.

When he opened them again a few seconds later, he saw a man, tattered and grubby, on a scooter speeding down the runway towards him. What was even stranger was the sight of two fat security guards running behind him. An airport police van squealed past them in an effort to run the scooter down.

It would have all been amusing had there not suddenly been the yellow muzzle flash and white smoke of handgun fire from the police. The sight made Ron uncomfortable, a feeling not eased when he realised that the scooter was heading straight for him. Which meant—

Crack! His windscreen split. Was it a bullet? No, but it was some flying pieces of runway torn up by the ridiculous onslaught of gunfire. What were these guys thinking?

'Ah, control, this guy's getting a little close, request permission to taxi, there's some gunfire here. Over.'

Nothing, static. 'Control?'

'Sorry there, Azulejo, permission denied. You're to sit tight in your location. Over and out.' The British voice of the control tower vanished. Not the usual guy.

Ron watched in unsettling fascination as the man on the scooter, who looked like Robinson Crusoe, weaved through the stationary fixtures all over the airport. Baggage cars, refuelling vehicles and cargo containers all provided moments of temporary cover from the police van that was chasing him. Then, quite suddenly, he was out in the open again, on the runway – and still headed straight for Ron's plane.

'Ah, control, I'm going to have to make a move from my location—'

'That's a negative,' the tower cut in. The tower never cut in. 'Hold your position.'

Ron stared at the man, speeding towards him, and further down the runway, the police van, still firing wildly. Ron knew that this was crazy, but he also realised that getting out of the plane would do nothing but expose him to the stray and inaccurate bullets being fired. The props were spinning at the front, giving a false sense of protection. The propellers only appeared to be everywhere at once, but he knew that they weren't.

He ducked down behind the dashboard of the small plane as the scooter man, now only twenty feet away, vanished from view. Ron sighed in relief; once the scooter had passed him, surely the police would have to stop firing in his direction?

No sooner had Ron begun to rise back into his seat than his passenger door opened and a ragged, bearded and sweat-covered man climbed up into his passenger seat. Why hadn't he locked the doors? Well, he justified to himself, maybe because he hadn't expected any more passengers once he'd gotten out on the runway ready for take-off.

He was too stunned to speak, but his passenger was not.

'Go!' the strange man commanded. '*Go now!*'

'Get the fuck out!' Ron swore at the man, who smelled like a sewer. The man looked around the cockpit and then reached forward, pulling something from under the front dash. The flare signal gun. Ron's eyes widened in terror as the man pointed the gun directly at his head.

'Go now! Those cops aren't really cops. They'll shoot me, and you – and if you don't take off now I will shoot you in the face and take off myself!' The man's voice was commanding, in contrast to his shabby appearance.

Ron looked into the man's eyes. This man was desperate, but he was not crazy. Slowly the pilot sat up and faced the front. The van rushed towards them at speed.

'Now!' the man yelled again.

A bullet zinged past and another slammed into the fuselage. They were shooting at his plane! Setting his jaw, Ron pushed the throttle into full ahead and the whirring sound of the propellers rose. The plane leaped forward. He gripped the steering column with both hands. The van was closing quickly; if he was going to make this, he had to get into the air as quickly as possible. Did he have enough runway between his aircraft and the speeding van? Could he get into the air in time? At the rate they were closing, he would know in about eight seconds.

The ground rushed by outside the tiny plane's windows, and Shaun looked down at the fixed landing gear, silently willing the wheels up. Another bullet made contact, this one far more accurate as the strut of the wing on his side was gashed.

Come on! Shaun's brain screamed, joining in the effort of will for both their survival.

The van rushed forward. The gap was closing.

Bullets. *Ping ping ping!* Glass shattered on Shaun's window. *Ping! SMASH!* Another bullet hit the very top of the windscreen, not directly enough to shatter it, but enough to increase the crack snaking across its length. *Ping! Ping ping ping!*

The Cessna sped forward. The van closed. Four seconds. Three. Shaun took the gun away from the pilot's head. Two. Ron pulled back with all his might on the steering column. 'Aaaarrrghhhh!' he growled, half with effort and half with terror. Shaun thrust the gun out his shattered window. One second. He fired.

Everything seemed to happen at once.

The Cessna lifted its nose and rose, the landing gear hitting the top of the speeding van and ripping off. But the flare had already found its mark. The van had barely cleared the speeding plane when the vehicle's front passenger cabin exploded. The engine beneath it did the same. The violence of the shockwave forced Ron to fight for control to stay in the air. He felt sick.

Shaun had the flare gun back at Ron's head in an instant, the second flare still loaded. He watched below him as they burst through the black smoke and saw the van disappear below and behind them. It still moved forward, out of control, with long flames billowing from underneath. Like a speeding fireball it shot through another safety barrier and sailed into a power terminal below. This explosion truly was spectacular. The intense voltage ignited the van's fifty-gallon fuel tank with an enormous *KABOOM!*

Ron's eyes were locked straight ahead, but even through his headphones he heard the noise. Explosion after explosion; a daisy chain of substation destruction.

'What was that?' he called, but Shaun could not hear him above the engine. Ron dared a glance at the man, who still had the flare gun trained on his temple. He gestured to the large headphones that hung on a peg on Shaun's side door. The wind rushed in where the window had blown out and it was not until he had put the headphones firmly over his ears that the howl of rushing wind quieted enough for him to hear his own thoughts.

'Where we headed?' Ron asked his passenger.

Shaun squinted at hearing the pilot's voice through his headphones.

'Just talk. The microphone is on a noise gate. It opens when you speak.'

Shaun did so. 'North. North and west. Towards Boone.'

The pilot nodded but said nothing. He did not want to show how terrified he was. He knew that panic was not a good state to fly in, and he still held hope of getting out of this alive.

'You know Grandfather Mountain?' Shaun asked, breaking the silence.

Ron nodded, and reached forward to twiddle some knobs. Shaun pressed the flare gun firmly onto Ron's head by way of response.

'I have to chart our course. If I don't they'll shoot us down. If you wanna get there, you have to let me do this.'

Shaun watched him for a moment, and then nodded.

'You're cleared north-west to Boone.' The tower crackled over the radio as if nothing unusual had happened.

'What was that?' Ron asked, motioning behind them.

'The van hit the power substation and exploded,' Shaun said simply.

'That's gonna cause some power cuts,' Ron remarked, hoping that soon the man's arm would tire and he would take the flare gun away from the side of his head.

'It does,' Shaun said, allowing himself to turn and look again at the pilot. He doubted that this guy would try to fight with him now – what could he do that would not endanger his own life?

'It took out the whole airport for the day,' he said, a little sadly. Ron missed the tense.

They flew on in silence for another twenty minutes, Shaun finally relaxing his arm. The scenery below changed dramatically over the time, going from the green of the Carolina hills to the awesome ruggedness of the Blue Ridge Mountains. Neither their size nor magnificence impressed Shaun today, though – not after the Khyber Pass.

'So, you mind me asking why the cops were after you?' Ron said.

'They weren't cops,' Shaun muttered in the same, distant tone.

'No? Well, they looked like cops to me,' Ron replied, trying not to sound antagonistic.

'They weren't. They were part of a group trying to get something from me. Well, something they think I have, but I don't have it yet.'

'What's your name?' Ron asked, hoping to make enough of a personal connection with the desperate man that he would decide not to flare gun him in the head.

'Shaun. Shaun Strickland,' he said so quietly that the microphone cut out and Ron didn't hear it clearly.

'Mind telling me what this is all about?' Ron asked, beginning to think that he might be able to talk his way out of flying across the state.

'Let's just say I'm a treasure hunter, looking for a map to lead me to my buried treasure,' he said, in a tone that signalled the end of the conversation.

It was perhaps half an hour later when the question came up. They had, after all, no landing gear.

'I don't suppose you've had any thoughts about how we're going to land us?' Shaun asked Ron.

The pilot smiled thinly. 'I've had lots of thoughts, and basically they all scare me to death. I've never done a belly flop before, but I'll notify Boone that we are going to need to make an emergency landing.' He pointed out the window. 'There's your mountain,' he said.

Shaun looked out. Even from above, Grandfather Mountain still looked higher than the surrounding peaks. It was rugged and beautiful. From the plane he could see the campsite where he had stayed with his brother Tim as a child; it looked tiny. It was more developed now and had a permanent amenities block and—

CRACK!

The sudden jolt of the plane alerted both men to the fact that the wing strut on Shaun's side had gone; the damage from the onslaught of bullets at the airport had finally taken its toll. Immediately warning lights flashed and a beep sounded through the headphones.

'What's that?' Shaun asked, not understanding.

'We're losing fuel. We're all right without a strut, but the fuel's stored in the wings, and I wasn't planning on flying to the state line today!'

Shaun looked out and saw the precious liquid streaming away into the air. His face perfectly portrayed his combined sense of panic and dread.

'It's in the wing? We're lucky they didn't hit it when they were shooting.'

Ron shot Shaun a sideways glance. Then the fuel ran out. 'Oh shit!' Ron cursed. 'We're too far short of the airport to try to make it. There's nowhere else to land!'

Shaun looked down at Carolina's Grandfather Mountain. No, it could not end like this.

'The campsite.'

'What?'

'The campsite, back there,' Shaun motioned. Ron looked at the clearing covered in tents and cabins. It was the only break in the treeline. He did not hesitate, he could not; they were losing altitude too quickly.

To call what happened a belly landing would be a stretch of the definition. Dropping more than gliding, the plane came down. People on the ground, not having the benefit of engine noise to alert them, realised too late what was happening. They only noticed the plane on its first earth-shattering impact.

Shaun and Ron had braced themselves, but they had pathetically little to grab onto. Ron had flown around and approached from the uphill side, trying to land down the slope to lessen the jolt. It did not matter. The first impact was immense and slammed both Shaun and Ron forward against the windshield, which finally succumbed to its crack and smashed. Because of the slope, the plane hit tail first, gouging the turf of the campsite. The fuselage broke in two, the tail section ripping free and catapulting the front section into a somersault after its initial bounce.

Shaun and Ron were thrown around the cabin like rag dolls, their seatbelts proving painfully inadequate. People dived out of the way, desperately trying to flee the cartwheeling plane. Several tents were collected along the way, but the body of the plane passed through the campsite and out the other end quickly.

Knocked unconscious, Ron's limp body saved itself simply by offering no resistance to the forces that flung it around. Shaun, however, bounced around the spinning cabin, smashing his head, body and limbs countless times, but nothing broke.

Eventually, on the fifth rotation, the cabin plunged through the trees and down an embankment. Shaun was thrown clear, flying out the open back of the cabin where the tail had been ripped off. He sailed through the air and landed hard, falling through branches on his way down and coming to rest in a mixture of mud, moss and foliage. He could not move, and as he slipped into unconsciousness he noted with interest that the cabin was still smashing its way through the trees. He wondered when it would finally stop moving, and whether Ron would be alive when it did.

CHAPTER 63

They had searched the hill for more than a year. They had come in every guise – as tourists, as campers; two of them had even become bona-fide hike leaders in order to search the trails – and what had they found? Nothing.

Grandfather Mountain was a big place. A very big place. It took tourists year round, and when the snows allowed, offered a range of hiking adventures from the hour-long nature walks to the three-week adventures across various trails. Every conceivable inch of the mountain that was accessible, and a lot of it that was not, had been searched by members employed, directly or indirectly, by a representative of the Holy Roman Catholic Church – Cardinal François Le Clerque. The search had begun just a month after the death of Pope Nicholas II in 2005, and led them here last year, the searchers knowing only that they were to look for an ancient diary and a map.

Not a lot changed up on Grandfather Mountain. The animals liked it that way, even though the crowds had become bigger in the past few years. The Blue Ridge Mountains were covered in forests most often found in Canada. The base rock that poked through to form cliffs and crags was more than a billion years old, pre-dating the formation of the continents themselves. Now, though, it had become a hiker's mecca, with a distinctive mile-high bridge measuring more than two hundred and thirty feet and spanning an eighty-foot chasm. The suspension bridge gave hikers who stayed late at night a whole new definition of the mile-high club.

Twenty-nine-year-old Georgina Milani had earned her membership to the club many times over, and rather liked her latest assignment. She had it easy, and all she had to do was search. Of course, it was Le Clerque's idea of punishment. She was one of his top assassins but had trouble controlling her temper. Her last assignment in Iran had ended abruptly when she took offence to one of her Persian counterparts' suggestion that women were not meant to be outside the house without proper covering, and that they were ineffective in this line of work. Georgina, a wild-blooded Italian, thought he was incorrect, and she proved it by killing him, his family and two witnesses.

It was she who had made the initial call back to the black-suited sentry, and alerted the four men who were also scouring the mountain that day. When Georgina arrived at the scene of the crash, she found that other hikers had already freed the unconscious pilot and were building a makeshift stretcher to carry him out. She walked over to the twisted wreckage; the word *Azulejo* was still visible on the side.

She moved around the crash site and wondered how the pilot had survived. Looking back up the hill to where the plane had cut its way through the trees, she visualised the violence of the crash. She superimposed the carriage in her mind's eye, tumbling and flipping out of control, collecting trees and branches as it bounced before slamming into *that* rock and coming to a halt.

Walking closer to the mangled wreckage, she noticed something else. The group of rocks where the plane had finally come to rest had been disturbed. A whole boulder, which had sat in place the whole time Georgina had been at the park, had been knocked a full two feet to the side, revealing a gap between the rocks. The fact that there was blood on the rocks prompted her to investigate further. Yes, someone had gone in here. There were footprints in the mud. Not shoe-prints, but footprints, bare feet.

She turned on the flashlight that always hung at her side and slid into the gap. The earth was freshly disturbed, but the small cavern was completely closed off from the outside world. The cave was air- and water-tight, or would have been until that plane knocked the boulder loose. Georgina knew that she would have walked past this a thousand times without a clue that there was a hollow inside. It could have remained undiscovered for years, or even centuries.

She scrambled back up through the cavern opening. The crowd had moved the man onto the stretcher and were preparing to take him away, but she got to him first. Shoving people roughly out of the way, she leaned over the pilot. He was a mess; alive but not awake. She slapped his cheek.

Nothing. Again, *SLAP!*

'Hey!' some guy objected.

She spoke in a thick Italian accent: 'Back the fuck off, I'm a professional!' She accented her words with another *SLAP!*

This time, the pilot groaned.

In an instant, Georgina pulled open his eyelids and withdrew a pen from her pack. She swivelled the pen until a bright green light illuminated one end. She moved the light across his face and watched his eyes follow.

'Sir, I need you to focus on the light. Focus on the light, sir. Good. That's good. Tell me who was with you in the plane. Was there someone else with you in the plane?'

Ron followed the light with his eyes. Man he hurt, but suddenly, things were getting easier. Easier when he followed the light. It started to dance and twirl in little patterns. Everything started to feel better.

'Sir, who was with you in the plane?'

She wanted to know about the crazy man. No, not crazy ... desperate. 'Sh,' he tried, but then coughed up blood. It was okay, the light was still there. Nothing hurt. He tried again. 'Shhtreetlund,' he gurgled.

'And what is he doing, why was he with you?' she pressed. He watched the light. He liked her voice.

'Treashhhure. Treashuure map,' he said. Then he died.

Georgina slapped him again, but got nothing. *Damn*. She raised the walkie-talkie to her mouth and spoke to the man in the black car.

'Someone else was in the crash. He survived and he has the map. I repeat, the map has been found and taken by a man called Streetlund.'

Static. It was a call the driver had never expected to come. He thought that perhaps one day they would find the map, but he never had expected to hear that it had been found and stolen all in the one broadcast.

'Do you read me, you stupid American bastard? Get down to the lower campsite straight away!'

'Copy.' She could not see it, but she knew that the black Mercedes would be squealing its tyres in an effort to get to her.

Where would he be? Where would he run to? He had just survived a plane crash that had killed the pilot, so he could not have gone far. She had seen the blood. She looked down the hill into the wilderness. Absently she thought about the word stencilled on the plane. *Azulejo* – Spanish for 'Bluebird'.

The mile-high bridge swung in the breeze. From where Shaun had found the bundle he now clung to, it was the shortest route to what he needed most right now: a car.

He had seen her. She did not know it, but he had seen her: the woman from the hospital. The cop. The woman whose face he had smashed into an unrecognisable mess. He had seen her. Her black hair, smooth skin and annoyingly attractive face.

He had been less than fifteen feet away as she entered the cave from which he had only just emerged, and the moment she disappeared, he had run. Uphill. She would not expect that.

Now he stood on the swaying bridge. There was no one here; everyone had cleared out when the plane came down. That was now nearly half an hour ago, but there were still a few cars in the parking lot on the other side. Without stopping to catch his breath, he limped and hobbled forward as best he could. The crash had knocked him about. He was missing four teeth, he had cracked several ribs, and the bruising to his body left welts that had already turned purple. The wound on his forehead had also reopened and blood streamed freely down over his eyes. He had found a leather pilot's cap strewn among the wreckage and grabbed it to act as a bandage for his bleeding scalp. It would scar. He looked like a dead man.

But you know what? his brain prompted as he moved out across the swinging structure. *You're not dead. You're alive, and you have the bundle, the diary and the map.*

The thought produced a gap-toothed smile, just seconds before another explosion in his head sent him sprawling forward. *BAM!* Images. His fingertips tingled, the lumps he had nearly forgotten about. What was happening?

You're falling, his brain told him while his mind played a slideshow of images.

You're falling ... off a bridge. Grab onto something.

'Oh.'

Shaun lashed out wildly with his hands and feet, still blinded by the pain. His hands locked around something and he pulled it to his chest instinctively. His ankle locked into something else. He curled his leg and hooked the bridge's rope railing behind his knee. When his vision returned and he realised what had just happened, his heartbeat tripled: he had fallen, dropped and then re-caught the bundle, and now hung off the side of mile-high bridge by his legs.

Shaun took a moment to gather himself. He looked down into the rocks and forest below him. He had survived a plane crash to nearly die falling off a bridge – why? No one was shooting at him; no one was chasing him. It had been the explosion in his head, the worst one yet.

Aware that his ragged clothes looked like the mud-caked skins of an animal, and that his blood and grime made him all but unrecognisable, he clambered back on the bridge's walkway and finished the crossing. He scanned the car park. Three choices: a van, blue and dating from about 1970, a small Hyundai hatchback, and, well of course, a red Porsche.

Window smashed.

Alarm screamed.

Attempts to hotwire.

Alarm screamed.

Attempts to hotwire continue.

Shaun admits to himself that he sucks as a car thief.

Three minutes pass. Alarm continues.

Ignition!

Shaun slammed the performance vehicle into reverse and spun the car a full one hundred and eighty degrees before launching on the gas to power down the mountain.

Georgina had heard the alarm and knew what was happening, but she had been too far down the hill to do anything about it. She saw the red Porsche speed past while she was still five minutes away, but had no doubt who drove the car at breakneck speed. It was the man who had stolen the map. The man she would catch. The man she would kill. The chase was on.

Unsure of exactly where he was, Shaun knew where he was going. He had to get the map to safety, to the only person he could trust – he had to get it to Tim.

He raced around the mountain curves and sped east towards Washington DC and his brother.

Tim had worked his way into the world of politics. He had gone from running his own mechanic shop in North Carolina to practising as a lawyer, and then being elected as a Senator in the nation's capital. Shaun was proud of his brother, but he had not seen him since that night four years ago, on the anniversary of their parents' deaths, when Shaun had said some things that he had immediately regretted.

Tim was so busy these days that Shaun had never really had a chance to apologise, and over the years it had become harder to even try. It had started with reminiscing about old times, and had escalated to his accusation of Tim abandoning him to seek his fame and fortune in the big city. Tim had left the house furious and deeply hurt. Shaun knew the truth of it; he knew that Tim had sacrificed a good deal of his own ambitions to change oil filters simply so Shaun could finish school.

All of the money Tim had earned had gone towards his little brother's tuition, and Shaun knew it. Shaun, though, had prided himself on never asking Tim for anything. Tim had seemed unusually provocative that night, but Shaun had hated himself for a long time over what had happened; pride, however, had stopped him from making the trip to DC.

Shaun looked at the bundle on the seat next to him and was thankful that this mass of animal skin would prove to be the catalyst for what should have been done a long time ago. That thought kept him company for the next two hours, the last uneventful hours Shaun would ever have.

CHAPTER 64

The only thing that looks cooler than a speeding red Porsche is a speeding red Porsche with bullet holes. Shaun would have agreed had he not been inside the Porsche in question, particularly considering that the number of holes was increasing rapidly. Every time he thought he had outrun the sleek black Mercedes, another identical car seemed to join the ranks from somewhere almost on top of him. His reprieve had come to an abrupt end twenty minutes ago.

There was nowhere to turn on these winding roads; nowhere he could swerve or duck and hide. All he could do was gun the engine and rely on the German-engineered sports car to do its thing. The problem was, no matter how fast he went, the bullets seemed to travel faster.

He thought there were five, maybe six of them now, but he could not be sure. It was a matter of odds when it finally happened. Although Shaun had managed to put distance between himself and his pursuers, he did not manage to completely escape the hail of sub-machinegun fire that spewed forth from the motorcade.

One stream zigged across his trunk, another tore into the side of the chassis, but it was a single round that punctured his rear right tyre that caused most of the problems.

The car's back end began to float and drift, and sparks flew as the metal rim ground on the asphalt. It was the next sharp corner that proved his final undoing. The left-hander sent the back end wide, and as Shaun tried to compensate, the Porsche fishtailed violently.

When the impact came, it hit hard. The solid pine tree did not yield an inch of its hundred-year-old trunk to the small red tin can that wrapped itself around the tree's base. Shaun was getting sick of crashes. It seemed that this time, he would surely be crushed, but as it happened the seatbelt held him tight and it was the front end of the car, near the axle, that bore the brunt of the impact.

Still they came.

He struggled to free himself. Popping the latch, he gathered the bundle and escaped through the passenger window. The glass further shredded his clothing and sliced his skin, but by now it was all part of one cumulative mess. The lights from the motorcade not a minute behind him now shone through the trees in the night. They were coming and Shaun had to—

BAM!

The explosion in his head knocked him to the ground again. He scraped around for the bundle he could not yet see through the blinding pain, and he fell flat on his stomach in the mud. He could hear them now. Close.

Again, his fingertips tingled and itched. Scrambling to his feet, now thoroughly caked in mud, blood and grime, Shaun plunged into the forest. His fingertips burned.

The forest was not kind in the dark. Branches lashed his face as he ran, whipping and poking at him. His bare feet were punctured and bruised, and his toenails were like the overgrown paws of an animal. Still he ran. He heard a screech behind him. They had arrived at the car.

Torches flashed their light past him. He ran on. *CRACK!* The shot rang into the night and somewhere off to his left a leaf fell from its branch. Shaun never saw it. He clung to the bundle in his arms for dear life. They must not get it. He had to keep going. Maybe he could reach the road, flag a car down. He was sure the road looped around here somewhere on its lazy meander down the mountain. *BAM!* Images. He was out for more than a second this time, and when he opened his eyes, he was face down in the mulch and mud of the forest floor. *Shit!* This had not happened to Fontéyne, had it? He was on his feet for only a few hundred yards this time before *BAM!* Again. 'Arrghh!!' Shaun clawed at his head with his free hand.

He scratched his face in the process. Blood streamed from the cut on his forehead again – it just would not close up properly – and the bumps on his fingertips throbbed like the pressure inside would make them burst. Man, what was going on ... *BAM!* Every few seconds now.

He could hear them behind him, but then, as he scrambled through the darkness he fell down something steeper. He felt the crunch of torn cartilage between his ribs as he rolled and bounced against rocks and trees. All the time he clung to the bundle. He could not stop. He was too exhausted. He relied on his inertia to carry him forward. He ran. Fell. Ran. Fell.

He did not run for himself anymore; he was nothing but a vessel for the diary, for the map. He carried it like his own child, using his body to shield the bundle when he fell. Still he sprinted on.

Blind in the night, downwards he rushed, the bushes whipping and tearing at him. *BAM!* He did not go down, but ran on like a footballer knocked off balance on his way to the end-zone.

CRACK! This gunshot was more distant, more ambient. He did not hear it land. On he ran.

The ground fell away down an embankment. Shaun half-tripped, half-ran as he burst through a thicket and the ground changed again.

Hard.

Road.

Lights.

BAM!

As Shaun Strickland flew through the air, his last thought was simply that the last explosion was not entirely in his head. He was unconscious before he hit the ground.

CHAPTER 65

Voices. Lights. Nothing.

Movement.

Neck burns.

Fingertips burn.

Nothing.

Gunfire.

Voices.

Nothing.

Shaun woke. Pain. The first thing he felt was the pain. Even before the light. His eyes were heavy, impossibly heavy. He was lying flat. His head fell to the side. He saw a man standing next to a bed. He saw the man reach out, brush the hair off someone's face. His eyes were so heavy.

Shaun fought to focus. To see the face. To see ... Lauren.

To see Lauren. Alive. Alive, lying on a bed. His eyes travelled up the arm. The man turned and walked to the end of the hall, to an open elevator door. The door started to close. The man turned, and though Shaun could not see his face, he thought he looked familiar. God, how long had he been asleep? Shaun refocused as another man, this one wearing all black, walked over to the bed. He raised his hand to the bed and pointed, pointed with the long silenced muzzle of a gun—

Shaun acted on instinct. He did not know whether he was awake or asleep or when exactly in time it was. All he saw was a man pointing a gun at Lauren. It was too far away. Too far to reach her. Thoughts raced faster than light.

Lying flat on a hospital bed, there was something running into his own arm. A tube. Connected to the tube, a stand.

Although it happened fast, for Shaun it seemed distorted into slow motion. He grabbed the stand with one hand and swung it. The heavy end of the stand, which contained the trestle wheels, slammed into the side of the man's head.

The man in black flew backwards, pulling the trigger twice as he fell. The cannula ripped from Shaun's arm as he rolled off the table and dropped to the floor. He scrambled on his hands and knees, feeling pain from every point in his body.

When he reached the man, he pounded with his fist. His hand, unknown to him until this moment, was broken. He gritted what teeth he had left and bared the pain as he pounded the man's face. There was no aim in his blows, there was only rage. And it took a woman's scream to break his trance.

The woman was Lauren.

Shaun scrambled to grab the gun that lay on the floor some feet away. He forced himself to stand. He turned to grab Lauren, but she pulled away from him.

He did not have time for this. They were coming. He knew this bit. He reached forward and pulled Lauren off the bed. As she screamed and lashed out at him, her fingernails biting chunks out of his cheek, he tried to speak, but no words came out of his dry, cracked throat. How long had he been out of it? He dragged Lauren down the hall as she kicked and screamed for her husband to help her. People stared, but thoughts of intervening disappeared as soon as they saw the black, silenced Heckler & Koch that Shaun carried in his free hand.

He noticed absently that some of his wounds had been dressed. His head was now wrapped in a large white bandage that looked like a headband against his grubby hair.

He pulled Lauren towards the stairs. *BAM!* His head exploded in pain again, but he noticed that his fingertips did not burn this time. Coming around the corner from the other end of the corridor, a man dressed in a police uniform lifted his gun and fired. Ceramics near Shaun's head exploded and Lauren screamed. Shaun spun and returned fire. The cop dropped, clutching his thigh.

Lauren did not understand. Reaching the stairwell, Shaun hurried his confused wife down at dangerous speed, causing her to miss steps and stumble. They hit the flat of the next level running and immediately spun left to where he knew the laundry chute would provide an escape. Yes, he knew this bit.

Shaun could hear the sounds of someone bounding up the stairs from below, and more than anything, he did not want to stop that desperate man. That earlier version of himself. He knew he must not interfere.

'What's going on?' Lauren demanded as they burst through the swinging door to the laundry. The occupants of the room, two orderlies, jumped in shock at the intrusion. Shaun tried to shout at them, but only a cracked shriek came out. When he waved his gun in the air, they got the point and cleared the room. He immediately began to dig into the open laundry trolleys and throw sheets down the chute. He had to let go of Lauren to do so, and he did not think twice about raising his weapon at her to deter her from trying to escape. As soon as he was satisfied, he motioned to Lauren with the gun, indicating she should jump.

'Whooa, no. No way buddy,' she said, shaking her head.

Shaun heard gunshots from the hallway and did not hesitate. He grabbed her roughly and, opening the chute, shoved her through.

Once he was sure there was enough time for her to clear the way, he dived after her. He landed with a thud. Words cannot describe the pain he felt at that moment. His ribs rolled over each other as the wind was knocked out of him. He could not even groan in pain.

After a second, he became aware of the sound of hard-soled shoes running across cement. It was Lauren leaving. Escaping. *No, no, no!*

Shaun forced himself up and off the pile of sheets. He pushed his way through the door and looked out into the familiar delivery bay where he had climbed aboard the DHL delivery truck; it seemed so long ago, but it had been only three weeks from his perspective.

There she was, running away out into the open. He tried to speak, but he could not. She was leaving, and she would never know. He had found her, and she was alive, and now she was running for her life, away from him. He moved to the edge of the bay and saw her back as she crossed out into the night. He could not lose her.

Not again.

'Lauren!' he called. She did not stop.

'*Lauren!*' he tried again. This time she slowed a little.

'Lauren, stop, please!' His voice, stronger now, was full of pain and grief. He was crying.

She slowed her pace, then she came to a walk. She turned and looked back into the delivery bay, expecting to see her husband's face to match his voice. Instead, she saw delivery trucks and the hobo. That crazy man they had saved and who had repaid them by taking her hostage. He could barely stand. She looked at him hard, and as she slowly took a step towards him, the voice came again. The raggedy-looking hobo lifted one arm towards her weakly and called out.

'Lauren. Please. Wait,' he sank down to his knees and bent forward, one arm still outstretched.

'How do you know my name?' she asked cautiously. He was still holding the gun.

'Lauren. Please, you have to—'

BAM! His head exploded with pain again, and once more images flashed in his head. Images of places, people, moments. He was not sure he recognised them all, but they were gone before they could be examined.

She knew the voice, but it was displaced. She walked towards the man as he looked up at her with pleading eyes. Crystal blue eyes that were filled with tears. His head dropped, but his arm still reached out towards her.

'Lauren, don't go. Please don't go.' Sobs broke the plea.

She could not reconcile the conflicting information from her eyes and ears. Finally Shaun's eyes came back up and his arm came down. He was spent. He could not see her walk away. He could not believe he was seeing her at all.

'Who are you?' Lauren said after a moment, looking at him like a cat trying to decide whether to rub up against a visitor's legs or to flee. Shaun looked back at her. He found it hard to believe she did not recognise him, but then he remembered the homeless bum they had hit with their car. As he lay there on the road, and even when he lay on the back seat of Shaun's own car, Shaun had not recognised the man. He looked old, mostly because of the missing teeth and unkempt facial hair. There was so much mud and blood on the man that distinguishing any features had been impossible.

Shaun knew now what was happening. The circle in his mind was complete. He was the hobo, and Lauren was alive.

'Lauren. Please,' he repeated quietly. She moved close, within arm's reach and stared at him. He raised his eyes and looked at her.

They had not seen the hobo's eyes when they brought him to the hospital, but as she looked into those eyes now, she knew them.

'Lauren,' he said again. She shrank back.

'Oh my God!' she said in a single gasp. Shaun's head dropped. He found it hard to breathe. Lauren moved to him and reached out. She touched his hair, but Shaun did not respond. She sank her fingers into the tangled mass, and felt him wince.

She did not, could not, understand, but as she lowered her face down to his, Shaun's hand reached out and touched her arm. Slowly, knowing he had to keep moving, he called on his strength and looked at her again.

'Shaun? What happened? I don't ...' she let it trail off.

'We have to go,' he said to her simply.

They were on the road and heading north soon after. They had taken the hospital truck, Shaun insisting that although the DHL one had the keys in it, they could not use it. He had also steered her away from the north gate, instead making Lauren drive over a garden and break a chain-link fence to escape the hospital. She had spent the first half hour in silent obedience, her brain occupied with running and re-running the events of the night.

Still affected by the drugs the hospital had given her to calm her down, she was groggy, and her arm hurt. Shaun had stayed conscious for long enough to give her directions towards DC, but then passed out again.

She looked over at him. This was her husband. The hobo. This was Shaun.

She drove on into the night and sped towards the home of Senator Tim Strickland in Washington DC.

PART 4

LOOPS AND WALNUTS

'Another time, another place, another life, another face –
Oh my love I know I'll see you again.
And the circle that starts with the beat of your heart,
Takes you back to the beginning again.'

'Round and Around', Christopher Davison

CHAPTER 66

It was five in the morning when the doorbell rang. He had not slept well, even though he knew he would have to be up early this morning. Professor Landus had left at a reasonable hour last night, claiming he had to fly into the 'hot zone' before events kicked off.

Tim Strickland was expecting visitors, although there was no way his visitors could know this. He had sent his housekeeper, who normally slept here during the week, home for the night, saying that he was having a lady friend visit. He partly wished that were true, but Tim had not had a regular lady friend for more than a year now. Anouska had run off with his political rival after meeting him at a function down in Louisiana.

He did not really mind. Like so many things about his life for the last ten years, he had come to expect it.

'Knowledge is power,' the professor from Cambridge had told him not long after they had met. The professor had a lot of knowledge; knowledge about what was to come. He had said he was from an institution called The Society for World Historical Accuracy. Tim had thought the name sucked, but had refrained from saying so.

Over the next little while, certain help was given to the would-be Senator. Important information about key events was passed along. Background and historical information on opponents in the political arena appeared in manila envelopes on his doorstep. With the help of The Society, Tim was able to make bold predictions about events and actions, and he was right every time, earning him a reputation for analysis and foresight. In the current climate, he was a valued advisor to the President, with whom he seemed to share a bond; they always seemed to see eye to eye on key issues.

So, on this of all nights, he had arranged to have his house occupied not by his regular hired help, but rather by a single trusted physician who had been installed in the guest room on the lower level. Tim had known the doorbell would ring, and he had prepared for the event in the way the professor had told him to. Throwing on his robe, he raced downstairs to face the moment that was to be his price for the aid he had received over the past decade.

The door opened in front of them, and Lauren looked at her brother-in-law. He was wearing a robe and seemed less surprised than she had expected. She had Shaun's arm around her shoulder and supported most of his weight. She looked up at the older statesman and smiled apologetically. She took a breath, ready to explain the reason for the unexpected intrusion, but the Senator beat her to it.

'Lauren. Come in, come in. Bring him through to the parlour,' Tim said, slinging Shaun's other arm over his shoulder. Trails of blood seeped through the saturated dressings that had been applied at the hospital. They laid him down on a makeshift bed that had been set up. Standing next to the bed was a man with a stethoscope around his neck and a tray of medical tools at his side.

'Lay him on his back ... gently,' the man said, taking scissors and beginning to cut open Shaun's shirt. Lauren looked confused, but then, the whole night had been one confusing mess. She was exhausted from the drive, and although she had had some sleep at the hospital she was hitting the wall again.

'Lauren, a drink?' Tim asked as he disappeared into the kitchen without waiting for an answer. He returned a moment later with a tall glass of orange juice, which she drank greedily. Tim looked up at the man examining his brother.

'Well?'

'There have been several bouts of trauma. This didn't all happen from one incident. It appears there's something of a gunshot wound on his upper arm here. It's slight, consistent with a grazing contact. Several ribs are gone, I'm sorry. That's going to be the difficulty, there's really not a lot besides time that can help them.'

Lauren broke in. 'I'm sorry, who are you?' she asked, looking at the tall man with glasses.

'Forgive me,' Tim said, 'this is my good friend and personal physician Dr Max Herringson. We've been expecting you.'

'Expecting us? How can you have been expecting us? Just what the hell is going on here?' Lauren asked, confused and getting a little angry. Tim smiled at her, trying to look reassuring.

'He's in good hands. What you both need now is rest. We'll be able to talk about it later in the day after you've both had a good sleep.'

'These bruises,' Dr Herringson continued as if he had not been interrupted, 'have been re-bruised. It looks like he's been in several car accidents, then beaten up.'

'We had a car accident earlier, we hit a ...' Then Lauren remembered what she was saying. 'Well, no, I mean, he was hit by a car last night, but was already looking pretty beat up.'

The doctor looked at her with a raised eyebrow. Tim took Lauren by the arm and led her into the next room.

'He'll be fine. Max is the best, and as I said, we've been expecting you. I promise we'll explain things a little later, but you really have to get some sleep now.'

Reluctantly, Lauren lay back on the couch, which had been prepared for her with fluffy pillows and a blanket. She wanted to complain and demand answers, but she was too tired from fighting the exhaustion that overcame her on the road. She had been sick with worry all night, but she had always liked and trusted Tim. So, as her eyes closed of their own accord, she did not fight to open them again. She slept deeply.

When she woke, the room was full of sunlight. She heard the clinking of spoons on mugs and threw back her covers. Entering the living area, she stopped at the sight of Tim, the physician and Shaun sitting and drinking coffee from what smelled like a freshly brewed pot. They looked up as she entered and beamed smiles, though Shaun was missing several teeth from his.

'Lauren!' Tim said smiling. 'Glad to see you're up. How are you feeling?'

'How am I feeling?' she asked. 'I'm totally fucking confused about everything! I'm feeling freaked out, is how I'm feeling.'

'Thank you,' Shaun said suddenly, standing. He was staring at her in the strangest way. 'Thank you for not leaving me.' It was definitely him again. Although he still wore a bandage around his head, it was fresh, and he had been thoroughly cleaned up. He had shaved, showered and changed clothes. His face was still cut and swollen, but the blood and dirt were gone. Those same blue eyes that had pleaded with her so desperately the night before, now looked at her again. Again, they welled with tears.

'Shaun, what's going on?' she asked as her husband limped towards her, looking at her intently. Tim and the doctor sat silently on the small couches in the living area. They knew what was happening, having listened to Shaun's story all morning.

'Lauren, do you know how much I love you?'

'I love you too, baby. But will you tell me what's going on? I just saw you at the hospital and then, suddenly you were the guy that we hit. I don't get it.'

'I thought you were dead,' was all Shaun could say as he wrapped his arms around her, in an embrace he had thought would never come. She held him, content for the moment just to be there, to hold him, to let the explanation wait. After a time she spoke.

'It's okay, baby, I'm right here,' she said. Shaun wept openly. 'Come on, baby, your snot's getting all over me,' she said after a while, pushing him back gently. He laughed a little through his tears.

'Sorry,' he snuffled.

'Okay, now what's all this about me being dead?'

The conversation took the rest of the afternoon. Lauren sat and listened, unable to take a lot of what Shaun said at face value, but he had gradually convinced her. The doctor had left shortly after Lauren woke, but had promised to return later. They thanked him profusely and as Shaun recounted the events of the past three weeks to her, several more pots of coffee were brewed and drunk. Tim sat and listened to the story again, picking up on details he had missed. Occasionally he would ask Shaun to elaborate, but mostly he sat quietly, allowing Lauren at the same time to absorb the details of the story. Of course, it was not all a complete surprise to Tim. The professor had told him much of this before.

When Shaun was finished, Lauren sat quietly. She had known the start of the story, but she found the rest of the tale incredible. The fact that Shaun had travelled back in time, something he had insisted for years was impossible, was also beyond Lauren's immediate comprehension. When she finally spoke, it was the question Tim had also asked earlier.

'So, where is the diary now?'

Shaun shuffled uncomfortably. 'It's, ah, still in the cave, or at least it will be in a day or two. Right now, it's tucked down my pants and I'm on my way to Spain.'

'So ... can't we warn you? Can't we get in touch with you or something and prepare you for the dangers coming up?'

'No!' Shaun said firmly. 'That was one thing the diary was very specific about. One thing Fontéyne kept saying. He called it The Rule of Knowledge. You can't change anything you know has happened. We mustn't try.'

'But what about me? What about the man you say shot me? You changed that and the universe hasn't exploded,' Lauren said.

'Ah, I thought about that. I admit, I acted on instinct at the time, but I've thought about that long and hard and I realised I didn't actually see you get shot. I turned as the doors were closing, saw the muzzle raised, then as the doors closed I heard two shots. I raced back up as quickly as I could and as I said, your bodies were gone. That female cop hypnotised me or something, and kept reinforcing that you were dead, so I didn't really question it.'

Lauren reached out and took his hand. 'I'm right here,' she smiled. Shaun smiled back.

'Well, you two seem to have sorted a few things out,' she said, looking at Tim. Her brother-in-law took off his glasses and lay them on the table. He wasn't sure exactly how much he was supposed to tell them, but decided restraint was the wisest approach. He was after all, a politician, and dealing with delicate information in his answers was something at which he excelled.

'Yeah, we've ah, straightened some things out. I've been very busy. It wasn't my intention to avoid you,' he lied. It had, in fact, been his exact intention for the past few years, as hard as it had been. But that was over now. He had had to play the bad guy as he made arrangements Shaun could never know about, but he knew it was for ultimate good.

'It's all true,' Shaun said then. 'If I'm really sitting here, and you're really alive, then it's all true. I need to get that diary. I can't believe I walked it right into their hands. They set everything up to lead me there, just so they could get their hands on the book. Looking back, I can't believe what a fool I was. Now they have the diary, and they have David.'

'Then, let's stop them!' Lauren said, exasperated. 'Why don't we just call this David character and warn him?'

Shaun looked at her. She knew the answer. 'But what if you're wrong?' she said. 'What if they're all wrong? What if you *can* change things?'

'I don't know,' he replied. It was too much to contemplate, and no matter how many times he went over it in his head, he always came to the same conclusion: he knew enough now to know that he did not know enough. 'I'm not sure you could actually change anything even if you tried, because it's already happened. I mean, if I stopped myself now from going to the mountains in Afghanistan, I wouldn't get sent back in time to stop myself, would I? So, it's a crazy loop. I have to go on the assumption that you can't change what you know has happened, but if you don't know it happened then who's to say that it didn't?'

'So, you want to go there again? You want to go and save your friend?' Lauren asked. 'I'm not sure I can let you leave me. I'm not sure I can let you go,' she said, reaching for his hand again as her mind continued to expand to absorb this new reality.

'She can stay with me,' Tim said.

Shaun closed his eyes and shook his head slowly. 'There's something else. It wasn't something I realised until this morning when I looked at you asleep on the couch. You know how you said—'

BAM! Shaun's hands shot up to his temples as more images flashed painfully in his mind.

'Baby, are you okay?' Lauren asked, worried.

'I'm fine. It's just that my head keeps exploding with these images. I'm okay. They seem to be getting a bit better. They got worse and worse right up to the moment of the accident, but it's like that point was a mountain that I'm coming down the other side of now. They're getting further apart.'

'What images? What do you mean?' Lauren asked.

'Events. Things. I don't know. Some of them seem like memories, and other things I know haven't happened,' Shaun paused, 'yet.'

Tim and Lauren remained silent.

'It's like the flash I had when I looked at you this morning. Like I was saying, you said yourself that we didn't recognise that the hobo we hit was me, because the idea was so impossible that it wasn't even something we were thinking about. Well, some of the images that flashed in my head were of the moments before I came through, as I was standing on the platform. I remembered looking up at the doorway and seeing a man and a woman. The man was me … and the woman … was you. It was me and you.'

'What? You're saying that you saw us? Are you sure?'

'I'm sure. I didn't think of it at the time, but why would I? But it *was* us Lauren, it was me and you, which means …'

'Which means you want me to come with you,' Lauren finished his thought.

'You were there, Lauren. It's already happened. I don't know why, but you were there. You *do* come with me.'

'And what if I choose not to?'

'You can't,' was his straightforward reply.

'And why not?'

'Because it would change something. It would make something different, and I might not be here now.'

'But you *are* here now!' Lauren insisted. 'And besides, how does me not going with you affect you being sent back in time anyway?'

'I don't know,' Shaun replied.

'See.'

'No, I mean that's exactly my point. I don't know how it would affect it, which would mean that it might not be how it is now. That's why it has to be the same, exactly the same, otherwise, this moment can't happen. Otherwise, I might not be here, I might not be able to ...' he choked at the thought, 'I might not be able to save your life.'

That silenced her. She thought back to the hospital bed; to seeing the husband she knew walk away down the hall to book them into a hotel. Then, she closed her eyes. Before she knew what was happening there were gunshots and the hobo they had hit with their car was bashing into a man. She replayed the moment in her mind's eye and shifted her perspective: it was Shaun, doing whatever he could in desperation to save her after having gone through the grief of losing her. He just did not want to mess with it. He would not risk the slightest chance of not being there to save her at that moment. It was all for love.

She smiled. What was she thinking?!

'I'm sorry, babe. Of course I'll go with you. Of course I will, it's just all a bit much to deal with. I mean, you suddenly believing all these things you were so adamantly against. And the fact that you're here, and I'm here and that you know what's going to happen, that means you're right, doesn't it? I mean, I know you're not making it up.'

'Why don't I get us some more coffee?' Tim said, rising. They both smiled and nodded.

Shaun leaned forward. 'Please understand. Nothing scares me more than putting you in danger. Nothing except you not coming with me and there existing the chance that I might not get back to save you.'

Tim reappeared a few moments later. He set a tray down on the coffee table. On it were two cups filled with steaming coffee, and an envelope with the initials PIA on it: Pakistani International Airlines. Sitting next to them were two fresh passports. Shaun looked at the envelope, then at Tim.

'You didn't. How did you ... I don't get it.'

'You don't have to. You'll get it, little brother. You'll get it when you need to, but for now, I'm sorry, I can't tell you any more. You know that Rule of Knowledge you keep talking about?'

Shaun felt sick. He suddenly felt very suspicious and very betrayed. What did his brother know? How had he known? He picked up the two airline tickets and examined them.

'Tim, these are for tonight! From Dulles International Airport.'

'There's a car waiting now. I have bags packed for you.'

Lauren turned to Shaun's brother. She had the distinct feeling that she was tangled up in some huge conspiracy she knew nothing about.

She was right.

CHAPTER 67

The flight touched down in Islamabad a little after eight the following morning. Shaun looked considerably better than he had for the past week, but his face and limbs were still bruised and swollen. Everywhere he went he attracted looks ranging from sympathy to fear.

Tim had equipped them with sturdy hiking boots and all-weather clothing. Shaun knew that the only way to find The Facility again was to locate and follow the former version of himself and David. He had no idea where they had been taken by the military, but remembered the key events and dates. It was tomorrow that they would arrive in Pakistan. That gave Lauren and him a day's start to get to the Khyber Pass.

This time he would not go alone. He planned to hire a bodyguard, or at least get a new gun – he knew that he would never get through airport security with the Heckler & Koch he had lifted from the hospital. Initially Lauren objected to the idea, but soon after landing in the nation's capital, she relented, feeling uneasy in the vastly different culture.

'The area we're heading to is a little wild,' Shaun told her once they were on the road, travelling in a privately chartered van with a driver and an armed guard. Tim had provided the necessary papers to get them through the various checkpoints along the way.

Shaun was pleasantly surprised to find that the mysterious sum of money that had appeared in his bank account the first time around had again surfaced; he was also surprised when Tim handed over a second ATM card for Shaun's account. He wondered about what else his brother had kept from him, but he trusted him nonetheless.

His trust, however, was not reserved for the people he was going back to confront. The Society. It was the element of the whole thing that really bothered Shaun. The Society had set him up. They had tricked him into delivering the diary right to them. But what about the map? The translation document Shaun had vomited onto Ernie's feet in the park had said that the diary and the map would be together.

Shaun had read the whole diary, but he was still no closer to knowing where Fontéyne's disc was hidden, or if it ever made it to its final resting place.

Shaun could only assume that the map was with the bundle of documents that had been buried in the cave at Grandfather Mountain, and then abandoned by Shaun and Lauren as they had fled the Motel 6 when all of this began. It seemed strange, then, that the men in black had continued to chase them – or at least the former versions of them – after the incident at the motel. Maybe they had the map but did not know what they were looking for? Maybe there was something in the diary he had missed?

Lauren clicked her fingers in front of Shaun's eyes. Shaun jerked his head, blinked, then stared at her.

'Whatcha thinking?' she asked.

'I'm just wondering why they want the diary so bad. I mean, it's all about finding the disc. There was supposed to be a map to the disc, that's what the last part of the diary said. It was written in some other language.'

'So, how would they know about the diary or the map at all?' Lauren asked as they bounced along, getting closer to the town that marked the start of the Khyber Pass. Shaun pulled out the piece of paper containing the translation, which he had kept in his back pocket.

'This,' he said, 'looks like a Vatican document. It's a translation of the last few pages of the diary. It talks about the map and refers to the diary. I think this English version, though, is a translation of another translation. An Italian version that was translated from the original that was hidden as part of the Dead Sea scrolls.'

'Alone, without the rest of the diary?'

'So even *that* was a copy of what was written in the diary,' Shaun realised.

'What if there's another copy of the diary?' Lauren asked offhandedly. Shaun went pale. He had not even considered that.

'I don't know. I don't know. If there was, I find it hard to believe they'd be so desperate for this one.'

'Well, they have it now, don't they?' his wife sighed.

'No. Not yet. They don't get it till tomorrow night blue time.'

'Blue time? What the hell's "blue time"?'

'Ah, sorry. It's just a way I use to think of things. This whole time-shift thing is making it hard to sort out past and future tense in my head, so I'm using this method to get it straight. Light coming towards you has a blue colour shift, and light moving away has a red colour shift. I kind of think of time like that. As we travel forward in time, the past is moving away from us – it's red time. The future is coming toward us – it's blue time.'

'Sorry I asked,' she smiled.

Shaun continued, 'They don't get the diary till tomorrow night from our perspective, our blue time, and now that I know that, I can stop it.'

'But you didn't want to change anything!' Lauren protested, holding Shaun to his logic.

'No, not change it. Not stop me taking it there, but stop them getting it. I know that I have the diary on me when the machine activates, when they trap me on that platform and send me back, but I don't know what happens after that. I mean, thinking back, I was naked when I came through. I didn't have it on me. I didn't have any clothes on me.'

'I like the sound of that,' Lauren curled her lip.

'Yeah, well, I don't think you would have liked it at the time. You probably wouldn't have recognised me,' he teased her.

'That's not fair. I like your new toothless look. And anyway, I still don't quite get what you're getting at. You think it didn't come through with you, is that it?'

Shaun thought a moment. Yeah, that was exactly it.

'I think they knew I would get sent back. I don't know who or how, but they led us there, tricked me into taking the diary there. They had people chasing us but the whole time they knew I would end up there. So, now I know something about them. I know how to find that cave, and I know where the diary will be. I can get it before they can.'

'But didn't you say that there were all those men with guns who surrounded your friend?'

'Yeah, well, I'll have to work out the details, but I'm sure that's why we were there, to get the book back. I'm still confused about why it's so important, though. I mean, obviously it has some cool stuff in it, but it doesn't say where the disc is.'

'But it does say what's on the disc, doesn't it? I mean, you said that this guy videotaped the whole execution thing.'

'Crucifixion. Jesus was crucified,' Shaun corrected. Lauren studied him for a moment, then let it pass.

'Maybe they want to know what they're looking for, what's on the disc.'

'Maybe. I still think maybe I missed something. This says that the disc and the map would be together. They got everything except the diary when they raided the motel.' Furrowing his brow, Shaun thought for a moment.

Then Lauren said what he was thinking. 'What if the map is *in* the diary, hidden somehow? Like in a code or something, you know, like every second word on every fourth page tells you exactly where it is?' she said, as if reading his mind.

He smiled, starting to feel excited at the theory.

'Maybe ...' Lauren made to continue, but her attention was drawn to the city they were entering. Shaun leaned forward and asked their driver to take them to the best hotel. He was paying these two enough that he had little doubt of their loyalty.

'I take you,' the driver said. 'I take you Pearl Continental! Very good hotel.'

'And have you tried to track down The Society you keep talking about?' Lauren asked Shaun.

'I Googled them when we were at Tim's. No luck.'

'What about this priest? How did he contact The Society?' Lauren asked, trying to fit it all together.

Shaun froze. Lauren had used the past tense about Giovanni contacting The Society, but suddenly it hit Shaun: that was not the case. In Shaun's reality, Giovanni was already dead. The event had happened in Shaun's red time. But not now. Now the event was blue. Shaun had come back in time far enough that Vincenso Giovanni was still alive. By Shaun's reckoning, he and David would meet with the Jesuit priest tomorrow. That meant—

'Stop the car!' he called. The driver spun, sensing the alarm in Shaun's voice. 'No, I mean, a phone. Take me to a telephone.'

'Telephone?' the driver repeated. Shaun nodded. The driver pulled a cell from his pocket and handed it to Shaun, who was suddenly bursting with excitement.

'Add it to my bill,' Shaun said as he rapidly dialled the international assistance operator.

'Yes, the Vatican. No. Yes, the one in Rome. The real one. Not the country club in Vegas. Thank you.' He waited. Lauren looked at him questioningly, but he shook his head in a gesture for her to wait.

'Yes, bon journo. Do you speak English?' Another pause. 'Yes, hello! I would like to speak to Father Vincenso Giovanni. I have ... what? No, listen to me, I know you have to say that, but tell him it's about The Facility and it's an emergency. Tell him—'

The line went dead.

'Shit!'

'What?'

'They hung up.'

'They did? Why are you calling the Vatican? You want to ask Giovanni if—'

The cell phone rang. Traced.

Scary.

'Hello?' Shaun answered without even thinking that the call might have been for the driver. It wasn't.

'Who is this?' a voice with a thick Italian accent asked.

'Who this is, is not important, what I can offer you is.'

'What is it that you want?' Giovanni asked, getting to the point.

'I want your contact at The Society.'

'No.'

'Then you will not get the player.' There was a pause.

'You have a player?' he asked.

'I have a player.'

'Where is it you want to meet?'

'You have a meeting tomorrow, with Mr Black. He will take you back to the hotel he is staying at. You will be shown something in the room. If it is something you desire, then you will excuse yourself and meet me downstairs in the hotel lobby saying that you have a meeting with the Holy Father.'

'At what time?'

'Three exactly.' Another silence.

'Three pm. How will I know you?'

'I guarantee you will know me.' Shaun hung up.

The driver pulled into the hotel.

'You want to fly to Rome, *arriving tomorrow*? Are you insane? We'd have to leave now! We'd have to drive back and—'

'Not yet. There's something unfortunate I have to arrange first,' Shaun said. The earlier version of himself and David had to be delayed here long enough to allow the trip back to Rome.

'Something unfortunate? Shaun—'

'We're in this now, Lauren. We can't just walk away and hope they'll leave us alone. We have to fulfil what's already happened. There are things that need to be done. If I can track down who's behind this Society and why we've been dragged into this, then I might be able to find a way out. A way we can be free of it. A way to get out of this crazy time loop.'

'Listen to yourself: "fulfil what's already happened"? I don't understand this.' She sighed. 'What do you want me to do?'

'How are your make-up skills these days?' he asked.

She cocked her head slightly. 'Fine. Why?'

CHAPTER 68

Sitting in the hotel lobby, Shaun did not feel good about what he had done. He knew, though, that he had had no choice; he needed to make sure of two things. One: that he could secure the player he knew would be left on the back seat of the journalist's car when the militants kidnapped he and David. And two: that his past version was delayed long enough to allow Lauren and him enough time to get back on their trail to The Facility. He touched his forehead and felt the healing wound. He hated the fact that he was responsible for the kidnapping, and by extension the death of the CNN journalist Craig Schwartz. The thought sickened him, but how could he change that?

He had paid his driver a significant sum of money to arrange for the militants and to secure the briefcase after the passengers were taken. He knew the consequences, for both the journalist and the captives; he knew that he and David would be beaten badly, and he knew that Schwartz would die, but he also knew that the delay was necessary so that he and Lauren could get back to Rome and have the meeting they were about to have now.

He looked at his watch. Five minutes to three. Lauren was set up in the lobby bathroom. Since their arrival that morning they had managed to acquire the necessary tools: latex, castor oil, food colouring and paint. They had also found clothing that resembled what Shaun recalled Giovanni wearing that day. Then, they had burned it. Shaun had been a little disturbed by how much Lauren seemed to enjoy that part of the process, burning and slashing and slicing the clothing, to make it resemble what it would look like if it had been in an explosion. Shaun was encouraged by the knowledge that the ruse had worked, even before they had enacted it. Who were they trying to fool now? They were trying to fool ... him. And he *had* been fooled. Not for a second had Shaun guessed that the explosion, or Giovanni's injuries, had been a hoax. He had not paid attention to the clothes the man had worn; he had been transfixed and horrified at the bubbling, bleeding burns on the priest's body. He knew the plan would work, simply because it already had.

He hoped.

The thing Shaun did not know, was the bomb. He had neither the time nor the know-how to source a car bomb, so he had to trust that the bomb was real. Someone really did want Giovanni dead. The plan meant that they would not only save Giovanni's life, but they had to make whoever wanted him dead believe they had been successful. It had to look real.

The alarm on Shaun's watch sounded. He looked up and saw the broad-shouldered priest descend the last step. Shaun sat, trying to look calm, trying to look collected, but he was as nervous as hell.

Giovanni politely weaved his way through the hotel lobby crowd and scanned the scene without giving the slightest hint he was doing so. He was a professional. He was on a high; he had just seen something he never thought he would witness in his lifetime: someone had cracked the codec, and more than that, they had developed a method that was capable of giving its user an experience never before attainable. That boy was a genius.

This meeting was unusual. The man had said the hotel lobby at three, but he had given no signal, no call phrase, no designated approach pattern, just, 'I guarantee you will know me.'

And he did. Giovanni did a double take as his eyes told him something that could not be possible. He turned and walked directly over to the man.

'You were right,' he said, taking a seat across from a battered version of the face he had just left upstairs.

'There isn't much time, so you must do exactly what I say. Do you understand?' Shaun asked seriously.

'I do exactly as I decide, and nothing else. Do *you* understand? Don't waste my time.' Giovanni rose and began to move off.

Damn, he was good. Not for a second would he accept a weakened position at the bargaining table.

'You're going to be killed,' Shaun said, a little too quickly. Giovanni stopped, turned and re-took his seat.

'How am I killed?' he asked, as if it were a foregone conclusion.

'Car bomb. In about fifteen minutes' time, the two men you have just met with will come racing down to an explosion in the car park, to find you lying on the ground, gasping your last breath.'

'Let us be ... frank, Mr Strickland. It is you upstairs, is it not?'

Shaun moved his head slightly by way of response.

'And if you are also here now, then I have to assume that you have indeed been to The Facility, and somehow been sent back. I therefore have no doubt that the knowledge you have is accurate, but why come and tell me this? If it has happened, it cannot be changed. It is, how you call it, The Rule of Knowledge.'

'Yes, and that's something I thought about,' Shaun said, letting his mask drop. 'I thought about exactly what I knew. I thought about what could happen to fulfil what I knew to be true, but that would have a different outcome. In the film industry they call it pre-production. Please,' Shaun said rising, 'follow me and we can continue our discussion.'

Giovanni rose and followed Shaun to the alcove that housed the restrooms. Knocking twice on the door of the disabled toilet, Shaun said, 'It's me.'

The door swung open and the two men entered. What Giovanni saw when he surveyed the cubicle caused his eye to twitch, the most indication he had given yet of surprise.

'All I really know, is what I saw. I put together what I thought happened in my head, but my wife here is a testament to the fact that what you think happened may not always be the case. I thought I saw her shot and killed, but all I saw was a raised gun, and then I heard shots. It turns out, those shots missed,' Shaun said, smiling at Lauren. 'Vincenso, this is Lauren.'

The priest kissed her hand. 'An honour.'

'Now, Lauren has prepared some things here ...' Shaun began.

'I can see,' he said, looking around at the collection of bottles, brushes and palettes. 'You intend to fake my death. Very clever, Mr Strickland. How long do we have?' Giovanni said, pulling off his shirt without having to be asked. Lauren got to work.

'We have as long as it takes – so long as that's not more than about ten minutes.'

It was perhaps twelve minutes later when they emerged from the disabled bathroom. A small boy standing outside in the hallway looked up at them open-mouthed. Giovanni, looking like he had just escaped the fires of Hell, offered a smile and wink to the boy, who turned and ran back to his parents, traumatised.

'Are you sure it's triggered from your unlock button?' Shaun asked as they brushed through the small lobby, trying not to be noticed.

'I know Le Clerque. It is only he who would do this. Only he would have the, how you say, balls. I know his team's methods. That will be the trigger.'

Shaun was satisfied and walked away with Lauren from the now hideous-looking old priest.

'You really should have gone into the movies,' he said to Lauren as they backed behind a hotel column.

'Yeah, I can see my dad agreeing to that!' she laughed, proud of her handiwork. Then she paused. 'Maybe I still will.'

Vincenso Raul Giovanni looked at his new white Alfa Romeo and sighed. He loved that car; it was the best one the Vatican had ever provided on its lease scheme, and it handled like a dream. Giovanni placed two quick calls: one to the fire department and another to his own people to drive an ambulance to retrieve them. Pulling out his keyring, he looked at the car once more. Then, he blew it up.

The explosion was enormous. It was far bigger than any of them had expected. Windows shattered, glass shards flew, the fireball engulfed the surrounding cars. The shockwave knocked Giovanni off his feet, and he had to get up and scramble to the spot Shaun had designated.

From behind the column, Lauren gasped as she saw David and her husband race down the stairs and push their way through the crowd. As much as she had already believed what Shaun had told her, seeing two versions of her husband in the same place did her head in.

As she watched Shaun push his way through the crowd, she imagined the pain he was in, believing that she was dead. Lauren wanted more than anything to call out to him and tell him it would be all right.

The commotion lasted only a couple of minutes before the ambulance and fire brigade arrived. Keeping out of sight of the bomb site, Shaun hustled Lauren out and into the ambulance, an eerie sense of déjà vu passing over them. Moments later they were on the road again and speeding away from the hotel.

Giovanni sat up and began to tear the prosthetics off his face. 'I did as you said: I told him to read. May I ask what that was about?'

Shaun withdrew the paper containing Giovanni's name. The priest examined it, recognising a translation he had authorised of a document found with the Dead Sea scrolls but only recently rediscovered in the painstaking cataloguing process.

'How did you get this?' he asked Shaun as they sped through the narrow Roman streets.

'From a walnut,' Shaun replied. 'Look, how I got it isn't important right now. What it says is. You're familiar with the document?'

'I am.'

'Who else has seen this?'

'Very few. Although, as you can imagine, Le Clerque and his men now have full access to everything I was working on. He has definitely seen this. He may have seen it years ago for all I know; he worked in translations.'

'The map it speaks of, and the diary, what do you know of these?'

'Not a lot, I'm afraid. We hadn't really discovered what was meant by "Caroline's grandfather". It seemed to be a very personal reference. We have been searching for this Caroline girl for a long time.'

Shaun smiled. Yes, it really was personal. 'It meant Grandfather Mountain in North Carolina in the United States.'

Giovanni, for the first time, looked at Shaun with genuine surprise. 'How do you know this?'

'Because I found the diary. I found everything.'

'You found the diary?' Giovanni almost shrieked. 'We must get it translated right away! Where is it? Does Le Clerque know about it?'

'Le Clerque knows about it. He had people at Grandfather Mountain. They worked it out, but they hadn't found anything.'

'And you did?'

'I did.'

'Where is it now? We must have it translated!'

'I'm afraid that's not possible. Your friends at The Society tricked David and me into carrying it right into The Facility. I had it on me when the machine was activated.'

'Then it is at The Facility?'

'It is, or it will be. But, the translation isn't necessary. The book was written in English.'

Giovanni stared. Slowly he began to nod. 'That would make sense, I suppose. It would prevent anyone from knowing what it said if it was found early. No one would be able to read it until very late this century. Then, you have ...' Giovanni swallowed. 'You have read the Fontéyne diary?'

'I have.'

Giovanni was very quiet as he processed everything he had heard.

'Let me ask you again, Vincenso. What is it that you want? You agreed to meet me on the pretence of trading information for a player.

Now, I've saved your life and told you I've read the diary. What is your motivation? No bullshit.'

Giovanni again was quiet. He then looked directly into Shaun's eyes and, for the first time in his life, he made the decision to share his innermost desire with another person.

'My friend. It is my wish, my deepest motivation, to recover the disc and see the face of our Lord Jesus Christ once again.'

'Again?'

'I ... I came to this calling through a vision. I need to know if ...' Giovanni looked down, as if ashamed.

'What would Le Clerque do if he found the disc?' Shaun pressed.

Giovanni took a deep breath. 'I have known François Le Clerque for a long time. A long time. We were friends back in seminary.' Giovanni looked into the distance, as if looking through the years. 'He was ... *is* ... a brilliant man. A man of exceptional intellect. Probably the most intelligent man I have ever known. He is passionate, and incredibly ambitious, but ...' Giovanni shook his head. 'He had these ideas. These, how you say, notions, about what really happened. He does not believe that Jesus died on the cross.'

'But he's a Catholic?' Lauren asked.

'Yes, yes,' Giovanni waved his hand, 'he kept these notions to himself, of course. Very few of us knew what he truly believed; only those of us he had tried to convert to his way of thinking. No, you are right, he was a Catholic, but not because he believed the doctrine of the Church. He was a Catholic for the power.'

'Why does being a Catholic have anything to do with power?' Shaun asked. This world was new to him.

Giovanni smiled. 'My friend, despite what outside observers may think, there are only three religions in the world that wield considerable political power: Judaism, Islam and Christianity. The Jews let their money do the talking and influence politics through financial aid of their preferred candidates. Islam is a divided religion; the Shiite and Sunni factions battle with each other. But it is only one religious branch, the Catholics, who have a nuclear weapon,' Giovanni said and then stopped. He let the point sink in.

'The Vatican?' Shaun said slowly. 'The Vatican has a nuclear weapon?'

'They have three,' Giovanni replied. 'This is a fact unknown to any government in the world. It is a fact known to only a very select few in the upper echelons of the Vatican, and to Le Clerque.'

CHAPTER 69

'Are you saying that all this is about Le Clerque wanting control of a nuclear arsenal?'

'Müller is dying. Pope Pius, as you know him, is in the advanced stages of pancreatic cancer. He intends to announce his retirement within the week. When he does so, the conclave of one hundred and fifteen cardinals from around the world will gather and vote. A new Pope will be elected.'

'But that could be any of them, right?' Lauren cut in.

Giovanni smiled. 'I'm afraid that today the decision is guided less by the Holy Spirit than by blackmail. I'm afraid that Le Clerque's ascent is a foregone conclusion.'

'So, he wants to become Pope, but why does he want to control the nukes?'

'It is the Pope, and he alone, who knows the launch codes to these devices. You see, Le Clerque believes fervently in what he is doing. He sees the threat to the world in the rising wave of Islam and the terrorism and hate it brings. He does not separate our Islamic brothers from those few who commit atrocities in the name of Allah. He calls Islam a "virus" and told me once that one day he would "cleanse the world" of it. Le Clerque's lust for power is absolute. He doesn't want to be the leader of one of the world's religions; he wants to be the leader of *the* world religion.'

'What? He can't just make other religions disappear!' Lauren cut in.

'He's going to start a war,' Shaun said quietly.

'He is going to start a war,' Giovanni echoed.

Shaun thought back to the diary, and what Hamza had told Fontéyne: '*Millions will die.*'

'I don't get it,' Lauren said, shaking her head.

'Where are these nuclear weapons housed?' Shaun asked.

The priest closed his eyes. 'Two are off the coast of Israel, and one is in Rome.'

'He's going to launch one against an Islamic nation ...' Shaun said, joining the dots.

'I believe he will launch a nuclear strike against Iran, and make it appear that Israel is responsible.'

'Iran will have no choice but to respond,' Shaun continued.

'Yes, Mr Strickland. They will launch against Israel, and of course this will draw in Israel's sworn allies, the United States and Britain, and many more. Iran will call upon their Muslim brothers for a Jihad against Israel and the West in defence of Islam ...'

'World War Three,' Shaun finished.

'Le Clerque will let the Jews and the Muslims wipe each other out, and then he will be the world's saviour through his own version of Christianity.'

There was silence in the back of the ambulance as the realisation sank in.

'And if *you* found this disc, Father Giovanni?' Shaun asked.

'I would take it to the Holy Father, and allow his ultimate wisdom to decide. But,' Giovanni paused, 'I believe that finding this disc, and presenting it to the conclave, is the only way to stop Le Clerque's rise to the papacy. The only way to stop this war.'

It made sense to Shaun now.

'You are assuming what's on the disc?' Shaun asked.

'I am. I have to go on the idea that it contains an interview with our Lord.'

'It was a contingency,' Shaun said quietly.

'Excuse me?'

Shaun put the pieces together. 'I'm afraid there is no interview on the disc.'

Giovanni stared wide-eyed. 'You ... you have seen the disc?'

'No, but I have read the diary. It seems Le Clerque had a contingency plan should someone else find the disc before he did. He hatched a plot to kill Pontius Pilate and stop the crucifixion of Jesus.'

Lauren looked at Shaun. She had never heard him talk about religion except to say how narrow-minded he thought it was.

'Then the agents you say he planted *inside* The Journalist Project, he would ...' Giovanni stammered.

'He succeeded. Delissio the Italian, and Barishnikov the Russian.'

'They were to kill Pilate?'

'They failed.'

'You know this from the diary?'

'I know this, and a lot more, from the diary. It cannot fall into the wrong hands; it contains too much information.'

Giovanni's eyes lit up. For a man who traded in information, the news could not have been more enticing.

'Then the disc is still our best hope! You say you have a player?' Giovanni asked.

'Ah, well, yes. I will by this time tomorrow.'

'You do not have one with you?' the Italian asked, sounding disappointed.

'No. I've employed someone to retrieve the player from where David and I were forced to abandon it. It will be returned to me tomorrow, and we will have just enough time to catch up with David and the other me as we – they – head into the mountains.'

'And for this, all you want is a phone number?'

'No. I want your contact at The Society. I want to know everything about them that you know. I need to find out whose side they're on.'

'The Society is, I believe, on no one's side. They have their own interests at heart.'

'Were they responsible for the attempt on Lauren's life?'

'I don't know.'

'Do they want me dead now?'

'I don't know.'

'Who's pulling the strings here? Who's running The Society?' There it was, the real question.

'Mr Strickland, these things I simply don't know. I will give you the number I use to contact them. They usually contact me, but when I do need to speak to them, I leave a message on the video-store answering machine stating my desired time and place of meeting, and a contact meets me. It is usually to trade information or as it was in this case, to tell them about Le Clerque. In the past they have requested a meeting to ask me to arrange components of technology or to use our influence on a particular government.'

'Government? Which government?' Shaun asked.

'Why, more than you can imagine. The Journalist Project involves many countries from every region on the planet, though most don't know they are involved. They are mostly blind to anything beyond their own small part; a pay-off here, a trade there. It is a very complex thing. The Vatican is seen as somewhat neutral on the political stage, and so our relationships are generally good, even with the Muslim countries. They politely respect our differences.'

'Call.'

'What? Now?' Giovanni asked as the ambulance made a sharp right turn.

'Now. Call.' Giovanni opened his phone on Shaun's command, but then stopped.

'I think ... I think it's better if you call, Mr Strickland. After all, Le Clerque now thinks I am dead. That can be an advantage. If The Society is indeed in cahoots with Le Clerque, then I do not want to give away our upper hand.'

Shaun nodded, seeing that the priest was right. He took Giovanni's phone and dialled, unsure of what he would say as he waited for the answering machine to click on.

'Yes.'

Shaun froze. This wasn't supposed to happen. He was supposed to leave a message. He covered the mouthpiece and mimed to Giovanni, who shrugged his shoulders and shook his head.

'Ah ... is this the video store?' Shaun asked.

'No, Mr Strickland, this is The Society for World Historical Accuracy,' the voice said. Shaun's blood ran cold. Was Giovanni setting him up?

Yet, Shaun knew the voice, although he could not place it. A man, perhaps forty or fifty years old; a British accent with a twang of something else. It waited patiently in silence.

'Ah ... I ... want to meet.'

'Agreed. Where?'

Shaun again covered the mouthpiece.

'Where? Where should we meet him?' Shaun asked Giovanni. The Italian again shrugged, still a little stunned that the phone had been answered.

'Ah, the ... Coliseum. No, no ... the Circus Maximus. The main gate.'

'Agreed. When?'

'Half an hour?' Shaun spat out.

'Half an hour,' the voice repeated, then continued. 'You will see a boy with olive skin and dark hair sitting at the corner of the gate. He will be wearing a Carolina Panthers cap. Approach the boy and he will give you something. You will know what to do with it. Take what the boy gives you to Pakistan. In the old city in Peshawar under the tip of the six o'clock shadow of the Bala Hisaar fort tomorrow, you will be met by an American. You will recognise him. His name is Allan

Johnston and he will take you to where you need to be. Your friends will have recovered the player for you, but you are not to give it to the priest. You must bring it with you to The Facility.'

'Wait a minute, just who are you and what—'

'Do not question me, Shaun,' the voice said, sounding uncomfortably like the way his father used to chastise him. 'Do as I say and you will live a long and happy life with Lauren.' *Shit!* How did he know about Lauren? 'You must make the priest come with you, believing he is going to get the player, but you will not give it to him. Tell him, after he has seen the player and again watched the Napoleon disc, that he needs to come with you to The Facility if he wants to expose Le Clerque to the Holy Father. You can tell him I told you this, but only after you get him to Peshawar with you, otherwise, he will not go. Oh, and I suggest you stay close enough to David and Shaun that you can hear some of their conversation, as it may make more sense to you this time.' The phone disconnected.

Shaun was silent.

'What did he say?' Lauren asked, seeing Shaun's face. 'He … ah … he's going to meet us. Half an hour at the Circus Maximus. Father Giovanni, can we get there through this traffic in half an hour?'

Giovanni smiled and said something to the driver in Italian. Suddenly the siren and lights blared their full glory over the Italian streets, and the ambulance cut through the city racing to save not one life, but millions.

CHAPTER 70

Standing before the massive ruin, Shaun Strickland took in the full glory of the Circus Maximus. Its stones spoke of the ages it had been standing, and Shaun's mind carried him back to a time when the crowds held Roman coins instead of cameras. He imagined the sounds, the roars of tens of thousands as mighty chariot races filled the arena. The spectacle played out in Shaun's mind even as he stood there, staring at the massive structure that once had the capacity to hold nearly a quarter of a million people.

Shaun walked forward through the crowd of tourists and locals. Sitting alone at the gate was a boy of perhaps twelve wearing the all too familiar Carolina Panthers cap – the cap of Shaun's local football team.

Shaun casually walked up to the boy, who looked Italian.

'Bon journo!' The boy kept his head down, but thrust his hand up in the air. He held something. Shaun took the item and examined it as the boy rose and walked away, disappearing into the crowd.

Shaun thumbed the object in his hand, then turned and walked back to where Giovanni and Lauren waited for him.

'Well?' Lauren asked. Shaun held out his hand. There, in his palm, was a large, tasty-looking walnut.

Giovanni made several calls before leaving Rome, and it bothered Shaun that he could not understand what was being said. He told himself that when he got back home and this was all over, if that day ever came, he would learn a language or two.

For the third time in a fortnight, Shaun travelled the road from Islamabad to Peshawar. The difference this time was that he had Lauren and Giovanni. Lauren was with him, and he knew that if that were the case, he could endure anything. Except losing her again. He was also armed with knowledge. Knowledge was power.

They had arrived at the hotel where he had left his driver. He met briefly with the mercenaries, who handed over the briefcase containing David's player and accepted their final cash payment. When asked if he needed to see the prisoners, Shaun had declined, and said that he knew they were fine. He also knew that the bastards who had beaten David and him to near death would soon be wiped out by a US military unit, but he neglected to mention this.

The conversation with Giovanni had not gone quite so smoothly. The Italian was incensed at the notion that he had been deceived, even if only for a short while.

'What do you mean I cannot have it? I gave you my contact, you give me the player! This was our deal.'

'I know, I'm sorry. But it was your contact who instructed this. He said that if you want to stop Le Clerque, then you would come with us to The Facility.'

'Come with you? You mean me? Go to The Facility? Well ...' Giovanni paused, then smiled. 'Yes, I see how this might be of benefit, but you shouldn't have lied to me. Lying is a sin, you know,'

'Would you have come with us to Pakistan if I had told you that you could not return with the player?'

'Well, no, I suppose I would not have. Very well.'

'And we *did* save your life,' Lauren added.

'Yes, my dear, you did. I suppose it is not you that I should be angry with. I have, after all, always wanted to go to The Facility. How do we find it?'

'We follow.'

'Follow who?'

'We follow me. The earlier version of me, the red me. But first I have to meet with Allan Johnston and give him this,' he said, taking the walnut from his pocket. He felt for its seam with his fingernail, then popped it open and unclasped it. He then took the piece of paper with the diary translation on it, and refolded it exactly the way it had originally been folded and placed it inside the walnut, which he then snapped shut.

Lauren looked dubious. 'So, that's really going to live inside your stomach and keep that piece of paper safe?'

'Something troubles me,' Giovanni said as Shaun nodded. 'If this is the version of the paper that you retrieved after you had been sent back, and you are now putting that same version back into this food to be digested by your earlier self, then does that not mean the paper is ... I mean ...'

'I've thought about that too,' Shaun said. 'It's caught in a time loop. I got it from the walnut, which got it from me, who got it from the walnut, and so on. The truth is, I don't know. It means this paper in my hands is infinitely old. It looks pretty good then, doesn't it?'

'It just can't happen!' Giovanni said. 'When you showed me the paper, one of the calls I made was to get a copy of this translation. They told me the document did not exist. It, how you say? Does my head in.'

'I'm sure a lot of this will.'

They had approached the massive fort. Originally built by Baber, the first of the Mongols, some time in the mid-sixteenth century, its huge battlements and ramparts rose above the cityscape with imposing presence. Its long shadow cast far back into the city, and it had taken the trio more time than they had expected to find the tip at exactly six in the evening. The tip of the shadow happened to fall on a small bench in a city plaza.

'Allan Johnston?' Shaun said, taking a seat next to a bald man in sunglasses and a green cap who continued to throw bread to pigeons that huddled about the cobblestones. He recognised the man.

'That's right, son. Captain Allan Johnston. I believe you have some baking ingredients for me?'

Shaun handed over the walnut.

'Okay then,' the Marine commander said, 'I have a present for you too.' He handed a brown parcel to Shaun. 'You need to get yourself and your friends up the Khyber. Our unit will hit the Pathans at o-nine-hundred hours tomorrow morning. We'll take the captives up to the drop-off location and then return for you. There's going to be a lot of activity around here by that time, so you need to be well clear of the ambush or they'll shoot you soon as look at you. You understand, son?'

'I do.'

'Good. There's a map in there. It has an X on it. Be there at nine-thirty in the morning. My unit will take you to where you need to be.'

Shaun took the package, which contained a small matte-black Glock 9-milllimetre; a semi-automatic pistol with a ten-loader magazine.

CHAPTER 71

Shaun and Lauren were woken from their cramped sleep in the station wagon by a tap on the windscreen.

The driver Shaun had paid so well had also sold his car to them for double what it was worth, and Shaun willingly paid the extra cash. Now the sun-silhouetted figure whose steamy breath gave testament to the temperature outside beckoned them and pointed to the road.

'I can hear our ride. It sounds like they're past us already – you'd best, how you say ... shine and rise?' Giovanni urged.

Barely awake, the trio raced through the cold air, clambering and jumping over rocks. Shaun was still injured, so Lauren raced ahead. At last she came around a rock and saw a large transport vehicle moving off.

'Hey!' she screamed, waving her arms. 'Hey! *Wait up!*' But the soldiers were too far away and the engine noise was too loud.

'They're leaving!' Lauren called back to Giovanni. Without question, the priest reached into his jacket and retrieved a small pistol, making sure to flick on the safety before hurling it high into the air. Lauren caught it on the full.

'The safety is on the lower left!' the panting priest called. Lauren took as careful an aim as she could and squeezed the trigger. A puff of white smoke kicked up from a rock next to the transport and the vehicle stopped. She fired again and immediately doors opened and troops spilled out, taking cover behind the multitude of rocks. Lauren dropped the gun and began to wave with both arms.

It was a good thing Shaun was so far behind and did not see his wife fire on the group of Marines; he may well have died of a heart attack then and there. Fortunately the captain had the presence of mind to command his troops not to fire on the crazy woman.

'... but it could have turned out very differently,' Shaun said to her as they bounced along in the transport a few minutes later.

'We're here, aren't we? And anyway, like you said, I can't die! Not yet anyway, because I make it to the cave with you.'

'Yeah, but I don't know if you've lost a limb or have a bullet wound.'

'Oh.'

'Here we are!' Captain Allan Johnston said as they pulled over. 'Your buddies are over the rise, so I suggest you move quietly. The bug is due to move in seven minutes, so I hope you're rested up.'

A few minutes later the transport vehicle moved off, and the three were left standing on the side of what could barely be called a road, amid an unfamiliar, aggressive landscape.

'Okay, this hike is going to be long and hard. We've got about eight hours ahead of us.'

'But then we reach The Facility, yes?' Giovanni asked.

'Yes. Then we see it. Then ... I don't know what happens next,' Shaun said. He had grown a little comfortable with the advantage of foresight, however slight, and the thought of losing it sent an unfamiliar pang through his spine.

'How are your headaches?' Lauren asked suddenly. It caught Shaun off guard. He had not thought about that all day, probably because he had not had one of his massive head throbs in a while now. Curious.

'Much better, thanks.'

The three snuck up to the rise and listened. There were no voices. Tentatively, Shaun peered over. He could barely believe it. Before his eyes, he saw himself in the flesh, from a different point of view. As an observer. He had not realised how tall he was, nor had he noticed that slight stoop he had when he relaxed. David was busy on his hands and knees examining the bug. Then without warning, it sprang to life. Lauren started a little at the sight of the small electronic creature as it hovered still for a moment. Then, like a dog beckoning its master, it moved off, pausing momentarily every few feet before moving again.

Shaun turned to Lauren and winked. 'Game on!'

CHAPTER 72

The next four or so hours were unrelenting torture. The trek was harder than Shaun remembered it, mostly because of the additional task of keeping out of sight. They had agreed that if they needed to communicate, they would scribble on a pad and show it to the others.

Shaun did not want to risk anything now. He recalled feeling inquisitive and a little excited the first time he had made the trek, but now there was a horrible sense of foreboding; of fate; of things being preordained. He remembered what he had been told by the voice on the phone, about staying close enough to his previous self and David to hear their conversation – but it was the voice itself he continued to hear in his head, over and over. Maybe he had heard it at a speech one night, or ... yes, his podcasts. It was one of those talks, he was sure of it. An English accent. Which talks had he downloaded from England? Oxford? Cambridge? Yes, Cambridge. What was that professor's name?

'Does that thing ever land?' Lauren whispered in his ear.

'Landus!' Shaun exploded far too loudly. Giovanni looked back at him with a death stare. Shaun caught his tongue. 'Sorry,' he mouthed.

The bug kept going, relentless, uncaring that those following it were made of aching flesh and brittle bone. It flew on. Never too far, but never stopping either.

Finally, the little drone entered the mouth of the cave, with the three of them following slowly and listening as the earlier version of Shaun and David talked and jabbered away as if they were on a family picnic.

As David touted the merits of compression, explaining the difference between the spatial and temporal methods, Shaun took Lauren's hand, and she took Giovanni's. They moved forward in the darkness. The cave light was eerie, and it was only David's endless babble that kept them moving in the right direction.

Shaun kept close enough that he could still see the lights of the bug, but they did not help illuminate the pitch darkness immediately in front of him. He felt his way along blindly as if reading giant Braille. Ahead,

David continued his detailed explanation, which both Shauns listened to intently. ✕

After a few more minutes the conversation died down again, giving Shaun more time to think, to process, to put the picture together.

The translation document said that the map and diary would be together, yet Le Clerque's men were in possession of all the documents that came with the diary. Shaun, therefore, had to assume that the map was *in* the diary; encoded somehow, and he had missed it.

Damn! If Le Clerque's seekers got their hands on the diary, they also got the map, which meant that they would find their way to the disc. And, Shaun suddenly realised, Le Clerque would almost certainly destroy the disc in order to ensure that nothing prevented his rise to the papacy. The disc offered proof, video evidence, that Jesus was killed on the cross; it also showed a genuine miracle. It confirmed for millions their faith and yet did no harm to any other. Why was it so important to him now, Shaun wondered. And then it hit him.

He believed.

The only thing Shaun Strickland had ever believed in was the power of scientific method. He had met hundreds who claimed to be Christians, Muslims, Jews, Hindu and none had been able to convince him. But now something was different.

There is no teacher like experience, Shaun realised, and what drove him now was not need – although he did not see any other way to stop Le Clerque's nuclear war – nor interest – although the fact someone had mastered time travel was the very heart of his intellectual pursuit. No, now that Lauren was alive, and perhaps even because Lauren was alive, Shaun was driven by belief ... by faith.

Suddenly Lauren bashed her shin hard against a rock.

'Oww!' she yelled. Giovanni had his hand on her mouth with lightning speed, but in the silence of the tunnels, the sound seemed to live forever. The two men froze and Lauren dropped to the ground, crying silently and hugging her shin. Shaun crouched next to her and hugged her tightly, letting her bury her face in his shoulder. Had they heard her? Of course they had. What if she had just screwed it all up?

'It's okay, baby,' he whispered. 'It's okay. They don't find us, I promise. It's okay.'

Shaun's words eased the fear that had raced through her body. She squeezed her shin tight and listened as she heard voices from up ahead. Shaun was yelling at the helicopter, telling it they were ready to go, but for the next few minutes it did not move. Just as Lauren struggled to her feet again and made sure she could bear the weight, the tiny bug moved forward into the tunnels.

The sound up ahead changed and Shaun remembered that it was this last hour that he had half-carried his injured friend. That meant they were almost there. The sensation was surreal, to remember the events before they happened. To be living in a state of déjà vu.

The last leg of the journey was the most painful. Finally Shaun had to come face to face with what he would do. What *could* he do once they had arrived? Shoot the men surrounding David? Shoot anyone who went near the diary?

No. His plan was to sneak in while Giovanni guarded the door. More importantly, he wanted the priest to guard Lauren. He remembered seeing the two figures, a man and a woman, so he knew that she was there with him. But he did not know what happened after that, and the last thing he wanted was to start a firefight with both David and Lauren in harm's way.

He should have stopped and worked out a better plan, but instead he just moved forward, towards that point, that epoch to which he was drawn beyond his will. He had to see the machine work. He had to see himself sent back in time.

Finally, Shaun called a halt. He peered around the passage and saw the bug, sitting on the floor of the cave. He took a deep breath and then, exactly as he had remembered it, the deep humming sound started again. The sound of inevitability.

CHAPTER 73

An eerie blue light bathed the two figures in front of them. Giovanni and Lauren stared in amazement as the rock parted.

The bug sat motionless, and David, his arm still slung around Shaun's shoulder, moved forward into the light. Soon, the two men passed away from view. When someone did speak, it was Giovanni.

'Those doors were made in China,' was all he had to say.

'Oh God, Shaun, what is that? The cave just opened.'

'Yeah, I would have told you about it, but I didn't want to spoil the surprise,' Shaun said, smiling. He was growing nervous. His brain was trying to tell him something, but he would not let it, not now.

Slowly they crept forward to look through the massive doors within the rock. Lauren and Giovanni could barely breathe.

'It's ...' Lauren started.

'... beautiful!' Giovanni finished.

They hid near the doorway, bathed in an angelic blue light, and beheld the impossible. In the middle of the Afghan mountains, at the end of a long, winding tunnel, hidden in a deep cave, was ... this: a complete and perfect city of technology and nature.

'Welcome to The Facility,' Shaun said, one edge of his lip curling upward. Though he smiled, he was suddenly very afraid. He had felt safe knowing that Lauren would come this far, but very soon, the future was all open again. He squeezed her hand. She looked up at him and saw that tears were again forming in the corners of his eyes.

'Hey!' she whispered teasingly. 'What's with all the waterworks—' She was silenced by a deep, passionate kiss as Shaun held her tightly. When he finally pulled away Lauren was lightheaded.

'Wow!' she gasped. 'So, all a girl's gotta do is die, come back to life, fake a priest's death then hike through mountains for eight hours? Why didn't you say so?'

Shaun smiled and kissed her again. After the longest time, he spoke.

'I don't know what happens now. I don't know after this ... but God, I missed you.'

'I had no idea,' Giovanni interrupted, looking back into the world beyond the doors. 'None. I mean, I knew so many of the components, but this, this is ... a miracle! Look, over there,' he pointed. 'There is grass growing. And there – so many buildings!'

'Don't get too close,' Shaun warned, keeping his friend back from the doors. 'In about five minutes I get trapped on that central dais and all hell breaks loose. Those quiet buildings and some of the passages around these railings are filled with guards.'

For minutes they watched David and Shaun explore The Facility. Shaun winced as he saw himself ascend the stairs to the central platform. Around and around he went, higher and higher, and all the while the two men spoke about relativity and worm holes. Shaun wanted more than anything to scream out, to warn himself that it was all a giant, waiting trap.

But he did not. He could not. He dared not.

He just watched in silent agony as he saw himself reach the top and walk out onto that ominous round platform.

What was it that his nagging brain was trying to say? What was he supposed to do? Slowly his eyes drifted upwards to the observation deck, hanging imposingly out from one of the far walls, as if to remind everyone that they were being watched. Shaun knew now that they *were* being watched.

'WELCOME, DR BLACK,' came the voice. Lauren jumped when she heard it.

'What the?'

The screen that David had been poking around on now flashed and sprang to life.

'David, what did you do?' Shaun heard himself ask in his school-teacher tone. Did he really sound like that?

'Nothing, I didn't do anything!' David said defensively, but a low whirring had begun.

'SEQUENCE INITIATED,' the voice spoke again.

'David!' Previous Shaun, red-time Shaun, called down. 'What's happening on that screen?'

Lauren hugged her husband tightly.

Shaun watched quietly, accepting.

Giovanni looked on in stunned silence.

David looked down at the screen to see a multitude of figures and graphics flashing by. Then, the beeps started.

'Ah ... I, um, I just touched the screen,' David said, starting to panic as the lighting in the room suddenly changed from blue to red.

'Shit! What's happening?' Shaun said as a low hum began in the arches above his head.

'COORDINATES CONFIRMED. SECONDARY CONFIRMATION AUTHORISED,' the woman's voice spoke again.

Shaun looked up at the observation deck and this time he saw movement. *Secondary confirmation authorised.* This was no accident. *You bastard!* Shaun screamed with all his mental will at the figure in the observation deck, the figure who had hit the button to authorise the event. Was it Le Clerque?

Just then the sound of hydraulics filled the cavern, and Shaun pushed Lauren backwards as doors down on the ground level slid open. From recesses in the walls on all four levels of the catwalks encircling the perimeter, a stream of men in blue-and-grey uniforms moved out with weapons at the ready, raised and pointed towards the central platform.

'David!' Shaun heard himself scream from the platform.

'Why are they pointing guns at you?' Lauren hissed. Then, looking a little closer, she asked, 'And why are you moving so slowly?'

Shaun followed the gun barrels of the guards who were no more than twenty feet from him, but looking the other way. They were all aimed at the platform where the other Shaun was trying to escape but seemed to be doing so at a leisurely pace. Another group of guards formed a circle around David, but none raised their weapons.

'Shit, Shaun, get down from there! What are you doing?' David screamed.

Then, an alarm shrieked, its 'Whoop! Whoop!' sounding throughout the city.

'*Shaun!*' David yelled again, but he was drowned out by the noise of the cavern.

'THIRTY SECONDS TO TRANSMIT,' came the same calm voice.

Lauren watched, frustrated and horrified as her husband moved as if he were on the moon. His hair seemed to bounce and fall more lightly, and his movements slowed with each step.

'COMPRESSION SCAN COMPLETE.' The voice came again, then almost without a pause it began to count. 'TWENTY ... NINETEEN ... EIGHTEEN ... SEVENTEEN ... SIXTEEN ...'

Shaun on the platform reached forward, but it was like he was under water, unable to fight through the density of the medium fast enough. David screamed and waved his arms helplessly.

'TWELVE ... ELEVEN ... TEN ...'

'I don't like it!' Lauren shouted in Shaun's ear. She gripped him tightly, like he might disappear at any moment. Shaun too felt uneasy. He looked from the dais up to the observation deck, imagining the smile, the evil, cruel, smug smile of the man whose shape he could just make out. *Bastard!*

Le Clerque, Shaun knew, was enjoying watching as the man on the platform struggled with the weight of his own movement, trying desperately to escape.

'NINE ... EIGHT ... SEVEN ... SIX ...'

Shaun stood up and Lauren stood beside him. A strange distortion had appeared around the circumference of the dais, and the arches seemed to emit some kind of heatwave that rippled and warped the air. Through it all, the man on the platform tried to move. He turned his eyes upwards, and for a brief moment locked his gaze on Lauren and Shaun standing hand in hand in the doorway.

During the second or so that their eyes stayed fixed, Shaun noticed several things: the Shaun on the platform was not touching the ground; the sweat falling from his face seemed to drift like soap bubbles to the floor; and, most strikingly, his eyes were filled with desperate, uncomprehending fear. It brought the memory back with force and he felt sick. God, he had been so scared and confused. All because that bastard up there wanted to get the diary, for what? To use it to decipher the map and find the disc. To wipe out Islam. To kill millions.

Anger rose in Shaun's chest.

'FIVE ... FOUR ... THREE ... TWO ...'

No. *No!* They would not have it. *No!*

'Protect her!' Shaun spat as he threw his gun to Giovanni and launched forward unnoticed by the guards.

'Shaun!' Lauren cried as her husband sprang forward onto the metal catwalk.

'Ground level!' he said, and the platform instantly started to move downwards, even though his words could not actually be heard in the chaos of the cavern.

'ONE ... ZERO ... INITIATE COMPRESSION TRANSMIT.'

As the catwalk section moved downwards, the guards barely noticed.

All eyes were fixed on the dais. The platform glowed with an intense blue light that fought to outshine the deep red the cavern had become.

The Shaun on the platform had stopped moving. Not only stopped moving; he had stopped in every sense of the word. He began to red-shift and grow dim as he froze in a silent scream.

Every particle that went into the making of Shaun Strickland separated. He became a cloud of himself and began to swirl. In the centre of his being, a black hole was forming, a black hole the size of an atom, contained within itself by all the power and design of the machine.

The particles spun, both individually and relative to one another, and then as each one was described by another, as the compression took place, the particle disappeared. Finally the last remaining particle, the one that represented Shaun Thomas Strickland, fell in through the event horizon of the microscopic black hole. It fell past its ultimate red shift to blink out of existence and disappear through the atomic-sized worm hole at the geometric centre of the platform.

Then, he was gone.

As the lights returned to blue and the siren ceased, Shaun charged screaming towards the central platform.

The first of the guards made to block his path but caught Shaun's fist in the jaw and was sent sprawling back into the second guard. The third moved as if to hold up his weapon, but Shaun, fuelled by rage and fear and adrenaline, grabbed its barrel and spun, pulling it free of the guard's hands. He charged on.

The fourth guard held up a hand but was met with the arcing rifle butt as Shaun completed his spin. The blow made a sickening thud as he hurtled the man and charged on. He was only a hundred feet from David now, and the platform was ten feet beyond that. The fifth guard fell from a boot kicked into his stomach, and the sixth flew backwards from a shoulder charge.

David, traumatised by the sight of his friend obliterated to nothingness, barely noticed as the ring of men around him was punctured by a flailing, lashing Shaun. It was only as Shaun bumped David's shoulder as he raced past that David noticed the screaming maniac at all.

Shaun took the stairs three at a time, using the railing to pull himself higher and faster. Forward and upward he sprang, not pausing when he heard David call out below him.

'Shaun? Shaun is that—'

'Not now David—'

'*Shaun!* Don't, it's a trap!'

He knew it was, but now he understood: nothing mattered except getting the diary and keeping it out of the hands of the men who had killed Lauren, who had killed Giovanni and who would ...

Neither of those two are dead, his brain politely interrupted. Shaun ignored it and began to scream again instead. He found a final burst of energy to carry him past the top step and out onto the platform.

There, in the centre of the large, circular floor were the clothes he had been wearing when the event had happened: his jeans, his shirt and his shoes. He skidded forward on his knees. Tangled up in his shirt was the diary. The Fontéyne diary. Graeme's diary. His diary.

'You didn't need to beat my guards so badly, you know,' said a voice that filled the cavern, coming from nowhere in particular but everywhere at the same time. Shaun looked up. He knew that voice. He rose slowly, calmed himself and surveyed the scene.

Everywhere, the blue light bathed the rock and buildings and pipes and screens. But unlike the last time he had looked out on the scene, this time it was not empty; far from it. He looked around at the catwalks encircling the whole place. Every twenty or so feet there stood the uniformed guards, but along the ground were hundreds of people. Many of them were guards, but many more now emerged wearing casual attire: trousers, jeans, coats.

All wore an overcoat of pale grey, mimicking the lab coat of the traditional scientist. Men and women, but no children. In fact, not a soul would have been under thirty. It was only then, seeing several of the guards still rolling on the floor nursing various injuries, that Shaun realised they had not put up much of a fight to stop him. The voice came again.

'Thank you for coming to see us, Mr Strickland. And thank you for bringing your book; we've been waiting for it for a very long time.'

'I know you!' Shaun shouted accusingly at the tinted windows of the observation deck high above him. There was no mistaking the voice now; he had listened to it in his study through many long nights as he worked on his theories. The voice of someone who thought the way Shaun thought, who Shaun admired and mimicked when giving his mock presentations to Lauren.

His eyes flicked up towards the entrance. No sign of Lauren or Giovanni. Good. No news is good news.

'You do? Well, how nice. I know you too,' the voice replied, as if the very soul of The Facility itself were speaking.

'You cannot have the diary, Landus!'

'I think it's Professor Landus to you!' the English accent replied.

David looked around at the scientists and guards. Each was transfixed, as if they were watching the greatest show on earth.

'I know you,' Shaun repeated, this time quietly. 'You ... you sent me an invitation,' he almost mumbled, his brain showing him the memory of the letter he had received in the mail from Cambridge. Suddenly, like a blurred picture coming into focus, it started to make sense.

'I ... I know you,' Shaun said again. 'You sent me, you ... it was you who sent me a letter. You asked me to go to Cambridge.'

'Your theories were impressive, I have to admit,' the voice replied.

'You made me leave home to go to England. You ... I know you.' He was almost babbling.

'Listen to it for once, Strickland.'

Yes, listen to me.

'You booked the tickets. They were already booked and paid for. From Charlotte. Why from Charlotte? Masonville has its own airport ... but from Charlotte ... too late to fly out ... we had to drive.'

'Shaun, what the hell's going on here, man?' David called up from below. He was still injured from the beating at the hands of the Pathans, and all the confusion was beginning to break him down again.

'You wanted us to drive. You wanted us to drive that night. You made it happen! Why did I never get a response from any of the other letters I sent out? None of the emails. Why in years did I never get a response?'

'No one else ever read your papers. No one could have, it was too dangerous. But I read them, Shaun. I read them, and what you see is the result of that. Your ideas, *your own ideas* made this possible.'

'But I said that it was *im*possible!' Shaun shot back, forgetting that he was speaking to a huge void, feeling more like his dialogue was internal.

'The key, Shaun, the key! You've seen it work, you've even felt it. You know it works. You stopped your research because you couldn't find the key. Your impasse.'

'A way to hold it open ...' Shaun said, remembering the frustration he had felt. Getting to the very moment of triumph and realising that there was not enough collective power in all the universe to hold a worm hole open. Even when he had theorised that these worm holes could be created, they could not be held intact long enough for anything to pass through. They would crush into oblivion anything that tried.

'You thought on the wrong scale, Shaun. You thought big when you should have thought small.'

Listen to me!

'Tell me, what happens when pool balls collide?' the voice asked like a school teacher.

'Huh?' Shaun said.

'What happens? Why do they bounce off each other?'

'Because ...' Shaun thought, 'because the electrons in each of the pool balls are negatively charged and they repel each other,' he yelled back up at the observation deck.

'No need to shout, I can hear you. Gentlemen.' On that word, movement filled The Facility. Everyone who was not a guard filed back into the buildings from which they had emerged. It was as if they were giving the two some privacy in this public arena.

'And what's really happening when you sit in an armchair?'

Shaun looked down and thought a moment. 'You're not touching it. You're levitating at the height of one angstrom.'

'What the hell is an angstrom?' David muttered. To his astonishment, one of the guards next to him, without taking his eyes off the central dais, replied: 'It's a unit of length equal to one hundred-millionth of a centimetre'.

'Oh,' David said, and shut up.

'That's it. The charge of an electron. The very fabric of our being, the stuff it's all made out of. You saw through your own calculations that time travel is possible on a microscopic scale.'

'But it can't be held open. There's not enough energy.'

'The key, Shaun: you thought of it once, you know what it is. Particles from *what* showed an inconsistency of energy? Why did you wake up naked? Whose numbers were out? Why are *we* unique in the universe?'

And then, unable to wait any longer, Shaun's brain took control of his mouth and spoke up.

'Life.'

'Yes.'

'*Life!*'

'That unknowable quantity that makes one thing alive, and another thing not. It's energy, Shaun. On a microscopic scale, nothing can crush it, not even a black hole. The particle integrity remains intact because the force is equal on all sides. Life, it's the energy of life. The breath of God.'

'But how do you get a man through a microscopic worm hole?' Shaun stammered.

David, whose own subconscious had been working away, popped the answer up like a light bulb. 'Compression!' he spat out.

Shaun looked down at him and frowned – this was not his conversation.

'You know what has to be done,' the voice said.

And at that moment, Shaun did know what had to be done, but he did not want to do it.

CHAPTER 74

The whir of the machine had stopped, and the guards made no sound. It was an eerie silence when compared to the chaos that had gone before.

Shaun stood silently. It had taken him so long to piece together, and now he had, he felt sick. All he wanted, more than anything, was to take Lauren back to North Carolina and live happily in their country home. He would not even mind teaching those tenth-graders; after all, they did not have guns.

Well, most of them didn't.

The sound of an elevator broke the stillness. Landus was coming down. David made to run, but guards around him raised their weapons to change his mind. Shaun did not move. He could not; he was stunned. His brain laid it all out to him and he recoiled at the idea. He nearly fell forward off the platform, but caught himself on the low railing.

He looked down at the diary and traced the symbol once again with his finger. It travelled up to the cross-bar, then made a small loop down, travelled up to the same point again, then a big loop back down. His journey.

'Shaun!' a voice called. It was Lauren. She and Giovanni were being marched by guards towards the base of the platform. Giovanni looked up at him as if to apologise, but Shaun did not register. Giovanni had unloaded a full clip on the men who had approached them in their hiding spot, but it had had no effect; the bullets were blanks. It had been planned. It had all been planned, down to the very last detail. Giovanni walked forward sombrely, still clutching the briefcase Shaun had given him charge of.

'Shaun, what's happening?' Lauren called up to him as she and Giovanni were forced into the ring of men who surrounded David. The engineer looked at the newcomers and his eyes grew wide with surprise.

'Father Giovanni?' he asked. 'But you were ... you're *dead*. The bomb ... I saw you!'

Giovanni allowed himself a smile.

'It seems, Mr Black, that it takes more than fire and brimstone to keep this old man down. I seem to, how you say, keep on keeping on?'

David appreciated the man's humour, and for that matter, simply seeing a familiar face. Then his eyes drifted over Giovanni's shoulder.

'Don't tell me ...' He let it hang. Lauren, however, stared up at her husband. He seemed to be ill. His eyes looked to the back of a long passageway between buildings, where the elevator door opened and a figure emerged. Lauren, David and Giovanni could not see that figure from where they stood, but Giovanni had also recognised the voice – it was the voice he had spoken to for years at The Society. His contact.

Shaun could see him, or at least, his silhouette. The man stepped out of the elevator and walked towards the base of the platform, where Lauren, David and Giovanni were assembled.

'But I just found her!' Shaun protested.

'And it's the only way you can keep her,' Landus said as he continued to walk forward.

Shaun's eyes lowered as tears began to run down his cheeks. 'But I just found her,' he repeated quietly.

'I'm sorry.'

Shaun knew what he had to do. He knew the way this went now. He finally understood.

'My parents?' Shaun asked then, the slightest glimmer of hope creeping into his voice.

Landus continued to walk. 'You cannot save them. You cannot change anything, not a single thing.'

Tears flowed freely now, running over Shaun's clenched jaw.

'You can see them, and say goodbye, though they will not know you,' Landus continued. Shaun smiled a little through his tears, then looked down at Lauren.

'Shaun! What's going on?' Lauren screamed, on the verge of hysteria.

'I love you so much, baby,' he said quietly. 'I'm so sorry. I'm so, so sorry.'

'Shaun! What the fuck is going on?' Lauren demanded.

Shaun continued to smile down at her.

'Now,' Landus continued, 'if you would be so kind ... the diary?' Shaun looked at the brown, animal-skin-bound book in his hands, then looked out at the approaching figure. He tossed it.

'No!' Giovanni called as the diary flew through the air. 'Shaun, the map!'

Shaun looked down at the old priest and breathed deeply.

'It's okay, Father.' He looked back up. 'It's taken me a long time to understand it, but now I do. The map has been with the diary the whole time, just as it was written.' He paused.

'What do you mean? I do not understand,' the priest said as the diary landed somewhere beyond his vision.

Shaun took a deep breath. He understood everything. He finally understood. He closed his eyes and, shaking his head, he spoke: 'I am the map.'

Silence.

No one else understood.

'The Rule of Knowledge. The translation document. Everything. I understand now. I understand why this happened to me ... Even why I got that book instead of a basketball as a child. It couldn't have happened any other way, could it?'

'No,' Landus said, coming around from the last building and holding the precious diary. 'It couldn't have happened any other way.'

'What do you mean, man? I don't get it!' David said, racking his brain.

'I had to see everything I saw. I had to read everything I read. I had to know all that I have come to know. I had to experience everything exactly as it happened, because it was the way it *had* happened. It was the only way I would *believe*. I had to believe. I didn't believe for the longest time, but I had to. The map isn't in the diary. It's not a code or a drawing. It's not a piece of parchment hidden in a cave. All of that was far too dangerous, too much of a risk. *I am the map.* The disc will be wherever I decide it will be. It's wherever I tell Fontéyne to put it. Isn't that right, Professor?'

'That's right,' said the man stepping forward into the light. He did not look like Lauren or David had expected him to look. He was taller and leaner. His hair was a salt-and-pepper grey, with flecks of what had once been sandy brown. He was dressed in a grey suit with a tweed jacket, and looked every inch the English professor. From his hand the light glinted off an intricately carved golden ring, the top etched with the crest of a Roman eagle. David had seen that ring before, in the video of Napoleon's escape, worn by the man called Fontéyne.

The professor watched them as the guards around the trio parted to allow him through. Lauren studied the man who now carried the diary. The man responsible for it all, for setting it up. He was handsome for his age, which she placed at around forty. He looked physically fit. He looked strong and determined. And he looked ... familiar.

The man looked at her with eyes of crystal blue and a blank expression. The man was Shaun.

CHAPTER 75

'Oh my God!' Lauren gasped.

'Holy shit, man' David said.

Giovanni smiled.

'Welcome to The Facility,' Landus said. 'I'll be right with you.'

He turned back to Shaun up on the dais. 'Now,' he said, 'you know it happens, you know it's worth it. The Rule of Knowledge is unbroken. It is absolute. Don't change a thing, not a single thing.'

'But so many people die,' Shaun began, shaking his head.

'It is out of your hands. You must not prevent it,' Landus said sternly. 'You *do* not prevent it.'

It was only then that Lauren noticed that the accent was gone. No longer was this the refined speech of a British university professor, but the relaxed and slightly less dramatic accent of a school teacher from North Carolina.

'Shaun,' Landus said reassuringly, 'it'll be okay.'

Shaun was silent. Then: 'How long?'

'Fifteen years, give or take,' Landus said flatly.

'Give or take how much?' Shaun asked without a hint of trust in his voice.

'Ah ... give or take a bit,' Landus said, then shot a sideways wink at Lauren. 'Don't want to give away all our secrets now, do we?'

Landus turned away. 'Gentlemen,' he said, seemingly to the air. At once the lights in The Facility flicked from blue to red, and the whole scene was once again bathed in an eerie, otherworldly glow.

'Wait!' Shaun called from the platform.

'No, I've waited long enough!' Landus shot back. 'You can't imagine how I have waited, Shaun, but you will. You will more than imagine. You will know. You will experience every second of my painstaking wait, and when you are me, you will understand. You will do the same.'

Landus began to walk forward but then stopped. 'Oh,' he said, 'I nearly forgot. David, if you will. Do you still have that specification you wrote on the plane? About the encryption?'

David looked confused, but then remembered the pages he had shoved into his pockets shortly before he had wiped himself out on the free alcohol service offered by the international carrier. He searched his body, and pulled out the pages. He stared at them for a moment, then smoothed them over before handing them to Landus. Landus took them with a smile and folded them into a fine, tight roll. Then, from his pocket, he pulled out a large, beige walnut. He flipped the casing open and closed it again around the papers.

'SEQUENCE INITIATED,' a woman's voice came over the speakers.

'There's no carrot cake this time, sorry, but you'll need this.' Landus turned and, in one motion, threw the walnut baseball style the one hundred and fifty feet up to the platform where Shaun stood. David looked at him. Shaun was moving backwards away from the edge. Slowly. Unnaturally slowly. The intense gravitational field being created on the dais caused time to slow down relative to the outside world. To Shaun, the outside world was happening all too fast.

'COORDINATES CONFIRMED,' the woman said, her voice filling the cavern. Landus walked over to the panel David had so fatefully examined a few minutes earlier and punched in a series of numbers.

The walnut travelled upwards to the platform but looked as if it would sail right past Shaun before he had a chance to grab it. A bad throw.

'SECONDARY CONFIRMATION AUTHORISED,' the voice came again.

Then a funny thing happened.

The instant the walnut passed the perimeter of the arches, it slowed dramatically, moving through the air like a child's balloon. Shaun rushed to catch it, and was thankful that it seemed to slow to a normal speed after the bullet-like projectile it had been from his perspective when Landus had thrown it. He heard the woman's voice. She had already started her twenty-second countdown and reached fifteen by the time Shaun had put the walnut in his mouth, slapped his chest and sent the smooth container sliding down his throat. His brain was trying to tell him something else, and he made a vow to himself to listen to it from now on. Of course – the memory loss. Shaun looked around frantically and saw, sitting conveniently near the centre of the platform, a small razor blade. Every detail planned.

'TEN ... NINE ... EIGHT ...' She was speeding up. He raced over and grabbed the blade, then, without hesitating, began to carve into his arm. From the outside his scream was low and drawn out.

'What's he doing?' asked Lauren in a panic.

It was David who answered. 'He's writing. He's cutting the word VOMIT into his arm so he knows what to do when he wakes up. The pain will draw his attention to it, and after he hurls, he'll see the walnut and the papers inside it.'

'It will bring back his memory?' Giovanni asked.

'Yeah. I'm not sure how it works, but yeah.'

'It works,' Landus said from over at the console, 'by forcing him to come into conscious contact with some element from his own time. The human brain is a delicate thing, and it adapts to whatever reality it is presented with. It needs to be shocked into waking up from the belief that it belongs in the past.'

'SEVEN ... SIX ... FIVE ... FOUR ...'

'Lauren!' Shaun cried again and ran towards the outside of the platform, or tried to. He felt so heavy.

'THREE ... TWO ...' He saw her standing there in the centre of the circle. Everything was moving so fast. He did not want this, he did not want to miss her again, he did not want to not be able to see her, to touch her, to kiss her for another fifteen years. It was worse than a prison term, it was Hell. As the countdown reached zero and the chipmunk voice said, 'INITIATE COMPRESSION TRANSMIT,' Shaun reached out for her with all his strength.

Frozen. That was the last moment Lauren saw her husband as she knew him. Frozen in mid-air, reaching for her with desperation in his eyes. Then, as they had seen only moments before, the man's molecules separated from each other. Then the atoms within the molecules separated, then the vibrating strings.

The cloud spun and swirled in a vortex, but Lauren could not look. She buried her head in Giovanni's chest and squeezed her eyes tight. It was over.

When she opened her eyes again, The Facility was bathed in a blue glow once more. Lauren looked up. Giovanni released the arm he had around her shoulders and looked past her.

She turned to David, whose attention was also focused behind her. Slowly, tentatively, she turned around.

Landus had taken off his tweed jacket and wore a blue collared shirt underneath. The sleeves were rolled up to just below his elbows, and

Lauren noticed the hint of a scar on his inner forearm. It was a word: VOMIT.

She scanned the man in front of her, raising her eyes to finally rest on his face. She breathed. Just breathed. There was no sound but her breath.

'It's me, baby,' Shaun said.

Lauren just breathed.

Shaun walked forward slowly. Lauren backed up. Shaun stopped. 'Lauren. It's me.'

She stared at him, quivering. 'I ... I ... just ... I just don't know ...'

He strode forward and stopped just short of her. Their eyes met. She studied his face.

For the first time in twenty-one years, Professor Maxwell S Landus, Shaun Strickland, began to cry. Slowly, deliberately, he looked deep into Lauren's eyes and spoke.

'That's it. It's done. Everything I know is done. I don't know what happens now, after this. All I know is ... God, I've missed you—'

Lauren's lips were on his. Her mouth was warm, her taste was sweet. In that moment, more than two decades of planning, waiting, sacrifice, torture and hell, were worth it. The moment lasted an eternity, and Shaun drank every instant with all of his being. He was free.

An uncomfortably long time later, David cleared his throat. 'Ahem ... ah ... sorry to ... well, you know ... but I just wondered what happens to us now? Are we going to be killed?' he asked.

Landus pulled away. Looking at David, he grinned.

'Kill you? Why then, how would we ever educate you about our compression technology?'

David's puffy eye went wide.

'You mean it?' he said, sounding like a kid who had just been told he could go for a ride in Santa's sleigh.

'Well, first we have to start you off on something small, like virtual stereoscopic codec development.' He motioned down to the briefcase in Giovanni's hand. 'I see you've already played with that a little, though. You like Napoleon on the TV? You should see it in our theatre!'

David went ashen white.

'You have a cinema,' he asked, 'that displays the disc like my player does?'

'Well, there's been a few improvements on your design – no glasses, for one,' Shaun said.

'Improvements? That codec was great, but my playback design is flawless! Who could improve on that?'

'I could.' It was a voice from behind David that answered. No one had seen him approach, all the focus being on the professor whom Shaun had become. David turned to look at the man. He had short, closely trimmed hair, and the same trim and healthy-looking physique the new version of Shaun possessed. There were no glasses on his face, but the enhanced brown of his iris gave a hint to the contact lenses he wore. David Black looked at the man who had posed the challenge, and saw what he would look like in fifteen years' time.

'My my, would you look at that gut?' the newcomer said. 'Really, David, the first thing you gotta do to get these abs is cut out all that high-sugar soft drink and maybe do a knee bend once in a while.'

David just stared. He had not been prepared for this. The man in front of him was definitely himself, but a shiny, polished version. He was what David imagined he would look like if he could win one of those extreme makeovers they have on television.

'I ... er ... well ...'

'Oh, here it comes,' the man said.

'It's a ... I ... umm ...' Instead of completing a coherent sentence, David wet his pants. The senior version rolled his eyes.

'Don't worry, both Shaun and I have gone through a lot of the training we put the agents through. One of the great scripts I had written into the subneural programming takes care of your little problem. Yes, it really does smell as bad as you think it does.'

David blushed bright red.

'But don't worry. You're about to have the best mind-screw of your life, man. Everyone here even calls me Dr Black,' the older version of David said with the same enthusiasm David had displayed when he talked about his work, but Dr Black was tempered, more measured.

Without knowing what to do, David held out his hand, as if to introduce himself. The doctor stepped back with his palms up in a surrender.

'Hey, man, you can keep that to yourself. I don't want any of those freakin' headaches Shaun was complaining about all the time. Rule number one: we can never touch. The fact that I know that we never do doesn't mean that it can't happen ... I think. We're actually still working on that one.'

'What happens if you touch?' Giovanni said, caught up in the show.

Dr Black turned to him. 'Well, let's just say that there's a Doppler effect. Waves of space–time fuck up, ah ... sorry, Father ... ripples in space–time, which manifest themselves as God-almighty explosions of head pain, leading up to and away from the event. The only experience we've really had with it was Max's ... ah ... I mean Shaun's experience when he checked his future version's pulse when he was hit by the car.'

Lauren squinted, remembering. 'You said something about that ...'

Shaun smiled and held up his three fingers. 'The blisters I thought I had on my fingertips here. When I checked the hobo's pulse, I touched skin. A part of my future version's matter transferred over to me. Miraculously, the lumps went away after I was hit by the car when I had the diary. When I had my pulse checked, the matter transferred back.'

'This is incredible!' the priest said, his accent growing thicker in his excitement.

'Cooooooool!' was all David could string together, still looking at the man in front of him.

'So, rule number one: we don't touch,' Dr Black continued. 'Rule number two: I'm always right. Whatever original thought you think you've come up with, I had it first, literally. There is nothing you can think, or know, that I don't know or haven't thought first.'

'But I—'

'David, listen, because I only say this once: get over your arrogance, and absorb. You have to accept what I tell you because you have so much to learn, you cannot imagine. Luckily for you, the first thing you will learn is all about our accelerated learning and neural programming technology. But first ...' Dr Black turned to one of the guards who stood in the circle around them. 'Eric, take our friend here back to get a shower and a new set of pants.'

David started to protest, but then realised he was in no state to have the conversations he wanted to have right now, to ask the questions he was dying to ask. As he walked off, he looked around and remembered that it had been his ambition over the past six years to meet the man who developed the codec he had spent his recent life cracking. He felt an overwhelming sense of something he had not allowed himself to feel many times before. A rare feeling, a warm feeling, washed over him when he realised that he was responsible for it all. He had invented the codec that had so amazed him. The feeling he had was one of unadulterated pride. His mind filled with awe and wonder and he swelled at the thought that he had had a hand in it all. Then he remembered that he had just wet his pants.

'Now,' Shaun said, watching David walk off with the guard, 'Father Giovanni. I'm glad you could finally join us here.' He turned to face the priest.

'I can barely believe it is you,' the priest said. He had seen Shaun's face before, of course; he had seen it for years. This man had been Giovanni's sole contact at The Society for World Historical Accuracy. This man, who had always referred to The Society as a larger entity, an organisation through which he would have to relay Giovanni's information in order to return a decision – this man *was* The Society. Giovanni had never thought much of it, but now he understood. He realised how clever it had been. Shaun seemed to read his thoughts.

'It's easier to keep a secret that way,' Shaun said, smiling. Giovanni's expression had turned blank as he realised the enormity of the task that Shaun had undertaken. Then, he followed the thought through. Shaun was the decision-maker behind The Society, which meant that he had willingly consorted with Le Clerque. He had been party to some unspeakable acts. Giovanni did not understand.

'Father, you have shown utmost support throughout the years. For that assistance I thank you greatly.'

'But I was removed as your Vatican contact. You have been dealing with a man I assure you has only his own interests at heart. He cares only about establishing a new Church, his Church, and starting a war that would kill millions of people. He has had people killed. He tried to kill me, and it was you yourself who prevented that, but there were others. There are things you must have known about, assassinations you did not stop. Murders you were a party to ...'

Shaun felt Lauren's eyes on him, and was cautious when he spoke.

'Father, I have been in a position over the past two decades that no one else has ever experienced. It's true that after the Holy Father, Pope Nicholas, passed, I knew you would be removed as the official spokesperson for the Vatican, and I knew that I would deal with Le Clerque. The thing is, Le Clerque did not know that I knew him. He planted two agents into our military recruitment program to steal the agent list, and to kill Pilate. He authorised the murders of many people, and it's true that I knew about these things. It's true also that I did not stop them.'

Lauren took a small step back from her husband. The reality that this man had led an entire life without her was starting to scrape the surface.

'These things are true. I cannot explain to you, to anyone, Father, what it's like to know something terrible is going to happen. To absolutely know it, and to have the power to do something about it *and to choose not to.* But, for me, these things were in the past. They were in my red time as we call it here. They were moving away from me. For me they had already happened and so I could not interfere, even if that meant making sure that they *did* happen.'

'You killed people?' Lauren stared at the man she had just met, the man who was once her husband.

'No,' Shaun said carefully. 'I never killed anyone. I did my best to remove responsibility from my own decision-making, but it's true that sometimes I allowed things, horrible, terrible things, to occur. But you must understand: I had no choice. If I changed anything, anything at all, then what is taking place right now, our reunion, may not have happened. I've been in a prison of my own knowledge.'

Giovanni tried to imagine it, but struggled with the idea.

'Look,' Shaun said, stepping forward to the Italian priest, 'nothing has happened that I did not allow. Le Clerque did not steal anything I did not allow. No one I did not know to be already dead was allowed to be harmed. But I couldn't risk anything being different; what we are doing is too important. For me, it was all red time.' He turned to Lauren. 'Seeing you again, being with you, is too important.' Then he pointed down at the case Giovanni held. 'You see, Father, I kept my promise. You have your player. But there is something else I have for you.'

Shaun reached back into his pocket. When he withdrew his hand it held a penny-sized disc.

'You liked the Napoleon movie that you saw, yes?' Shaun asked.

'I ... the ... it is what I need to prove to the Holy Father that time travel is possible so he will believe that Le Clerque is a traitor to the Church.'

'I see. Then I think, Father, you may wish to take this movie as well. It will interest you greatly. Take it to Müller and let him do with it as he sees fit.'

Giovanni's eyes bulged at the tiny disc in Shaun's hand. He dared not hope, but he decided to ask the question anyway. He did not have to – Shaun was already nodding slowly.

'You had it all this time?' Giovanni asked.

'Take it. It's your responsibility now.' With that, he let the disc fall into Giovanni's palm. 'My work is done,' Shaun said with a sense of fatality. As if the weight of the universe had been lifted from his shoulders, Shaun suddenly seemed lighter. He breathed deeper, and appeared to lose several years of age before their very eyes.

'This whole time?' Giovanni asked again.

'Yes, this whole time. I knew where it would be, remember? It was the first thing I did when I woke up twenty-one years ago. Well, after I found some clothes ... which didn't last long because I vomited almost straight away and found my walnut. I very nearly missed it. That would have been ironic.

'The first thing I did was decide *where* the disc would be, and then I went and got it. From that moment on, I was locked in. It meant that I couldn't change my mind about the disc's location, nor could I decide not to go ahead and build The Facility, because I had the disc, which meant that it had all happened. It's funny, effect creating cause, rather than cause creating effect. I've had very little free will over the past twenty-one years. I knew what had to be done and I had to make sure nothing prevented it from happening. Making sure none of Shaun's papers ever reached further than his own outbox. Making sure he never got a university scholarship. Everything happened when it was supposed to. Creating my new persona, and ensuring that Shaun knew the works of Professor Landus; building a career at Cambridge and fostering the contacts I would need to help me see it all through. Getting Presidents elected, making wise investments and placing several large bets on sporting events to get the capital I needed. There are more details that could be explained, Father, but know this: now, it's out of my hands. Now, it's up to you. What you have in your hand is the culmination of something that has been in progress for more than two thousand years. That's it, all of it, that's what the whole thing was about, and I've done my bit. Now I just want to take my wife home and live the life that was taken from me.'

He reached out his hand to Lauren, and she took it gingerly.

'You have to give me some time,' she said slowly.

'I know,' Shaun answered.

CHAPTER 76

Three days later, Cardinal Vincenso Raul Giovanni sat in the sun at his favourite cafe not far from Vatican City. He finished the last of his extra-strong short-black coffee and wiped his lips. He was a different man. Only twice before in history had men been as totally transformed as the priest was now. One of them had seen the disc Giovanni had just watched; the other had made it. Both knew the face.

Giovanni breathed deeply, then strode towards the Vatican. It was early, and the sun was just beginning to filter through the city's tallest peaks as he passed through the gates.

'I have an appointment with the Holy Father,' Giovanni said as he approached the Pope's chamberlain. The man looked up and smiled.

'Ah, Father Giovanni, he is expecting you,' the man replied. 'Please, go straight up.' Giovanni marched with an ordinary-looking black-and-silver briefcase at his side. He navigated the hallways he had known intimately for the past thirty-three years, but now they seemed different. When he had completed the formalities outside the Pope's chamber, he walked through the Holy Father's doors with confidence and purpose.

Cardinal Joseph Müller, elected Pope Pius XIII, sat alone at a large mahogany desk, a fountain pen in his hand. He preferred to write most of his communications and then let his secretary enter them into the computer, and now he was penning his retirement speech in a thick black ink. He looked up over thin-rimmed glasses at the priest's approach.

'Ah, welcome Vincenso!' the Pope said in Italian. 'How good to see you. It has been a while since we have had some time together, has it not?'

'It has, Holy Father.'

'Please, Vincenso, there is no need for that.'

'I'm sorry, Joseph, but what I have to talk to you about will require you to truly be the leader you have been elected to be. In fact, there has never been a moment that has more greatly required the divine infallibility of the station of Pope.'

Müller put his pen down, hearing his friend's tone.

'There is something on your mind?' Pope Pius asked. In response, Giovanni put his briefcase on the table and opened it.

'What is this?' Müller asked.

'Holy Father, I beg a few moments of your time to listen to me. I ask you to hear me in full before you pass judgement on what I have to say,' Giovanni said. 'What I have to tell you and, through this device on the table here, to show you, will require you to have an open mind and be prepared to accept some challenging ideas. It will be the most important thing that has occurred in your life so far.' He paused. 'Yes, a very open mind. Do you think you can do that?'

Müller had not been spoken to in this way for many years, and it commanded his full attention. He slipped the speech he was writing to the side and interwove his fingers on the desk. He gave Giovanni his undivided focus.

'Please, Vincenso, begin.'

Vincenso Raul Giovanni did begin, and for the next twelve hours, deep into the evening, he held the Pope's attention. All other appointments were cancelled or postponed. When Giovanni emerged from the Pope's chamber at eight o'clock that evening, the sun cast a deep red light through the hallway windows. Giovanni navigated his way back through the corridors, passing other members of the clergy as he walked with an air of completion. He knew now how Shaun Strickland had felt as he had handed over the disc. To know he had successfully played his part in something larger brought contentment to his soul.

It was as Giovanni rounded a corner and entered one of the lower ornate hallways of the major wing that he saw Cardinal François Le Clerque walking in the opposite direction. He had two assistants with him, one of whom was taking his dictation of a homily on racial tolerance. The cardinal spoke without looking at the junior priest. When he looked ahead down the corridor, he did not speak at all. Le Clerque stopped, frozen.

Striding towards him was a ghost. In an instant, a thousand facts flashed through the Frenchman's mind. The car had been totally destroyed; his agent had reported that Giovanni had been hideously burned and taken away in an ambulance, dead. Le Clerque had sent 'visitors' to the local medical facilities to make sure that the job had been properly completed, but they had not been able to trace which hospital Giovanni had been admitted to.

Now, in that instant, Le Clerque knew why.

Giovanni continued to close the distance, the appearance of Le Clerque at the opposite end of the hallway not faltering the Italian's stride one iota. After a brief pause, the Frenchman resumed his walk. They were barely twenty feet away when Le Clerque absently allowed his eyes to drift down the Italian's arm to the briefcase he carried. François Le Clerque's blood ran cold. How had he? The player had been secured in his own personal safe … there was no way that what the Italian carried could be the same case, but it looked identical. And what was Giovanni doing in this part of the Vatican? He was stationed outside the—

Then he put it all together.

The Pope.

Giovanni had been to see the Pope. But how? He had nothing to show him – the disc had not been found, and Müller was to announce his retirement this very evening.

The fat French cardinal began to jog, then to run towards Giovanni. They stared each other in the eyes in the moment of passing, François wearing a look of confusion and panic, Giovanni wearing one of knowing contentment.

'Eminence! Eminence!' the confused assistants stammered as they chased after their scrambling cardinal.

Giovanni continued to march forward. His part was done.

What would be, would be.

CHAPTER 77

'This is amazing,' Shaun remarked as he ate the best apple crumble of his life. As he had promised himself for the past twenty-one years, the first thing he did upon his return was to buy Lauren a bag of fresh apples, and he had come to repeat the gesture for the next few weeks.

'You shouldn't be eating that yet!' Lauren chastised him as she dashed about the kitchen trying to complete the trimmings for the Thanksgiving turkey before their guests arrived.

Shaun grinned, sucking the remnants of his indiscretion from his fingers, one of which held a golden Roman ring given to him by his friend X7. It had been passed down through the Fontéyne family for generations, and Graeme had presented it to Shaun just before embarking on his mission.

Ever since his older self had sent him back in time twenty-one years, Shaun had dreamed of living this life again. He had woken up in England, naked, confused and in pain from the cuts on his forearm. Soon enough, though, he had remembered, and had set about doing what needed to be done despite the pain of losing Lauren again. For the past nineteen years he had been Professor Landus, and had distinguished himself with incredible predictions and amazing science. He had pioneered ideas, and had access to the resources and people he had needed to realise those ideas.

Of course, there was much more that he had access to. It had started quickly enough, once he had completed the first task of securing funds and reinventing himself. Shaun Strickland had become Maxwell S Landus because he already knew that that was who he had become; it was the first of many such choices where Shaun had to learn that he had no choice at all. He did well on a few football matches with the bookies, and then he compiled a list of everything he knew. Every election result, world event, sporting victory, newsworthy affair. He entered himself into hypnotic regression therapy and was able to recall far more. The compilation became his bible.

It was six years before he heard a voice say, 'I'd like to sign up for your advanced Afghanistan hiking class.'

He had looked up from his desk into the eyes of a leaner, more sober-looking David Black, fresh from six years of training and learning in a Facility that did not yet exist. Shaun had not expected him, but the joy he felt when David arrived was overwhelming. David had arrived with instructions and knowledge from The Facility that allowed Professor Landus to start his preparations in earnest. Tim had been a great help, his most trusted ally and consort.

The true challenge had been one of self-discipline. One of stopping himself from arriving on the doorstep of his North Carolina home and taking Lauren in his arms. Of course he had not, but he had had the couple closely monitored. He had not realised he was such a putz, and he loved his wife all the more for putting up with him. Through it all, though, he had known that eventually it would be worth it. He knew that if he just obeyed The Rule of Knowledge, then he would be with her again. He had seen it, and so had been inspired to continue his work. He knew also that millions were counting on him, though they didn't know it.

Now, as he cleaned up the spillage of tonight's dessert that he had prematurely sampled, he felt that everything had been worthwhile. Fitting back into Masonville High had been a challenge. He had dyed his hair and done his best to look the same age as he had been when he had left the previous week, but he knew that the students talked about him behind his back. He was clearly not the same man.

His teaching had improved considerably, however, as had his ability to guide and counsel the kids who came to him with more personal problems.

Tonight he would see his friends for the first time in more than a month. David would arrive shortly, as would David senior's wife, a research scientist from Spain who spent her spare time writing compression algorithms. 'There's someone for everyone,' Shaun had mused as he saw the fireworks ignite between the two. He once caught sight of a flirting text message that read: 'There are 00000010 kinds of people in this world, those who understand binary, and those who don't.'

It was now about five-thirty on a Sunday, and the ball game Shaun had on in the background held particular interest for him. It was the first World Series in more than a decade where he did not know the result.

He had decided to bet anyway, mainly because this time held the thrill of possible loss. He did not need the money. No, money was something he would never have to worry about again. Ever.

It was probably because he had not heard the score for a while that he walked into the lounge room to see what was wrong. What he saw made the apple he was snacking on fall from his mouth.

CHAPTER 78

Eight-year-old Diego Mannuel sat fidgeting with his parents in the Quito hospital waiting room. He was not fidgeting from boredom, but more because he was so involved with what was happening on the television. He was so excited that he could not sit still. His parents too had their eyes fixed on the screen, just as they had for the past two hours. So had everyone else in the waiting room. Since the program had begun, none of the patients had hit their call buttons, none of them had complained. They all sat watching, forgetting, for the moment at least, their various ailments.

Initially Diego had liked it because of the action. He had started to pay attention as soon as the man began to battle the lions. It was more the way it was filmed, though – he had never seen anything like it. He felt like he was living the events as they happened. He did not like it when they whipped the sad man. He had wanted to turn away, but he had not. He expected his father to tell him he was not allowed to watch it, that it was too violent, but his father had not. Now as he watched, they were speaking in Spanish.

Elizabeth Jones hated the television. She hated the news that it brought, like this morning when she had heard about that terrible tragedy of a cardinal leaping to his death from the top of the Vatican roof. He was French, they had said, and she did not like the French. Nor did she like Germans, Blacks or Asians. She especially didn't like the television, but today was different. Today there was something happening that had never been done before on British television, and it had grabbed her attention. She had missed the tube to work because, try as she might, she just could not look away from the screen. It was a British production, she was sure, but it was fresh and new, and so incredibly addictive. She tried to call in sick, but she could not get a line out on her phone.

Miyako Matsui lay with her lover. Tadaka Yamishita was the man she would marry, she was sure of it. He came from a good family, had an honourable trade as an investment banker and lived in an upper-city thirty-second-floor Tokyo apartment. She loved staying with him on the weekends like this, because the view of the city at night never failed to seduce her. The blues, greens, reds and yellows weaved a living tapestry of life and energy. She particularly loved his one-hundred-and-sixty-four-centimetre flat-panel television. It sat against the window and was framed by the blurred backdrop of the night sky. They usually watched a movie after making love, but tonight there was something amazing on television. It had what she assumed were American actors, but they spoke perfect Japanese. It had been ages since she had seen anything natively Japanese that had this much money spent on it, but the new technique was cutting edge, and she knew that Japanese animators and film-makers were renowned for that. She cuddled up closer to Tadaka and listened in awe to what was being said.

Graeme Fontéyne sat alone in a cave on the outskirts of Jerusalem. He had been sitting and thinking for about two hours now. He replayed again and again the events of a few days before. The iron spikes had been driven cleanly through the palms of the man's hands, not through the wrists as had been debated among scholars. It had rained, which was something no one had documented; that evening it had rained and thundered all night.

His mother had been there, with his other followers, but the guards had kept them well back. Graeme had taken the spear, the one that pierced the man's side. The Roman had laid it down on a rock as he had helped remove the body, and Graeme had taken it and broken it into three parts in order to fit it beneath his tunic.

He was not thinking clearly. He had not done so for days now. He flexed his hand and rolled his fingers. They were all there. His fingers were all there. One of them now wore an intricately carved gold ring that danced in the firelight. It had been Pilate's ring, and was the Governor's show of gratitude for saving his life. Graeme had seen, and owned, this ring before, a gift from his grandfather. Graeme would pass it on.

He was not sure what to do now, so he just sat. It was late and dark, and Malbool had taken Mishca to an inn so they could rest. So now Graeme sat alone and stared at the flame as it danced in the occasional breeze that filtered into the cave. He absently flicked his tongue on the back of his teeth, starting and stopping the recording with each pass. He had captured it all, and now there was nothing to record but the dance of the flame.

'How is your hand?'

The voice startled him.

Graeme looked around but did not see anyone. No one had known he was coming here. Only seconds later did he realise the question had come in English. An agent.

'I never thanked you,' came the voice again, and this time Graeme pinpointed its origin. He stared deep into the shadows at the back of the cave as a figure stepped forward into the light. The shadows danced and flickered on the man's face, and the orange of the flame gave vibrancy to his olive skin. Graeme scrambled backwards and slipped over. His heart began to pound, and that all too familiar surge of adrenaline filled his system. This time, though, it was through a sense that was unfamiliar to Graeme Fontéyne: fear.

'Relax,' the man said. 'It's all right. This is what you're here for, isn't it?' The man beamed a smile through his beard, which now appeared soft and well groomed. In fact, everything about the wavy-haired, brown-eyed man glowed. Graeme had seen this man before, not three days earlier, with impossible injuries and bruises. This iridescent version of that same man was not possible.

'We all have our part to play. Yours and mine, Graeme, are interwoven. You must complete your mission, and I must complete mine.' He made it sound so simple.

Graeme's heart calmed just a little, and his sense of awe replaced that of fear. The man had used his name. His real name. Not the one by which he went in this ancient time, but the name his mother would give him two thousand years from now.

'Come, sit with me. You have many questions you wish to ask me. Am I right?' Joshua Ben Jacob, the man they called Jesus, asked. 'But first I want to thank you,' he said kindly.

'For … for helping you when … helping you when you fell?' Graeme stammered, finding his voice, shaky as it was.

'For not killing him. I know you wanted to. Thank you for your restraint,' Jesus said. Graeme thought of the guard who had whipped and driven the Jew ever onwards, without remorse or pity.

'Now, please, sit with me. Ask everything you have been told to ask. Ask also whatever it is that you want to know for your own sake.'

Graeme sat, dumbfounded. He looked into the eyes of the man before him and saw no hint of malice. No hint of judgement or deceit. He saw only endless patience. The man was in no rush. Graeme gathered himself, running a mental finger over the files organised in his mind and structured his questions. There were many of them, and it had taken one of The Facility's advanced memory techniques to allow him to recall them in order: questions of science, of philosophy, of meaning.

After taking a deep breath, he began to speak.

The conclave of cardinals sat in silence. They had been called together to do their duty. Only once before had a Pope announced retirement from the papacy. Müller had cited the cancer that had taken his health, and his subsequent inability to lead any longer.

When they had first arrived, most had already known which way they would vote, and were prepared to sit through the days of deliberation merely as a formality – but now Le Clerque was dead. He had thrown himself from the roof of the Vatican in a fit of remorse, or so it had been reported.

This particular session had lasted longer than any previously. Thirteen hours. Twelve of those hours had been spent watching the presentation that had just finished. There was no longer any need to vote. The man who would lead the Church, a radically different Church, had already been named by the man who spoke out from the screen. The man who had been chosen to 'Bring me to my people.'

The doorbell rang. Shaun drew away from the television and walked over to open it. The turkey had been proudly placed in the centre of the dining table, which was set ornately with condiments and cutlery. Smells of rich, basted meat and roasted potatoes filled the room. When the door swung open, Shaun smiled at his guests. He embraced David Senior and smiled, bidding him to come in. He politely kissed David's wife, Anna, on the cheek as they embraced. Then Shaun looked at David, the young David, the David he had not known personally for years. David Junior shuffled nervously from one foot to another, before Shaun stepped forward and embraced him too.

'Hey! How's the education?' Shaun asked as he ushered David in.

'Ah, man, it's ... unbelievable. I can't ... I had no idea. I mean, you're incredible ... I can't ...' David stammered.

'Settle down!' He gave David a playful jab in the ribs. The engineer recoiled and walked inside to see where Shaun lived. A modest yet comfortable North Carolina home. David had been studying and living at The Facility for the past few months, and this was his first venture out.

He was nervous to meet this new Shaun, a man he didn't know. The man who apparently had worked with the senior version of himself to engineer a feat unheard of in human history ... and what was his greatest desire? To sit and eat turkey with his wife and friends.

They all sat after greeting Lauren and congratulating her on the feast she had prepared. They also congratulated her on the news of an addition to the Strickland family, who would join them in the not too distant future. Shaun excused himself from the table to turn down the television ...

'... so much correct or incorrect. What you have come to call science is a method, it is not a thing. It is a way of testing things, a way of describing them. It is a structure that allows you to explore and move forward.

'Take the medium that I have chosen to use to deliver this message to the world. Science will say that there are red, green and blue dots grouped together, phosphors illuminated by a cathode ray at varying intensities, or liquid crystals displaying one of a finite number of pixel hues. Religion would step back from the screen and say, "It's a picture of a face." Both are correct, but they look at different aspects of the same thing. Things are the way they are; it is only your description and understanding of them that changes. When ...'

Shaun pressed the mute button. He had seen this show before, and he knew he would see it again. He sat back at the table. For now he would enjoy the night with his friends. A night during which he did not know what the conversation would be, or what would happen. A night where anything was possible. One thing was certain, however: like a thief in the night, the 'second coming' had arrived. It played now simultaneously all over the world. It played so everyone heard it in their own language, so everyone understood. Shaun knew that he had played his part, and that everything had come full circle. He knew that tomorrow, the world would be a different place.

ACKNOWLEDGEMENTS

There are many people I would like to thank for this book becoming a reality:

Mum and Dad, thanks for conceiving me. I couldn't have done this without you going through the birthing process. Oh, and thanks for all the support that came after that too! Thanks to my brother Brett for your faith in me.

To the team at Hachette for your belief and hard work: Vanessa, Matt, Kate, Shaun, Nicola, Claire and all who work tirelessly behind the scenes. A special thanks to Matthew Reilly, a man with more courage than any of his action heroes.

To my wonderful, talented Sarah, who tolerates, supports and encourages me in equal measure. To Gavin, Eddy and Lindz – the 'make look awesome' filters for any situation; and to all those who took the time to read my early drafts – your patience with my typos and enthusiasm for the story has helped more than you can ever know. If I have missed anyone, I sincerely apologise, I blame my small brain – you are allowed to punch me in the stomach, (Careful, I have abs of steel!)

To my real-time feedback friend Guida, for devouring the story as quickly as I could write it and everyone else who took the plunge: Vera, Lissa, Sean, Naari, Chris, Bethany, Jesse, Liena, Katie, Adam, Grace, Lyn, Alex, Sam, Chelsea, Nils, my much-loved late Uncle Joe (who said I had verbal diarrhoea), Kate, Hannah, Emilijo, Brendon, Christina, John, Bec, Ian, Miranda, Jed, Riley, Michelle, Brendan, Natalie – you live forever in our hearts, Dimi, Sam, Laura, Mel, Caz, Ken, and the others – you know who you are. (See how I covered that?)

Thanks to the genius of Paul Davies, and Mr Berto Einstein – you make me want to build a time machine. Thanks to the musical imagery of Chris DeBurgh, you inspire emotion onto my page. Thanks to Kenny Thompson for kind permission to reprint lyrics.

Finally, thank you, dear readers. I sincerely hope you enjoyed reading this tale as much as I enjoyed writing it. Tell me what you think! There's many more to come …

Scott Baker is a writer and film-maker who has recently returned from Middle Earth – after working on *The Hobbit* films. Scott was a storyteller from a young age, making up elaborate reasons why he wasn't able to tidy his room – shifting the blame onto his older brother. Scott grew up in the Blue Mountains learning martial arts, reading novels and watching movies. He teaches film and lives somewhere on the highway between Sydney and Canberra in a little silver Mazda 3. *The Rule of Knowledge* is Scott's first novel. He has recently directed the film version of his second.

Find out up-to-date information at www.ruleofknowledge.com

Milton Keynes UK
Ingram Content Group UK Ltd.
UKHW031042020824
446373UK00004B/160